Into the Long Dark Night

The Journals of
Corrie Belle Hollister

Into the Long Dark Night

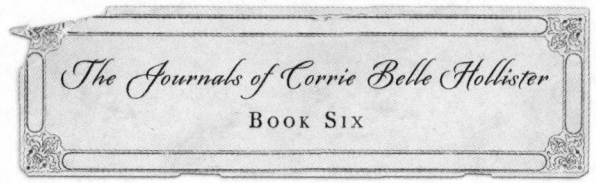

The Journals of Corrie Belle Hollister

BOOK SIX

MICHAEL PHILLIPS

HENDRICKSON
PUBLISHERS

Into the Long Dark Night

Hendrickson Publishers Marketing, LLC
P. O. Box 3473
Peabody, Massachusetts 01961-3473

ISBN 978-1-59856-963-6

Printed in the United States of America

Second Hendrickson Edition Printing — March 2016

Cover Photo Credit: Mike Habermann Photography

To

Sandy Loyd Bean

A Note to the Reader

The idea for the story of Corrie was born two decades ago in the living room of a Eureka, California, home. Michael Phillips had gotten to know Judith Pella from a Bible study they both attended, and their common interest in writing began the conversations that ultimately resulted in a collaboration and the launch of THE JOURNALS OF CORRIE BELLE HOLLISTER series.

Then these talented and dedicated novelists had the idea for a totally different historical series, THE RUSSIANS, and decided to work on the two projects simultaneously! Their enthusiasm and discipline got them through the first two novels in both series, but reality raised its head—they decided that each would continue on with one series. As it turned out, Michael was captivated by courageous Corrie and the frontier setting not too far from his home, and Judith loved the drama, complexity, and the intensive research required by the Russian story. So this is the reason Michael Phillips' name appears solo after book two of the series.

Judith and Michael went on to collaborate on several other historical series over the years. They love to hear from their readers.

The authors may be contacted at:

Michael Phillips	Judith Pella
P. O. Box 7003	judithpella.com
Eureka, CA 95502	
macdonaldphillips.com	

Contents

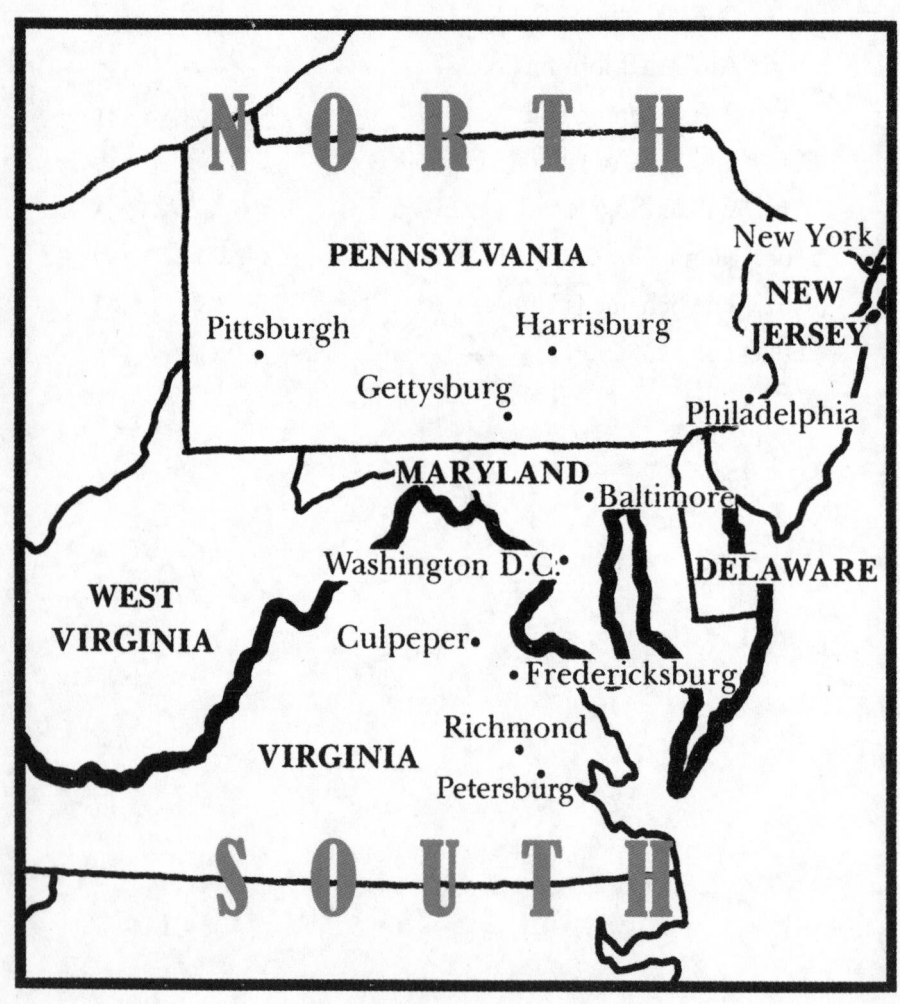

Getting Ready to Go East

CHAPTER ONE

*W*here you bound for, Miss?" a voice rasped beside me.

I glanced up nervously. "Oh . . . the East Coast," I said. He must have gotten aboard at the last little town we stopped at. I hadn't even seen him sit down.

"Long ways for a young girl like yourself to be going," the man said. "You alone?"

I nodded. His question reminded me again just what an incredible thing this whole adventure was. I had ridden in the train around Sacramento a few times. But it was nothing compared to *this* huge, fast modern train and the locomotive pulling it.

I was about an hour east of St. Joseph, Missouri, now, and I was still pretty awestruck that I was halfway across the country and on my way to Washington, D.C.

It had been twenty-one days since I had left my family in Miracle Springs and boarded the Wells Fargo stagecoach bound for Salt Lake City. Then I changed to the Holladay Overland Mail and Stage. We mostly followed the Oregon and Mormon trails from there, over the Rockies and through Wyoming, down through Nebraska, and finally to the Missouri River and St. Joseph. After a night in a St. Joseph boardinghouse, this morning I had boarded the train to St. Louis.

I still couldn't believe it was actually happening. I was alone, on a train bound for St. Louis, Columbus, Ohio, through the Cumberland Gap of eastern Pennsylvania, and finally Washington, D.C, and the East Coast! And—the most unbelievable thing of all—in my bag I was carrying a letter from the President of the United States. Abraham Lincoln himself had invited me to visit the White House, and to help him with the war effort against the Confederacy.

For a long time I thought I was dreaming. But it was all real, and here I was!

It *was* a long way for me to be going alone—the man was right about that. I glanced over at him and smiled. He had a kind face and was well-dressed, although his raspy voice reminded me of Alkali Jones.

"Well, I work for the railroad, Miss," he said. "I'm not going far, just to the next stop. But if you have any trouble, or need anything, you be sure to talk to the conductor. We're here to help you any way we can."

I thanked him, and we chatted for a few minutes more. Then he excused himself and went to talk to the conductor.

I gazed out the window, listening to the rhythmic sound of the steel wheels thrumming underneath me, and thought about the months since receiving Mr. Lincoln's letter. That had been the week just before Christmas last year, after I'd come back from Sacramento. At first I was so mixed up about Cal—feeling angry, foolish, stupid, and immature. I wanted to go out and chase him down and get back the Union's money, and make sure he wasn't able to tell his uncle or anyone else something that would hurt the Northern cause. A lot of my initial thoughts weren't altogether rational!

But Pa soon talked some sense into me. It was winter, and I couldn't go just yet, not unless I wanted to risk getting snowed in somewhere on the stageline, and neither Pa nor Almeda liked that idea much. Not unless I wanted to take the Butterfield Overland stage that went through the South, as Cal had done. But I didn't want to travel through the Confederacy. There was a lot of fighting going on by now down in the region of the country the Butterfield went through—not so much during the winter months, but I didn't want to take any chances!

In the end we all decided it would be best for me to wait until spring and take the Wells Fargo and Holladay route. In the meantime, I wrote a letter to Mr. Lincoln, thanking him for his kindness and telling him I'd be proud to take him up on his offer to visit. I said I hoped to be there sometime in late June 1863.

Besides the weather, I also had to wait several months because the first book of my journals got published in January. The whole family was so excited—especially me!

Mr. Kemble had already talked by telegraph to Mr. MacPherson. In spite of all that was happening, there had already been considerable interest in the book in the East, and he wanted me to get started gathering up material from my journals to make into a second book.

None of us could believe it! I hardly had a chance to get used to the notion of being an author, and now Mr. Kemble and I had to get working on another book. I had enough stuff written in all my diaries and journals, that much was for sure. But I couldn't quite understand the idea of putting into a book what I'd written down just for myself—I still had a hard time figuring out why anyone would be interested in any of it. Of course the story of how the five of us kids got to California, and how we found Pa, might interest folks, especially because it happened in the middle of the gold rush. But the other, more personal, writing—well, I didn't know.

"What parts of my journals do you want?" I had asked Mr. Kemble. "There's nothing much that seems like it'd make a book."

"Your pa's trouble with Buck Krebbs and him writing back East for Katie and Becky getting kidnapped and rescued—you don't think that's plenty exciting?"

"Sure, I guess so," I answered. "I guess I was wondering more about my private thoughts."

"Put some of that in, too. It's all interesting. It's all interesting, Corrie."

With his help, we got it all written down in a form that he thought would make a good book, and sent it off to Mr. MacPherson in Chicago. Even while we were doing that, mail started coming to me from people who had read the first book about our trip west and finding Pa, and that encouraged me about the work Mr. Kemble and I were doing.

So for all these reasons, the first several months of 1863 were busy ones before I could be ready to leave for the East.

By the time I stepped onto that Wells Fargo stagecoach in the second week of May, one book about California with my name on it was being read, according to Mr. Kemble and some of the mail, all across the country, and another one was on the way. I found myself wondering if I'd someday write another book about what was happening now in the East for the people back in California.

Looking Back with Different Eyes
CHAPTER TWO

*E*ven after the excitement of seeing the book get published and anticipating getting to visit Mr. Lincoln, still it might have been a foolhardy thing to do, heading across the country alone in the middle of all the fighting that was going on!

That just wasn't the kind of thing most ordinary young women did. But I don't suppose most folks would accuse me of being "ordinary"—in how I thought about things *or* in what I did.

Pa and Almeda both tried to talk me out of going more than once between Christmas and the middle of May when I left. I even talked myself out of it a time or two.

But they both had enough of the adventurer's blood in them to understand why I had to go. Pa and Uncle Nick had gotten into trouble, but they had their share of wanderlust when they were young, too. And after Mr. Parrish had died, Almeda had the drive and determination to do some things that other women didn't do, and to succeed at them no matter what all the men may have thought.

Ma, too, had been a mighty determined, headstrong lady before she died. The older I got the more I realized how extraordinary she must have been. Just bringing us all out across the country as she'd done was a pretty remarkable thing to do. And that was eleven years ago, when the prairie and plains were a lot less tame than they were now. And California wasn't tame, either!

Not until you grow up yourself can you see what was *inside* your ma and pa and other people around you. When you're young, you see their faces, but you don't know what they're thinking. You hear their words, but you don't understand why they said them. You see what they do, but don't know the motives causing them to do things. It takes growing up, doing a lot of thinking, and looking inside your own self, before you can understand all those *inside* things about your own ma and pa.

I was seeing that I had little bits of all of them inside me— lots of Pa and Ma, of course, but parts of Uncle Nick and Almeda, too. Sometimes I was scared, but another part of me wanted to go and see places and do things I'd never done before. I suppose I had a good share of Ma's and Almeda's strong wills, too. Maybe other women hadn't done some of the things I was trying to do before. But that didn't mean I couldn't try. I might fail, but I just might succeed, too!

Pa and Almeda had both left home when they were younger than I was now. I had just turned twenty-six, and if I wasn't ready to try something out on my own by now, I figured I never would be. Life in the West had been a lot rougher and more primitive when Almeda had come around by steamer to California and when Pa and Uncle Nick had come west. Now I had a nice bright Concord stagecoach to ride in halfway—a little bumpy, perhaps, but better than a wagon train!—and now a smooth, fast train coach for the rest of the journey. This was positively luxurious compared to how they had traveled, and how it was when Ma and the five of us kids had struck out in 1852.

The only thing to worry about was the war.

It was easy to forget about that sometimes—it seemed so distant and far away. I couldn't help wondering if it was really true that the country was torn apart, with the two sides hating each other, and that thousands of boys were getting killed.

I could see the anxiety in Pa's and Almeda's faces when they waved goodbye to me in Sacramento. But we had talked and prayed it all through, and I told them that if I heard about or saw any fighting within a hundred miles, I'd jump on the fastest horse I could find, and fly due north as fast as his legs would carry me, no matter where I was at the time.

"I'm going to see President Lincoln," I said, "and to write an article or two *about* the war—who knows, maybe even part of a book. But I don't figure on getting anywhere near it myself!"

"Just don't forget it," said Pa. He smiled, but he was serious.

"We want you back," added Almeda, giving me a tight squeeze.

"You know I've got to go?" I said.

They both nodded.

"When the President himself invites you for a visit, and even to help him, there isn't anything you can do *but* go!"

So I rode off eastward on the stage, and my family all got in the big buggy they'd brought me down in and headed back north to Miracle Springs.

Who could tell how long it would be until I saw them all again? I cried quite a bit between Sacramento and Carson City. But they weren't just tears of sadness. Though I would miss my family, I was excited about the adventure ahead of me.

An Interesting Journey
CHAPTER THREE

$\mathscr{S}$tagecoach travel had to be the most intimate way imaginable of getting from one place to another. There was no escaping the close quarters. Whether you liked it or not, you were jammed in with people you didn't know for long hours every day.

Most of the Concord stagecoaches I had traveled in back in California were built to carry nine passengers—three facing forward, three to the rear, and three in a seat in the center. But between most of the stations on the trip across the country, they used smaller coaches that didn't have the middle seat. There was also room on top and beside the driver if needed. I'd read about a stage several years ago running between Sacramento and Shasta in the north of California that held thirty-five people—the largest coach I'd ever heard of. But I never saw it.

During my trip, there were between three and eight of us along various stretches of the route. When the six seats inside were filled, two other men sat on top, one beside the driver and guard, and the other on the very top with the luggage.

The seats were upholstered in nice leather and were reasonably comfortable, except where the roads were so rough that we bounced up and down all day long. Then we all got mighty sore in our hindquarters!

The most interesting fellow on the way was an Englishman by the name of Sir Jeremy Mawr. He sat opposite me all the way from Salt Lake City to St. Joseph. He spoke in the most wonderful accent and was really quite friendly, in a stuffed-up kind of way. He said he had come here to learn about the gold rush and see the West firsthand, and was now on his way back to England. For someone interested enough to have come all that way, he did a lot of complaining about how uncivilized and uncouth everything was, although even then he made it sound appealing and attractive. Something about the voice and the accent made *everything* sound educated and full of more meaning than if an ordinary person had said it. Every once in a while he'd mumble some comment about the appalling conditions and the lack of a first-class compartment for gentlemen to ride in. His attitude was pretty uppity, but I just enjoyed listening to him talk, and didn't say anything.

One of the other passengers, a gun dealer from Denver, didn't have much patience with him. After one of Sir Jeremy's comments about the dust and bumps, the dealer said right out, "Look here, Mawr . . . if you don't like it, then get out and ride on top, or else hire yourself a horse and make the trip yourself. The West ain't for sissies, and maybe it ain't for high-falutin' Englishmen, neither!"

After that Sir Jeremy, and everyone else in the coach, too, was quiet for a spell. I think the rest of us were glad when Mr. Thackery, the gun dealer, got off. Sir Jeremy's funny ways were more pleasant than Mr. Thackery's loud jokes and rudeness.

After a while I had a long talk with Sir Jeremy, and found him to be a man I really liked. He even invited me to England to visit him on his estate. I don't know if he was just being polite or not, but I found myself thinking about it a lot afterward. And when I told him what I did and about my writing, and showed him the letter from Mr. Lincoln, then he started asking *me* a lot of questions, and pretty soon the others were as well. I had been a little shy during the first few days, getting used to being away from home and being mixed in with so many people I didn't know, people who were older than I was. But once we started to find out about each other, everyone got more friendly, and I found myself more and more comfortable. By the time we'd been on the road several days, we almost felt like family.

Every station stop was interesting in its own way. The terrain kept changing, of course, but all the people tending the stations had stories to tell that kept us entertained during meals and during the nights we'd spend at the overnight stops. Some of the men reminded me of Mr. Tavish, and had stagecoaching tales about robbers and Indians just as exciting as the Pony Express stories Tavish had told.

I'd listen to the stories, and I'd also wander out to the barns and stables where they kept the horses and repaired the coaches. I talked to the hands and learned all kinds of interesting things.

The Concords were so well made that all the men who worked on them spoke with pride, almost as if they'd designed them themselves. One man got to talking so much that he showed me practically every inch of the coach and how it had been put together. He said it was built lower down to the ground than the English mail coaches so that it would be able to round the curves and handle the rough terrain of the West better. The tops were built out of thin basswood, curved at all the edges to reduce the wind resistance. Being heavier on the bottom like that enabled the coaches to take the sharp curves faster. One Concord, he told me, was being shipped from Boston to San Francisco and went down when the ship sank. But a month later, when the coach was pulled out of the water, it was put into service, and was still on the road to that day.

"Just look at them wheels, Miss," the maintenance man went on. "Why, every one of them spokes is of seasoned ash and hand-fitted to the rim and hub."

You could tell they were strong, and had to be, because the wheels were big—three feet in diameter in the front and five feet in the back. The hardwood spokes held them together and took all the weight as the wheels were spinning around.

Most of the luggage went up on the flat roof. The strongbox for valuables was stored under the driver's seat. On the back was another rack with leather over the top of it to protect everything inside from the dust that the coach kicked up. This was called the boot, and it carried extra luggage as well as tools, water buckets, and sometimes mail and other packages.

The coach body had two long, heavy leather straps underneath, running from front to back as supports. These acted as suspension, to absorb the bouncy, rutted, rocky roads. The leather worked much better than iron springs, which were used on most kinds of wagons.

We stopped every fifteen miles or so for changes of horses, and once during the day and once about nightfall at the home stations. There was still lots of snow on the ground going through the mountain passes, and the nights got cold in those small sod houses. The trip from Sacramento to the Missouri River cost over $500, which was a lot of money for Pa to part with for my sake.

I sure hoped it would turn out to be worth it!

Growing-Up Tears

CHAPTER FOUR

*E*very mile of the road we traveled had memories, and I was surprised at the things I recalled because I had been so young when we'd come this way before with Ma.

Ever since South Pass beyond Fort Bridger, the stage followed the same route we had come across by wagon with Captain Dixon. As I looked at the countryside passing by, I thought of Ma nearly all the time. Memories of that wagon trip kept flooding over me—the mountains . . . Fort Laramie . . . the descending plains . . . Indians . . . buffalo . . . talks we'd had . . . things Ma had said to us . . . ways she was always trying to prepare us for growing up.

And now I was grown up and on my way to St. Louis. Ma had gotten a good price on a wagon there, and had bought most of our supplies before we crossed Missouri to Independence to join Captain Dixon's wagon train. Everything was full of heart-stirring, sad, melancholy memories.

My memory of Ma dying brought me to tears a few times during the weeks of the trip. But as I saw places that stirred up the past, I felt a quiet melancholy that seemed to have nothing to do with Ma. When in the distance I saw the wooden walls of Fort Laramie, something out of another world came up from inside me, touching my heart with a significance that could not be understood by the mind, only *felt*.

As we approached the fort, I began to hear voices in my mind—Tad and Becky clamoring in the back, Emily asking questions, Zack exclaiming over the troop of soldiers escorting the wagons toward the fort, Ma trying to keep us all calm. I remember her turning, with words meant only for me, as she did so often. Even though I was only fifteen, she tried to treat me as a woman. So many voices, so much laughter, so many poignant memories . . .

Perhaps facing the past and feeling the pain of it is part of growing up. I was twenty-six, and I had a lot more growing yet to do. But the tears I cried as I traveled east somehow felt like the tears of growing up. I was experiencing emotions impossible for children to feel—the aching nostalgia of the past, and the significance of memories that ran too deep for words.

The farther east we went, the more I found myself thinking about New York and the farm where we'd lived. I wondered if it was still there, and if there might still be people there who'd known Ma and Pa, or even us kids, or any relatives, or the church.

A different feeling started to come over me. I wanted to see the place where we had lived, wanted to walk through the fields and the house, wanted to climb the oak tree again—oh, there were so many memories! I began to anticipate going there to visit.

What would it be like? Would there be anyone I'd know? Would it feel like *home*?

At the same time, I couldn't help wondering if there would be tears, and if the land and town and farm and fields and oak tree would have that sad kind of meaning, too, that couldn't be explained.

There was only one way I'd know. One way or another, I had to go back there to visit and see the place.

Insides of Things

CHAPTER FIVE

*T*raveling all the way across the country, I had a lot of time to myself—time to think and time to write. My journal was filled with pages of thoughts and observations and feelings that didn't have much to do with where I was or what was happening around me.

I have always felt as if I were living two lives at once—one, what I was on the outside, the part of me that other people *saw*. The other, what I was on the inside, the part of me that was *thinking* all the time.

That's why I kept a journal. I had to let the thoughts out someplace, and writing them down somehow made it feel like the thoughts were completed, and then I could move on to think about something else.

One of these little thought-journeys happened just the night before we arrived in St. Joseph, and I found myself thinking about it that last day on the stagecoach. I had been talking with the wife of the stationman after supper when she said she wanted to go out to the chicken coop to check and see if there'd been any eggs laid in the last couple of hours. I went with her, and there was a big brown egg, freshly laid.

"Isn't that a beautiful big egg," she said, reaching down to pick it up. "My husband will love that for his breakfast tomorrow."

Just those few words set my mind racing. I got to thinking what it would be like if, instead of fixing the egg for breakfast, she set it up on the mantel to admire. What if it was the most beautiful egg ever seen, and she didn't want to destroy it by breaking it? So to preserve it she set it there, and took good care of it, and showed it to everyone who came through the station.

Now there's no doubt that an eggshell *is* a wonderful creation of God's. It has got a unique shape. It's strong enough to hold a little baby chick until it's ready to come out into the world.

I found myself thinking how lots of folks do that with many things—they set the shells up on the mantel to look at and admire. But they never get *inside* the shell because they're so busy looking at the outside.

But it's the inside where the life is, not the shell. The yoke of the egg becomes a baby chick, and the white feeds the chick while it's growing in its shell. An egg is no good if all you do is look at the shell. If you put it up on the mantel and leave it there, it will eventually spoil. The life in it will die if it's left there in the shell. The purpose of an eggshell is to be broken, so that the life inside can come out. The shell has no meaning all by itself. It's only a container for the life. Yet it's easy to see the outside and *think* you're seeing the egg, when really you're only seeing the shell, the husk, the container.

It almost seems as if God intentionally hides the important insides of things, surrounding them with attractive, unusual, attention-drawing outside skins. We look at and admire a tree's bark and leaves and branches and shapes, but its real *life* flows invisibly in the sap deep inside. The dirt and soil deep under the ground give life to the roots and enable plants to grow above ground where they are seen.

And people, too, have an outside shell that folks see—our body, our looks, our voice, our behavior and mannerisms, even our personalities are really part of the outside skin, our shell. But the real person is inside, in the soul. Just like the white and yolk of an egg. And like with eggs, if all we ever do is relate to the shells, the outsides of people, we'll never know the real life inside them.

After that, I found myself looking differently at people, trying to catch their eyes and seeing if I could use them like windows to see inside, past the shell into some part of their soul. I found myself listening to people differently, too, watching for glimpses of the inside *real* self that might be revealed.

Why, God, I asked silently as I sat there bouncing along and thinking about the five other people in the stagecoach with me, *did you make it like this? Why did you hide the inside life of things behind shells that sometimes we can't see past?*

Then I thought of the time Jesus was telling stories to the people and trying to explain spiritual truths to them. His disciples came to him afterward, confused about what they'd heard and full of questions. Jesus said to them, "The secret of the kingdom of God has been given to you. But to those on the *outside* everything is said in parables, so that they may see but not perceive, and hear and not understand."

I was confused, too, when I thought of that. It seemed as if God were intentionally obscuring truth so that some people would be able to see and understand it, and other people wouldn't. Why would he do that? Why would the kingdom of God be a "secret"? Then I remembered another place where the Bible talked about the "mystery" of the gospel.

I thought about all this for a long time, and I kept coming back to Jesus' other words to his disciples after he'd finished telling the parables: "He who has ears to hear, let him hear." What did that mean? Did God intentionally hide the whites and yolks inside shells to keep some people from seeing where the real life was? At first that didn't sound much like God.

But then I got to thinking about God himself. He was life, the life of the whole universe! He was the one who gave *everything* else its life! If the whole universe was like an outside shell, God was inside it—like the yolk which feeds the developing chick, like a heart, like a soul, like the sap inside a tree—giving it life and energy and meaning.

But why did God make it so that the most important things are the hardest to see? I remembered one of Jesus' parables about this very question. He said the kingdom of heaven is like finding a treasure buried in a field that is so valuable you go and sell everything you have in order to get it. Buried . . . hidden . . . secretive . . . a mystery. Why did God hide himself and the truths of the kingdom of heaven? Was it because he *wanted* people to have to dig and search and look for them? Why did God show himself only through the insides of the things he made? Was it so that only those who really wanted to search and look and dig in the field for the hidden treasure would discover the hidden meaning and life? Was there something about God's being, something about truth, something about the kingdom of heaven that *required* being sought and searched after and dug for?

I never did come up with any real answers to all my questions. But I sure did find myself looking at things differently after that—looking to see where I might be able to catch a glimpse of God *inside* of something he had made.

Especially people.

Caverns of Pain and Joy
CHAPTER SIX

Clackity clack . . . clackity clack . . . The steady vibration of the engine and the cars speeding along the tracks had a sound and feel all its own. Now that I was out of St. Joseph and well across Missouri, the stagecoach part of my journey already seemed like a distant memory. This was so different than riding in the horse-drawn Concord!

The clattering and swaying of the train coach put me in a thoughtful mood, and I found it much easier to write in my journal than for the last three weeks, even though I had to be careful not to spill the ink! The sounds and rhythm were like rain on the roof, and rain had always made me thoughtful. Even though I was just getting used to it for the first time, the sound of the train hurrying along the tracks was already making me feel reflective.

The train was a remarkable invention. And it wouldn't be long before there would be trains going all the way to California! This very track I was now on would eventually take people from coast to coast!

There'd been a groundbreaking in Sacramento on January 8, just four months earlier. It was pouring rain, but that didn't stop Governor Stanford from turning the day into a great celebration. There were speeches, and then he turned over the first shovelful of dirt where the beginning of the transcontinental railroad would start toward the Sierras.

Immediately the work had started, clearing out the railbed and building bridges through the mountains between Sacramento and Nevada. But none of the actual rail for the tracks, or train engines and cars themselves arrived for a long time after that. They would all have to be brought the 18,000 miles around the Horn by ship. Nevertheless, the building of the Central Pacific Railroad had begun.

On the other side, the Union Pacific was slower to get started. They were supposed to begin laying down track westward from Omaha, Nebraska, but I hadn't heard that they had done anything yet.

Thinking about Mr. Stanford reminded me of Cal and everything that had happened. As much as I tried not to think about it, the memories were too fresh, and I couldn't help it.

I suppose that's another part of growing up—loving something or someone that gets taken away from you. Almeda said it made a person older and wiser. Sadness and pain somehow make you see things you couldn't see before, give you a clearer vision even if there's a hurt to go along with it. Any kind of pain—the loss of a good friend, a faithful dog, or horse, the disappointment of not getting something you wanted, or wanting to do something that didn't happen—all those disappointments bring with them a kind of sadness that opens a place in you that can't get opened any other way—a special place in your heart. God wants to get in so that he can live there himself, but the door to that place can be opened only by the experience of pain or sadness. It seems kind of funny that God wants to give us life and happiness and fullness and joy, but, as Rev. Rutledge often said, one of the ways he uses to do that is pain and hurt and suffering.

But I had also learned from Rev. Rutledge that God often does things in a way that seems backward to us, completely different from the way we think he should. The last time Rev. Rutledge preached about the "upside-down ways of God," he had talked about a place—he called it a cavity, a hole—that's down inside us all. This place next to the heart is where the *fullness* of God's life and joy lives.

Rev. Rutledge compared it to a big cavern, a mine. The bigger the mine, the more of God's life and joy and wisdom you can hold. He made us picture in our minds two gold mines in a hillside—one a tiny little one going in only a few feet, and the other a huge cavern that men had been working on for years that went way inside the mountain and was huge inside and where there were many different veins of gold.

"In the same way," he said, "we all have different-sized mines or caverns inside us. The bigger the cavity, the more of God's fullness we are able to hold."

But what he said next really made me think. "The way God works inside us to make the caverns bigger," he said, "is usually with painful circumstances. The trials and hurts, the bumps and bruises, the heartaches and sadnesses of life—*those* are his tools, just like the picks and shovels and sledge hammers you miners use! God has tools, too, and he can't widen and deepen out our mines without using them. The greater a man's or woman's suffering, the deeper the cavern is hollowed out for holding all the more of the abundance of God's life and being and character. The greater the sadness has been, the greater potential there is for joy. The deeper the hurt, the more of God's love it is possible to feel."

I'd heard him say things like this before. But this time it struck so deep in me because I *was* feeling pain just then in my life. And I hoped it was making a place bigger inside me to be able to hold all the more of God's joy someday!

Thinking about Marriage

CHAPTER SEVEN

*T*he hurt I felt as I rode east, wishing I could forget the events of the previous year, was more from foolishness than anything. For all my talk about growing up, I had behaved so immaturely. I had allowed myself to get swept off my feet.

I thought back to my twenty-first birthday, to the day I had ridden up the hill early in the morning and had talked to God about my future and what I hoped my life would be.

Everything had been so clear then! My heart was focused on God, and I wanted nothing but what he wanted for me. I wanted to be pure and to love him with every part of my soul. I wanted to love other people, and to tell them what was in my heart toward God.

I had even thought about marriage back then. I had en-visioned the kind of man I might like to marry, *if* I ever did— sensitive, gentle, strong, open, emotional, tender. But most of all, a man who shared the desire I had in my heart to follow God with his whole heart. I had asked myself back then how a man and woman could possibly be friends and companions for a lifetime if they didn't share that most important thing of all—that inner direction of where you want to go and what you want to be in life.

All of that I had known and thought about and felt deeply and prayed to God about at the age of twenty-one. Then, only at twenty-five, I seemed to forget every word of it!

The moment that tall, handsome man with the brown hair and deep blue eyes had walked up to me in San Francisco, all my good intentions had flown out of my head like a bird leaving its perch. I felt like a foolish, silly young girl! Everything Cal had said to me, and even all the happy times we had shared, totally blinded me to the one simple and most important fact of all—we *didn't* share that same desire in our hearts to follow God completely in everything.

At the beginning, I think he was being as sincere as he knew how to be—maybe as sincere as he was capable of being. He was kind and gracious, and treated me with courtesy and respect. I think he meant the nice things he said to me, and genuinely did like me for the person I was.

But a man like Cal just isn't capable of being *completely* sincere. He wasn't capable of it because he didn't have the desire to follow God down deep in his heart. Down at the very bottom, Cal was following what *he* wanted to do and be in life, nothing else. And people who are not following God with their whole hearts *will* end up just like Cal—following their own way.

I knew all these things. I had known them for a long time. I knew them before I met Cal. Yet when I *did* meet him and spent time around him, my eyes clouded over and I couldn't see things clearly. I lost sight of how important it is what someone *wants* deep down in his heart. If what he wants is for *himself,* it's going to affect everything about him.

I didn't see that in Cal. I really believed he cared about me. But when his plans and ambitions got upset, the deeper part of him that was only looking out for himself gradually started to show. I only wish I had seen it sooner. I could have saved myself a lot of the hurt.

I suppose God was using even the hurt to carve and chisel and pick the cavern inside me and make it bigger. But it still didn't feel too good!

I found myself thinking all over again about the kind of man I hoped to meet someday. I didn't really *wish* to get married. I wasn't sure that was a right and proper thing to hope for. If I had placed my life in God's hands—which I figure I had done a dozen or more times, a little deeper and more completely the older I got—then what business did I have *hoping* for something that I had committed to God?

Hoping to get married seemed to me like taking it right back out of God's hands. And hoping to get married is just about one of the surest ways to make a big mistake and either marry the wrong person or else get married too soon.

Ever since I was a little girl, I had always assumed I probably *wouldn't* marry. And even after I was older and did think about it occasionally, I only wondered *what if . . . ?* I didn't want to start hoping for something that God might not want for me. I wanted to be willing to let God make my life turn out the way he wanted it to. I would have been perfectly happy to marry or not, just so long as God had *his* way.

But thinking about it all did get my mind imagining what kind of man I would want to marry if marrying was what God had in mind for me.

Cal had viewed everything in the light of opportunity. I knew there were lots of men who looked at success in life in terms of getting rich. There were lots of people like that in California, that was for sure!

I knew, too, that some men figured they had to be tough and strong and loud, or good-looking, or able to do things other men couldn't do in order to prove how much a man they were. Those were the kinds of things most women were attracted to in a man, and I could never make much sense of that. Why would a woman want a man for what his outside shell looked like instead of looking down to the yolk and the white—the life, the real heart of who he was inside? An egg-shell is a pretty durable thing. But a human being is altogether different. Our bodies get old and slow and wrinkly and fat and sick, while our souls—some people's, I should say, but not everybody's—get bigger and wiser and more full of life and love the older they get. It seemed logical that women should be looking for a wise and growing soul to fall in love with rather than just an attractive body and strong personality.

For Cal—and I suppose for lots of men—life and opportunity had to do with what benefits there were to *him*. Maybe it wasn't easy to see such a tendency in men at first. I suppose that's why women often fall in love with men who are self-centered and only out for their own gain. But the man I would look twice at in the future would be one who was constantly seeking out opportunities to do things that would benefit others.

I hoped my time with Cal had taught me this lesson once and for all—to look past the surface in men to what their souls were like. As nice as he had been to me, Cal put himself first in everything. But the Bible says that the wisest people are those who put others first. Getting and achieving was Cal's motive. He wanted to climb high in life. If I ever did have a husband, I wanted his motive to be serving others rather than striving to achieve something for himself.

Most of all, I had come to see in Cal an approach to people and relationships that originated in the question of what they could do for him. As much as I would have liked to believe that he was trying to be sincere toward me, I can't help but wonder if he didn't think that I—and maybe Pa, too—were the kind of people he wanted to associate with because he thought we might be important someday. I wondered if he would have acted as interested in us if Pa hadn't been a mayor and hadn't been asked to run for the Assembly, and if I hadn't been one of the only women newspaper writers in the state.

I think Cal was looking for opportunities for himself—in the people he met, in the conversations he was part of, in everything.

But the kind of man I'd like to meet would think about helping other people, about what he could do for them. It would never occur to him to think how he himself could use others to get ahead.

Well, that would be quite some man, whether I ever married him or not! Always thinking about truth, putting others first, doing things to benefit those around him instead of himself, looking for opportunities to help, serving however he could, trying to do good, always growing more kind and loving on the *inside* whatever the outside might look like . . . that's the kind of person I wanted to be, too!

God, I prayed, *I am so sorry for forgetting all the things you've shown me and taught me. Help me to learn and grow from what happened. Make my cavern bigger inside. Give me eyes to see people as you do, and to see into the heart of things. I pray that you would open Cal's mind and heart to you and to the truth. Forgive me for not being more aware of you last year. And whatever you have for me, whether it's being married or not, give me a thankful heart. Keep me growing, Lord, as a person whose inner life shows more and more of your life. Give me eyes to see whatever you're trying to show me and ears to hear whatever you're saying.*

North vs. South

CHAPTER EIGHT

$\mathscr{T}$he train passed through St. Louis in the early afternoon. We were there for two hours before starting off eastward again. Suddenly the sight of soldiers in the city brought me back to the reality that I was heading straight into a war! I had been so absorbed in my own thoughts, I had forgotten about it for long stretches at a time.

Missouri itself had long been a slaveholding state, even though it remained in the Union when war broke out. But the border of the Confederacy was pretty close. I was traveling just about a hundred and fifty miles north of it right now—a lot closer than California! In St. Louis we crossed the Mississippi River, and that brought the war close to mind, too, because already there had been a lot of fighting along its shores. Both sides wanted to control the vital inland waterway.

The two best-known generals, Lee of the South and Grant of the North, were leading their troops in two completely different areas—what were called the "theaters" of the war. Lee, being a Virginian himself, was still concentrating his efforts in the north of the Confederacy toward the east. His goal was to conquer the capital at Washington, D.C., and win the war for the South that way. All the activities and battles for the last two years had taken place between the two capitals, Washington and Richmond.

The North's capital was at the very southernmost part of the Union and the South's capital was in its northernmost state of Virginia. The two cities were separated by only a little more than a hundred miles. How different the war might have been if the capital of the Union had been in Maine or Massachusetts, and if the capital of the Confederacy had been located in Florida! But as it was, a lot of the fighting took place in northern Virginia and Maryland.

But another whole arena of fighting was going on at the same time, along the Tennessee and Mississippi rivers. In the same way that the South wanted to get control of Washington, the North wanted to capture New Orleans. That city controlled the mouth of the huge Mississippi River, and whoever controlled the Mississippi also controlled the Missouri, the Tennessee, the Arkansas, and the Ohio rivers, too—and controlled the shipping to and from about fifteen states. When compared with New York's million or Philadelphia's half million, I don't suppose New Orleans with its 170,000 people seemed that big. But it was still by far the largest city in all the South. In fact, it was more than four times larger than any other Confederate city. Right from the beginning, Mr. Lincoln had seen its importance, and had sent troops westward to try to swing around and encircle the South from behind and get possession of the whole Mississippi.

So in one way, the war was fought over the two cities of Washington and New Orleans. And leading those two efforts were the two great generals: Lee in Virginia and Grant along the Tennessee River and later the Mississippi.

And right then, as I bounced and rode and clattered along toward the east, first by stagecoach and then by train, events were building to a climax in both places. After a whole springtime of maneuvering and minor skirmishes here and there, that summer of 1863 was predicted to be the turning point of the whole war.

And although I was absorbed in my own thoughts and writing in my journal and thinking about Cal and marriage and my family, I might be riding right into the thick of it!

Another thing that made 1863 a turning point was that the Negro people and slaves were all free now. I heard people talking about it on the train and in the stagecoach and in the cities I went through and at the boardinghouses I stayed in. How it would affect the country and what would come of Negroes and slaves being equal with white folks and being free and having the same rights, no one knew. But everyone was talking about it. There were people for and against it, even in the North and West. Some people called Mr. Lincoln a brave and courageous Christian man. Others called him a fool and said it would never work.

President Lincoln had signed and issued what was called the "Emancipation Proclamation" back in September of the previous year, but it wasn't made official until January 1 of 1863. So now all of the South's slaves were officially "free" men and women, and it was against the law to hold slaves at all. Jefferson Davis and the *Confederate* States of America didn't recognize Mr. Lincoln's new law. But if the North won the war and got us back being one country again, all the slaves would be free.

The South was already in such disarray that a lot of slaves were just leaving the plantations and heading north.

As uneducated as most of the Negroes were, they had heard the news and wanted to get north of the Mason-Dixon line, where they might really have a chance to be free for the first time in their lives.

None of them had any money. But they were rugged and strong and determined, and freedom was a powerful incentive. Of course, the whites of the South wanted to prevent the Negroes from going north. They were fighting for slavery in the first place. Many of the poor black folks were killed trying to get out of the South.

President Lincoln's announcement said: "All persons held as slaves within any state—the people whereof shall then be in rebellion against the United States—shall be then, thence-forward, and forever free."

About two hours after the railroad man had gotten on, the train stopped again and he got off. He walked by, sat down, and visited with me for a minute or two as the train was coming into the station, and his friendliness helped me feel relaxed and at ease for the rest of that day. It seems that God often sends somebody along like that, even if just briefly, to give you a little dose of encouragement right when you need it. And they probably never know how much their kind words mean! The coach was nearly empty, and I rode most of the next day without talking to anybody.

As we were preparing to leave Cincinnati, a lot of people had come aboard and were walking through the coaches to find seats. A Catholic nun took the seat beside me. She gave me a nice smile. I was happy for the company, and so glad not to find myself next to some of the rough-looking men who wandered through occasionally. We began talking immediately.

She introduced herself as Sister Janette, and one of the first things I noticed was the ring—it looked like a wedding ring—on her fourth finger. She was traveling back to her convent from visiting her family after the death of her father. She called her home a "cloister," and said it was in southern

Pennsylvania. She was taking the train to Pittsburgh, then about halfway across Pennsylvania, to where some of her sister nuns would meet her with a wagon. I told her I was on my way to Washington, D.C., and she said she was happy to hear we'd be traveling a long way together.

I had never met a nun, but I liked her right away.

We visited a while, mostly about the ride and the scenery. Then we talked about the war. Sister Janette had grown up in Ohio and she told me about that, and of course asked about me, and so eventually I told her my story. I had always been curious about what it was like to be a nun, and I didn't know much about being a Catholic in general, so I was full of questions.

"But what do you nuns actually *do?*" I asked after she had been telling me about the small community where she lived. "I mean, besides praying and going to Mass every day. What do you do the rest of the time?"

A curious smile came over Sister Janette's face. At first I thought I might have offended her with my question, but as soon as I heard her soft voice again, I was reassured that I hadn't.

"Do you know what an *order* is, Corrie?" she asked. I shook my head.

"The Catholic church is made up of many different *orders* of priests and nuns which focus their teaching and work and worship differently. Some monasteries and convents are devoted to little more than worship and prayer. Other orders actively work to help the poor, others to establish schools. Some are devoted to nursing and medicine, some to evangelism or religious writing."

"What is the order of your convent?" I asked. Again she smiled.

"In one way, I suppose you could say we have *no* order," she answered. "Our cloister is something of an experiment. We are represented by several different orders living and working together. That's why we are called the Sisters of Unity, although that is not the name of an official order of the church."

"Why do you say it is an experiment?"

"Because it's an unusual idea—crossing the lines of your own vision and ideas and purposes and becoming involved with someone else's. At least it's unusual in the church. And it's especially unusual in the wider aspects of what I have been seeking for us to do throughout our community and area."

"Did you start the convent?" I asked in surprise. Sister Janette looked much too young for that.

"Oh no," she laughed.

"But you are in charge, then?"

"Not officially. I am not the mother superior, and as you can see I am still a young woman. But you could say that the Order of Unity is my brainchild. The convent itself is old, dating back to the early eighteenth century. But some years ago it fell upon hard times, and was eventually closed. I grew up not far away, in Lancaster, and after I decided to give my life to the church and become a nun, the thought began to grow in me to reopen the convent. After I took my vows, I spoke to the mother superior and the head abbot of the diocese in Philadelphia of my plan."

"They must have liked it," I said.

Sister Janette laughed. "No, I can hardly say they *liked* it. As I said, unity is not a particularly strong element in Catholic doctrine—especially unity with Protestants! But the older I grew, ever since I was a teenager, I found my heart open in so many ways to *all* of God's people. And it didn't seem right for us each to remain behind the walls of our own private little enclaves, never mixing, never communicating, never having anything to do with one another, pretending that no other Christians even existed."

She paused. "Well . . . there's no need to bore you with details. I'll just say that I was *very* persistent, and eventually they reluctantly agreed to reopen the convent for a temporary period to allow me to do what I could with my small new 'unofficial' order. That was six years ago, and we are twice as many in number as we were then, and so they allow us to continue. I think they are even beginning to realize that the work is valuable, although it will probably be after my lifetime that anyone will admit it!"

"Why is that?"

"Oh, the church bureaucracy is the *last* of man's institutions ever to admit they were wrong about something. You can't imagine how organizationally tied in knots the church is. We're supposed to be ministering to people's souls, and yet sometimes I think all we do is feed and perpetuate our own organization. But, be that as it may, I do love the church and at least I am able to carry on what I think is an important function among people in my little corner of it."

"How many of you are there?"

"Seventeen, mostly younger than I. I am thirty-two, the second oldest. I suppose if you had to categorize us, you might even call us a collection of misfits—sisters who love our Lord and who have given ourselves to his work and his church, but don't seem to fit very well in any of the church's more rigidly structured compartments. Slowly and gradually some of the young sisters have heard of our Unity order and have come out of other orders to join with us."

She smiled and shrugged. "The bishop looks upon us with a skeptical eye, and yet even he cannot deny the reality of the spiritual life that is among us. For some reason that is still very strange to me, it seems that those whose hearts yearn for unity among the wider spheres of God's people always find themselves dissatisfied with the existing traditions that so many are comfortable with. And it seems inevitable that when they attempt to express the yearnings of their hearts, they are looked upon as rebellious instead of full of love for the whole and complete Church of Christ. I will no doubt spend the remainder of my life trying to understand that perplexity. But that is why I say we are misfits. Yet we love one another, and we love the small community God has made of us. And we love what we do."

"What do you do?"

"Back to the question you asked in the first place! I'm sorry, I never answered you, did I?"

"I'm very interested in everything you were saying, though."

"Well, Corrie, what we really *do* is simply seek to be involved in our community, and especially with other religious groups within the vicinity of the convent."

"*Involved* . . . how?"

"Oh, many different things. We might help the Amish with one of their barn raisings, or—"

"The *Amish?*"

Again Sister Janette laughed. "I forget that you are from California!" she said. "The Amish are a Protestant sect that live in great numbers in southeastern Pennsylvania. They mostly keep to themselves, and to be frank with you, they don't like Catholics much. The beginnings of their church had to do with resistance to Catholic ways several hundred years ago. But we love them in spite of it, and wherever we find an open door to help them, we walk through it. No one, even the most stubborn Protestant, can resist a smile and a helping hand."

I laughed. I couldn't help thinking of how Pa and Avery Rutledge first got on together! I wondered if what she had called a "barn raising" was anything like when the Miracle Springs church had been built.

"So you go about helping people in your community?"

"Whenever we find opportunity. But it's more than helping with a specific job or project. We try to mix in a spiritual way with other communities and sects and groups of God's people. Our desire is not merely to *do* things, although that certainly is part of it, but to share life, to break down walls of division that exist between different groups of Christians, to let people inside our hearts and get inside theirs so that we no longer look at one another as Catholic or Amish or Presbyterian or Brethren, but simply as brothers and sisters."

"How do you do that?"

"In whatever ways we can. We invite families of other church affiliations to visit us. We welcome visitors to our convent and treat them as part of our body of life, whether they are Catholic or not. Gradually word has spread that we are there to help anyone with any need he might have, and one by one people have stopped being afraid of the fact that we are Catholics and are looking upon us as friends. Some even come occasionally to our times of Bible reading and prayer."

"Do you go to other churches' meetings, too?"

"Oh yes. If you want to see unity happening between Christians, you have *got* to do that. You can't wait and expect people to come to you. Unity is an active, outflowing thing. It will never happen if you expect to see it manifested in others before you do anything about it yourself. So yes, we are constantly moving out and among other Christian groups, wherever we can do so without causing offense. You should have seen it the first time four of us appeared on Sunday morning at the Amish church meeting!"

"What happened?"

Sister Janette laughed.

"I didn't know whether they were going to throw us out, or whether they might cancel the service right there on the spot! The eyes of every man, woman, and child in that little church house turned around and stared as if they were going to pop right out of their sockets!"

"Did they say anything?"

"No. There was just a long silence as they tried to figure out what four nuns dressed in Catholic habit were doing in their Amish gathering. But eventually the minister went on with the service."

"And afterward?" I asked.

"Not a word. They ignored us completely, as if we weren't even there, and we quietly left. But I wasn't offended by their silence. It takes time for people to get used to something new. We went back the next Sunday, and the next. Finally some of the children began to come up to us and ask questions. The prejudices of children don't run so deep, and their universal humanity is usually more ready to show itself. Once the children broke the ice, some of the women began to smile timidly at us. Then conversations started, until after a couple months those stiff, proud, bearded Amish men were laughing and talking with us about their crops and the weather, surprised, I think, to find out how much we knew about such things from our own experiences in our *own* fields. Since then there's been wonderful fellowship between the sisters of our convent and the dear people of that Amish community."

"And you've done the same thing with others?"

"Similar things, yes. We've attended many meetings and services all around the area—going in groups of two, three, and four. In some we've been welcomed. In others, shunned, sometimes coming into fellowship and relationship after a time, as was the case with the Amish. Sometimes the ice never thawed, and eventually we left to try elsewhere. Unity is just not something all Christians are open to."

"And when they're not?"

"You can't be obnoxious, Corrie. You can't force yourself upon those who don't want relationship with you. So eventually we have had to give up with some and move elsewhere, remaining open but not pushing. But over the years we've established contact and harmony to varying degrees with not only the Amish but also the Brethren, some Mennonites, Methodists, even a few Baptists. And yet even with those, some people are more open than others. In every church and congregation, you find those with hearts hungry and open for wider relationship with God's body, and those who are only content if they are surrounded by people just as narrow as they themselves. God's body is indeed huge and diverse!"

"And what do your own church leaders think?"

"The bishop and the others? Oh, they're still skeptical and rather aloof about the whole thing. They can't deny that we've grown, that there's enthusiasm among the sisters and the community for what we're doing, and so they tolerate our little 'order.' But to be honest, Corrie, they don't care about unity with Protestant churches and people any more than most Amish and Baptists do with Catholics. There's *so* much mistrust and suspicion on *both* sides, it's enough to make my heart break. What must the Savior think of us? I'm sure it breaks his heart even more to see his people so divided and selfish and narrow."

I didn't say anything, and a long silence followed. The conversation seemed to have reached one of those natural breaking points where both of us needed to be quiet for a while and think about everything we'd heard and said. I'd almost forgotten we were in a train. Now suddenly the bouncing and jostling came back to my senses, and we rode along for a while looking out the window, meditating to the clacking along underneath us.

*W*hy did you get interested in unity?" I said after a while, turning again toward Sister Janette.

She continued staring outside, but I could tell from the look on her face that she was thinking deeply about how to answer my question. Finally she turned back toward me.

"Two reasons, I suppose, Corrie," she said. "I grew up with two childhood friends I loved very much. The three of us were inseparable. My parents were staunch Catholics, but neither of my friends was. One was from a family of unbelievers, as far as I know, and the parents of the other were Plymouth Brethren. Of course the three of us neither knew nor cared about such distinctions. We didn't even know what they meant. The two of us who came from 'church' families attended church with our own parents every Sunday and never thought much about it the rest of the time. But when we began to get older, there began to be things said about the 'unsuitability' of our continued friendship, especially on the part of the parents of my Brethren friend. According to the things my friend repeated to me, Catholics were worse than atheists. In the end my friend was eventually forbidden to see me again."

"What did you do?" I asked, amazed at such a thing.

"I was devastated. I was only eleven at the time, and couldn't begin to understand. It was the most horrible thing I could imagine, not to see her anymore, and I must admit I came very near hating her parents for a time, God forgive me. But in the years since, that experience actually proved very maturing, for it deepened within me the determination to make my life count in bringing people *together*. My friend's parents were instrumental in my life, even if in a negative way. The memory of their confining and restrictive view of Catholics has always kept before me what I *don't* want to become myself. Unfortunately, their perspective is not so unusual. Both Catholics and Protestants suffer from the disease of self-absorption. Anyway, that is the first reason I am so committed to breaking down the walls between God's people."

"And the second?" I asked.

"Just the fact of where I grew up . . . Pennsylvania."

"How do you mean—I don't understand?"

"Do you know anything about the history of Pennsylvania, Corrie?"

"Not much, I suppose. Just what we learned about the Pilgrims in school."

"The Pilgrims were actually farther north, in the New England states. Pennsylvania was settled later. And in the very beginning people came here for unity. So I guess you could say I am just following in the footsteps of Pennsylvania's founders and first inhabitants by wanting to carry on that vision today."

"Was Pennsylvania that much different from the other states? I thought all the colonies were settled for religious freedom."

Sister Janette smiled. "In one way, of course, you're exactly right. But it was a very selective kind of religious freedom the Pilgrims wanted. They were selective in just the same way as most churches and religious groups and institutions are today, selective like my childhood friend's Brethren parents, selective like my own bishop."

"*Selective* . . ." I repeated. "I don't think I quite know what you mean."

"They wanted religious freedom," Sister Janette said, "but more for themselves than anybody else. The Pilgrims first came to America in the seventeenth century to escape the persecution and intolerance they had faced in Holland and England. They sought *freedom* to view spirituality in their own way and to worship as they wanted—neither of which they had been able to do in the old countries of Europe. Yet as soon as they were settled in New England, they established an equally intolerant religious climate of their own. The very thing they had left in Europe, they brought with them and planted in the new soil of America. It wasn't long before these Puritans were persecuting those who didn't believe as they did, running dissenters out of their settlements, burning witches at the stake, rooting out those they viewed as heretics for so much as one word misspoken about one of their own narrow doctrines."

"It sounds as if they became just as bad as those they left behind in Europe," I said.

"I'm not so much talking about rightness or wrongness of what they actually believed," Sister Janette went on. "For all I know, many of the early colonists held to many true doctrines, and I have no doubt they were sincerely trying to adhere to the Scriptures. To be honest with you, I haven't studied their actual beliefs that carefully. Beliefs and doctrines and viewpoints have never really interested me as

much as the *relationships* between God's people. So whatever
they believed about this or that doctrinal issue, and however
much truth they may have discovered, I have never been able
to get beyond the fact of their extreme intolerance of others
who believed differently. It seems to me they simply extended
and spread still further the very sins of persecution and intolerance and disunity they had left behind in Europe."

"The history I was taught about the founding of our country never said much about that," I said.

"Of course not. Because the people writing history books
try to pretend that everything about their spiritual predecessors
was wonderful and perfect. But the fact is, the Puritans were at
times a pretty ruthless lot, all in the name of Christ. It's been
the way of many, many Christian movements. My own Catholic church was the worst of all. So many horrible atrocities have
been done throughout history by Catholic leaders who, in my
opinion, were no more Christians than Attila the Hun.

"But then the reformers came along, men like John Knox
and John Calvin, and before you knew it, *they* were behead-
ing and burning people at the stake and treating those who
differed with them with no less cruelty than the Vatican had
two centuries before. No matter what a movement's roots, it
seems eventually intolerance and narrowness and persecution
creep in. Jesus Christ himself began what eventually became
the Roman Catholic Church. Yet look what a mockery of his
teachings we made of it. Martin Luther's motivations to break
with the church were pure and scripturally based. Yet look
what narrow zealots like Knox and Calvin did to Luther's inspired message. The Puritans sought freedom, and yet within
a hundred years they were putting people to death whom they
saw as a threat to the purity of their beliefs."

She paused and looked directly into my eyes. "Wherever you look, it seems that narrowness is the eventual result of spiritual movements, churches, and organizations. I tell you, Corrie, when I look at the sorry state of what has been the history of God's people, I am mortified and dismayed. It is hardly any wonder the world pays us so little attention. We have not been faithful stewards of the message Christ gave us to proclaim—a message which has unity among his people at its very foundation."

"Why, then, are you still so committed to unity? How can you maintain your enthusiasm? Everything you said seems so discouraging."

"Because it does not *have* to be so! It is not supposed to be so! And I believe we *can* make a difference. If God's people at some time and in some place don't make unity and *tolerance* a priority, nothing about this dismal pattern will change. But it *has* to change! And I believe I, and the sisters of my convent, and you, and others like us—I believe we *can* be the kind of people Jesus wants us to be."

"What does all this have to do with Pennsylvania?" I asked.

"Now you see why my bishop has been skeptical!" laughed Sister Janette. "When I get talking like this, I'm afraid I become rather too zealous myself for my own good! He once said I sounded like a Methodist street preacher instead of a Catholic nun!"

I didn't know what a street preacher might sound like, because I'd never heard one. But I had an idea, and laughed along with her.

"To answer your question, William Penn was a man whose vision was unity, too. He saw many of these very problems I've been telling you about. The intolerance and cruelty between Christians and their sects grieved his heart just as it does mine. That's why he devoted *his* land—*Pennsylvania, Penn's Woods*—to *all* segments of Christendom in the new world. He invited anyone to come and make a home there, no matter what his beliefs. He offered his land to be what the Pilgrims had come to New England to find but then had not extended toward anyone else—a land where spiritual freedom and unity would exist."

"What happened?"

"People *did* come. Intolerance in New England, and the continued narrowness of the followers of Calvin in Europe, led many to Pennsylvania, where they found homes and established churches, free from persecution—Baptists, Shakers, Methodists, Presbyterians, Quakers, Anabaptists, Brethren, yes, and even Pilgrims and Catholics and Calvinists and Lutherans, too!"

"But what does all this have to do with *you?*"

"Just growing up in Pennsylvania, I suppose, infected me with some of William Penn's own vision. I heard about him from a young age, then later read about him. I knew what had been on his heart to accomplish with the vast woodland that was known by his name. And then there were such visible and constant reminders all around me of the reality of his vision of unity. Within thirty miles of my childhood home of Lancaster, besides the strong Amish and Mennonite influence, every one of those other Christian groups I mentioned had a church or a community. Even though my young Brethren friend was taken from me, as I grew older and began to widen my viewpoint, I saw close by such an enormous variety of expression of the Christian faith. And I could not think it to be anything but wonderful! I found welling up within my heart such a desire to know people in *all* these other sects and churches, to be part of their lives and to share my life with them.

"I happened to be a Catholic, and I wanted to remain a Catholic, but that didn't mean I didn't want to mix and interact with others who *weren't* Catholics—not to try to make them like me or to see all matters of belief as I did, but to share life with them. Oh, Corrie, don't you see how wonderful is the very idea of God's people living together in harmony?"

"Yes . . . yes, I do," I said. "But I must confess I hadn't ever thought as much about such things as you have. Back home, we have just one community church and nobody talks about all the differences. I've never even heard half the names of the groups you've told me about."

"California is young. But here in the East there are so many, many different groups. In time they will spread across this huge land, and California too will become a hodgepodge of ten or fifteen separate sects of the Christian faith."

"Has William Penn's vision of unity come about?" I asked. "Is Pennsylvania still as he hoped it would be?"

Sister Janette's face fell, and her previous enthusiasm seemed to leave her altogether.

"Oh, Corrie, it's so sad. No—Pennsylvania has become just like New England, just like every other place. From such glorious beginnings, most of the groups that came here eventually became just as isolationist in their ways of thinking as the Pilgrims before them. Even though freedom was extended to them to come here, very few actually shared William Penn's vision. They were reluctant to extend the same openness and sense of unity outward to others as had been extended to them originally when they came to Pennsylvania."

She looked out the window with a wistful gaze. "I find it so hard to imagine! It looks so double-minded to me. And yet, there they are, worshiping freely in Pennsylvania, and yet with an inwardness and skepticism and resistance toward unity with everyone else. My mind just cannot absorb the inconsistency, even the hypocrisy of it. I know that is a strong word, but that is how I feel about the matter."

"Yet you are still excited about the work of your convent?"

"Oh yes! What a perfect place for us to be—right in the midst of so many different expressions of Christianity! We could find no more perfect soil for our experiment, as the bishop calls it, than among the diversity represented in Pennsylvania. Maybe most of the groups there have lost sight of the vision that brought them there, but *we* haven't!"

Silence fell as I thought about all she had said. At last I asked Sister Janette another question, although it was far different than what we had previously been talking about.

"If unity is what your heart longs for, then this war between the Northern and Southern states must seem awful to you," I said.

"Oh yes, it's absolutely heartbreaking," sighed Sister Janette. "The other sisters and I have given as much time in prayer to the country as to all our other work. This division and strife *cannot* be God's will, no matter how much each side tries to believe God is on its side."

"How can that be?" I asked. "How can people think that God is with them, when they view things so differently?"

"Unity, Corrie . . . for the same reason that unity does not yet exist between his people."

"What do you mean?"

"Because people put their *own* self-interests above those of their neighbors, even their Christian neighbors. And then they attach God's name to those self-interests and pretend *he* originated what they believe rather than admitting that they came from their *own* biases. It's the cause of all the world's strife—putting ourselves above our neighbors. It's the very thing Jesus warned us we couldn't do without ruining all he came to do for mankind."

She sighed. "This civil war in our nation is the extreme extension of the disunity that exists between all the segments of God's people. North and South are fighting each other with guns and cannons, while the different groups of Christendom fight one another with words and doctrines and by isolating themselves and shutting out all those who do not believe as they do. But at the root, I see nothing so very different there as in this awful war we are now engaged in. In the kingdom of heaven, which lasts forever, I'm not certain that the silent strife and divisions among God's people don't have even more serious consequences than this war which is tearing our country apart."

A Different View of Marriage

CHAPTER ELEVEN

$\mathscr{S}$ister Janette's words were strong ones, like nothing I'd ever heard before. Everybody has been talking about this war as if it is the most terrible thing that has ever happened in all of history. Her idea that the intolerance between Christians might even be worse was a thought that took some getting used to.

We sat quietly for most of the rest of the day, talking every once in a while but not as seriously as we had before. Late in the afternoon my eye chanced to fall on her hand again, and I suddenly remembered the question that had been raised in my mind when I first met her.

"Do you mind if I ask you about your ring?" I said. "I thought nuns weren't married, but isn't that a wedding band on your finger?"

Sister Janette looked up at me and smiled. "But we *are* married, Corrie," she answered. "When we take our vows, it is like a marriage ceremony, and afterward we wear a wedding ring."

"I . . . I don't understand."

"Not very many non-Catholics do," she said. "But when we take vows of chastity and give our lives to the church, we are not devoting ourselves to Catholicism or to a certain order or to a life of loneliness. At least it was not so for me. I gave my heart and my whole life to Jesus. I truly consider him my husband. I am married to him. The Bible speaks about God's people as the bride of Christ. And I live out the devotion of my love for him in service to his church and the people he sends me. That is why I wear a ring. My heart and my life and all that I am belong to him."

"I've never heard anything like that before," I said. "It's beautiful."

Again she smiled. "I'm glad you think so," she said. "So many people look upon women such as I—nuns, with our distinctive dress and peculiar lifestyle—and feel sorry for us. I think we are looked upon as a lonely sort, like religious spinsters who could never hope to be married and so became nuns because there is nothing else for us to do."

"Do you really believe people think that?"

She laughed lightly. "You would be surprised at the things I've heard about how Catholic sisters are looked upon! But for me, being a nun is entirely a free choice. There were some young men who paid attention to me when I was seventeen or eighteen. But I *wanted* to give my life to Jesus and him only. I could have had all sorts of marriage proposals, but it would not have changed anything. *Jesus* was my first choice as a husband. I wanted to devote my life to him and no other. And I have never been sorry—not for a minute. I made that choice, and I make it anew every day."

She looked at me with an intensity that obviously came out of deep feelings. "I love Christ, Corrie. I love his people, I love his church, I love doing his work, I love the world he made, I love his Word, the Bible, and I love being part of all he is doing in the world. I would have no other life than exactly the one I have chosen. I am a happy, contented woman, Corrie, and I wear my wedding ring with pride and a heart full of love. The life I have with him of purity and chastity gives me a fulfillment that goes beyond the mere personal satisfaction of what some might consider earthly pleasures and happiness. Some might look upon mine as a life of sacrifice and denial. But for me it is a chosen life of laying down my complete being in submission and service and devotion to him. It has *brought* me happiness, not taken it from me!"

After all the thinking I had been doing before meeting Sister Janette about Cal and marriage and my future, her words gave a whole new direction to my thoughts. Since almost before I could remember, all the way back to when Ma and I talked about my probably not being the marrying sort, marriage had always been *the* thing a young girl looked forward to. If you didn't marry, there must be something wrong with you. But now Sister Janette said that she wouldn't have married no matter how many offers she had, because she chose and *wanted* to be devoted to Christ and no one else. It was something I had never heard before.

I couldn't stop thinking about it all the rest of that day, and the next. And I couldn't help wondering what, if anything, it all might have to do with me. Was I, like Ma'd said, not the marrying sort? Or even if I was, might Jesus want me to be married to him like Sister Janette was?

I didn't know what to think of that—and I didn't know if I liked the notion or not! I didn't want to be a Catholic nun . . . or I didn't think I wanted to be. Could I be married to Christ and *not* be a nun . . . not even be a Catholic? What might "service to the church . . . service to Jesus" mean for me, a Protestant, with no convent to go to . . . no order to join?

The ideas got confused and mixed up in my mind as I considered everything she had said. I wanted to belong to Jesus, but I didn't know if that meant I shouldn't be married to someone else.

I never did get it all resolved. I tried to pray quietly, but even that was hard right then. This whole way of thinking about it was so altogether new that even prayer came hard.

Then right in the middle of my thoughts, Sister Janette's voice interrupted.

"Corrie," she said excitedly, "I've just had the most wonderful idea! Why don't you stop with me and spend a few days with the sisters at the convent? I want them to meet you, and you can see for yourself everything I've been telling you about!"

I thought about it, and the offer seemed very attractive to me. I *did* want to see Sister Janette's convent and meet the other nuns, to find out just what this new way of life was really like.

I turned the idea over in my mind. I had told President Lincoln I would be coming to Washington sometime in late June, and it was only the first week in June. Surely I could spend a few days in Pennsylvania, and then go on to Washington to meet the President.

"Thank you," I said at last. "I think I would like that."

The Sisters of Unity

CHAPTER TWELVE

I accepted Sister Janette's offer, and in two days I found myself in as different a place from Miracle Springs as anything I could ever have imagined. Suddenly there I was, with a small community of Catholic women, most of them not much older than I was—three or four of them even younger. But they were all just as nice as Sister Janette, and immediately made me feel very much at home among them. I especially took to one of the sisters whose name was Jane. She took me under her wing and let me in on the goings-on of the place.

I had a tiny little room to myself, with only a narrow bed and a small writing desk. But after the stagecoach and train, it was a welcome change. After I had been there for two days, they began calling it "Corrie's room."

After talking with Sister Janette on the train and listening to her enthusiasm about all they were doing among Christians of the community, I expected something quite different from what I found. I thought there would be "activity," more things *happening.* But the atmosphere around the Convent of John Seventeen was very quiet and subdued, hushed, peaceful. Sometimes I felt I was supposed to whisper all the time. It took me a day or two to get used to the change.

They had Mass every morning, which was unlike any church service I'd ever been in before. I hardly understood any of it. The nuns ate all their meals together in the large room beside the kitchen. That was a lot of fun, with talking and laughter. After lunch they went to their own rooms or to the chapel for quiet and prayer and meditation. Actually, prayer and meditation went on all throughout the day, but I never could completely understand the pattern, even though Sister Janette was very good about trying to explain it all to me and make me as comfortable as she could. There were many chores, too—tending the garden and the sheep and goats and chickens and two cows, fixing meals and cleaning up afterward, laundry, and other work. They all stayed very busy all day long, besides praying and reading their Bibles and meditating, and I helped with the work as much as they'd let me.

Being part of a community of women was very different for me. The spirit of love and cooperation and unselfishness was extremely appealing. It almost made me want to stay there with them. But at the same time, it was so very *Catholic*, so different. I couldn't help feeling like a stranger.

How could Christians be so different? I wondered. But even as I asked myself the question, I realized that the Sisters of Unity were trying to lessen those differences. As totally different from them and un-Catholic as I was, they accepted me among them entirely, and never once tried to make me act or behave like them. They just let me be myself, and seemed to love me as I was.

After a few days at the convent, I went with several of the sisters to an Amish barn raising. That was a day I'll never forget! The men had funny beards without mustaches, and the women wore dresses that all looked the same with little white caps over their hair. There was a sternness about them on the one hand, but, like the Catholic sisters, they made me feel as if I were one of them. And once the work started, there wasn't a second wasted! The men and teenage boys began carrying and sawing and hammering and tying big beams with heavy ropes, and in less than an hour were calling for everyone—women included—to come and pitch in together to hoist the first huge wall up off the foundation slab and into place. I found myself squeezed in between a young Amish man and one of the sisters from the convent. When the signal was given, a team of horses pulled at the ropes, the end of the wall lifted off the ground, and then we all got in underneath and lifted the wall boards up higher. In a few seconds our hands were outstretched and the great line of people standing side-by-side slowly inched forward, holding the wall above our heads, walking it gradually higher and higher, while the horses pulled the ropes attached to the top, and the strongest of the men held the bottom of the wall in place to keep it from slipping.

At last the wall reached perpendicular, another shout called off the tugging of the horses, the command was given to release the wall, and suddenly there it stood, twenty or more feet in the air, standing tall and true on its own. We all stepped back, and a great cheer of triumph went up. The first wall was in place, and the morning's dew was still not off the ground! But there wasn't a moment to lose! Even as we were shouting in our victory, half a dozen of the men were hammering diagonal boards in place at the wall's ends to hold it steady and keep it from crashing down.

I was already sweating, and the day had hardly begun! This was hard work! If the sisters from the convent made it a practice of attending barn raisings and getting their frocks dirty and their hands blistered helping with the men's work, and bringing food to help feed everyone, I could see why these Amish people could hardly help but accept them and consider them their friends. There was more unity going on in that barn raising between a handful of Catholic sisters and a small community of Amish farmers and their families than any book or sermon by an Amish pastor or a Catholic priest could ever achieve.

By the end of the day I was thoroughly exhausted! As we rode back to the convent in the back of the wagon, we were nearly falling asleep. The sun was setting over the Pennsylvania fields toward the west. Every muscle in my body ached— but what a satisfied feeling it was!

Four walls and the joists of a great roof stood where there had been nothing but a wood foundation when the sun had risen that same morning. There had been laughter and good food and many conversations throughout the day in the midst of the work. It seemed as if we'd been there a week, not just twelve hours. Not only were these women from the convent truly my sisters by this time, I now felt I had an equal number of friends among the Amish community who would welcome me into their homes just as fully.

Part of me hated to leave. My heart longed to get to know them better, and I was beginning to understand why Sister Janette was so deeply stirred when she spoke of unity. It was *love* that burned in her heart. I understood that at last, because I now felt it myself for many new people—Catholic and Amish—that I'd never even known existed a week earlier. And feeling love for them only served to stir up even deeper longings to be connected with even *more* of God's people.

I truly was beginning to feel some of the yearnings that gripped Sister Janette's heart. As we bounced along slowly in the wagon, talking and laughing and quietly recounting the events of the day with pleasure, in a deep place within me I found many thoughts and feelings I had never had before stirring into life.

Oh, how I slept that night! And the next morning when I woke up and tried to move, I discovered two hundred muscles I never knew I had—and every one of them was screaming in pain!

I crawled out of bed, only to discover that I'd slept away half the morning!

"Hard work, Corrie?" Sister Jane greeted me. I was amazed that all the sisters had been about their tasks as if yesterday's barn raising was nothing out of the ordinary.

"Yes," I answered, rubbing at my arms and shoulders. "Aren't *you* sore?"

"A little," she laughed. "Believe me, every one of us knows what you are feeling. We went through that at first, too. But we are used to it now. You'll just have to stay here long enough with us to raise two or three barns. Then you'll think nothing of it!"

I tried to laugh. But even that hurt.

But as much as the thought of raising *another* barn any time in the near future seemed an impossibility to my aching body, Sister Jane's words remained with me all that day and well into the next.

You'll just have to stay here. . . .

I couldn't get the words out of my mind. For the next few days after the barn raising, I kept to myself. I stayed in my room, resting, spent some time in the chapel praying, and went for a couple of long walks in the countryside. All the time I was thinking over and over about what Sister Jane's words might mean for me.

This was like no other place I'd ever been, and within me were thoughts like none other I'd ever had. I found myself thinking not so much about unity or about the Amish and the barn raising but about the sisters, about the life they had chosen to live. I remembered over and over what Sister Janette had said about having chosen to be married to Jesus and to serve him completely. *I am a happy, contented young woman, Corrie,* I recalled her saying. *My devotion to him has brought me happiness. . . . I would have no other life than exactly the one I have chosen.*

I had grown up for years thinking that for a young woman not to marry meant failure in life. The image of the spinster was one everybody was familiar with, and the silent dread of every girl once she got to be sixteen or seventeen. Ma had helped prepare me for it, of course, so the thought of living my life unmarried was not fearsome to me. But there was still something about being single that most folks seemed to think was unnatural. I know Uncle Nick and Pa worried about me from time to time, even though I was doing fine by myself.

But here was a whole community of women—most of them young, and several of them a lot prettier than I was— who didn't even *want* to be married, who had *chosen* not to be married because there was something else they wanted even more: to be devoted servants of Jesus—devoted to him just as much as being married to him! It wouldn't be right for them to think of themselves as his wife, even though they considered him their husband. But the word I had heard them use was *handmaiden.* They were Christ's handmaidens, his servants, and he was their Master, their protector . . . their only love.

It struck a deep chord in me. This was a level of devotion and commitment and love to Jesus beyond any I had ever seen before. Faith was not something these women did just on Sunday. It was not something that concerned only their minds and what they *thought* was true about God and the Bible and spiritual things. This was real life, daily life. They had given themselves to him *completely*—minds, hearts, hands, feet . . . everything. They had given their whole lives to serve him. They had kept nothing back for themselves—not even their own clothes! They had no money. They had left their families. *Everything!* They had no future apart from him.

I thought of Almeda. She had been my closest friend, and much of what I thought, even the person I was inside, had been influenced by her. And yet even her life wasn't devoted to Jesus in the same way as I saw here. Maybe on the inside it was, but on the outside she still ran her business and thought about family things.

I didn't have any critical feelings toward Almeda. She had done more for me than I ever thought any person could do for another, and I loved her so much! But her life as a Christian was very different from the lives of the sisters at the convent.

As I thought about it, I realized that, except for Sister Janette, the sisters didn't talk as much about spiritual things as Almeda did. They just went about their work and said their prayers and had their Masses without talking too much about it. So I could see that even in living a more normal life, Almeda's openness to talk about spiritual things had helped me understand more about them than I might have been able to.

As I pondered my future and thought about Almeda, I began to wonder what it all had to do with *me*. What kind of woman did *I* want to be? Everything I saw here in this life of separation from the world and devotion to the Lord brought out from within me deep feelings of wanting to be part of it myself.

I felt as if one part of me was considering what it would be like to *become* a nun. The question of becoming a Catholic never occurred to me, but only what it would be like to live this way, to join an order or a convent, to live with other women dedicated to God. At the same time, another part of me would remember my life back home at Miracle Springs and my family and would immediately think that the very thought of my joining a convent was absurd.

But I was twenty-six years old, after all—and perhaps it was time I found a new home. Maybe God didn't intend for me to go back to Miracle Springs. Maybe he had led me here to be part of this convent, and that's why he had kept me unmarried all this time. Could *this* be where I belonged now?

It was very confusing. I had never experienced such thoughts before. I had never thought of my life much beyond the landscape of it I could see at present. Now I was straining to look past the horizon, asking myself what purpose there might be for my future.

But even in the midst of my confusion and unsettledness, the idea held something wonderfully exciting and exhilarating. I thought about living a life *completely* in the hands of Jesus and no one else, doing nothing but *his* work, thinking nothing but *his* thoughts, being with people who were committed to the same purposes and goals. What a life that would be! What was writing, what was marriage, what even was an invitation to the White House alongside that?

The thought of the White House—and the President's invitation—drew me up short. It was already the end of June, and I had said I would be at the White House before the month's end.

Yet I was reluctant to leave the convent—to leave behind the peaceful calmness of this place, to leave the sisters, and their focus on commitment to Christ.

Could it be that God really was calling me to stay? I had to decide soon . . . but how could I know for sure?

I thought and prayed about it for two or three days. All I could think of was the single question: *Was I supposed to be part of this life I saw at the convent . . . perhaps some purpose here for me beyond just a casual visit of a few days?*

As I walked through the fields and countryside, a quiet sense of deep calm gradually stole over me as I reflected and asked God all these questions. Before long my thoughts became occupied, not just with what I ought to *do*, but with God himself. I became aware of his presence, as if Jesus himself were walking along right beside me.

Even though I was alone and far from home, and wondering about myself and my life and my future, I felt as if God had wrapped himself around me like a cloak, giving me his love and protection.

I had never been married, so I didn't know what feelings a wife might have toward her husband. But I knew what it was like to feel Pa's care and protection watching over us all, and I remembered how I felt when I was very young, lying in bed on a winter night, knowing that Ma was in the other room, tending the fire and watching over all of us.

This feeling of God's closeness was even more real than those memories. All I could think of was wanting to give more of myself to him, wanting to be totally his, wanting to be *one* with him, even in a deeper way than a wife gives herself to a husband. I could think of nothing so wonderful as being his . . . forever and completely!

Finally, on one of my long walks, I found myself a mile from the convent, walking through a little grove of trees. As I came out of the wooded area, a little clearing opened in front of me, gently rising upward toward a knoll in the distance, where a great oak tree stood. Somehow it reminded me of the hill overlooking Miracle Springs, or the mountains where I had ridden Raspberry early on the morning of my twenty-first birthday. I always felt best able to hear God when I was alone in the country, someplace high.

As I came out of that wood, and my eyes fell on that oak tree in the distance, and with my thoughts full of God's love and care for me, suddenly a great joy welled up within my

heart as though I could no longer contain it. It was a happiness just in being alive, in being in God's hands, in being his
daughter and knowing that he loved me and had a good life
for me to live with him . . . whatever that life might be. I felt
as though my heart would burst for very ecstasy!

I ran straight to the oak tree, then jumped up and grabbed
its lowest branch, swinging back and forth for a minute. Then
I let go and fell to the ground, laughing and panting at the
same time.

I breathed in the warm afternoon air deeply and leaned my
back up against the tree. A deep quiet settled over me, as I imagine Moses must have felt when looking on the burning bush. A
hush descended over the whole little meadow and knoll. I heard
no sound, not even a bird or a breath of wind. I sensed that the
Lord himself was everywhere, calming and stilling and quieting
the grass and the leaves of the tree and the very air itself.

Then from within me I found prayers rising up, and I
began speaking to Jesus as if he were right there.

"God," I said, "I do so want to be yours . . . completely."
The words weren't many, but they said everything that had
been building up within me for days, perhaps even for years.
I had prayed such prayers before, but something was different
this time. Was it that I was older? Was it that I was so far from
home? Was it that I was doing something I'd never dreamed
of doing—going to visit the President?

Maybe it was all those things. All I know is that I had
never felt such a complete abandonment to God's control,
keeping nothing back for myself. And soon I found myself
telling him even more of what was in my heart.

"Whatever you want for me, Lord," I said, "that is what I
want. Whatever future you have for me, whether as a writer or

not, whether married or not—I will be happy just to know I am with you. I will do whatever you want me to do, Father. Let me just know that I am yours, as completely as Sister Janette and Sister Jane and the others are yours. I want to be your bride as they are, and to serve your people and to work for unity as they do. Oh, God, use me and fill me with yourself, and let me be as happy and content as they are! If you want me to remain here with them, if you want me to become a nun, it would give my heart joy to do so. I am devoted to you, Lord Jesus. Let me love you and serve you. And if you want me to continue to write, speak to me about what you would have me say."

My words trailed away and finally stopped, but my thoughts did not. I found myself continuing on, talking silently with Jesus, turning first one thing, then another over and over in my mind, and then handing it to him and saying, "Here, this belongs to you now." Everything I thought about—my friendships and relationships, even things that I couldn't see yet, like this trip east and what would become of it, what I should write, whether I should marry or be single, where to live—everything, one by one, I gave to him.

I don't know how long I sat there. It might have been ten minutes, or it might have been two hours. I lost all track of time. It must have been quite a while, though, because when I again became aware of myself sitting there under the great oak, the sun was a lot farther down toward the western horizon than it was when I had left the convent.

And I found myself quiet again—quiet inside. All the words were gone, as if the well of my thoughts had run dry. I had given everything over to Jesus, and I had a quiet, almost empty feeling. But the emptiness I felt was an emptiness of *self*, not anything else. I felt marvelously *full* of his love.

When I finally rose up from the ground, I stood and took a deep breath. I had not been aware of it at the time, but my tears had been flowing as I'd been sitting there. They were certainly not tears of sadness, nor were they tears of pure happiness. Maybe there was a bit of a lonely feeling, a knowledge that my life wasn't my own anymore. Not only had I given over to the Lord the external concerns of my life, I had also given him something else. I had given him *me*, and everything I was!

As odd as it may sound, I felt almost *married* to Christ, as Sister Janette had talked about. I had given myself completely to him, as a wife does when she marries her husband, as Almeda did with Pa. I had given my heart to God, and no matter what else ever happened in my life, nothing could change that, or make me take it back. If I never married, I knew after this day that I would never be sorry about it. I also felt like a daughter feels when her father is there to take care of everything.

I got up and stood for a moment beside the great tree. All at once I became aware of a sound—a low, rumbling, thunderous noise, yet the sky was clear.

Then I saw the first rider and realized that what I had heard were horses' hooves.

He was followed not by a second rider, as in a single column, but by a massive horde of riders, all dressed in dark blue, probably ten or more abreast, and galloping hard. The thundering blue column was maybe two hundred or so yards from me, across several more fields, and they were riding west.

I stood mesmerized, watching them gallop past in the distance. Now and then a cry would go up, a yell to a horse, a commander's shout. But mostly I heard only the deep sound of hundreds of horses rumbling by. I could feel the ground shaking under my feet as I watched. One of the riders, following right behind the leader, carried a flag which waved silently in the air above him. It was the United States flag, and the blue of their uniforms was that of the Union army.

I gave a little shudder and felt suddenly cold, even though the day was a warm one.

I had never seen soldiers since the day Mr. Grant had visited Miracle Springs so many years ago. That had been a happy day. The uniforms had been bright and colorful, and the men wore them so proudly. But this day was different, and the uniforms were those of an army at war.

I watched, and then as suddenly as they had appeared, they were gone, followed by the retreating sounds of the last of the horses, until once more I was left alone in the field.

Slowly I began making my way back toward the convent, and gradually my thoughts returned to the time I had spent praying under the oak tree. Before long I had forgotten about the riders altogether, and the mood of calm serenity and peacefulness stole over me again. The noisy intrusion had not disturbed the deep sense of having abandoned myself completely to someone I loved in the depths of my being. I had the strong feeling that this was a day I would never forget, that what I'd done out there under the oak tree was something that would change my life no matter where my steps took me in future years.

The War Again!

CHAPTER FOURTEEN

The minute I got back to the convent from my walk, things started to happen rapidly. In the midst of my quiet communion with Jesus, unanticipated events came crashing in upon me. I found myself learning again that high lofty things in your mind and heart have to get down and mix with the dirt under your feet and the work of your hands or they don't mean much in the end. The minute you have some revelation of truth in your mind, or some spiritual experience with the Lord in your heart, God throws you into something you have to do with your hands and feet. It seems he doesn't want us to spend *too* much time sitting around just thinking about him without doing something about it.

"Corrie, Corrie!" I heard a voice shouting frantically at me as I approached the convent. "Where have you been? We've been looking all over for you!"

I looked up in the middle of my reverie to see Sister Janette running toward me. Behind her I could see all the other sisters scurrying and running about. Two of them were hitching up one of the wagons. Sister Jane was just coming out of the stable with one of the horses, and all the others were carrying supplies and loading them into both wagons.

I quickened my pace and hurried toward them. "What . . . what is it?" I said as Sister Janette ran up to me.

"Word has just come to us of dreadful fighting," she said. "Some soldiers were just through here—"

"I saw hundreds riding by out where I was, too," I said.

"There were only a dozen or so who stopped here," she said.

"They were on their way to rejoin their regiment, but were looking for food and boots."

"What did they say?"

"That the Confederate army had invaded the North and that they had to stop them, and that terrible fighting had already started. It's not far from here—across the river, about forty miles west, outside of a little town called Gettysburg."

"What are you doing?" I asked, glancing around again at all the activity and bustle.

"We're going there," she replied. "It will take us a day to reach the battle, so we must be off without delay."

"*Going* there . . . ?" I repeated. I don't know if I was shocked or afraid, or merely surprised.

"Yes," she said, and by now we had turned back and were walking toward the others. "They are sure to need our help. There isn't a moment to lose!"

Now I saw what the nuns were piling into the wagons— blankets and water, medical supplies, bandages, alcohol, as well as food and provisions for themselves.

"What . . . what will you do?" I said, taking a handful of blankets and a doctor's kit from one of the sisters and lifting it up to Sister Janette, who had climbed up into the wagon to stow in the provisions.

"Whatever is necessary. Nuns have to do anything God sends our way, you know. We have two nurses among us—they will tell us what to do. And willing, tender hands and loving words do more sometimes to comfort the sick and wounded and dying than any amount of medical knowledge."

"The *dying!*" I gasped. I don't suppose the full reality of what Sister Janette was saying had yet sunk into me.

"There is a terrible war going on, Corrie. Many, many young men *are* dying, but perhaps we can help a few survive, and ease the final moments of others with words of hope and love. It's Christ's work, Corrie, and we must be about it, as he is always about it."

She glanced up and paused in her work for a moment. Her eyes met mine, and I could tell she knew I was shocked and bewildered and frightened by this sudden intrusion of the war so close to our lives. In that moment I felt so naïve, so like a child again, and saw such a difference in Sister Janette's eyes. She was so calm, so at peace in the midst of the commotion, so unafraid of the danger, and so confident that the Lord would take care of his handmaidens. There was no fear in her voice, only the desire to be about the same work that her Master was doing to meet the needs of men.

"Sister Mary will be staying here to watch over the convent and tend the animals," she said after a brief pause. "You will be fine with her, but I wanted to see you before we left."

She paused again, then reached out and gave my hand a squeeze. "Corrie," she said, "I am so thankful to the Lord for sending you here. I am so glad to know you. I hope you will remain until our return, though it could easily be three or four days. So if you do have to continue your journey,

Sister Mary will be able to make arrangements for you to meet the train."

I returned her gaze, and then without even thinking what I was saying, I found myself blurting out: "No, I'm not going to continue just yet. I'm . . . I'm going with you!"

The war hadn't been going as well for the South as they had hoped. At first it seemed that the Confederacy would win over the Union in a year or less. But by the middle of 1863, the tide was gradually shifting.

Only two months before, in May, the Confederate Army of Northern Virginia, under General Robert E. Lee, had struck one of their strongest victories against the Federal Army at Chancellorsville. Yet the victory greatly weakened Lee's army. And the Union forces, with far more manpower and resources to draw upon, was able to recover itself much more quickly. By summer, Lee's Virginia army was still weak, while the Union's forces in the North had recuperated from the loss.

In addition to this, in the Mississippi Valley, General Grant had laid siege to the fortress of Vicksburg ever since the end of May, and it was now clear to the leaders of the Confederacy that Vicksburg was doomed, and that very soon the Federals would control the entire Mississippi. For the South, it was a crisis of the war that could spell its final defeat. If they still hoped to win, something drastic and dramatic had to be done. Since Grant was winning the battle in the West, action had to be taken in the East—and quickly.

General Lee proposed a daring plan to invade the North. If Vicksburg was to fall, then *he* would attack and take Philadelphia and Washington! With the largest part of the Union army busy under General Grant, a successful strike against the North might, Lee hoped, force Lincoln to quit the fight. Surely, the great Southern general thought, Lincoln would surrender and recognize the Confederacy's independence before allowing the capital of Washington to be destroyed.

Other factors prompted Lee's bold move, despite the continued weakness of his army. Ever since the beginning of the war, the Confederacy had sought to be recognized as a country of its own by the foreign powers of Europe, especially England and France. Lee hoped that a successful invasion of the North would secure such foreign recognition. This might mean financial aid, in exchange for cotton, which the factories of Europe needed in large supply. It might also mean pressure from England and France upon the United States— the *Union* states, that is—to recognize the *Confederate* States. Lee also thought that the presence of his army in the North would strike great fear into the people of Pennsylvania and New York and Ohio and the New England states. They were already weary of the war, and if he could destroy their morale further, it might lead to a Northern surrender.

In addition, moving the battle north of the Mason-Dixon line would relieve Lee's home state of Virginia from the great strain of having to support his huge army for over two years. Many battles had been fought on Virginia soil. The fields had been ravaged, and supplies were low. Since it was probably inevitable that there would be fighting somewhere during that summer of 1863, why not move north for a time and get supplies and food and meat and leather and grain from the lush farmlands and towns of Pennsylvania? Lee wanted to let Virginia farmers grow their crops without armies trampling all over them, taking everything in sight!

The very name Robert E. Lee struck fear into the hearts of loyal Northerners. He had won most of his battles, and his army seemed nearly invincible. So when news of his invasion came, many in Pennsylvania were filled with dread.

But there was one man in the Union who realized that Lee's coming into Pennsylvania might actually give the North the opportunity to turn the war in its own favor. That man was Abraham Lincoln, the man whom people had considered uneducated in military affairs. He saw the danger Lee was exposing himself to by stretching out his tired army so far from home and so far from supplies.

With Grant about to take the Mississippi Valley, if they maneuvered with skill and could cut Lee's invading army off, they could destroy it once and for all, and the war would nearly be over. President Lincoln was not afraid of Lee's reputation, for he saw what most others did not—both the weakness of Lee's army and of his plan to invade the North.

Therefore, he kept careful watch on Lee's movements throughout May and June. And when mounted Union spies brought word back that Lee's forces were moving north from Hagerstown, Maryland, into Pennsylvania toward Chambersburg and Harrisburg, Lincoln ordered the generals of his Army of the Potomac to march northwest to meet him. The climax of the war had come, though none of those involved yet knew it.

The two armies were enormous. There were approximately 77,000 Southern men marching under Lee, and 85,000 Union soldiers. It was sheer accident that the two huge armies met where they did. For the whole last week of June, Lee's scouts failed him, and no reports reached him of the Northern army's position. He continued his march—with his infantry divisions spread out and dispersed dangerously far behind him—thinking that the Federal troops were far away and that there was still no threat.

But on June 28, a week after I arrived at the convent with Sister Janette, Lee received word that the Union army was massed and very close. He realized instantly the danger his army was in. Immediately he sent couriers galloping off that night through the fields and along the roads of southern Pennsylvania, calling all the scattered legions and divisions together. He had to get all his troops together as a solid unit or they would be destroyed!

The orders all these couriers carried were simple enough. The Army of Northern Virginia would assemble and prepare for battle outside the little town of Gettysburg. It was close to Lee's present position, and many of the country roads led there. Once together, Lee would continue the march, depending on what the Union forces were doing.

The Federal Army didn't care about Gettysburg. It held no particular importance. They were simply scouring the countryside trying to find where Lee's army was, and Gettysburg happened to be where they found it.

As the month of June came to an end, therefore, and as I was walking about the fields and countryside thinking and praying, destiny was bringing thousands of young American soldiers across those same fields and through those same Pennsylvania woods and along the dirt roads toward Gettysburg, where their fateful and deadly collision would take place.

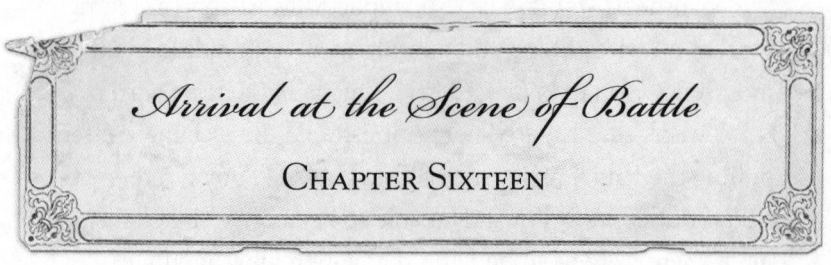

*W*here are we going . . . what will we do?" I asked as we bounced along in the back of the wagon along the rutted dirt road. It was nearly dark. We had been riding for about two hours, and had just a little before crossed a covered wood bridge over the Susquehanna.

"There is a small convent and church in New Prospect," replied Sister Janette. "It should only be about another thirty minutes. They will put us up for the night."

"I mean when we reach Gettysburg," I said. I don't suppose I hid the lingering fear from my voice very well, because Sister Janette immediately tried to reassure me.

"We will see what the Lord will have us do," she replied. "Don't be afraid, Corrie. No harm will come to us, not when we are about his work of helping people. The fighting will no doubt be long over, though even if something should happen, nothing can take us out of God's divine care. We will not reach Gettysburg until the middle of the day tomorrow, even if we leave New Prospect before dawn. But there will be many, many wounded, and the doctors and nurses there will need all the help we can give them."

"But I know nothing about all that," I said.

"Neither do most of us," she replied. "More than anything, it takes a heart of love and a kind voice, with a dose of common sense. You'll do fine, Corrie. I'm glad you came with us."

I wasn't sure I shared her optimism. I'd nearly fainted after pulling the Paiute arrow out of Tavish at the Pony Express station. I didn't know how I'd be able to keep my stomach inside me if there were wounded and dying men all around me!

We slept at the convent and were in the wagon again before the sun was up the next morning. It was about thirty miles to Gettysburg from the convent, and we reached the town about two o'clock the next afternoon.

Sister Janette had said that the fighting would be over, but we began to hear the shots of guns and cannon fire when we were still an hour away from the town. The mood of the fifteen or sixteen women in the two wagons—all nuns but me—hadn't exactly been jubilant. Everyone knew we were about serious business. Yet when we heard the dull sounds of explosions and sharp crack of gunfire off in the distance, an even greater somber mood settled over us, and hardly anything was said that whole last hour. Word had come to the convent the day before, on July 1, that the fighting had already begun. And if it was still going on as fiercely as it sounded the closer we drew to the town, it must surely have been an awful fight.

Nothing in my wildest imagination could have prepared me for what I saw. I would give almost anything to have the memory of that day and the next two erased from my mind. That brother could commit such horrible atrocities against brother—loyal Americans every one—is a crime against our country I doubt I shall ever be able to forgive the leaders of the Confederacy for. Nothing—no amount of freedom, no amount of financial or economic power, no principle they believed in, and certainly not slavery itself—could be worth having caused the horrible suffering and massive death that their rebellion against the government of our country caused. I couldn't help but think again of Cal, and it made me angry all over again, not for what he'd done to *me,* but that he could give his loyalty to the Confederacy at all. The South's cause just wasn't right!

But at the moment, there were more urgent things to think about. We had come to help, and there were plenty of innocent boys and young men—wearing *both* blue and gray— that needed tending to. And it didn't take long for us to find them. There was suffering everywhere!

Several miles outside Gettysburg we began encountering straggling groups of retreating wounded, teams of medics, sometimes officers on horseback. The closer we got, the more activity there was—moving both away from and toward the battle. Occasionally a troop of reinforcements rode swiftly by in bright, unsoiled uniforms. But those limping back in the opposite direction were dirty, torn, and blood-smeared, moving slowly, with no smiles on their faces.

Sister Jane, who was driving the lead wagon, stopped as we passed one such group and asked a man, his attire clearly identifying him as a medic or doctor of some kind, what we could all do to help.

"You see these men, Sister?" he said. "There's thousands more like them up there."

He nodded his head back over his shoulder in the direction from which he'd come, where we could hear the sounds of battle.

"Strewn out all over the place for miles. I don't know what to tell you, but if you're looking for men that need patching up or just hauling out of there, you won't have no trouble finding them. Just stay away from the front lines. The lead's flying so thick you can almost see it!"

Sister Jane thanked him and we continued on. I was already starting to feel sick to my stomach just from looking at the battle-worn men who were going away from the battle, and we weren't even there yet!

We had seen only Union soldiers, but as we entered the town of Gettysburg itself, now we began to see the gray of the Confederacy. At first the very sight of their uniforms struck fear into me, although I don't know why. There weren't many soldiers in the town at all, but there was a lot of activity just to the south. We could even see the edges of it as we came, which I later found out was a major battle going on right then for what was called Culp's Hill. The hill was held by Union forces, and they were being attacked by the Confederate soldiers between the town and the hill. So the Southern commanders were doing a lot of riding back and forth between the outskirts of the town and the battle.

Sister Jane led the horses right into town and straight to the St. Francis Xavier church. She had a feeling there would be plenty to do there, and she was right. As we approached, we could see great activity both inside and outside the church, which had already been set up as a makeshift hospital. Immediately, all the sisters jumped out of our wagons and rushed forward, talking to the nuns and one or two priests of St. Xavier's.

They were glad for the help! It was clear from one glance that they were not prepared for the deluge of wounded.

Almost before I had the chance to wonder what I should be doing in the midst of all the activity, Sister Janette was running back to me from where she'd been talking to one of the priests.

"We must get all the supplies inside first, Corrie," she said. "Why don't you get up there and start handing them down to me from the wagon."

I did so, and as Sister Janette left for the church with an armful, other sisters were there to cart in their share. Once started, I hardly had the chance to stop to think for the rest of the day. Every moment was filled with not only new experiences but awful sights and sounds, and everything so unexpected. I'd never dreamed of any of this when I started east!

I saw a doctor cut off the end of a young man's mangled arm that had been blown apart by an explosion of cannon fire. I don't mean I actually *watched,* but I knew what he was doing, and I heard the poor man's tortured screaming. I saw more blood that one day than I'd ever seen in my life—outside the church and even inside it, on the blankets where we put the wounded to lie on the floor. I saw men coming in without hands, without legs, wounded and bleeding from every part of their bodies. They'd come in from the battlefield, sometimes still bleeding from fresh wounds, or sometimes with makeshift bandages wrapped around an arm or a shoulder or even all the way around the chest, and then we'd have to unwrap them and dress the wounds.

At first I hung back, aghast at how horrible it all was. I gaped with my eyes wide and my mouth hanging open, while Sister Janette and Sister Jane and all the others rushed forward to help without seeming squeamish at any of it. They couldn't ever have seen anything like this before, yet their hearts were so full of sympathy and compassion for the poor wounded young men that they never stopped to worry about what they felt.

Even as I was carrying the last load inside from the wagon, Sister Janette called out to me from where she knelt on the other side of the church beside a boy who had just come in on a stretcher.

"Corrie, come help me for a minute," she said, glancing up at me. I rushed toward her, throwing the blankets down on the floor against the wall. "This poor lad's got a dreadful gash from his shoulder down across his chest," she said. "Would you help me bandage it up?"

I don't know what I said, but the next moment I was kneeling down on the floor beside her, the boy staring blankly up at us. I didn't realize it until later, but what Sister Janette was doing was initiating me into the role of nurse's assistant with a mild wound that wouldn't be too difficult to deal with nor would repulse me too badly. Before the next two days were over I would see so much worse. But for my first exposure to battlefield nursing, even this young boy's wound was bad enough. As she unbuttoned his tunic and peeled it away to reveal his skin, I couldn't help looking away. There was a long red gash, still bleeding a little, about eight or nine inches long. It was a clean cut and didn't look dirty, although I could hardly stand the mere thought of how painful it must be for him.

"What . . . what happened?" I found myself asking as Sister Janette dabbed alcohol on a clean white rag.

"I got thrown off my horse," he said, "and a da—"

He winced sharply in pain as Sister Janette applied the soaked cloth to the cut and gingerly cleaned the whole area of his chest.

"—a Yankee swatted down at me with his sword," the boy went on, still grimacing from the alcohol.

"That's awful!" I exclaimed.

"Nothing more'n I'd have done to him if I'd had the chance!" he said. "I'm just lucky my lieutenant shot him before he ran me through a second time."

"He shot him?"

"Yep, killed him dead in a second."

I winced and looked away, but not from the pain. I couldn't believe how casually he spoke about another man dying. All the while Sister Janette was dabbing away at the cut.

"Did . . . did it hurt terribly?" I asked.

"Yeah, but only at first. It kinda went away. 'Course, I think I fainted for a spell, too, before I woke up here. That alcohol there, that hurts worst of all." He turned toward Sister Janette. "But I'm obliged to you, Sister," he said, "for helping me out. Don't want you to get the wrong idea."

She smiled down sweetly at him.

"Corrie," she said, turning to me. "There's some salve there in that bag just to your left. Will you get it for me? We'll dress the wound."

I found it and handed it to her.

"Now, Corrie," she went on, "get some of it out of the bottle and apply it—use your fingers—up and down the cut."

I did. There was nothing any worse about it than Claude Tavish's arrow, though I couldn't help shuddering when I first touched the open wound. The boy lay there calmly as I put the ointment on. After the alcohol, I suppose it was a relief.

"Now that roll of gauze," Sister Janette said.

I got it out and handed it to her. She unrolled several lengths, wrapping it over the wound, then up and around his shoulder, diagonally across his back, under the opposite arm, and around across his chest and over the wound again. She repeated the process several times until there were three or four thicknesses over the cut. Then she cut it off and tied it firmly in place. We would not follow that pattern too long, because there were far more wounds to treat than there were supplies. By the end of the day we were forced to be stingy with bandages and ointment. But as yet we did not know the full extent of the battle's severity.

"There you are, young man," she said cheerily. "That wound should heal just fine."

He nodded, thanked us both again, and we rose and moved away.

"You did very well, Corrie," said Sister Janette. "We will see where else we might be useful. Did everything get in from the wagons?"

"Yes," I answered.

"Good," she said, stooping down beside another wounded man, again dressed in gray, although much older this time, and with his eyes closed.

"Are you in much pain?" she asked, laying her hand gently across the man's white forehead. Slowly he opened his eyes, saw that it was a nun speaking to him, tried to force a smile, then closed them again.

"Yes, Sister," he whispered, "but nothing that will kill me. Take care of the others first. I'll live."

"Where is it?" she asked.

He nodded his head and tried to lift his hand to point. "Down there . . . my leg," he whispered.

I looked and could see instantly by the shape of his twisted leg that the bone was broken. No wonder he was so white! It was probably even more painful than the boy's saber wound, though not life-threatening.

"I see," said Sister Janette, stopping to think for a moment. "It will need a splint to set properly." She glanced around the room. "Hmm . . . I'll go find out what provisions we have. But first," she added, turning her attention back to the man, "we'll do what we can. Corrie," she said, speaking to me, "you get up by his head and hold on to his shoulders. You know what we have to do?" she said down to the man.

"Yes, ma'am," he whispered. "I'm afraid I do."

"It may hurt for a moment."

"Has to be done, Sister."

Sister Janette took a deep breath, then took hold of the dirty boot of the broken leg. "Now, Corrie, you hang on hard while I pull this leg straight and get the bone back into position."

I stretched my hands under the man's arms and held on tightly to his shoulders. Sister Janette gave a hard tug at the other end. I could feel the man crying out in pain, though hardly a sound escaped his lips. It only lasted a second or two. I felt Sister Janette's pressure at the other end relax, so I eased my hold, too. The poor man breathed out a sigh of relief. If anything his face was even whiter than before and beads of sweat were on his forehead. But one look at his leg showed that she had been successful and that it was straight again.

"There," she said, "I hope that eases the pain after a while. As long as you lie still, it will be fine until we can get it splinted."

For the rest of the afternoon, Sister Janette remained close by me, though occasionally giving me something to do alone or leaving me for a while and then returning to see how I was doing.

I can't say that I became comfortable with any of it, but I gradually got more used to it, and even ventured out on my own now and then to see where I might be able to help someone. I dressed a lot of wounds, helped attach several splints to broken arms and legs, and just talked to a lot of soldiers—most of them younger than I was, and nearly all from the South. Some were crude and angry and used foul language; others were nice and spoke gently. Some said they were from Hill's Corps and others had come back from Ewell's charge against Siocum at Culp's Hill, and others had been with Early striking up Cemetery Hill. I didn't know what any of them were talking about.

All the ones who could speak were anxious to keep talking about the various battles they'd been in, but from the sound of it, none of them had been victorious. It sounded as if nothing had yet been decided and that the battle was going to continue for some time. All during the afternoon, as we were tending to the constant flow of wounded, in the distance we could hear the sounds of guns and cannons, though after a while you quit hearing it altogether. Whenever I'd go outside the church to help unload new men from a wagon and help carry them in by stretcher, I could see smoke and fire in the distance.

People from the town were helping, too, and all the churches had been set up as makeshift hospitals just like St. Xavier's. After we'd done what we could, the men who could be moved were transferred to neighboring houses where the people of Gettysburg were taking them in, or to small hospital tents that had been set up for them.

The day passed so quickly, it seemed as though we'd only just arrived when the darkness of night closed in. The fighting slowed and finally ceased, with only a few scattered spats of rifle fire now and then. We got the hundreds of wounded, in the church and outside and in nearby tents, as comfortable as possible. And then in the priests' and nuns' private quarters of the church, we took turns getting something to eat and then finding a corner to lie down in with a blanket to get some sleep. It was hot, and the floors were hard. Sleep was difficult. But I didn't realize how exhausted I was until suddenly I found myself opening my eyes to the light of morning.

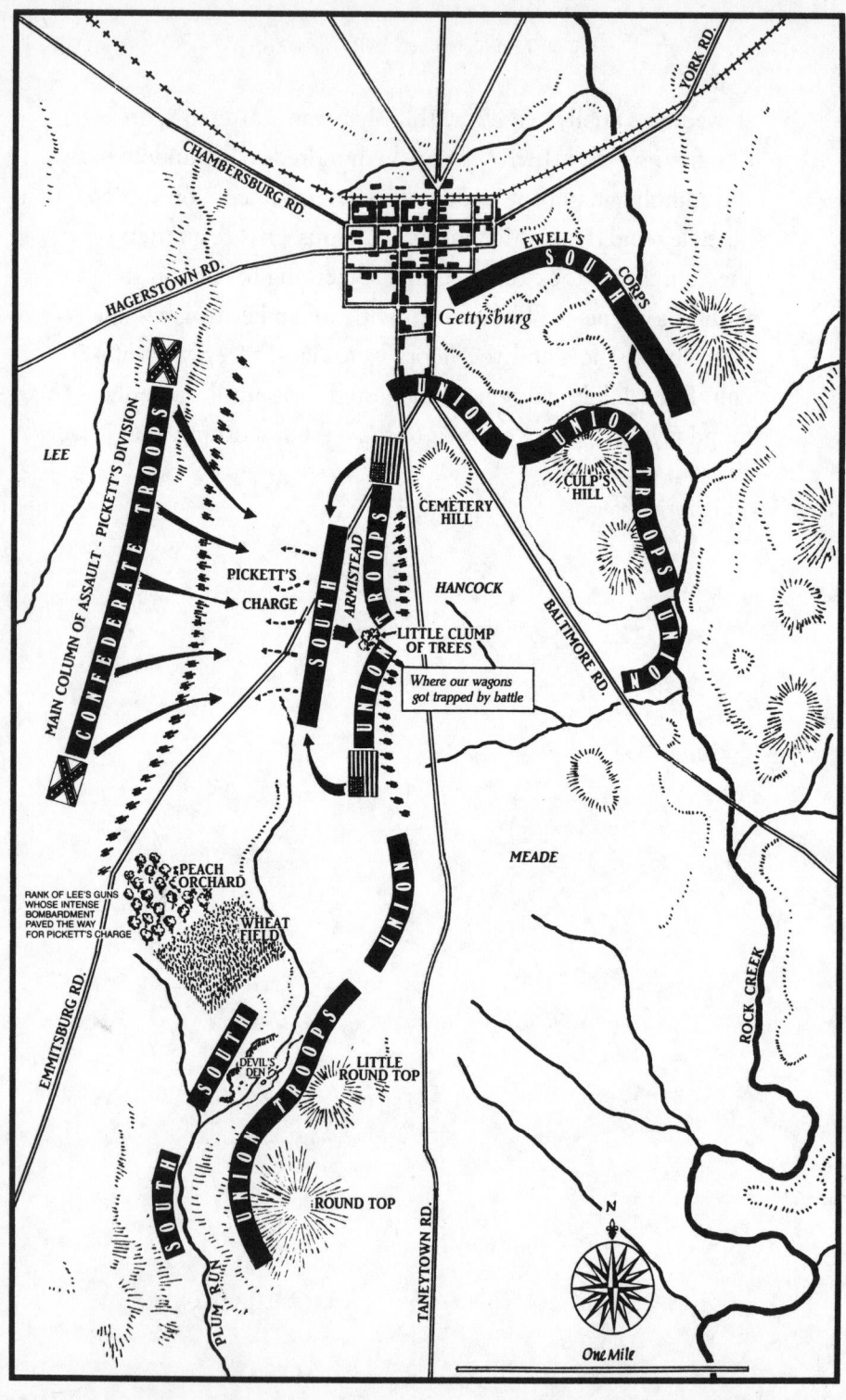

CHAMBERSBURG RD.

YORK RD.

HAGERSTOWN RD.

Gettysburg

EWELL'S CORPS

SOUTH

LEE

UNION

CEMETERY HILL

UNION TROOPS

CULP'S HILL

UNION

MAIN COLUMN OF ASSAULT - PICKETT'S DIVISION

CONFEDERATE TROOPS

PICKETT'S CHARGE

ARMISTEAD

SOUTH

UNION TROOPS

HANCOCK

BALTIMORE RD.

LITTLE CLUMP OF TREES

Where our wagons got trapped by battle

MEADE

PEACH ORCHARD

RANK OF LEE'S GUNS WHOSE INTENSE BOMBARDMENT PAVED THE WAY FOR PICKETT'S CHARGE

WHEAT FIELD

EMMITSBURG RD.

SOUTH

SOUTH

DEVIL'S DEN

UNION

UNION TROOPS

LITTLE ROUND TOP

ROCK CREEK

PLUM RUN

ROUND TOP

TANEYTOWN RD.

N

One Mile

*W*hen I woke up, there were still no sounds from the battlefields. Others were already moving about. I could smell food being prepared in the kitchen, but most of the sisters had already gone to the church or were moving through the rows of tents outside in the field next to the church, checking on the men, reapplying bandages, bringing them bread and tea and milk and whatever other provisions there were. From the relative calm, I thought perhaps the fighting was over for good.

"Good morning, Corrie," Sister May greeted me.

I turned to see her approaching me from the kitchen.

"Are you hungry?"

"Famished," I answered.

"Some of the local women are baking bread as fast as they are able," she went on, "both for us and for the men. I have some tea in the kitchen, if you'd like. And Janette's next door at the Wade home. Jennie's one of the parishioners here, and she and her sister and mother are mixing and baking us a good supply."

"Are all the citizens helping like that?" I asked.

"A good many—although when the bullets fly too close by, most stay in their cellars. But from what the sisters here tell me, Jennie's never been one to be afraid of anything, and when there's a job to do or someone in need of help, she's always there with her sleeves rolled up."

"What should I do?" I asked.

"You could go over to the Wade home and see if they need any help. There was talk a little while ago, too, of sending a few wagons out into the countryside to bring wounded into town."

"Is that safe?" I asked. "Is the fighting over?"

"We hope so. It's been quiet."

Even before the words were out of her mouth, a sudden eruption of gunfire rang out, very close by. Sister May and I looked at each other apprehensively, but neither of us said anything, hoping it would quickly die down.

It didn't. Gradually the sounds of ongoing fighting made it clear that the battle of Gettysburg wasn't over at all, but was now going into its third day. Within an hour, more wounded began arriving again, and the work of patching and bandaging and cleaning and nursing the casualties once more occupied every available hand.

The first few men to come in that morning with fresh wounds were talking about the reason for the renewed fighting. The Confederate troops under Ewell were making one last attempt to take Culp's Hill from Slocum's and Newton's Union troops. If they could, the men said, Ewell would be able to overrun Hancock's position on Cemetery Ridge. They could break through the Union line from the rear, while Pickett attacked frontally. Even the wounded were speaking of the brilliance of Lee's strategy, their eyes aglow, as if they fully expected to rout the Union army by the end of the day.

As I listened, I was unable to keep a great fear from rising up inside me. What if they did, indeed, smash through the

Union line and continue their march to the coast and the eastern cities? I was on my way to Washington, D.C.—and so was the Rebel army of Robert E. Lee!

Maybe this *would* be a good time to become a nun, join the Convent of John Seventeen, and hide myself away from all this until the war was over!

I walked across the grass to the house next door, a two-story brick home, where Sister Janette introduced me to Jennie Wade, her mother and sister, and her sister's little three-day-old baby. I learned that this was Jennie's sister's house. Jennie and her mother had come to stay with her after the birth of the baby.

"You're baking bread besides tending to your sister?" I asked.

"My sister takes no care," laughed Jennie. "It's the baby! But idle hands are the devil's workshop, you know, Corrie. And when you and the sisters arrived yesterday, I went straight over to Sister May and told her that I would do my best to keep bread baked so you would all have plenty to eat."

"It is very kind of you," said Sister Janette.

"And delicious, too, if that was your bread I ate last evening," I added.

Jennie laughed again. "It probably was. Thank you both, but really—it's the least someone like me can do. Not as important as what you and the nurses and medics do."

"If nuns and nurses and medics and helpers like Corrie don't eat," said Sister Janette, "they won't do the wounded much good. Everyone's part is just as important as the next person's."

"Thank you, Sister," Jennie replied with a smile, attacking again the large mass of dough she had been kneading.

I liked Jennie immediately. She was several years younger than I was, but so outgoing and friendly that I knew if we had the chance, we could become good friends in no time. I'd never had a close friend—a girl—my own age before, and even as Sister Janette and I walked back to St. Xavier's, I found myself thinking what it would be like to know Jennie better. A few days earlier I had been thinking about remaining at the convent and becoming a nun. Now I was thinking about wanting to stay in Gettysburg after the battle because of a new friendship with a young girl I'd only just met. I laughed at myself. I was becoming so unsettled, I didn't know *where* my future home was! Every place I went, I wanted to stay and live there. Every person I met I wanted to remain with forever. Where was my home supposed to be, anyway?

The sound of gunfire was increasing as we walked through the field. "Does it seem as if it's coming closer?" I said, half to myself.

Sister Janette must have been thinking the same thing, because she looked around with a concerned expression in her eyes, then nodded and said, "It does seem to be, doesn't it, Corrie? Yes, I think it is."

We quickened our pace, and in a couple of minutes were back inside the church building.

Within a short time, the wounded began arriving even more rapidly, and soon we were busier than we had been the day before. Steadily the sounds of the battle seemed to get louder and louder.

An hour later, I heard the rumble of perhaps a dozen horses galloping through town. Then more activity—wagons, men dragging cannons, infantrymen walking, some running . . . all Confederate soldiers. There was a lot of talk among the wounded. And from those coming in fresh from the lines, we managed to piece together the information that Ewell's

Corps had failed at Culp's Hill. They had been repulsed by the Union troops and were now rapidly falling back toward the town. That accounted for all the Confederate activity. It wasn't what you'd exactly call a full retreat, and the Union army wasn't chasing them. There was no danger of Gettysburg being overrun. But the fire from Howard's Corps was following the Rebels as they fell back, and as it did the battle encroached upon the outskirts of the town itself.

I was working next to the southern wall of the church, just inside the door, when I heard a sound that sent my stomach into my throat. A dull thud sounded in the wall beside me, accompanied by the splintering of wood. A bullet had struck the church!

Suddenly a barrage of tiny whacks sounded all against the southern wall, peppering the whole church with lead slugs. A second or two later a great explosive outburst of gunfire sounded, much closer than we had heard before.

Then came the sound of breaking glass from one of the windows, and the delayed sound of gunfire echoed as the glass tinkled onto the floor below. Father Adams yelled above the din, "Everybody onto the floor!"

I dropped the gauze pads that were in my hands and in an instant was lying on my stomach, just as another window exploded into tiny pieces. The bullet ricocheted off a bell on the opposite side of the church, then thudded into a wall. Suddenly the battle had come too close for comfort!

More shots sounded, and all around the church slugs could be heard pecking the walls of wood. Then came a calm and silence.

Father Adams stood, went to the door and peered out. I don't know what he saw, but he didn't say anything. Some of the wounded men were talking, the rest of us breathing sighs of relief and rising again to our feet.

But the silence didn't last long. Suddenly gunfire erupted again. We all fell to the floor once more, but this time there were no sounds of bullets against the church. The direction of the shots had shifted. I got to my knees, listening.

Between the deafening explosions, I could hear a sound I couldn't identify at first. Then I realized it was the sound of bullets striking against a wall. But they were no longer hitting the church. It was the sound of bullets against brick—hundreds of them in rapid-fire succession. The fire had shifted and was blasting against the house next door—the home of Jennie's sister!

I had risen to my feet and unconsciously moved toward the window that looked out over the little field up in the direction of Baltimore Street. I could see dust and tiny bits of brick flying about the walls.

Sister Janette had apparently noticed the change, too, because I saw her standing at the back door of the church, a look of fear on her face as she made the sign of the cross on her chest. I had never seen her look that way before. The fearlessness she possessed with regard to herself was one thing. But now she was clearly afraid for the home of these friends of the parish. Her lips were moving in silent prayer.

Suddenly there was a scream. I glanced back out the window. It had come from the house!

I looked back toward Sister Janette. She was no longer standing at the door but was already running out across the field.

Father Adams called after her. She continued on, heedless of the danger or her own safety. Before I knew it, I was flying through the back door of the church after her.

I heard voices calling, and think I faintly heard my name. I felt a hand tugging against my arm, trying to restrain me, but I pulled away and continued outside, following Sister Janette.

My mind was a blur. I was running, though I scarcely knew why, thinking in some vague way, I suppose, of helping my new friend. There was still gunfire sounding in the distance, though it had shifted and was no longer concentrating its deathly fury in our direction. I did not know that at the time, nor care. Impulse guided my steps, not thought or reason. Neither did I hear the shouts behind me urging me to come back, nor the cries ahead from the brick home.

On I ran, following Sister Janette by ten or fifteen seconds into the house. Suddenly as I burst through the door, I stopped. My mind seemed to come once more into focus.

The room was empty. All was quiet and still. Even the gunfire had abated momentarily.

Only a second or two passed while I stood there, suddenly aware of myself. The first sensation to come to me was the smell of warm bread baking in the oven. It was such a homey smell, so deliciously fragrant, so in contrast to the horrible battle going on all around us. For an instant the smell of bread which filled the house seemed to say, *It is not so bad as it seems. Good will triumph in the end. Peace will come, and we will all enjoy life's goodness together again.*

But the feeling of tranquility was illusory. Even as I was drawing in a deep breath of the fresh aroma, I heard crying coming from the rear of the house. I headed toward the sound.

But I did not get far. Sister Janette met me, her face white and her expression somber.

Sensing the truth, I struggled to get by.

"Corrie, please—" she said.

"Let me go!" I cried. "I want to go to Jennie."

But Sister Janette restrained me. "No, come with me," she said, trying to turn me in the opposite direction and lead me back the way we both had come.

I wrestled against her, more vigorously now. "I want to see Jennie!"

"Corrie . . . Corrie, please!" she implored. "You don't want to go in there. Now, come with me."

Her voice was tender yet commanding. I continued to struggle and finally pushed my way past her.

"Corrie!" she yelled after me. "Corrie, don't go in there! Corrie, please . . . Jennie is dead."

Pickett's Charge up Cemetery Ridge
CHAPTER EIGHTEEN

The rest of that morning is lost in a blur in my memory.

When I sat down to try to reconstruct the events to write them down in my journal, I could remember nothing for a long time after falling into Sister Janette's arms and sobbing. It was several hours before the day began to fit into a pattern that made sense to my mind again.

The gunfire ended shortly after the volley that had hit the brick house and ended poor Jennie Wade's life. Within fifteen minutes there was silence throughout the town. The fight for Culp's Hill and the retreat of Ewell's troops were over, and no more significant fighting took place for several hours. All there was for us to do was try to find room for the new wounded that kept being brought to us, even after the sharp explosions of gunfire had died away.

When my mind finally began to refocus, I was in the church, walking among the wounded, a towel draped over one arm, and a container of water in my hand. I think I had been helping Father Adams wash and clean some of the fresh wounds, because there was blood on the towel. But as I came to myself I was standing alone.

Suddenly my eyes took in the scene around me. I remembered where I was, I remembered about Jennie, and pangs of new grief shot through me. I stood there in the middle of the room—probably not for more than five or ten seconds, but it seemed like an hour—while thought after thought flooded through me like a dream.

As I glanced about at the wounded, I couldn't help but wonder why we had to be in a war at all. So much blood . . . too much fighting . . . and altogether too much dying! What was it all about . . . what was the purpose . . . why did it have to be?

I thought of Jennie, tears again rising to my eyes. I found myself wondering what it was like to die. What did Jennie *feel* at the exact moment the bullet crashed into her and she felt life slipping away? Or did she even know? Maybe she just fell asleep, and the next instant her soul was in heaven.

I continued to look around the room, wondering what was going to happen to all these poor young men lying here. I wondered if they were afraid of dying, or if they were brave like soldiers are supposed to be and had no such fears. Did any of them have a faith in God that gave hope and courage to face whatever came? I found myself thinking of their families and friends in far off places. They wouldn't even know that their sons and brothers and husbands had been wounded.

I thought of mothers worrying and praying that their sons would be safe, and asking God to bring them back safely. Many of them were Confederate mothers, and yet they were praying to the same God that I prayed to and that all the mothers in the North prayed to—everybody asking God for protection and safety, while the sons of these mothers on both sides did their best to kill one another. It didn't seem to make much sense! How could God answer the prayers on both sides?

Wondering what the parents of these soldier-sons might be thinking and praying made me think of Pa, and I thanked the Lord again for giving him back to me. I wondered what *he* was thinking right now. Did he miss me, was he anxious about me, was he praying for me? How much harder it must be for the parents of these soldiers to have their sons so far away from home, and to be so powerless to help them.

In the middle of my daydreaming, I felt a tap on my shoulder and heard Sister Agatha's voice. "You seem deep in thought, Corrie . . . are you all right?"

Startled, I came to myself and saw her standing at my side. "Yes . . . yes, I think so. I just found myself filled with more thoughts than I knew what to do with for a moment, that's all."

"Do I see some tears?"

Then I remembered. "I can't stop thinking about poor Jennie," I replied.

Sister Agatha put her arm tenderly around me. "Neither can any of us, dear."

"And then I couldn't help thinking about my family back home," I went on, "and about the parents of these wounded boys."

"Well, their parents are far away right now. So we've got to be the ones to take care of them for a while."

I sighed, then nodded.

"So would you like to help me?" she asked. "I'm about to change the dressing on a dreadful back wound, and I need another set of hands."

"Yes . . . of course."

"Good . . . you're sure you feel up to it?"

"Yes . . . I'm fine now." I drew in a deep breath. "Thank you, Sister Agatha," I said.

She smiled, then led me in the direction of the boy who had been shot in the back.

We did what we could to make the wounded comfortable throughout the morning, hearing virtually nothing from the surrounding countryside. We ate lunch, and I cried again at the sight of some of the very bread Jennie had baked the day before. Two of the sisters spent the morning with Jennie's sister and mother, helping tend the little one, and helping to get Jennie's body to the undertaker.

Around two o'clock, Father McFey suggested that, the battle seeming to be over, two of the wagons be taken out into the region south of town with supplies to see what might be done for the wounded who were farther away and had not been fortunate enough to have been carried or transported back to town.

The wagons were hitched up, supplies loaded aboard, and six or eight of the sisters piled in to accompany him.

"Corrie, what about you?" Sister Janette asked me, thinking, I suppose, that it might be good to get me busy away from the church. I had never faced having someone die like that, so close by, especially so suddenly, and from a gunshot! It was different than with Ma, who had been sick. And that was a long time ago. Sister Janette could see how shaken I was and was probably right about my needing something to occupy my hands and mind.

I nodded in agreement, and ten minutes later found myself jostling along in the back of the wagon with the others on the Taneytown Road going south.

We had gone two or three miles from town, stopping every now and then to help someone and leaving supplies at some of the makeshift tents behind the lines where some of the wounded had been taken. Around three in the afternoon, the first noises of renewed battle sounded in the distance.

It all broke loose so suddenly that we were too far into the thick of it to turn back. There was a great uproar, with smoke and fire and explosions, and within minutes the air was so thick we couldn't see more than a hundred yards ahead.

We turned the wagons around, but by then the battle had engulfed us.

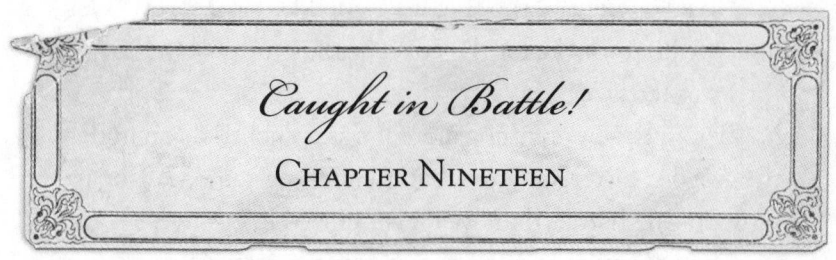

Caught in Battle!

CHAPTER NINETEEN

There was a small clump of trees right in the middle of the Union line at the crest of the ridge, and straight toward that clump of trees Pickett's men charged.

We were on the other side, the east side of the ridge, behind the Union soldiers. But we could see the trees to our left as we attempted to go back the way we'd come. As the Confederates charged up the hill, though they fought them off, the Union line crept down toward us. And then one small detachment of Confederate troops actually broke through the Union line right near the clump of trees! For a short time there was pandemonium. Union soldiers were falling back right toward us, with shouts and orders filling the air!

In the midst of what had been a sea of dark blue uniforms, suddenly there were two or three hundred gray-clad men surging through, led by General Armistead, who had stuck his slouch hat on the end of his sword and was holding it high in the air to lead his men on. At the same time, Hancock's men tried desperately to fight them back!

Within minutes, the battle between Armistead's Southerners and Hancock's Northerners for control of the hill and the clump of trees had swooped down upon us!

"Everyone out of the wagons!" cried Father McFey. "Get underneath, or make for the cover of the brush behind us."

I was terrified!

Before I knew anything more, I was crouched down under the wagon, Sister Janette's hand clutching mine. All of us were praying harder than we'd ever prayed in our lives!

I had never been so close to a battle before. All the shots of guns and cannons we had heard before now had been in the distance. Now it was right beside us, all around us! And the most awful thing was seeing the actual men, so close, fighting and shooting and trying to kill one another! I smelled smoke and gunpowder. I heard the sounds of horses neighing in terror, screams of men in pain, and the constant explosions of cannons and sharp cracking reports of thousands of guns! It was so close, I could even hear, in the midst of all the noise, the groans of men who knew they had no hope, that it was just a matter of time before they bled to death.

Suddenly I became aware that Sister Janette's hand was no longer on mine. In fact, she wasn't beside me at all! I glanced around and saw her creeping out from under the wagon. She was crawling right toward the thick of the battle! A young man had fallen only about twenty feet away, and she was going to see what she might do for him—that is, if he was still alive at all!

Now most of the other sisters, as well as Father McFey, were doing the same, some crouched down, some on their hands and knees, moving out toward the fallen men in both blue and gray, who were scattered about the battlefield.

My first reaction was that I should go help them. It seemed like the right thing to do, even though I was terrified at the thought. But the impulse was just as strong to stay right where I was and protect myself! Yet in an even deeper place inside my heart, there was *another* thought. And that was the feeling that I had to obey the impulse to help instead of the impulse to keep myself safe. I may not have liked it, but I knew what I had to do—I had to get out from under the safety of the wagon and follow Sister Janette's example.

"Oh, God, help me!" I breathed, then crept out slowly toward the field of battle.

I made my way, seeing all about in every direction bodies of horses and men, some dead, some still alive. A sick feeling came over me like I had never known before. By this time all the others were working with the wounded, moving from man to man to see what could be done. But I couldn't bring myself to start. I was paralyzed—not by fear exactly, but just by the awfulness of it all.

I was still near the wagon, separated from the others. And as I stood there, the sights and sounds of the battle grew dim. Suddenly I was alone, in a cocoon, while my senses blocked out everything else but what I was thinking.

What good would it do, I thought, to help a few people? Hundreds . . . thousands of men were spread out all over these fields and hills! Some of those lying on the ground might need only a bandage to cover a wound, yet they would bleed to death because nobody was there to help them. We couldn't possibly help them all! For every one we could save, hundreds of others would die helplessly! The little good we could do— what difference would it make?

If ever I had felt like giving up completely, just lying down and crying and waiting for it all to be over, this was the moment. It all seemed so hopeless! Despair was around us—everywhere! I could find not the smallest ray of hope anywhere within me!

As I stood there, my eyes on the ground in front of me, I managed to move my head and glance about. Bodies lay everywhere. The very grass of the field was splotched with blood!

But then my eyes fell upon something else in the midst of the sickening field of death. Ten feet away, growing bravely up out of the soil, unconcerned with the chaos and noise all about it, was a little lonely flower. It was white, with touches of blue on the tops of its petals. I don't know what kind of flower it was. I had never seen one like it.

At any other time, in any other place, I might not have noticed anything of significance in the sight. Yet today it caught my attention. This little bit of purity, here, in the midst of all the death surrounding it, touched my heart. For a moment I was able to forget that only a few paces away men were killing one another. It was God's way of speaking to me, saying, *You see, Corrie, even when it doesn't look like it, and even when you can't see me, I am still here. No matter how bad it may look, I never forget my people.*

I cannot say exactly how, but somehow that flower put hope back into my heart—hope which gave me the strength to get on again with what needed to be done. Even if it were true that thousands of people were dying all around me, if I could help just a few . . . if I could help just *one,* I knew that it *would* be worth it.

If I could do but one little deed of kindness to someone here, bandaging a wound or speaking a word of comfort, I could be like the little white and blue flower in the midst of *their* despair. Who could tell—perhaps I might help someone who would go on to save others someday. No act of kindness was too small. You could never know what might come of it in the end.

All these thoughts passed through my mind in a few brief seconds. Then just as suddenly the sounds and smells and sights of the battle raging all around returned upon me. But at last I was ready to do my part in it, whatever came to me.

I breathed in deeply, then ran forward to rejoin the sisters as fast as I could.

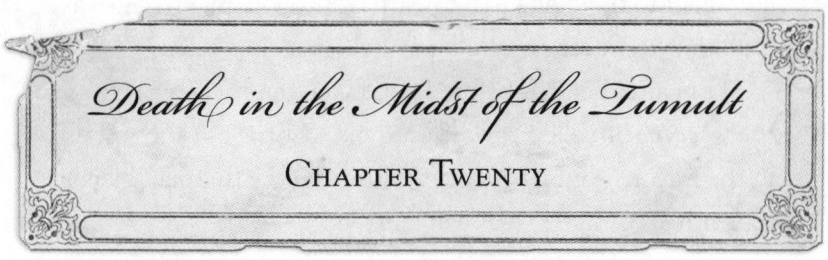

Death in the Midst of the Tumult
Chapter Twenty

*S*ister Janette was nearby. I ran to her and knelt down. But she turned, then rose and motioned me away.

"It's too late for him, Corrie, God bless him. Come, there are many others who need us."

I followed her, glancing down with dumb sickening horror at the corpse lying at her feet.

I went with her, and in another minute was kneeling beside a man who was groaning in agony with what looked like a broken leg.

"Are you wounded?" asked Sister Janette, laying a tender hand on his forehead.

"No, sister. It's just my leg. It hurts something fierce!"

"If you can stand the pain, we will carry and drag you as best we can over to our wagon. I think you'll be able to lie there in safety."

"No place is safe with them bloody Rebs on the attack!" he said.

"It will be better than out here on the open field. Corrie," she said to me, "take hold of his shoulders and I'll do my best to ease the pressure on the leg."

With a great deal of effort, with groans and grimaces from the man—as well as some words I won't repeat—we finally got him into the shade underneath the wagon. Even as he was thanking us, Sister Janette hastened off again.

I ran after her, but before I had taken ten paces away from the wagon, she yelled back toward me. "Corrie . . . in that box in the wagon—bring bandages! Hurry, before this man bleeds to death!"

I spun around, found the bandages, and ran back. To my horror, I saw Sister Janette's hand literally stuck *into* the man's stomach, plugging what must have been a terrible wound. Her arm was red with blood almost up to the elbow, and her habit was smeared all over with splotches of red.

"Tear off a big piece, Corrie!" she cried. "Here . . . stick it in here. We've no time for medicine . . . he's already lost too much blood!"

The only consolation was that the man appeared unconscious and not in pain.

"Is . . . is he alive?" I asked.

"Yes . . . his heart is pumping and he's breathing well. If I can just stop—" She didn't even finish, taking the cloth from my hand and crudely attempting to fashion a makeshift bandage that would be tight enough to stop the flow. Even as I was ripping off more pieces and helping her with them, my eyes were diverted up the hill, where a horrible scene was taking place about thirty or forty yards away. Two men were fencing fiercely. One was an officer in the Confederate army, and appeared to be about forty-five. The other, dressed in the dark blue of the Union, was a foot soldier, much younger.

The awful thought swept through my mind that within a few short minutes, one of these proud soldiers would probably be lying on the ground, either dead or in unimaginable pain.

But then my attention was again brought back to the young man lying unconscious in front of me.

When I glanced up again, suddenly the Yankee lunged forward with his blade. The gruesome scene was too much for me, and I hid my eyes.

When I again dared to look up, the old soldier was sprawled out on the ground. His slayer was nowhere to be seen.

I was no longer thinking about Sister Janette and the man whose life she was trying to save. Suddenly I was on my feet. I darted toward the wounded man, hardly conscious that I was running straight toward the little clump of trees!

The poor man's shabby gray uniform had a big red spot on the left side of the chest. The blood glistened in the sun, still wet, the wound obviously fresh. I thought he was dead. I stooped down. Then I saw him half open one eye.

"What's . . . what's a girl like—"

He struggled to speak, but his voice came out only in a faint raspy whisper.

I took out some of the strips of bandage I was still carrying, then reached out and placed them over the hole in his chest.

"What is your name?" I asked him, looking into his face contorted with pain.

When he answered his voice was weak. "Lieutenant Isaac Tomlinson," he replied, uttering the name with pride.

"Would you like some water?" I said.

"Just . . . just wet my face . . . I'm—I'm so hot."

I dabbled some drops from the canteen I was carrying onto a cloth and spread it across his forehead and cheeks.

"That feels good . . . are you an angel? What are you doing here?"

"I'm just someone who got caught in the battle like you,"
I said.

"I didn't just get caught, girl. I joined up . . . to get the
Yankees for what they done. I—I used to own a large planta-
tion in New Orleans. It was a good life . . . but then they came
. . . and the slaves all up and left, some of us were burned out
. . . they killed my wife. So I went to war with my son."

His voice was still soft, but full of passion at the memory. He seemed to be using his last ounce of strength, even
if it was with words instead of his sword, against the hated
Northerners.

"Where is your son?" I asked.

"He was killed last month."

"I'm sorry."

"Thank you, but . . . but don't—don't worry. . . ." His
words were filled with pain for his son rather than himself.
"Now I have nothing . . . nothing more to live for. Death will
not be hard to bear."

"You are not going to die," I said, wiping his face again
and doing my best to keep my tears away.

"No, girl. You do not . . . how can you understand? Death
. . . it is close at hand . . . I can feel it closing in. . . ."

I didn't know what to say. He seemed to be giving up.
How could I convince him that life was worth living, worth
fighting for?

"At last my sorrowful life will be ended . . . I will not be
sorry to leave it behind."

I struggled to find words of consolation for this wounded,
bitter man. "But God—" I began.

"Yes," he mocked. "God. You think there could be a God
who would take everything from me, and . . . and then leave

me here to die?" His voice, still gravelly and labored, had suddenly turned its bitterness away from the Yankees who had killed his wife and son, blaming God instead for the tragic circumstances that had befallen him.

His words made my heart sick! I *had* to find a way to make him see that God *loved* him and was not at all like he thought! "Perhaps . . . he was just trying to reach you."

"Well, he certainly went about it the wrong way." His words were accompanied by a sharp look of pain that swept over his face.

"He loves everybody," I said. "Even in the midst of all this, you mustn't forget that. He is sometimes all we have left to hang on to."

"I used to believe all that. My wife . . . my wife and I . . . we used to—" He grimaced in agony and took in a quick breath or two. "We used to go to church . . . every Sunday . . . believed all that. But when she—"

"We mustn't blame God for what men do," I said in desperation.

But no more words from the Confederate soldier came back in reply. I looked down into his face, waiting for an answer.

But no answer came. He had shut his eyes for the final time. Lieutenant Isaac Tomlinson was dead.

I could not hold back the tears. In a rush they suddenly flowed from my eyes, and with them came a sense of dejection and failure. I had not been able to help the poor man either physically *or* spiritually! If I had had just a few more minutes with him . . .

But I could not think that way. I could not let my spirit be broken in the same way as his had been. I had told him he could not blame God. Neither could *I* blame myself.

I stood, tears still streaming down my cheeks, and looked down at the dead man. Peace was on his face. For that much I could be grateful. I could not understand how he could be glad to leave this earth. But he did not understand the true reason for living, so how could he possibly understand the true meaning of dying? "Oh, God . . . take care of him!" was all I could pray.

I returned to Sister Janette and helped with other men fallen in battle. I suppose I did help to save others that day. But the face and words of Lt. Tomlinson stayed with me.

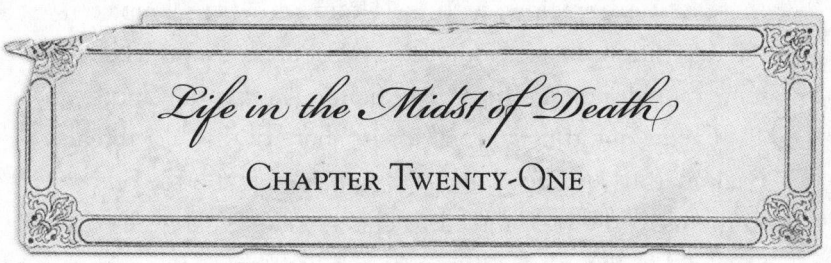

Life in the Midst of Death

Chapter Twenty-One

*T*he next two hours passed like five minutes! And yet as I try to recall the events, the time stretches out in my mind as if it were five days. I saw more death, more hand-to-hand fighting, and heard what must have been a million shots of gunfire. But in the midst of the smoke and tumultuous din, we were able to help a few men here and there who might not have survived the day otherwise.

The surge of General Armistead's Confederate troops didn't succeed in dislodging the strong Union position along the ridge. After breaking through temporarily, Hancock's men once again closed ranks, and eventually succeeded in killing or taking prisoner nearly every one of Armistead's men. It was probably the most dramatic moment, the high-water mark of the Confederate attack. And it came close to winning the day for General Robert E. Lee, who was observing from the opposite ridge behind Pickett's charge.

Prior to the outbreak of the war, the regular army of the United States had been rather small. Most of the high-ranking officers knew one another professionally, and many lasting friendships went back to shared experiences at West Point and years of service together in various forts and posts of the army. When the country suddenly broke apart, some of these officers remained with the Union, others took up command positions in the Confederacy. Suddenly friends and former comrades found themselves fighting *against* one another!

Even California came in for its share of this heartbreak. Back in 1861, as the Union was splitting up and the officers of the old army were forced to choose sides, a farewell party was held in the officers' quarters of a little army post outside of Los Angeles. The host was Captain Winfield Hancock, and he was giving the party in honor of his companions and fellow officers who were resigning in order to join the Southern army. One of those present was another captain by the name of Lewis Armistead, one of Hancock's close friends. When the party was over, Armistead shook Hancock's hand with tears in his eyes. "You'll never know," he said, "what grief this decision has cost me. Goodbye, my friend."

He and Hancock would not see each other again. Now they were generals in opposing armies. And Armistead led the spearhead of Pickett's charge up Cemetery Ridge, straight toward the little clump of trees, and straight toward his old friend Hancock, who was waiting for him at the top with his huge battery of Federal forces.

The fighting was fierce, and the smoke so thick that sometimes the soldiers could hardly tell their own comrades from the enemy. Riding up into the middle of the fray to make sure the hole in his lines had been plugged, General Hancock was shot from his horse. He was immediately carried back to the rear of the fighting, seriously wounded but still alive. At nearly the same time, on the Southern side, General Armistead kept waving his black felt hat, but the tip of his sword had pierced through and now the hat had slipped all the way down to the hilt. Then suddenly a bullet slammed into his body and he, too, fell. Both generals had now fallen, yet still the battle raged on.

As much horror as I had seen, the most awful moment of the day was yet to come. It had been probably an hour since I had seen Sister Janette. All the sisters and Father McFey and I were scattered so widely over the battlefield, we only seemed to meet occasionally when one or more of us would be running back to fetch something from the wagons, or when one of us needed another's help. By this time twenty or thirty men had been dragged or carried back to the relative safety of our wagons. At one of these times I ran into Sister Janette.

"Corrie," she called out when she saw me, "could you help me? There's a fellow I can't budge by myself."

I looked up toward her voice and saw her running toward me. She was an absolute mess—blood all over her habit, her face blotched with sweat and dirt. She looked exhausted, but as full of life as ever. I ran immediately to join her.

"He's a huge man," she went on, leading me up the slope in the direction of the fighting. "I'm afraid for him if he stays where he is, but I can't move him an inch by myself, even though he still has one good leg."

In another minute we were at the man's side and Sister Janette was helping him to a sitting position. Then she stood behind him, grabbing at his broad shoulders and grunting and lifting, trying to help the man get his strong leg underneath him. She was right about his size . . . he must have weighed three hundred pounds! His left leg was badly shattered and bleeding.

I got under one of his arms, and with his weight on both of us, he pulled himself up by using the butt of his rifle as a cane. Eventually the three of us managed to struggle to our feet.

We turned and, with the man hobbling along with the two of us on either side helping to prop him up, we slowly staggered down the hill away from the fighting.

I never heard the shot. They say you never hear the gun that kills you because the bullet gets to you before the sound of the gunfire. And there was so much fighting and gunfire filling the air that it was impossible to distinguish one shot from any of the other thousand shots going off every second. But the first thing I knew, I was toppling over onto the ground beside the big man. He swore a little, and cried out from the pain as his wounded leg crumpled beneath him.

At first I thought we'd lost our balance. I scrambled out from amidst our tangled arms and legs to see what could be done to get the motley trio back on our feet. The man grunted and swore and got himself back to a sitting position. I jumped up and took my position again under one of his arms.

Then suddenly I noticed Sister Janette lying face down on the ground on the other side of him. She wasn't moving. The back of her shoulder was covered with blood—and not the blood of those she had been helping.

"Sister Janette!" I screamed, rushing around the big girth of the man to her. "Oh, God . . . no . . . God, please!" I cried, gingerly turning her body over. Her eyes were closed, her face a ghastly pale white.

I forgot about the wounded man completely, although there was nothing more I could do to move him by myself. Without even thinking what I was doing, I found myself lifting the limp body into my arms, unconscious of the blood of my dear friend spilling all over my own arms and chest. I hardly even felt the weight, even though Sister Janette was a larger woman than I was. With one of my arms under her knees, and the other under her shoulders, and with her head dangling back lifelessly, I staggered and half-ran the rest of the way down the slope and across the field to the wagons.

I was completely out of breath when I arrived. Immediately the other sisters were at my side, sensing that a crisis was at hand that touched us all more closely than anything we had yet encountered.

They took her from my arms, and before I could even catch my breath, had laid her gently in the wagon. The two sisters who were nurses were working frantically and talking between themselves.

"Is she . . . is she—?"

"No, Corrie," replied one, "she is not dead. She has lost a lot of blood, but it appears that the bullet passed all the way through her arm. You probably saved her life by getting her to us so quickly. We have already managed to stop the bleeding."

I felt no relief at her words, but rather a numbness. Before I knew it, I was wandering away from the scene. I had tried to help others, but I guess I knew Sister Janette had the best care she could get right now, and I didn't want to be in the way.

I was walking almost aimlessly. I should have gotten someone else to go back and help me with the heavy man with the wounded leg, but I'm ashamed to say I had already forgotten about him. Not even knowing it, I went off in a different direction altogether, and then found myself almost stumbling over a man lying on the ground. He wore a Union uniform.

"What are you doing out in the middle of all this, Miss?" he said.

I glanced toward the voice, then stopped and knelt down beside him.

"Trying to help, whenever I can," I replied. "What can I do for you?"

"I ain't hurt too bad. I think the bullet broke the bone in my arm. I couldn't hold my gun no more, so I figured I might as well sit myself down before I got myself killed outright. What's your name?"

"Corrie Hollister," I answered, looking his arm over and pulling out some bandages I had shoved into the pocket of my dress when Sister Janette and I had begun lifting the big man. The fellow was right—his arm did look broken. But besides that, his ribs were pretty badly shot up, too. "What's yours?" I said.

"Alan Smith." As friendly as he was, his voice was soft and he was in obvious pain. He wore a beard that was probably a week old, his clothes were scruffy, and he looked to be in his early twenties.

"Where are you from?" I asked.

"Texas."

"But Texas is a slave state. And your uniform . . . ?"

"Oh, I'm in the Union army, all right. But I live in Texas. My pa was a friend of Sam Houston's. When they kicked Sam out of the governorship of the state 'cause he didn't want slavery and wouldn't go along with the Confederacy, why he up and left the state and came north. My pa and some of Sam's other followers came with him, and I came with my pa, 'cause I ain't no friend of Jefferson Davis neither. So I joined up with the Union army. Maybe I'll go back when it's all over, who knows? I reckon I'll always be a Texan at heart, and I sure don't consider myself a traitor to Texas. Why, shoot, I'm on the side of the tallest Texan ever, on the same side as Sam Houston. By the way, where you from?"

"California," I answered.

All of a sudden a sharp pain seemed to come over his face. He closed his eyes and lay still. I was scared. I thought maybe he'd died. But then gradually he opened them again and started to breathe more easily. The jovial look he'd had just a moment before was completely gone. He seemed to have something much different than Texas on his mind.

"How do you feel?" I asked him.

"It ain't the pain I mind so much, Miss . . . what did you say your name was?"

"Corrie," I said.

"It ain't so much the pain, Miss Corrie," he went on, "although that last one was a real doozer. I thought I might be done for all over again. But the worst of it is realizing how close I come to dying back there without never really being prepared for it. What I'm trying to say is, I never really thought about what's to become of anyone when they die."

"You're pretty young to be thinking about dying," I said. "If it hadn't been for my ma, I'd probably never have thought much about it either."

"Your ma?"

"She died when I was fifteen."

"How old are you now?"

"Twenty-six," I said.

"Well, I'm twenty-three. But I'm a soldier, and it don't seem too smart for someone like me to go twenty-three years of his life never thinking about what might become of me later, after this life. Especially for a soldier. But the minute I was hit a little while back, suddenly I realized I'd faced what might have been a certain death if the bullet had been a couple inches one way or the other. I *still* might die of this thing!"

"I think you'll be fine, Mr. Smith," I said. He was certainly in better shape than most of the other wounded men I'd seen.

"What if you can't stop the bleeding? What if I get shot again? You know what I'm getting at, Miss? What's to happen? You understand what I'm trying to say?"

"I think so," I answered. "You're wondering if there really is a heaven to go to after you die, is that it?"

"I reckon that's just about the size of the question exactly," he said. "Or a hell, too, for that matter. Heaven ain't guaranteed for fellows like me that ain't been all they maybe ought to have been!"

"I certainly believe there is," I said.

"A heaven and hell?"

"I don't think too much about hell. But I know there's a heaven because Jesus said so, and I believe in him more than I believe in anything."

"In Jesus? How do you mean that you *believe* in him?"

"I mean he lives in my heart—his Spirit, I mean, not his actual bodily self that lived back so long ago in history."

"That don't sound altogether reasonable. I mean, it don't make no sense that somebody could live inside somebody else like that. That ain't exactly what I meant about believing in God and heaven and hell."

"But that's what God means by believing. Jesus said that his Spirit—his real deepest self, the part of him that was God's Son—he said that part of him would live on and would come and dwell in the hearts of anybody that wanted to share life with him. He talked about it in the Bible a lot. That's why he rose from the dead, so he could share life like that with us—in our hearts. That's what he said belief was, and that's why I know I'll go to heaven when I die—because that's his home, and he promised to take us there to live with him."

"That's a heap more than I ever heard about in church when I was a kid! How do you know it's all true?"

"Because the Bible says so, and Jesus said so. And that's enough for me to believe it. I reckon that's what faith is, too, just believing because God says something."

"But how do you know?"

"I guess because Jesus is my friend, too. I've been sharing things with him in my mind and heart for long enough that I know I can trust him."

He didn't say anything for a minute, and seemed to be real thoughtful.

"I reckon it's like this," he said at length. "If anything *should* happen to me, like I was saying, like if I was to die or something, well, I want to make sure that I do go to be with God. I ain't never thought about all this before. I always just took life as it came. To tell you the truth, Miss, I can't even say as I know there's a God at all."

"I don't suppose I can answer every doubt you have," I said. "I've had doubts from time to time myself, but I still know that God's love for me is as real as anything there is in the world. And his love for you is just as real."

Again Alan was quiet for a while.

"What about all my buddies who died?" he asked. "People like Sergeant Thomas and Corporal Harry—what if they never make it to heaven? One thing I know for sure, and that is that they weren't Christians! Are they all doomed? I ain't sure I'd want to go to heaven if none of my buddies are there."

"But if God *is* real, and if he's the one that made you, and if he does love you like I say, then wouldn't you rather be with him?"

"I don't know. I never thought much about what being with God would be like."

"I don't know what to tell you about your friends, Alan," I said. "I don't know what happens to people like them. But I know that God knows. And I also know that he knows what is best, and that he will be completely fair and just and loving in everything he does. We're not supposed to know everything about him. And where we don't know, we can trust him to do whatever is best."

There was a long silence.

"Well, I do reckon there's a lot of sense in what you're saying," he said at last. "And the way you put it, a person'd be a fool not to want to know God better, especially if it's all you say it is."

"Oh, it is," I said, "and even more."

"Well then, how do you get to be Jesus' friend, like you said? How do you get to believing him like you talked about, you know—with him in your heart and all that? What do you have to do?"

"Just pray to him," I said, "and tell him you want to be his friend, and that you *want* him to live inside you."

"That's all . . . ain't nothing more to it than that?"

"That's all."

"Sounds too simple."

"It is simple. All it takes is someone who wants to be friends with Jesus, because he's more anxious to live with us and help us through life than we can even imagine. It's just that most folks don't want his company."

"Well, maybe it's high time I quit being that way myself. So you just go ahead and tell me what I gotta do."

"Just pray to him and tell him just what you're telling me. He'll do the rest. Would you like me to pray for you?"

"Would you? I'd be much obliged."

I closed my eyes and put my arm around Alan's shoulder. "Lord," I prayed, "I thank you for leading my steps here to my new friend, Alan Smith. I ask you to come into his heart and be his friend, and to live with him for the rest of his days. Take care of him, Lord Jesus. Heal him of these wounds he got today. Make him strong again, and protect him through-out the rest of this war. And most of all, show him what you are like. Show him how much you love him. And make every little part of his life such that he'll want to share it all with you. Thank you, Lord, for giving us *both* your life and your love inside us. Amen."

I looked over at Alan. His eyes were still closed, but I could see a tear or two escaping out from under the lids. I knew that he had indeed opened his heart to the presence of Jesus. *Oh, Father,* I breathed silently, *thank you . . . thank you so much for this dear new life!*

When I opened my eyes again, Alan was looking at me, a bright smile on his rough, dirty, unshaven face.

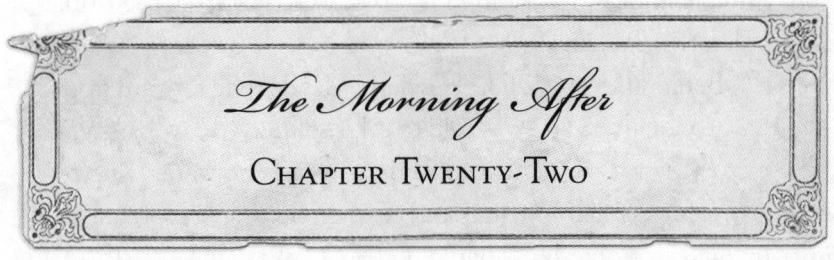

The Morning After

CHAPTER TWENTY-TWO

From their advantage on top of Cemetery Ridge, the Union army had held their line together, repelling the enormous wave of Confederate troops. The fighting had been so fierce, and the day so hot and still, that the smoke from the guns and the dust from fifty thousand human and hoofed feet clung in the air like a vapor from the pits of hell, burning the eyes and choking the lungs . . . and smelling of death.

Eventually the Confederate charge began to break down. The formations fell apart. The tight assault, designed to break the Union line in half, frayed and splintered. And before the afternoon was over, thousands of gray-uniformed Southerners began drifting back down the long slope, not in outright retreat but in a slow return to their position of the morning.

The Union army made no attempt to follow them down the hill to try to turn its victory into a slaughter. They had successfully beaten back the supreme effort Lee's army could muster, and they were satisfied with the victory. Besides, they were exhausted, too, and were content just to see the enemy backing away down the hill.

Lee's invasion of the North had been stopped, right there on Cemetery Ridge, during those two hours of fighting.

Philadelphia and Washington, D.C., were safe from the Confederate army!

Behind the line, Union General Meade rode forward from his headquarters and was told that his soldiers had won a great victory. For a moment it looked as though he were going to give a huge shout of triumph. But then he simply took off his hat and said quietly, "Thank God!"

A mile away to the west, General Lee rode among the men of Pickett's Corps who had made the charge, trying to encourage them, telling them that he was proud of their efforts, and adding, "It is all my fault."

Probably one of the most poignant and ironic moments of all came not far from where we'd been. After most of the fighting had stopped, and after all the Confederate soldiers under General Armistead had either retreated, been killed, or taken prisoner, Union medics found the Southern general himself, barely alive, lying amid the dead on the battlefield. He had only the strength left to whisper a last message for them to take to his old friend Hancock before he died. Not yet knowing his friend's fate, General Hancock himself had been carried from the field bleeding from his wound, but he would survive to serve his country again.

Though the Confederate army had been defeated in their attempt, and was certainly crippled, it was far from broken. The Union army had lost nearly as many men, and the Rebels were ready to take the battle of Gettysburg into a fourth day if the Yankees tried to attack. They had failed in their own attack, but they were still confident they could smash any offensive General Meade might try.

It was evening when we arrived back in town at the church—exhausted, dirty, bloody . . . and silent. We had seen things no human being ought to see. We had been part of something God never intended the humans of his creation to do—fighting and killing one another.

It was a day none of us would ever forget . . . *could* ever forget!

As night fell, ending July 3, it was silent in every direction in the fields surrounding Gettysburg. But none of us knew whether there might not be still more fighting to be resumed the next day.

My thoughts were nearly entirely occupied with trying to make Sister Janette comfortable. My heart had been turned inside-out and upside-down so many times in the last two days that I scarcely was thinking now, just going through the motions of doing what had to be done. Everyone was concerned about Sister Janette, yet there were so many others to look after, too, that most of the nuns kept busy with the soldiers—redressing wounds, feeding, washing, taking water around. I remained mostly at Sister Janette's side. Whenever she regained consciousness, even if only for a moment, I wanted to be there to hear what she might say or to get anything for her she might want.

Shortly after dark a man suddenly strode into the church. His boots echoed heavily on the wood floor, and every head immediately turned in his direction. His gray uniform immediately identified him as a Confederate officer.

"We're pulling out, men!" he called out. "All of you that can travel, wagons'll be coming through town for you in less than an hour."

"We surrendering, Captain?" asked one of the wounded.

"No, we ain't surrendering!" he shot back angrily. "We're just getting you men out of here and back to Virginia."

A few whoops and hollers sounded at the mention of their home state, but mostly it remained quiet. The captain turned and left as quickly as he had come.

About forty minutes later, the sounds of several wagons approached along the street outside. They had been combing through the fields for wounded, and had already stopped at the tent hospital nearby, so a good many men had been loaded up. Half a dozen men walked in with stretchers and began transporting the wounded out of the church. We helped those who could walk or hobble. In half an hour the place was nearly deserted, and the wagons disappeared down the street and out of town to the west. Only three men remained, all unconscious, whom the medics didn't expect to live. I didn't know then what happened to all the dead, though I hardly wondered about it at the time.

All through that night, General Lee pulled his men together from their scattered positions—those around the town who had fought for Culp's Hill, Longstreet's Corps down at the peach orchard and Devil's Den opposite the Little Round Top. Most of the night Confederate wagons began making their way toward the South Mountain gaps before swinging south for the crossing over the Potomac.

The next day dawned quiet. It was July 4. But it was a somber and dreadful national anniversary. No one was thinking happy thoughts.

I went out early for a walk. I wouldn't have dared to do so the day before, but something about this day was different. There was a stillness you could not only hear, but could *feel*. The troops who had been around for a day or two as part of Ewell's Corps were all gone. A lot of the Southern wounded had been taken, and their wagons were now far away. Smoke from a few fires still rose quietly into the warm morning air. Outside of town, a tent village for the wounded showed signs of activity.

I walked south, along the very road we had taken yesterday. The only soldiers I saw now were dressed in the dark blue of the Union army, but they didn't pay much attention to me.

As awful as the previous day had been, there was something even worse about what I saw that morning. The farther from town I went, the greater were the indescribable horrors—dead horses and dead men lying everywhere, some of them barefoot, their boots pulled off by survivors in desperate need of new footwear. Now I knew what had been done with all the dead—nothing! Bodies clad in both blue and gray were strewn everywhere.

There would probably be huge mass graves dug, and townspeople and medics and church people and the soldiers themselves would all eventually come to remove the evidence of battle—corpses and broken wagons and shattered weapons and discarded supplies. But for now, on this morning so soon after the smoke had settled, all the horrible scars of destruction and violence and death lay everywhere for all eyes to see.

As I was gazing out over a field into the distance, my careless steps stumbled, and I nearly fell. I pulled my eyes back in front of me and looked down. I had nearly toppled right onto a corpse.

Aghast, I stepped back, but not before I saw the dreadful look of the dead boy's eyes staring straight up at me. A look of anguished fear remained on his face, caught there and preserved at the very moment of death! I would never get it out of my mind as long as I lived. I felt as though he were looking at me, from the other side of the curtain of death, still asking—asking me!—what all the nonsense of killing was supposed to be about, asking why *he* had had to die.

Suddenly my stomach churned. Choking, and my eyes stinging with tears, I backed away from the body, then turned and began to run. Faster and faster I flew, and ran the entire distance back to the church, crying all the way.

The Train Again

Chapter Twenty-Three

*T*he fighting did not resume.

Most of that time the two great armies watched each other warily, each wondering if the other was going to attack. Neither did. The Confederates half expected Meade to come after them, but when he didn't, Lee finally made the decision to call off his hoped-for invasion and to retreat back into northern Virginia. He gave the order, his army began the long retreat the way they had come, and General Meade followed at a distance. Lee was still dangerous, and Meade wanted to make sure the general did indeed go back to Virginia.

The great battle of Gettysburg was over. Lee had tried to invade the North and had failed. But he had also made good his escape, even if in defeat.

Those of us from the Convent of John Seventeen remained another two days in Gettysburg. By then Sister Janette had recovered sufficiently to travel, although she remained very weak.

Gettysburg was the bloodiest battle of the whole war. Over 50,000 men were killed—23,000 from the North, 28,000 from the South! The dead lay everywhere surrounding the town. And once the armies departed, the 2,400 inhabitants were left with ten times that number of wounded to do their best to care for. The wounded were brought into homes, even as graves were being dug for the dead, and the town's churches did even more than they had been able to do during the fighting to help care for them. Carpets and walls and floorboards and blankets and pillows and books used for pillows—all were saturated with blood! The U.S. Sanitary Commission, for whom I'd helped raise money at the start of the war, sent in doctors and nurses and supplies to help with the effort, too. They erected many more tents outside town, which eventually relieved the burden on the townspeople.

Several of the sisters, including the two who were nurses, remained behind in Gettysburg. But now that General Lee's invasion had been stopped, I felt I ought to continue on to Washington. And I did not want to leave Sister Janette's side. We again spent the night in East Prospect, and then arrived back at the convent late the following day.

Whatever my future held as far as marriage or being single, becoming a nun or joining a convent, writing or not writing, of one thing I *was* certain. I needed to continue on to see President Lincoln before anything. It was for that reason I had come, and I had to follow through. He had asked for my help with the war effort, and now more than ever I wanted to do whatever I could.

Now I had been part of what the Sanitary Commission did and saw how valuable and necessary their work was in caring for the wounded. I had seen firsthand where the money raised for the Sanitary Fund went. And if I could help with that again, perhaps I could do more good in that way than I'd been able to do with actual bandages and medicine in my hands.

Four days later, therefore, I found myself back on the train and again heading northeastward toward Harrisburg, where

I could connect with another train to take me south to the nation's capital.

What an unbelievable three weeks it had been since I'd met Sister Janette on the train and decided to get off with her and visit the convent!

It would be a long time before I'd know which had affected my life the most—my talks with her, being with the Sisters of Unity, or witnessing the battle of Gettysburg. How could I ever be the same again? All three experiences had enlarged the world of my mind. Never had I encountered so many new things to think about in such a short time.

I sat in the train all that first day, staring blankly out the window, unable to focus my thoughts. All the enthusiasm and jubilation of the earlier part of my journey were gone. I felt very isolated and alone. A huge dark cloud settled over my spirit, and I couldn't get out from under its oppression. I had felt so cared for, so safe, so at home with the sisters at the convent. Why I hadn't felt lonely before meeting Sister Janette I didn't know. Nothing had changed. This had been my plan all along. Yet now that I *had* met her, met them all—everything was different. I had left a part of myself behind, a piece of my heart. And now I didn't feel altogether whole because a part of me had remained with them.

Even the thought of seeing President Lincoln was no longer exciting in the same way. What is meeting the President of the United States alongside a friendship that stirs deep bonds of attachment and love inside your heart? I felt as if I'd left home all over again. In fact, I felt more sadness in my spirit now than I had felt leaving Miracle Springs.

I pulled from my pocket a small silver cross the sister had given me the night before. It was a simple little token of friendship, yet merely holding it in my palm and gazing on it with my eyes sent stabs of painful longing deep into my heart.

I turned it over. There on the reverse, in letters so tiny I could just barely make them out, were the words: Sisters of Unity, New Providence, Pennsylvania. I read them over and over, three more times. Would this, I wondered almost wistfully, one day be my home, too? Why did I feel such a longing to remain there at the convent? Was it their life of dedication to Jesus that had penetrated so deeply into my soul, or merely the friendship of other young women whose spirits hungered for the same kind of life I did?

Perhaps it had to do with what had taken place at Gettysburg. Perhaps what I felt was a melancholy lingering from Jennie Wade's death and watching Sister Janette fall to the ground with a bullet in her shoulder—seeing the face of death so close all around me.

Whatever the reason, part of me didn't want to be on this train anymore. I wanted to turn around and go back . . . back to the convent . . . even all the way back to Miracle Springs.

But I knew I couldn't turn around. I had to finish what I'd started out to do.

Sister Janette's final words of parting came back to me. "You will always have a home here with us, Corrie," she had said. "And you will always occupy a special place in my own heart. You are a dear friend. I thank God for allowing our paths to cross, and I shall pray for the day when I see you once more."

I looked out the window at the passing countryside. Everything seemed gray and dreary. I tried to take in a deep breath, but it was no use. I choked on the very air, and my eyes filled with tears of sadness.

I arrived at the Capital early in the afternoon. The station was in the center of town. I left my bags there and walked straight to the White House.

There were soldiers and guards all around, I suppose on account of the war and the danger there could be to the President. Something was going on, but I couldn't make out what. There seemed to be an unusual amount of scurrying around, and then all of a sudden I saw three policemen come out of a gate holding on to a handcuffed man. They shoved him into a waiting enclosed carriage, got in after him, and the driver called to the two horses, and they lurched off down the street.

Once all the hubbub had settled, I remembered what I was doing there. I asked one of the guards in front near one of the fences surrounding the grounds where the gate was where I could get in. He gave me a funny look, but then directed me around to the side.

I walked around toward where he had pointed and came to a gate where there were even more guards. People were coming and going into the grounds. It was the same gate the three policemen had just come out of. There was a little guardhouse where two men with guns were in charge of opening and shutting the gate and letting people go through, and there still was quite a bit of activity and bustle after the incident I had just witnessed.

I walked up to the men standing in front of the guardhouse. "I would like to see Mr. Lincoln," I said.

One of the men eyed me carefully, then answered roughly, "Beat it, little girl. No one sees the President, especially not today."

"But I've—"

"Scram, you hear me?"

He made a menacing move toward me and I immediately backed away. There was enough of a crowd around that I quickly found myself surrounded by people and moving away from the gate. But after a minute or two I stopped and glanced back at the man who had spoken so harshly to me.

He was still watching me—and not with a friendly look, either. I was sick inside. What was I going to do?

I turned again and stumbled along, following the leisurely crowd of people wandering around the White House. My mind was swimming. I didn't know what to do. Maybe there was another entrance, somebody else I could talk to. I kept moving along the walkway, eventually walking around the entire perimeter of the White House grounds, until I found myself back at the guardhouse. There was that same meanlooking man standing there, holding a rifle!

I walked away again, this time back in the general direction of the train station. I didn't have anywhere else to go, though what I intended to do there, I'm not sure. I wanted to run away and hide, to get on the first westbound train and go back to the convent in Pennsylvania.

I felt so alone and so foolish. What had I thought, that I would just walk up to the White House and walk in as if it were the house next door? How could I have been so naïve? That was where the President of the United States lived! Who was I to think I could just walk up and knock on the door? He probably wouldn't remember me at all. He probably wrote nice notes like that to hundreds of people, never expecting them to do anything so outlandish as actually come to the White House and try to see him! It was all so clear now! He had never intended me to visit him at all. It was just his way of being nice and expressing his gratitude, and I had misunderstood the whole thing by thinking of it as an actual invitation.

Oh, I felt like such a stupid fool! I had come all this way for nothing! And what was I to do now? I was three thousand miles from California. I didn't even know where home was anymore! What should I do?

If a train had been available right then to take me back where I'd come from, I would have bought a ticket and boarded it at once. I was so discouraged I could not even think clearly! But after checking the schedule, I found that there *weren't* any trains leaving until the next day. So I would be stuck in Washington at least overnight. I'd have to find someplace to stay, and then I'd leave the city the following afternoon.

I retrieved my bags and asked the man behind the window about boardinghouses nearby. He told me of one just down the street and around the corner.

"You want me to get you a cab, ma'am?" he asked.

"Yes . . . yes, I suppose so. Thank you," I replied.

He signaled to one of the boys around the place, and when a twelve- or thirteen-year-old boy ran up to take me to where a horse-drawn cab was waiting, I couldn't help thinking of the first time I saw Robin O'Flaridy in the lobby of the Oriental Hotel. This little fellow had exactly Robin's flair and manner.

He led me to the cab with all the confidence of a street-wise grown man, and when I gave him a quarter as I climbed into the carriage, he flashed me a bright smile, kissed the coin, and ran back inside the station.

Ten minutes later I was inside the boardinghouse making arrangements for the night.

The lady whose house it was wasn't as friendly as either Miss Baxter or Miss Bean, and the house wasn't as clean or as nice either. She looked me over a minute, as if wondering why I would want a room. Finally she agreed to let me stay the night, acting as if she were doing *me* a favor. She took me to the room and told me that dinner, if I wanted it, was served promptly at six o'clock.

"Don't be late," she added. "I don't have time to be keeping things warm or serving any longer than I have to."

And with those words she shut the door behind me and I found myself alone. I set my bags down on the floor and glanced around. The room was small and plain, and from the looks of it I judged that mostly men stayed here. It wasn't very clean, and not at all homey. The blanket on the bed was a plain, drab olive green, and the curtains on the windows were so faded and threadbare they looked as if they'd been up for fifteen years.

I walked to the window and pulled back the curtain. Dust fell from it and settled to the sill. Outside, the only view was the back of the station, train tracks, and parked train cars. I hadn't needed the cab. I could have walked from the station.

I turned again back to the room. As I took everything in, the room was even smaller and uglier than I had first realized. I sighed, thinking to myself that I ought to try to make the best of a bad situation.

But my heart wasn't really in it, and before I knew it I had flopped across the bed and was crying from sheer loneliness.

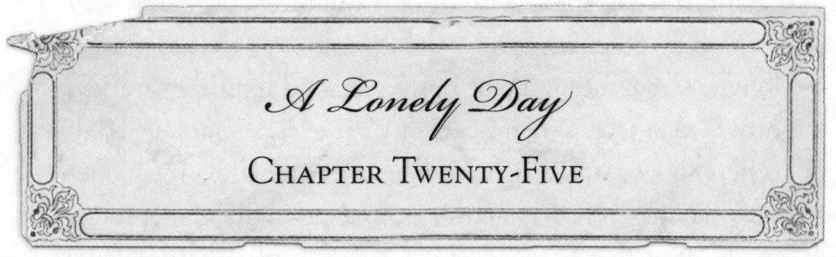

A Lonely Day

CHAPTER TWENTY-FIVE

I didn't have the energy or desire to make use of the rest of the day to see anything in the city. All I could think of was getting out and away from there!

I cried for a while, then fell asleep. When I woke up my stark surroundings seemed even more dingy than they had earlier. I got up off the bed and washed my face, put on some fresh clothes, and went out for a walk, hoping that would raise my spirits.

But it didn't.

I just walked around for a while in the vicinity of the train station. It was not a pretty part of the city. I should have taken a cab to see some of the buildings and monuments, but I just didn't have the heart to go back toward the Capitol or White House. Anything, though, would have been better than the smelly slaughterhouses and sooty brick buildings where I found myself. There were even what looked to have been slave-auctioning platforms, now in disuse. I was too depressed in my own thoughts to be afraid, although perhaps I should have been. The people I passed looked none too friendly.

I forced myself to look into people's faces. Once you saw someone's eyes, really saw *into* them, and knew they had seen you as well, people usually stopped seeming so fearsome. I

began to see in the faces of people I didn't know a look that
I can only describe as *vulnerable*. I could see that they were
lonely, sometimes sad, but in deeper ways than they wanted
others to detect. When I caught their eyes, some smiled, but
others sort of stared right through me, and I saw the aloneness. They could cover and shield and guard their inner selves
in the way they walked or dressed or spoke or conducted
themselves. But not in their eyes. Once I made contact there,
even if only for a second, it was like a window opened into a
deeper part of their being.

At times my heart went out to such people, and I found
myself wanting to touch them with more than just a look, just
a passing glance, or just a brief smile. Yet I didn't know what
to do. How do you touch another person, someone you don't
even know, when all you're doing is passing by for a second or
two? I found myself wondering how it was when Jesus caught
people's eyes? What did he do, what did he say to them?

And then in the midst of my thoughts, a stab of renewed
pain went through my heart. I was lonely, too. I was vulnerable and exposed and isolated, just like everyone else.

The sad melancholy I had felt before deepened all the
more. I was almost glad for the rain that started pouring
down. It fit the dreary loneliness of my mood perfectly, and
the drops falling down over my face helped to hide the fresh
tears spilling from my eyes.

By the time I reached the boardinghouse again, I was
soaked nearly to the skin. I just had time to change into dry
clothes before making my appearance in the dining room a
minute or two after six.

"I told you six, prompt, young lady," said the landlady
abruptly.

"I'm sorry," I said. "I'm afraid I got caught in the rain."

"Makes no nevermind to me what happened. Just don't be late again."

"I won't be here tomorrow," I said. "I'm leaving town on tomorrow's train."

"Just as well," said the woman grumpily, serving a plate with potatoes and a slice of meat and handing it to me. She certainly didn't seem very appreciative of having my room occupied! All the other guests were men. No one said a word throughout the whole meal except one of them, who seemed as if he just might have a bit of friendliness to him.

"Don't be too hard on her, Marge," he said, giving me a smile. "Can't you see she's new in town?"

"I got my rules, Mac," she replied to him, no more friendly in spite of the fact that they obviously knew each other. "They've got to apply to young ladies traveling through where maybe they oughtn't to be, just as well as to you working men. Besides, how I treat my guests is my own affair, so keep your nose out of it."

"I'm your guest too, Marge," he said, grinning at one of the other men.

"If you don't like the service, Mac," she grumbled, "then find yourself another place!"

Mac apparently thought better of any further exchange with the surly landlady, and his momentary speaking out on my behalf didn't lead to any more friendliness on his part. He and the other men continued to fill themselves with enormous quantities of Marge's bland dinner. She served them all seconds, and scarcely another word around the table was said. She took no more notice of me and offered me nothing further, although I had trouble enough finishing even the meager first portion. Finally I excused myself and went back to my room.

It was too early to go to bed, but I was too depressed to do much of anything else. I lay down on the bed and cried some more. All I could think of were the people I loved so dearly and missed so painfully.

Under normal circumstances, the people around the edges of our lives come and go, and we hardly notice. Then suddenly when we're lonely, they all come back into our memories, making us aware of the huge tapestry of relationships into which our lives have been woven.

Of all people, I found myself thinking of Mr. Ashton at the Mine and Freight office, missing his smile and kind, "Good morning, Corrie," he always greeted me with. Even more surprising, I thought of Mr. Royce. It would be wonderful even to see *him* right now! I'd probably give him a huge hug and scare him half out of his wits! Robin O'Flaridy . . . Mr. Kemble . . . Patrick Shaw . . . the Wards . . . oh, and dear Marcus Weber! I would have traded everything I owned right then for just a glimpse of any one of them! I felt so alone, so far away!

I thought of the sisters at the convent. I wondered how Sister Janette was doing, and if she was up and around again, if her shoulder hurt. I would see them all again . . . and soon! They weren't so far away, and it didn't hurt quite so deeply to imagine all the faces at the convent. I would get back on the train tomorrow, and before another two days were gone, I *would* be with them again. This time I would stay as long as I pleased! I would relish being with them, sharing life with them, and working alongside them. Maybe there would be another barn raising! I could help with their garden and the animals and other work around the convent. And such talks we would have!

There was so much I wanted to ask them about their life, to find out if it was the kind of life I wanted to live. Oh, I did want to be not just God's daughter but his woman! Completely his . . . married to him . . . devoted to him . . . serving him with all my life and everything I did!

Perhaps the convent was the place for me to begin. Perhaps I would stay . . . for a time. If I didn't become a nun exactly, well . . . maybe I could be *like* a nun! Were there such things as *Protestant* nuns? I didn't know, but I could find out! They probably weren't called nuns. But whatever they were called, that's what I would become—a woman devoted in service to God in every way, with time to pray and to read and study and contemplate everything about my Father in heaven.

And then I would write . . . yes, I would keep writing, and would write not just newspaper articles and stories but about my life of devotion to God.

I closed my eyes, and images started to crowd into my mind. My thoughts were racing now—with the faces of everyone I knew. I could even hear their voices, but couldn't exactly tell what they were saying. Everybody seemed to be saying something different, calling to me, urging me to do something . . . but I couldn't tell quite what.

Corrie . . . *Corrie* . . . I thought I heard them calling, but then as soon as my name faded from their lips, the words all became jumbled and confused, as if they were speaking in a foreign language. But it wasn't a foreign language! They were speaking English, and I knew the words, but I couldn't understand what they were saying.

Of course . . . that was the problem! They were all speaking at once, and so all the multitude of words tumbled over each other, confusing and garbling everything. There were too many voices, too many people calling my name, trying to say things to me.

Why wouldn't they all just speak one at a time? Why didn't they stop shouting and interrupting each other so I could make out their words? If only they would just slow down a little! I could see their lips moving . . . I could hear the words . . . they just didn't quite make sense. The meaning was so close . . . I could almost—if I could just listen a little more intently. . . .

"Corrie . . . Corrie . . ." The voice was distant, almost in a wail, as if calling me to come back from someplace far away.

Suddenly Mr. Ashton's face loomed huge right in front of me. He had been calling to me. "Corrie . . . Corrie," I heard him say again, "Corrie . . . you're late for work . . . there's an order that has to be written up for Chase and Baxter in Colfax."

"I . . . I'll . . ." I struggled to find the words to tell him I was on my way to the office, but the words wouldn't come.

Even as I was trying to answer him, all of a sudden there was Mr. Kemble. His voice was even more insistent. "Corrie . . . you've got to get in here to talk to me about . . ."

But his voice faded away, and I couldn't hear him finish. I opened my mouth to try to say something, but then it was Sister Janette's voice speaking softly to me.

"Corrie . . . Corrie," she said, "you have to stay here with us."

Over and over came the words: "*Stay here with us . . . stay here with us . . . come, Corrie, stay here with us . . . don't leave . . . don't go away . . . come back, stay here with us . . . come back, Corrie . . . come back . . . come back. . . .*"

The words began to fade. I tried desperately to cling to the sound of Sister Janette's voice. As it drifted into the distance, a terrible pang of loss stabbed through my heart. Suddenly Jennie Wade's pretty young face appeared! She opened her mouth to speak, but no words were there. A look of pain instantly came into her eyes, but then they slowly closed. She was dying!

"Jennie . . . Jennie!" I tried to cry out, but my mouth opened with the same silent impotence as hers. I could feel my lips moving, but they were mute and soundless. *Jennie . . . no . . . Jennie, don't die . . . !* But they were only thoughts, not words. I could not make her hear me! Oh, dear God . . . horror of horrors! All of a sudden, a tiny red splotch appeared on Jennie's forehead, just above her left eye! It grew in size, and began to drip down over her eyebrow into her eye. *God . . . oh, God . . . no!*

I tried to look away, but could not move my head! Then Jennie's face faded away, along with Sister Janette's . . . and in another second both were gone.

The faces from the battlefield began to haunt me—young Alan Smith in dark blue and Lt. Tomlinson in his red-stained gray . . . all the faces in the church, and the men I'd seen lying on the ground . . . passing through my memory in a second or two. I seemed to relive every moment of the awfulness of Gettysburg. Then before me was the grotesque face of the dead soldier I'd stumbled over the day after the battle, his eyes wide open, staring into my heart, though I knew he was dead and could see nothing!

God, take away the memory of that face! I tried to cry out, I tried to pray, I tried to run, but I couldn't move. I could feel the dead soldier's body against my feet. I tried to step over him . . . I tried to turn around, to get away . . . but it was useless! Suddenly I felt myself stumbling and starting to fall . . . I fell and fell . . . tumbling down and down . . . falling right on top of the hideous corpse!

But as I fell, all of a sudden there I was in my bed back at the house in Miracle Springs, and the next thing I heard were the playful musical voices of my brothers and sisters. They were young again! There they all were—Zack, Emily, Becky, and Tad—calling to me, trying to get me out of bed, urging me to get up and play with them.

"Corrie . . . Corrie . . . get up!" they all cried in unison. "The sun's been in the sky for hours. Come play with us, Corrie . . . please, get up . . . come . . . what's the matter, Corrie? . . . why won't you come with us? . . . come back, Corrie. . . ."

Tad was so young, and Zack was still a boy with a high-pitched voice, and Becky was giggling in her happiest way, and Emily was still young and innocent. All four were imploring me to join them, tugging at my arms and legs. But I couldn't get out of bed. And try as I might, I couldn't answer them, though my heart was filled with such longings of love that I couldn't stand it.

Then another voice intruded over the din, and from behind them I heard Pa approaching.

"Come on now, Corrie Belle," he said. "You've been away from us too long . . . I know you got lots of notions and ideas in that writer's mind of yours, but it's high time you came back to the real world where your family—"

Oh, Pa . . . Pa . . . I want to come back! I tried to say.

His tender face was looking over me now, full in my mind's eye. Oh, how dearly I loved him! What a good man! How thankful I was that God had given him back to me!

"Come, Corrie . . . I tell you, it's time you was back where you belong—"

His voice was interrupted by a sound from the room.

"Hee . . . hee . . . hee . . . tell her we ain't gonna put up with her gallivanting much longer . . . tell her that from Alkali, Drum, hee, hee, hee!"

Still Pa's face loomed before me. He had tears in his eyes
. . . and I knew they were there because he loved me.

Pa . . . Pa . . . I love . . . I love—

But I couldn't get the words out. I loved him, but I couldn't
make him hear . . . I couldn't make him understand!

His face began to grow pale and distant.

*Pa, please . . . don't go away, Pa . . . don't leave me again. Pa,
I want to come back . . . help me, I don't know which way to go
. . . Pa. . . .*

The next voice I heard was soothing and comforting.

"The Lord is with you, Corrie." It was a man's voice . . . it
was Avery Rutledge!

*Oh, Rev. Rutledge. I've . . . I've been away, and I don't know
what the Lord wants me—*

"Yes, Corrie, I know all about it. He has heard your
prayers, and you need have no worries."

*But . . . but I don't know what he wants me to do . . . there's
so much I don't understand, and—*

"He will make sure you know when the time comes."

But . . . but I—

Suddenly Almeda was at my bedside, sitting beside me,
stroking my forehead. I could still hear the children clamoring
outside for me to join them, but a great sigh of relief washed
through my whole being at Almeda's soft voice.

"There, there, Corrie," she said tenderly, "I am here now.
You've been ill . . . your mind has been wandering. . . ."

*Oh, Almeda . . . it was so dreadful . . . there were boys younger
than Zack . . . they were dying all around me!*

"It's all right now, Corrie. Dr. Shoemaker says the fever
has passed, and that you will be yourself again in twenty-
four hours."

It was so awful . . . I didn't know if I'd . . . oh, Almeda, I was so afraid . . . so lonely . . . I missed you so much. . . .

"Yes, dear. You were talking in your sleep about the train and the nuns and a battle you were in, and about someone named Jennie—"

Oh, Almeda . . . it was so awful . . . there was so much blood and death!

"Just relax, Corrie . . . everything will be all right now. It was all a dreadful dream . . . from the fever. You are with us again now . . . you are with us . . . you don't ever need to leave us again."

I started to cry. *Thank you . . . thank you! You can't imagine how alone I felt! I wanted to be with you so much!*

"But you are not alone now. I am here with you, dear Corrie."

She stretched out her arms to embrace me. Her touch felt so warm and good. I was still crying, for sheer joy, to feel Almeda's arms around me.

I struggled to lift my own arms from the bed. I had tried so desperately to speak to everyone else who had come into my mind. But I hadn't been able to open my mouth . . . I hadn't been able to move . . . I had been powerless and silent.

But now, with a groaning of agony, I forced myself to raise my arms. Slowly I felt them leave my side. I stretched them upward and encircled Almeda's waist, returning her warm embrace.

It felt so good to have her there at my bedside, to send the dark cloud of loneliness away with her loving presence.

I squeezed her tightly, crying freely now for joy. But why wouldn't she return the pressure? I felt her arms around me and her hands on my back, but they seemed weak and limp.

A sudden chill swept through my body. Why was I suddenly so cold? But . . . but . . . of course, that was the reason . . . Almeda's arms had grown cold . . . that was what I felt.

I hugged her tightly, but then felt her arms fall from around me lifelessly. I glanced up into her face.

Oh, God . . . God . . . no!

It wasn't Almeda's face at all! My arms were clutched around Jennie's cold, dead body, where she lay, eyes closed, in a wooden coffin somewhere.

I tried to jump back, aghast. But once again I couldn't move. My arms were locked in an embrace around the corpse that had once contained the life of young Jennie Wade!

But my head did move. I glanced to the right and left. All around me, stretching for as far as I could see in every direction, lay coffins . . . coffins . . . with the bodies of the dead. . . .

With sickening horror I realized I knew every face! There were the soldiers—Smith and Tomlinson, the lieutenant, with the sword that had killed him sticking morbidly out of his body . . . there was the dead face with open eyes . . . *Oh, God, no it can't be!* . . . there lay Sister Janette! She had died from the wound in her shoulder!

I shut my eyes and tried to scream. I couldn't look at another single coffin—it was too terrifying. I was afraid that in one of them I'd see my own face, and that the moment my eyes fell upon it . . . I'd be dead.

I squeezed my eyes shut, but could not stop the flow of tears. Still my arms clung to the cold body in the coffin. I could not pull them away.

I felt tears pouring out from under my closed lids and falling down onto the body beneath me.

Some inner compulsion forced my eyes to open. But I squeezed them tight . . . I didn't want to look!

The cold was now beyond endurance. My arms felt as though they were wrapped around an iceberg. Slowly my eyes opened.

There, just inches from my face, my arms about the body her soul had once called home, was the white, pale, dead face of my mother.

Oh, Ma! I wailed in forlorn and bitter agony.

The cry of my own voice woke me suddenly. I jumped up with a start, glancing around wildly in the middle of the darkened room. My lungs were heaving, my body drenched with sweat. My arms were clasped around a pillow that was wet from my weeping.

For five or six seconds I stared into the darkness, bewildered and disoriented. As wakefulness gradually stole back over me, I remembered where I was.

The reality was nearly as bad as the dream. For with the return of consciousness the acrid reality of my aloneness returned as well. I slumped back onto the pillow and wept once more.

Nighttime Thoughts
Chapter Twenty-Six

*S*leep did not return for a long while.

I cried, at first from the renewed despondency of finding myself again so far removed from all those I loved, and then for a while from nothing more than a sorrowful sadness over my plight and the disappointment of the day before. Then I relived my dream, trying to sort through everything it caused me to think about. It was a long, dark night.

I didn't have any idea what time it was, but finally I crawled off the bed. I was still wearing my clothes from the previous evening. I felt around for a match, lit the kerosene lantern, and once again beheld my dingy little quarters. The dress I had worn in the rain still hung damp over the wardrobe door. Outside I heard the continuing sounds of rainfall.

Slowly I undressed and changed into my bedclothes, then lay back down. Somehow the dream and the crying had taken my loneliness through the deepest valley of despair. And now as my tears began to dry, I found myself taking a few deep breaths of air, and with them drawing in the first breeze of a reviving hope.

I turned the wet pillow over, then stretched out on my back, staring up at the ceiling. I was here, I thought. I couldn't leave just yet. The soonest I could leave would be tomorrow afternoon. Why not at least try again to make the best of it? Even if I missed tomorrow's train, what would be the real harm to me? If worse came to worst and I had to remain another night, I could endure the sour disposition of the landlady through one more mealtime. And I'd be sure to be on time!

She was lonely, too, I thought. Lonely and growing old . . . her husband was probably dead, or maybe she'd never married at all. What business did I have to be so absorbed in my own self-pity that I would ignore one of God's children in such obvious need of graciousness and love as this lady?

I determined that I *would* stay another day, and that I *would* find an opportunity to return the landlady's grumpiness with as much good cheer as I could muster! Maybe I *was* homesick, but that was no excuse for not doing what Jesus told me to do. And he said to do good and be kind and to treat others as I wanted to be treated. So I would make an effort to do just that tomorrow . . . at the first opportunity that presented itself, which would be at breakfast. I would be there at 7:29, with a smile and a kind word for every one of her cranky ones!

After that . . . well, who could tell? I would determine to make it a better day than the one just past. Even if circumstances didn't go right—even if they all went miserably—I would make it a better day by my attitude toward it. I would be thankful for all things that came my way, for every person who crossed my path, and for every word that was spoken to me!

I found myself thinking about the White House again and what had happened there. I don't suppose I should have expected anything different. Who was I, anyway, to be given an audience with President Abraham Lincoln? But, I thought further, *had* I indeed mistaken his meaning? I had been so sure that coming to Washington was what I was supposed to do. Where had I misunderstood?

I jumped off the bed, went to my suitcase, and pulled out the letter. I opened it and read it again, though I hardly know why—I'd already read it enough times to have memorized it ten times over!

MISS CORNELIA BELLE HOLLISTER,

I have been made aware of all your work for the Republican party on behalf of my election, as well as your efforts to raise money for our Union forces in this present conflict. I want to express my deepest appreciation on behalf of the nation, to tell you that your patriotism has not gone unnoticed. It would be my pleasure to meet you here at the White House in Washington, if circumstances would permit you to make the journey. I would very much like to give you my personal hand of gratitude, as well as ask you to help me in the war effort with a new project here in Washington.

Yours sincerely,
A. LINCOLN
President

How *could* there be a mistake? What could I possibly have misread about his words? *It would be my pleasure to meet you here at the White House. . . . I would very much like to give you my personal hand of gratitude . . . as well as ask you to help. . . .* Surely, if the man at the White House gate knew what the President had said, he would realize his mistake.

I had to try again! I wouldn't be so easily discouraged this time. I would tell them that I was *supposed* to see Mr. Lincoln

. . . that he'd invited me. How could everyone around the grounds be expected to know everything the President said or did? I should have expected them to turn me away. I had been completely unprepared. But I wouldn't be next time.

Making a mental resolve is the quickest way out of an emotional valley. Engaging your will and deciding to *do* something, however small a thing it may be, is the surest method for battling feelings of discouragement. And now that I'd decided upon two things I was going to *do* the next morning—smile and be nice to the landlady, and go back to the White House—I felt a great deal better.

I still didn't know what I'd do the day after tomorrow. But one day was enough to worry about, and usually paved the way well enough for the next.

It was probably only an hour or two before dawn, but with a considerably lighter heart, I finally fell asleep.

The next morning, despite the rough night and lack of sleep, I appeared in the dining room at 7:28. The other men were already there. A couple of them nodded at me as I entered. We sat down, and the lady called Marge served us. There wasn't much more conversation than the previous evening, but I tried to smile whenever I could catch anyone's eye.

When I was through, as the men were finishing up, I stood, picked up a couple of the dishes from the table, and followed the landlady as she was heading back into the kitchen.

"Would you like some help?"

She hesitated briefly, looked at me from under a suspicious bushy black eyebrow, then replied, "If you want to."

I followed her the rest of the way in, deposited my load on a sideboard, then turned to go back out to the dining room.

"I'll get the rest of them," I said. She didn't reply, but she didn't follow me back out, and when I returned to the kitchen again she had begun washing the other dishes, and let me continue until the men had gone and the table in the dining room was clean.

It was a rather silent affair, but I remained a while longer, found a dish towel, dried the dishes as she washed them, and then finally excused myself.

"If it won't be too much trouble," I said, "I have decided that I would like to remain at least one more night, maybe two."

"Suit yourself," she said. "I got nobody else for the room."

"Oh, thank you," I said. "I'll probably be gone all day," I added.

She said nothing.

"I hope you have a pleasant day," I said. "I'll see you tonight."

I turned and left. It wasn't much of a conversation, I'll admit, but at least I felt better for having tried.

I went back upstairs, got my bonnet, and set off again for the city. Forty minutes later I was approaching the White House. I went straight around to the east gate where I had gone yesterday, greatly relieved *not* to see the man who had been gruff to me before. Two men, both with guns, stood there letting people in and out. It seemed considerably calmer and more orderly than it had been yesterday.

I walked up to them.

"I'm here to see the President," I said as cheerfully as I could.

One of the men stared rather blankly at me, looked over at his partner with the hint of a grin, then back at me.

"The President," he repeated. "President *Lincoln?*"

"Yes," I nodded. "The President."

Again he glanced at his partner, this time with a definite grin. I didn't altogether like his expression.

"She says she wants to see the President," he said, and it was obvious from his tone he was mocking me.

"Look, Miss." said the other man to me, "we can't let just anybody who wants to see the President in here." At least his tone was more friendly.

"Why, there was a crazy man just yesterday who got over the fence, had a gun, and was trying to shoot the President.

Luckily we nabbed him in time. But there are constant threats, and protecting him is our job. I'm sorry."

Everything he said made perfect sense, and now I understood what I'd seen yesterday. But as he spoke I found myself forgetting everything I'd planned to say.

"But I've been traveling for a long time, just to see him," I said.

"I'm sorry. Those are our orders. That's why we're here—to *keep* people from getting in."

My face fell. I tried to collect my shattered thoughts so I could think. But before I had much of a chance to, the first man spoke again, and at least he wasn't teasing me anymore.

"How far did you come, Miss?" he asked.

"From California," I answered.

Both men looked at each other with wide expressions of surprise. "That is some distance. We ever had anyone come that far, Joe?" he asked the other guard. "Private citizen, I mean?"

"Not that I can recall."

"Please, I've just got to see him!" I interrupted, suddenly seeing a ray of hope.

"Suppose we ought to tell Hank?" said one of the men.

"Couldn't hurt," replied the one called Joe.

He turned and began walking toward the building behind him, while his partner, acting very nice and friendly now, spoke to me again.

"I'm sorry, Miss. We don't mean to be gruff with you. But with the war on, and with the battles of Gettysburg and Vicksburg just over with, it's been mighty tense around here. Lots of comings and goings—generals and couriers. There have always been lots of warnings of possible danger to the President.

But then after yesterday, suddenly everything tensed up a whole lot more. I'm sure you can understand."

"I was at Gettysburg," I said.

"I thought you said you came from California."

"I did. But on the way I was at Gettysburg, right during the battle."

The man looked at me with an expression of mild interest and surprise. But after a couple of seconds, he apparently decided against whatever he had been thinking, and said with finality. "I'm sorry, Miss, but we're under orders not to let *anybody* in without a thorough check."

I nodded.

"We just don't get many visitors from quite as far away as you've come. Most folks write the President first. He does get lots of mail."

"Oh, but I *did* write him!" I said, suddenly remembering the letter.

"Oh?" One of his eyebrows raised slightly. "Did you receive a reply?"

"No," I answered. "I was replying to *him*."

"Who?"

"The President."

"President Lincoln?"

"Yes."

"He wrote *you* a letter?"

"Yes, and my letter was in reply to that, telling him I'd come."

"That you'd come where?"

"Here . . . to visit him, just like he asked."

"The President wrote you, inviting you here . . . for a visit?" By now the man's voice was incredulous.

"Yes, that's why I'm here." I pulled the letter out of my pocket. "Here it is," I said, handing it to the guard.

He didn't look at it long enough to read it, only long enough to see the signature at the bottom.

"Hey, Joe!" he called out to the other man, who was just entering the building across the wide walkway. "Wait a minute . . . come back. I don't think we need to bother Hank about this."

Joe turned and came part of the way back to the guard-house, while the man I had been talking to thought a moment.

"I think you'd better go call Mr. Hay."

Joe hesitated. "You sure you know what you're doing?"

"I think so. And I think once he meets Miss Hollister here, he's going to ask us why we didn't call him down immediately."

Joe turned and went into the building. When he returned, the other man led me inside to a waiting room, where I sat down. In less than ten minutes I was talking with John Hay, Mr. Lincoln's private secretary. I showed him the letter I had received. He read it over carefully.

"Well, Miss Hollister," he said at last, "you certainly have come a long way to see our President."

"Yes, sir," I replied nervously. "I would have been here sooner—in June, as my letter stated. But I got caught up in the fighting at Gettysburg, and it seemed like the right thing to stay and help out with the wounded."

"Certainly," he said. "We're very grateful for your help." He paused. "We, uh . . . we would like to speak with you, of course, but you must understand—not knowing exactly when you would arrive—it will be a matter of fitting you into the President's schedule."

"Yes . . . I understand."

"And after that terrible business yesterday, things are in a bit of a stir around here. The President is out of town. We got him out of the city to safety immediately, just in case there was a larger plot afoot—there have been some nasty rumors floating about, and we just can't be too cautious about the President's safety."

I nodded.

"He will be out of town, we think, until the day after to-morrow. Might you be available, let me see—"

He glanced down at a notebook in his hand, turning the pages, then pausing.

"The day after that. Friday, that would be . . . how would that work out for you, Miss Hollister?"

"That will be fine," I said.

"Shall we pencil it in for three o'clock in the afternoon?"

"Yes, sir."

"Fine—very good!" He rose, then shook my hand. "Where are you staying, Miss Hollister, just in the event I should find it necessary to reach you for any reason?"

I gave him the address of the boardinghouse.

"Why, that's old Marge Surratt's place!"

"I believe that's correct."

"Nobody but railroaders and hobos stay there!"

"It's not so bad," I said, trying to put the best construction on it.

"Not so bad? It's a dreadful place! Marge Surratt is the surliest, nastiest landlady in this town. Everybody knows her . . . and stays away from her!"

"Do *you* know her, Mr. Hay?" I asked.

"Sure. Like I said, nearly everyone in town does."

"Where do you know her from if everybody tries to avoid her?"

"Oh, it wasn't always this way with Marge. She used to be quite the political dilettante. She was married to a senator, and the two of them hobnobbed with all of Washington's society. Why, Marge has been right here in the White House dozens of times."

"What happened to her?" I asked.

"Nobody knows quite the whole story in detail," answered Mr. Hay, "least of all me. There were rumors of trouble even before the election, to the effect that Surratt was in league with some big-money fellows from the South—you've probably never heard of Senator Goldwin?"

The very name suddenly filled my mind with memories of Derrick Gregory and my daring ride to Sonora and the whole plot against John Fremont. But it was too long a story to tell Mr. Hay about!

So I merely nodded. "Yes . . . yes, I have heard of him," I answered.

"And you know what kind of man *he* is?"

"I think so."

"Well, as I said, rumors started flying, including some that said there was trouble between Surratt and his wife—that's Marge. Surratt was defeated in fifty-eight. He went back to Ohio, but Marge stayed on. Word had it that she was still in league with Goldwin. If you ask me, she just couldn't stand to suddenly be cast adrift after years in the limelight. I suppose she thought that if she remained in Washington, the glow of power and prestige would linger about her life. Then he died the next year."

"And did it?"

"No. She never set foot in the White House again, as I understand it. Even James Buchanan, Southern sympathizer and ineffective as he was, was shrewd enough to realize that having her anywhere near his administration would tarnish his already shaky reputation. After her husband died there were reports of all manner of nefarious things Marge was mixed up in. Probably more than half of them aren't true, but once people began to talk about her in connection with slave-selling and gold-running, and even more serious plots on behalf of Goldwin and the Southern cause, she became a pariah among the honest and upright politicians in the city.

"Once Mr. Lincoln was elected and the war broke out, Marge faced three choices: go back to Ohio where she was from, go South and join the Confederacy, or stay here. By then, I think, Goldwin had no more use for her. With the war on, he had bigger problems than the fading star of an aging woman in the North. For whatever reasons, she remained here, broken, embittered, and angry at the whole world. She opened that run-down, dilapidated boardinghouse and has been there ever since."

"And she's no longer involved in politics or anything like that?"

Mr. Hay laughed with a curious expression. "Politics . . . no," he said. "But as to *anything like that*, it is hard to say. There continue to be persistent rumors that float about from time to time about what Marge is associated with. Gutter stuff, mostly, but sometimes more serious."

"What kind of things?"

"Well, you can imagine her feelings of antipathy toward the North, with her years of Southern connections. She hates Mr. Lincoln with a passion rivaled only on the streets of Atlanta or Montgomery! Nothing against her has ever been proven, but as I said, rumors persist of her association with low causes that would stir up trouble for the Union, and especially with people intent on the President's defeat and the victory of the Confederate cause."

I was silent. Mr. Hay had certainly given me a great deal to think about. I had wanted something more tangible to pray for the landlady about, and some insight into her that might make it easier for me to be nice to her. Now all at once I knew *too* much about her! Knowing how she felt about Mr. Lincoln, whom I admired, and about the Union cause, which I supported, would make it harder, not easier, to love her in a Christian way! And yet it still seemed that that was what I had to try to do. She wasn't exactly my "enemy," but when Jesus said to love your enemies, it probably applied to situations like this as well.

"In any event, Miss Hollister," Mr. Hay went on, "we can't have you staying at Marge's place. Whatever may or may not be true about Marge herself, the boardinghouse itself is run-down and dirty, and certainly not suitable for a young lady such as you."

"It's really not so bad," I said.

"Hmm . . . well, let's see . . . we shall have to make some other arrangements for you. Something closer by would be good."

"I . . . it isn't necessary for you to go to any trouble . . . not for me," I said.

"Nonsense, Miss Hollister," said Mr. Hay. "You just wait here for a few minutes. I will arrange for a carriage for you, and I will have one of the women on the staff accompany you and see what can be done. I'm sure after the letter the President sent, he would not take it kindly if we did not do everything possible to make your stay in Washington comfortable. You will be the President's guest . . . we will see to everything."

There was a slight pause, then he rose. I didn't want to be stubborn. After all, he could take it wrong. He might even suspect *my* loyalty and cancel my appointment on Friday. But something inside told me I had to do it anyway. I had prayed for an opportunity, and now that I had one, I couldn't let the offer of more plush quarters make me self-ishly lose sight of it.

"I'm sorry. I don't mean to be difficult," I said, "but I really feel I need to stay where I am, for another night or two at least. I told her I would be back."

"It's nothing but a flea trap, Miss Hollister!"

"I'm sorry. It's just . . . well, I feel I wasn't altogether as gracious to . . . to Mrs. Surratt as I ought to have been."

"Gracious . . . heavens! That's the last word I would ever associate with Marge! She hasn't a gracious bone in her body, and certainly would not return any graciousness she was shown."

"Nevertheless, it's *my* duty to be gracious to her, whether she returns it or not."

At length Mr. Hay shook his head in consternation.

"Have it your own way, Miss Hollister," he said, "although it makes not an ounce of sense to me! You won't object, will you, to my arranging the carriage for you?"

"No, sir," I replied. "You're very kind, and I appreciate it."

"Nor to the White House, and paying the tab for your expenses? You are the President's guest, wherever you choose to stay."

"That will be fine. Thank you again."

"And when you have discharged what you feel is your duty to Mrs. Surratt, you *will* allow me to put you up in a more suitable place?"

"Yes, sir, I will," I said with a smile.

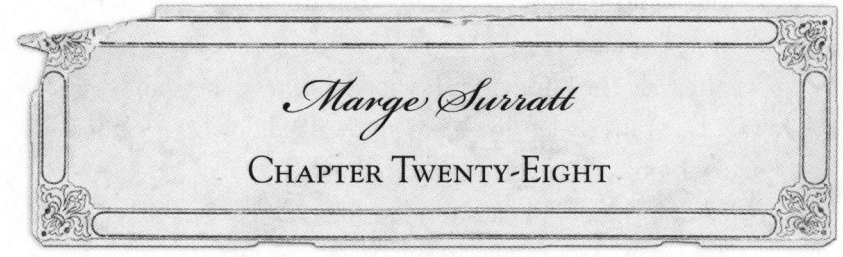

Marge Surratt
CHAPTER TWENTY-EIGHT

*H*ow could I possibly make Mr. Hay understand my feelings about Marge Surratt? I had prayed for some kind of a chink to open into her crusty, crabby, lonely heart. And now that I knew something about her, I couldn't just turn my back and walk away. But how could he understand? All he could see was that it was a dingy place and that I might have a much nicer room somewhere else. For me, however, it was a matter of the heart, not how nice the linens and blankets might be, or what kind of curtains hung in the window.

Maybe nothing would come of it. Marge Surratt could just as easily take offense at my trying to be nice to her as receive it kindly. Still, I had to try.

But Mr. Hay was very kind in every other way. He arranged for a carriage to take me back, and the lady who took me spent several hours with me, showing me around Washington. I saw the Capitol building, where the big dome for the top was in the middle of construction, the Washington monument, and some of the other important buildings. When she left me I had plenty to occupy my attention, and I spent the rest of the day walking.

Just the day before I had thought the whole thing a terrible mistake. But now I was gradually warming up to the city and thought maybe I did like it here, after all.

My opportunity to talk to Mrs. Surratt didn't come till the following evening.

After all the dinner dishes had been washed and put away, I tentatively left my room and walked downstairs, then knocked softly on her sitting room door.

"Who's there?" I heard from inside.

"Corrie . . . Corrie Hollister," I said.

I opened the door a crack and looked in. "I wondered if you'd mind if I talked to you for a minute," I said.

"Yes, I *would* mind," she answered irritably. "What is it?"

I opened the door enough to step across the threshold. As I did so I went on, hoping not to give her the chance to throw me out.

"I was at the White House yesterday," I said quickly, "and Mr. Hay said he knew you, that you used to be at the White House a lot, and that you knew President Buchanan."

"Yeah, that's right, a regular politician I was! What of it? And what were you doing with John Hay, anyway?"

I didn't want to tell her that I'd come to see President Lincoln, if it was true she hated him.

"What was it like to know a President so well?" I asked. For the first time since I'd knocked on the door, she looked up at me. She eyed me cautiously for a moment or two. I couldn't tell what she was thinking. But if it bothered her that I hadn't answered her question, she didn't show it, because finally she answered mine.

"Aw, it wasn't much. It was my husband who knew him. That was the only reason we got invited to the White House."

Her voice betrayed the hint of pain at the memory. It was the first time she'd let down the tough mask she was wearing, letting out just a thin beam of light from her inner self.

"Your husband?"

"Yeah, he was a senator."

"Where from?"

"Ohio."

"So you were a senator's wife!" I said.

"Yeah, yeah, it wasn't no big thing."

"It seems pretty important to me."

"Don't seem to mean much now, does it?" she said, then laughed bitterly at the irony, glancing around at the poverty of her surroundings.

The laugh contained no joy, but through it I glimpsed a little deeper place in her heart.

"What happened? Did he—"

"He got himself defeated, that's what. Then he went back to Ohio and died."

"But you wanted to stay here?"

"Look around for yourself. Can't you see that I stayed?"

"Why did you?" I asked, inching still farther into the room.

For the first time she seemed to grow thoughtful for a passing moment. A look came over her face that was more than hurt. It was a pensive kind of pain, as if she were wondering whether she had done the right thing. Finally she spoke, but her words didn't have an enthusiastic ring to them.

"I had friends, professional associates, things I didn't want to leave behind. That fool of a husband of mine was going back to Ohio to retire, right when everything was getting interesting and when they needed us more than ever. So I figured I'd start a business and stay."

"Who needed you?"

"Never mind who—it's none of your concern."

"I'm sorry. I didn't mean to pry."

"Aw, forget it, dearie. It's just that there's too many loose tongues and long ears in this town—especially now. Someone like me who used to know important people—people on the other side of the fence, if you get my meaning—someone like me's got to be careful every minute."

I was dying to ask what she meant, but didn't dare.

"Well, you have your business, anyway," I said.

She laughed sardonically. "Yeah, some business!"

"It's a nice place," I said, trying to be positive, "and you seem to be busy with plenty of people."

She glared at me and didn't respond. "So what do you want?" she asked at last. "You said you wanted to talk to me."

"Oh, nothing in particular. I'm a long way from home, and I don't know anyone in Washington, and I just wanted to visit with you."

"Visit . . . with me?"

"Yes—you know, just get to know you a little better."

The laugh she gave at my words sounded like a grunt of disbelief, as if the idea of someone wanting to get to know *her* was too preposterous to even be thinkable.

"Well, suit yourself," she said. "And you might as well sit yourself down instead of standing there like that," she added. I think she was as surprised as I was to hear coming out of her mouth words that were *almost* an invitation to join her. From her look and tone, I don't think anybody had ever sat down with her right here in her sitting room just to chat.

I took the chance while I had it, and grabbed the nearest chair to the door.

We talked for a while longer. The conversation didn't get lively, and she didn't warm up much to the idea. But at least she put up with it, although I was hard pressed to find things to ask her, and she remained as tight-lipped as ever. So I told her a little about my life and about Miracle Springs. She didn't seem particularly interested in anything, but listened.

Finally I could tell I had stretched it about as far as I could. I had hoped to find some way to get in where I could touch the real human soul of the woman, but the fences she had up around her heart were too thick and too high. Still, I hoped it was a beginning and that more might come of it. In the meantime, I intended to pray for Marge Surratt that God would soften her crusty exterior enough so that he might find a way in.

I stood up and thanked her for letting me spend the time with her.

She nodded an acknowledgment, but said nothing.

"Well," I added, "I hope you have a pleasant evening and a good sleep. Good night."

She grunted again, and I left, closing the door quietly behind me, wondering what the poor lonely lady was thinking.

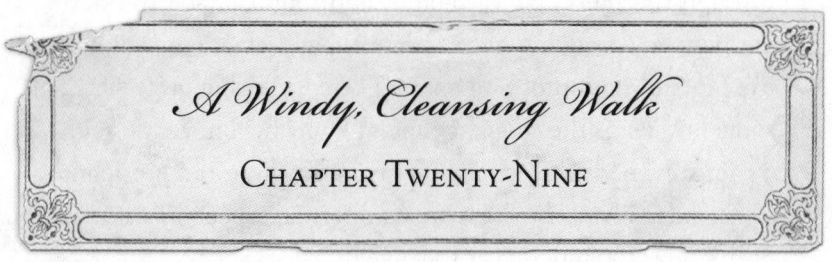

A Windy, Cleansing Walk
Chapter Twenty-Nine

My talk with Marge Surratt had an unsettling effect on me. And as I lay down that night to go to sleep, lots of anxieties gnawed at me.

I slept all right, but when I awoke it was still with a sense of inner agitation. It was Thursday. I had another twenty-four hours to wait before my appointment with President Lincoln. As much as I hoped for another chance to find some opportunity to speak with the landlady, I didn't much like the prospect of spending the whole day cooped up in my tiny room. So after breakfast I went out.

A storm had blown in as I'd slept, and the day was windy and blustery, with a fitful shower now and then. The rain would pour down, then stop suddenly. But it was warm, and when it was not raining, it felt comfortable. The smell was somehow different than the storms at home. Maybe it had something to do with the Atlantic, or with the fact that it was a summer storm. There was never rain in Miracle Springs during the summer.

I enjoyed the warm wind and the wetness in the air, and when the downpours came, I found the protection of some building to take shelter in until it passed. During one of the particularly long showers early in the afternoon, I wandered through the halls of the Capitol, and found myself wondering how Pa was doing in Sacramento, and even entertaining the fanciful notion of him coming *here* to Washington, D.C., someday. Yet as the thought came, I knew he'd never do such a thing, even with an engraved invitation from the President himself. He loved the West and California, especially Miracle Springs, far too much ever to leave it!

I went outside again, walking for miles, it seemed.

Part of me couldn't help feeling small, lonely, and insignificant in the midst of all the important things that Washington, D.C., represented. Moments would sweep over me, as they had two nights earlier, when I thought I had made a mistake in interpreting God's intention that I come here. Who was I? . . . what did I matter to the country, to the President . . . to anything? Then I'd remember the loneliness and the people I missed, and would feel sad and isolated and far away again.

But such feelings didn't usually stay with me for too long. Mostly I found thoughts of deep reflection that were directed at *me*—what kind of person I was becoming through all this. There was a certain melancholy to it, and yet something that felt good at the same time. I found myself taking in deep breaths of the warm, stormy air, almost as a symbol of taking in the thoughts and experiences and conversations I'd had since leaving Miracle Springs.

I suppose if I tried to put it into words, I was struggling with the deeper reality of what it meant for me to be growing fully into an adult—for me to be becoming someone completely *my own*, disconnected from home and Pa and my family and everything that had come before. Of course I would never *really* be disconnected. Yet being so far away from home was forcing me to step into a new level of individuality. I was meeting people and getting into situations as *me*. Not as Corrie Belle *Hollister*—my father's daughter and part of his family. Not as Corrie *Belle* Hollister, who was associated with Ma and Uncle Nick and the past generations of my family name. Here I was *Corrie*, a person of my very own. Myself . . . alone . . . God's daughter . . . an adult . . . with no one but myself to fall back on. It was a scary sensation, but it was strengthening at the same time.

The security of home was far away. I thought a lot about my life. I had had many adventures, but compared to being so far away, as I was now—somehow my early life seemed almost protected. Now the person I had become had to stand up to the test of whatever I might face—every day! There was no comfortable nest to return to at night, no secure arms to rest in, no shoulders to cry on. It was time for me to find out what kind of fiber I was made of, what kind of person I was down at the deepest parts of my being, my soul.

I thought about all the encounters I'd had with people thus far. Even the Englishman in the stagecoach, for all his pomp, had character and personality. Did I? Sister Janette and the rest of the nuns . . . their lives seemed to contain so much purpose and significance. Did mine? Lt. Tomlinson and Alan Smith and all the soldiers at Gettysburg had fought for their beliefs. Would I be willing to do that?

Everything I had been through had gone much deeper into me than I realized at the time of each encounter. I found myself comparing my life all over again to the Sisters of Unity, wondering anew if there was something for me there.

Who had I been? . . . who was I now? . . . who would I be a year from now? Was there any significance to my life, my being, to the person I was—any significance alongside the lives of Sister Janette and Jennie Wade and Alan Smith and even Abraham Lincoln? Toward what purpose in life had God been leading me?

I was going to see the President of the United States tomorrow! Why me? Who was I that he would care to see me? Why not one of the nuns, one of the soldiers wounded in battle—*anyone* but me?

And yet . . . *my* name was written down in his secretary's book for tomorrow afternoon at three o'clock!

And where did God fit into the whole maze of questions?

I *knew* where he fit. *He* was the force behind everything, the fountain of my life and everything in it, the one who had led me into every encounter I'd had, the one to whom I'd given my life, the one who directed my steps even when I didn't know it. If my life was a story, a progression of events and situations, then *he* was the author!

And if I didn't know what the next chapter held, or even if I didn't know what the chapter just written meant, it didn't matter. I was just a character on the page. But it was *his* book, not mine! And as long as *he* knew what the past meant and where the future was going, then all was well.

Did I possess the fiber, the character, the strength, the wisdom, the integrity to walk as a mature adult—as a *woman* of God at the same time as I was his daughter?

I didn't know. Perhaps I wasn't supposed to know just yet. But *he* knew. And if I didn't, well, he would see to it in his good time. He knew how the story of my life was supposed to progress, and who was I to worry about it?

As my swirling thoughts finally began to settle, I realized again that what I hungered for more than anything—a need which went deeper than people or experiences, beyond ideas and ambitions and dreams and goals, that settled fears and questions and uncertainties—was simply for more of God in my life. That hunger swallowed up all other desires. Intimacy with God absorbed and gave meaning to every other relationship. And being part of God's story gave purpose and direction and significance to all other of life's passing events, large and small. In God's story, my few moments with Alan Smith on the field behind Cemetery Ridge might be more significant than the time I hoped to spend with President Lincoln tomorrow. I did not need to fret in any way about *any* of these questions that had occupied my mind all day as I'd walked.

The presence and nearness of God . . . *that* is what mattered more than any significance my life might have, more than what I understood or didn't understand, more than whether I was strong or weak, mature or immature, more than whether I was a "woman" or still in many ways only a little girl.

"God, stay near me," I prayed, "and put in my heart a trust in you to take care of *everything* else."

The President

CHAPTER THIRTY

*T*he moment I stepped into the room where Mr. Lincoln was waiting, a great sense of awe came over me.

He was tall and thin, his face tired and his voice soft. Everything about him, from his black suit to the familiar beard, was exactly like the pictures I'd seen. And yet no picture could capture the aura of what it was like to be in the presence of a man of such stature and dignity.

His secretary introduced me.

The President came forward slowly, then extended his hand. I shook it, trying not to act as timid as I felt. At the touch of his grip, a thrilling surge of thrill passed through me. All over again it hit me—*this is the President of the United States. This is Abraham Lincoln himself!*

"Miss Hollister," he said softly. "I am so pleased to finally meet you, and pleased that you wanted to make the long trip here to Washington."

I swallowed and tried to say something, but couldn't get anything out!

"As I told you in my letter," he went on, "I'm most appreciative of how you helped with my election, and with raising money on behalf of the Union and the Sanitary Fund. It is important work they do, especially now with so many wounded, and of course they need money to continue their humanitarian operations. It is people such as you that the country has to thank for allowing such a work to continue. So when I tell you thank you, it is from the bottom of my heart."

It was clear he really meant what he said. I was humbled for him to speak so graciously to me, but at last I managed to find my own tongue.

"I . . . I saw some of the Sanitary Commission's people at Gettysburg," I said. My voice sounded so small! I felt like a tiny little fly in the presence of the President.

"Yes, I did hear from one of our guards, through Mr. Hay, that you *were* at Gettysburg. I would like to know more about it. Surely you weren't near the actual fighting?" As he spoke, Mr. Lincoln took a chair, motioning me to sit down opposite him. I did so.

"It was dreadful," I said.

"The fighting itself?" he said. "Were you near enough to actually see what was going on?"

"Oh yes . . . everything about it was terrible! And yes, we were very close."

"We?"

"I was with some Catholic nuns. We were helping the wounded however we could. Although with as much dying as there was, our efforts didn't seem to amount to much."

He asked how we came to be there, and I told him the whole story.

Mr. Lincoln listened quietly and patiently, and, it seemed, with great interest and thoughtfulness, asking me a question now and then, but mostly just letting me tell him about everything. I almost forgot where I was, and who *he* was! When I stopped, he was quiet for a minute, just thinking about what he'd heard. At length he let out a long sigh, then rose from the chair he'd been sitting in and walked slowly to the window and gazed out. When he turned back to the room, anguish and heartache were evident in every line of his face.

"Ah, Corrie," he said, "this is indeed a dark night for our country. Perhaps the darkest hour we have ever faced as a nation."

He paused briefly, then went on, more as if thinking aloud than talking to me. I almost felt as if I were intruding into some private place in his mind.

"Will we endure it? That is the question," he said. "And if we do, what will be the cost? Is freedom for the Negroes and keeping this nation united as one—is it worth the terrible price we have paid? Will this nation survive, or will the fallen have died in vain? Will freedom survive . . . or will this noble experiment we call the United States of America one day perish from the earth?"

Again he paused, and I was surprised to hear my own voice speaking in response.

"It *will* survive, Mr. President," I said. "It *has* to . . . I am sure of it."

"But again the question—at what price?" he replied. "How much longer will the night of conflict last? Oh, that the dawn would soon break through!"

It was the first time the great passion locked away inside his large frame had revealed itself. He was obviously very moved.

"Wasn't Gettysburg a great victory?" I said. "Perhaps the end of the war will come soon. Perhaps it *is* nearly over," I added hopefully.

"Perhaps," he said, nodding his head thoughtfully. "And Vicksburg."

"Vicksburg?" I repeated.

"The huge bastion of the Confederacy on the Mississippi. General Grant finally took it the day after Gettysburg, on the fourth."

"That's wonderful news!" I said.

"Yes . . . yes, I suppose it is."

I told him of seeing Mr. Grant long ago in California.

"My, but you have seen a great deal for one so young—the gold rush, Ulysses Grant, two national election campaigns, Gettysburg. . . ."

"I am more honored to be able, to meet *you*, Mr. Lincoln," I said, "than all the rest of it."

He gave a slight chuckle at my words, and I was immediately embarrassed.

"Do you think, then, that the war will be over quickly," I asked, "now that the Southern army has been defeated both at Vicksburg and Gettysburg?"

"We can only hope so," he replied. "Yes, the war in the West has culminated and it would appear the Mississippi Valley is at last ours for good. I doubt they will give us more serious trouble in that region. Their supplies and troops are thinning badly, from the reports I have. But—"

He stopped abruptly and suddenly an altogether different look than I had yet seen came over his face.

"But Lee," he went on after a moment, "is a skilled and crafty officer. I fear we let him off too easily."

I didn't understand what he meant. Lee's army had been turned back and his invasion of the North stopped. I thought it had been a great Union victory.

About that same time, Mr. Hay came back into the room.

"Excuse me, Mr. President," he said, "but this telegram just came in from General Meade. I thought you should see it. He is still following Lee's retreat."

Mr. Lincoln took the paper from his secretary, scanned it briefly, then replied heatedly.

"Lee has crossed back into Virginia and is in full retreat toward the south, he says! He rejoices that he has been driven away from *our soil,* as he puts it!"

He tossed the telegram onto his desk behind him, then slammed the fist of his right hand into the open palm of his left. His face was red, and he didn't look tired anymore.

"Will our generals never get that idea out of their heads!" he exclaimed angrily. "The whole country is our soil! The Union has been endangered for three years, not merely because Lee attempted an invasion of Pennsylvania. His army moving north of the Potomac isn't the threat, but rather that Lee's army exists in the first place!"

Mr. Hay excused himself. Mr. Lincoln gradually calmed, then looked back to where I was sitting, still wondering what I was doing listening to such talk between the most important man in the country and his private secretary!

"I'm sorry you had to witness that, Miss Hollister," he said. "But, you see, that is exactly the point I was trying to make to you before. When word came to me from Gettysburg, calling it a great triumph, I found myself seriously displeased rather than enthusiastic."

"Why, sir? I'm not sure I understand."

"Because it was our opportunity to destroy Lee's army completely. Once Lee cut his ties with Virginia and marched his men deep into the North, he was isolated. We could have compelled him to surrender, or perhaps to destroy himself if he tried to escape. We should *never* have allowed him to escape! But Meade didn't pursue him, and now the wounded lion will live to fight against us another day—mark my words."

It was surprising to hear him talk so ruthlessly about destroying General Lee. I had always taken him for a peaceful and gentle man.

"But surely you wouldn't want to have seen *more* men killed?" I said.

"Of course not. But there *will* be more killing, and the war will be prolonged now, I fear. You must understand, the ruthless pursuit of Lee I was advocating would have, I am convinced, shortened the war. We might have exacted a surrender at any moment. But now, alas, Lee will rebuild his army, the senseless killing will go on, and the war may drag out for another year."

"I think I understand now."

"We may have won the battle, yet we had an opportunity to end the war, and *that* mission we did not accomplish. I hate the killing! Yet sometimes to get to the light at the end of a tunnel, we must go through a long darkness first. Every day reports come to me of more death, more killing, more destruction of our nation, and every time it breaks my heart to realize the means by which we are being forced to obtain freedom for all our people—white *and* black, North *and* South."

"Do you think that aim is worth a war—freedom, I mean?" I asked.

Mr. Lincoln sighed deeply. "Ah, you've asked the question of my life, Corrie," he replied, his voice soft again and far away. "I shall go to my grave trying to find the answer. I know that when I became President, it looked to many as though I had run for this office just to start a war. You cannot imagine how such talk grieves my heart. Yes, we are engaged in a dreadful conflict—but not because I *wanted* it. There are two reasons. One, to keep these United States whole without being divided, and second, to declare to all the world that all men *are* created equal. That is, of course, the question of slavery."

Suddenly he seemed to catch himself. He stopped, gave a little chuckle, then added, "I'm sorry. I still have an old lawyer's habit of thinking out loud. I'm sure you didn't come here to hear an old man ramble on about his woes."

I was shocked to hear him refer to himself as an old man. But I didn't say anything, and when he spoke again it was in a different vein altogether.

"As I told you earlier, Corrie," he said, "I am grateful for your help in the past. And now that I have met you face-to-face and heard of your experiences at Gettysburg, I am doubly glad for inviting you here and that you were willing to come. I think you may indeed be able to help the Union cause."

"I would, of course, be happy to do anything I could . . . but I don't see how . . ."

"Don't you see how your testimony of having actually been on the battlefield could galvanize the citizens of the Union? You could tell of the crying need for supplies and volunteers and money on behalf of the Sanitary Commission. As long as this war continues, there will be more bloodshed, more wounded, and more need for volunteers to help with them, just as you and the sisters from the convent did. You can help us make this crying need known."

"I might be able to write an article about the battle," I suggested, "telling people how important it is they contribute to the Sanitary Fund."

"Exactly. It could be telegraphed back to your home state of California, and we might arrange for several of the eastern papers to run it as well. Yes, I think that is a splendid idea!"

Even as he was finishing his statement, Mr. Hay walked into the room again.

"Mr. President," he said, "I'm sorry to interrupt, but there's your four o'clock appointment with the French Ambassador."

"Ah, yes . . . has he arrived?"

"Yes, sir, he's waiting down in the east parlor."

"Miss Hollister . . . Corrie . . . I am sorry to have to cut our visit short like this," Mr. Lincoln said, turning toward me again. "I have so enjoyed talking with you."

"Thank you," I replied, standing up. He approached and shook my hand again, very affectionately, I thought.

"I meant every word," he said. "I sincerely hope you will be able to help in some of the ways we discussed. I'll leave you and Mr. Hay here to make the arrangements for the remainder of your time in Washington. Good-day, Corrie, and thank you again for a fine visit."

Mr. Hay's Big Plans

CHAPTER THIRTY-ONE

*P*resident Lincoln had been gracious, humble, and at the same time so honest and down-to-earth. Even though I had been in his presence, and even though now his face still filled my memory along with everything he'd said, it would be a long time later before I'd really comprehend what I had just experienced. And when it began to dawn on me what a unique and treasured encounter this had been, I found my-self thinking that America would surely remember Abraham Lincoln, for years to come, as one of the nation's greatest presidents ever.

And I had actually spent an hour with him! He had lis-tened to me talk. He had seemed interested. And he had, just as in his letter, asked me to help the country and the cause of the war! All my doubts and reservations about coming East suddenly evaporated. I walked out of the White House more full of enthusiasm and a sense of purpose than I had for months. I said goodbye to the two guards at the gate, Joe and Al, who were now very friendly to me every time I passed, and fairly skipped on down the street.

Mr. Hay asked me to come back and see him the follow-ing day, even though it was Saturday. When I did, he made arrangements for all kinds of things for me to do. He was very businesslike, but not like Almeda and Mr. Ashton. White House business was a lot different than Miracle Springs gold-country business!

When I left after my interview with the President's secretary, I had a list of things a whole page long to do. I just hoped I'd remember everything!

There wasn't much chance of my forgetting, of course, because Mr. Hay had written down the same list and had said he'd take care of everything.

There were many people he wanted me to meet, he said, beginning on Monday. Mrs. Harding, a nurse who had been out on the field, was now recruiting and training volunteers for the Sanitary Commission to send them out behind the troops where battles were anticipated. Mr. Vargo, the Sanitary Commission chairman in Washington, was primarily in charge of fund raising.

Both of them, Mr. Hay said, would have plenty for me to do. Once Mrs. Harding heard what I'd been through in Gettysburg, he said, she would be putting me up in front of women's and church groups all over the North to tell about it and to encourage others to help them save lives.

"And Vargo, too," he went on, "will be anxious to enlist your support on behalf of his financial efforts, especially once he learns that you already have experience in that sort of thing out in California."

I was starting to get tired just listening to him make plans for me. It sounded like a busy schedule!

"How long did you plan to be in Washington, Miss Hollister?" he asked me.

"I . . . I didn't really have specific plans," I replied. "I don't know, a few weeks perhaps. . . ."

"Hmm," thought Mr. Hay, "two or three weeks . . . that doesn't give us much time. We'll have to make use of every minute we can."

"Mr. Lincoln mentioned something about writing, too," I reminded him.

I was willing to talk to people if the subject was something I believed in enough and could talk naturally about. But "speechmaking," as I had heard politicians do plenty of times, was not something I *could* do, or *wanted* to do. Besides, I felt more comfortable expressing my thoughts on paper.

So I didn't want Mr. Hay to forget what the President had said about article-writing. I had already become excited about writing something to be telegraphed back to the West Coast. Wouldn't Mr. Kemble and Robin O'Flaridy come out of their chairs when it came across the wire!

I could just see them! Robin would be jealous, but he'd try not to let it show. Mr. Kemble would try to pretend that it wasn't anything so out of the ordinary, as if his reporters went to Washington and talked to people in the White House all the time! But then when he was alone, he'd mutter something like, "C. B. Hollister . . . I can hardly believe it! I didn't think you had it in you . . . but you've done all right, Corrie!" If I were there in his office, though, his next words would probably be, "But don't you go getting a swelled sense of your own importance to this newspaper . . . I'm *still* only going to pay you six dollars for the article, even if you are supposedly a friend of Abraham Lincoln's!"

I laughed at the thought. I didn't care if he paid me a cent! *This article's on me, Mr. Kemble!* I thought.

And when everybody in Miracle Springs got the paper and saw an article from the national capital with *my* name on it, what a day that would be! The thought brought a great lump to my chest, and I wanted to burst out laughing and crying both at once! I didn't know if I could stand not being there with them all when that happened!

"Look . . . look here! It's Corrie!"

"Why didn't she tell us. . . ?"

"How could she have told us, Drum? She's all the way back—"

"Why, if that don't beat all! Miz Corrie's done met Mister Lincoln himself. . . ."

"Let me look at it!"

"Hold your horses, Tad, son—we'll all get a chance to read it."

"We're all gonna be famous now, hee, hee, hee!"

"Aw, nobody's gonna be nothin', Alkali, you old goat!"

"Don't be so sure, Nick. . . . Corrie might put Miracle Springs on the map yet."

Voices and faces crowded into my mind all at once . . . laughing, grabbing at the *Alta* . . . all talking about me, and yet with me not there with them.

All these thoughts about writing and home flew swiftly through my mind in two or three seconds, even as Mr. Hay was nodding his head and replying to what I'd said.

"Yes . . . hmm, that's right," he said. "He spoke to me about that when we were discussing you this morning."

"I want to do whatever I can, but writing's what I do best."

"And indeed, we want you to do it. Are you still set on staying at the Surratt woman's place? It doesn't seem that the atmosphere would be terribly conducive to what you have in mind."

"I suppose you're right. . . . There isn't even a desk in the room."

"There, you see! It's imperative that you let me make arrangements for more suitable quarters. Why, you're practically working for the President now, Miss Hollister!"

"Yes, I see the practicality in what you're saying. Just give me another couple of days, and then I'll be happy for you to put me anywhere you like."

"Fine! Early in the week I'll have everything arranged! And in the meantime, I'll have your itinerary set as well. Why don't you come see me again on Tuesday morning? We'll send someone over to pick up your things, get you settled in one of the better boardinghouses close by—*with* a desk!—and by noon you can be hard at work on your first article. How does that sound?"

"Just fine, Mr. Hay," I replied, "but I . . . uh, I don't know if I can . . . that is, I don't have a great deal of money, and until the articles—"

"Miss Hollister," he interrupted, "I told you before, don't worry a thing about it. As I said, you are our guest. We will see to all your expenses—lodging, meals, cabs, whatever else you might need. And if the newspapers pay you for your articles besides, keep the remuneration with our blessings."

"That's awfully kind of you."

"The President was quite taken with you. He's counting on you to help him in this fight to preserve the Union. He feels it's the least he can do in return."

My First Assignment
CHAPTER THIRTY-TWO

$\mathcal{T}$he next few days I spent mostly at the boardinghouse, either in my room or trying to find opportunities to visit with Mrs. Surratt. Neither was particularly fruitful. Mr. Hay had certainly been right—it was not a place where I could work very well. And even with all the friendliness I could muster, Mrs. Surratt remained distant and untalkative.

Actually, my greatest worry became one of making a pest of myself. Something about the poor, lonely old lady had gone into my heart. It would be exaggerating to say that I *loved* her. Jesus told us to love people, especially those who were difficult to love, those who treated us badly, and even our neighbors. I doubt he meant we were to feel the same kinds of things for those kinds of people as we did our family and friends and the folks we called our *loved ones*. Yet he still said we were supposed to *love* them.

I found myself wondering exactly what he did mean when he told us that. It seemed like a contradiction to tell us to love people we don't, and maybe even *couldn't* love in the way we think of the word. All I could figure out was that he must have been telling us either to *try* to love them, or else to *do* nice things for them and to be kind to them no matter what we felt. In either case, it was still confusing.

But confusing or not, Jesus didn't leave much room for doubt about the matter. He said we *were* to do it—whatever it meant. We *had* to love people—enemies, friends, people we liked, and people we didn't like. So that meant I had to love Marge Surratt, whether I liked her or not. And I figured that meant I had to do my best to *try* to love her by being kind and nice and looking out for opportunities to help her or speak kindly to her, however I could. I didn't know if that was all Jesus meant, but it's all I could lay hold of for the time being, and I knew I'd better do that much.

So I puttered around the boardinghouse, and I'm afraid *did* make kind of a nuisance of myself. Nothing much came of it. She still spoke harshly to me. But we did have some more conversations, and she didn't object when I helped her with the meals from then on. And she seemed halfway interested when I told her what I was going to be doing, and even asked a question or two. I made sure I didn't get into things when we were talking that would have turned into an argument over different viewpoints about the country or the war or Mr. Lincoln or anything like that. If she really had been for the South, as Mr. Hay said, and if she disliked Mr. Lincoln as much as he'd said, then I knew there could be nothing worse than getting on different sides of issues like that. Arguing or talking about things you disagreed about was the *worst* thing you could do if you were trying to love somebody as Jesus commanded.

When Tuesday came and it was time for me to leave, she gave me a halfway sort of smile and said I'd be welcome back anytime. My heart jumped inside me, and I almost felt like telling Mr. Hay I'd changed my mind and I was going to keep staying with Marge Surratt! One of the interesting things I learned from my time with her was that when you do try to do what Jesus said, whether you love somebody or not, eventually something starts to happen inside your *own* heart just from the effort, and by and by you *do* find yourself starting to love them. I was surprised to find myself a little regretful about leaving her. I had already grown more fond of her than I realized.

Yet I knew there were other important things I had to do. So I packed up my things as planned and said goodbye to Marge Surratt, but told her I'd be back to see her sometime.

I did have to admit, though, that the new boardinghouse where Mr. Hay'd arranged a room for me was so much nicer. Not that niceness all by itself mattered so much. Some of the soundest sleeps I'd enjoyed had been around a campfire with Zack or Pa, and even a time or two by myself, on hard ground with nothing for company but the crickets and owls and distant coyote howls. So it wasn't the large bed with pretty yellow and white quilt, or the ruffly curtains, or looking out from my second floor room right out on the White House half a mile away . . . it wasn't those things alone that made the new boardinghouse so perfect. But the room had a nice desk where I could work, and it was quiet, without the sounds of trains coming and going. And seeing the White House out the window as I sat there at my writing table helped keep me inspired about why I was there and how important it was that I do a good job at what Mr. Lincoln had asked of me.

And I did get right to work as soon as I had my things put away in the wardrobe. It had been a long time since I had actually sat down with pen and paper and ink in front of me. Once I started, I realized how much I'd missed writing.

When I did start, something happened that I'd never felt before in any of the articles I'd done. I don't know if it was being so far away from home, or because of what I was writing about, or because of the importance of it—Mr. Lincoln had stressed that people needed to understand about what being at war really meant and how urgent was the need for money and help and supplies and medicine and volunteers. Maybe it was all those things together. But I found myself thinking more "personally" about what I was writing, and imagining myself talking to *real* people as I was doing it, as if I were standing up talking to them. I felt as if I were talking especially to the people in California—just as if I were writing a letter home.

It certainly didn't feel as if I were writing an "article." Before I knew it, I'd written what I'd seen at Gettysburg and what I'd thought and felt, too. I showed it to Mr. Hay the next day. He showed it to the President and some of the Washington newspaper editors, and by the following week what I'd written was appearing in the papers of Washington, Philadelphia, Boston, and Chicago. Mr. Hay said he'd wired it to Mr. Kemble at the *Alta* as well, and then told me to get working on another.

"But I thought—" I started to say.

"Never mind what you thought," said Mr. Hay. "I thought perhaps one article and a speech or two might be all we'd need. But the President says what you wrote about Gettysburg is better and more to the heart of the matter than three-fourths of the war journalism he's seen so far. I have to tell you, Miss Hollister, he likes what you've done very much. This is a man who's seen a great deal and is not easily impressed or swayed. 'A breath of fresh air,' that's what he called your story. And he wants more of the same. He says you're just what the war effort in the North has needed to rouse the people out of their complacency and to strengthen their resolve once again to fight on to preserve the Union."

"It pleases me that he liked it," I said.

"*Liked it!*" Mr. Hay exclaimed. "I should say he liked it! Now you get your mind and your pen busy. In the meantime, I am lining up some things for you with Mrs. Harding and Mr. Vargo."

The moment I saw the actual article in the paper, I had to laugh. What *would* Mr. Kemble say when he saw it? However it came to him over the telegraph, once he actually *saw* the printed copy in the *Post* and the *Mirror* and the *Globe* when they came to him later, he was sure to make some exclamation. There were the words in black and white! I could hardly believe them myself, even as I read them:

By Corrie Belle Hollister, reporter for the California Alta, *on special assignment with the White House.*

What a byline for a girl who'd started writing just to keep a journal, and whose first articles were about leaves, trees, and snow! I almost didn't believe it myself . . . but there it was! What had Almeda begun by giving me a journal and then by running for mayor? She'd gotten me writing, then interested in politics, and look where it had led!

I settled back in the chair and began to read the article. Even though I had written it, somehow it was different to read it once it was actually in the paper. They always made a few changes, of course, and I wanted to see those. But most of all I wanted to read my words as if I were a reader myself, seeing them for the first time. I'd written *When I came . . .* , but they changed the first sentence to the third person. I was glad they let me get onto the page as *myself* a little farther on.

When this reporter came East from California, she had no intention of getting involved in the war up close. But war seems to have a nasty way of intruding into life in ways that aren't always expected. And that is certainly what happened to me as I was traveling by train through Pennsylvania.

I had never heard of Gettysburg. Probably neither had most of you a month ago. It used to be just a sleepy little farming community in the rich heartland of southern Pennsylvania. But ever after this, whenever the name of that place is heard—that place where the fate of North and South collided—the very word will call to mind images in my memory that will bring tears to my eyes and a wrenching feeling of hurtful loss to my heart. For I will never hear the word *Gettysburg* without seeing in my mind's eye the faces of friends I knew there, some of whom I shall never see again.

I then went on to tell about how I had come to be at Gettysburg, and about Jennie Wade, Isaac Tomlinson, Alan Smith, and Sister Janette.

One was on the side of the North, the other fought for the South. The two women did not fight at all. Their only involvement was in trying to help. None of the four were bad people. They had all been swept up into events larger than their own lives. None deserved to die.

Yet today, only two of them are alive. The other two—an aging Southerner and an innocent citizen of Gettysburg—are dead. The two who live are still, even as these words are written, nursing serious wounds, and their recoveries may never be complete.

Yes, war always intrudes into life when we least expect it. And its intrusions are always cruel. For war takes life.

But even in the midst of war, people can *give* life. Wars are fought about large issues of national importance, and perhaps individuals like you and me—as well as Jennie and Alan and Isaac and Sister Janette—cannot stop them from coming. The terrible civil war that is tearing at the very fabric of this nation is perhaps one that must be fought so that the liberties and freedoms upon which the Constitution is based might be preserved. But if it must be fought, we must nevertheless save life wherever opportunity is given us.

I then explained about the Sanitary Commission's work of caring for the wounded, and about what we'd done at St. Xavier's, and told everyone how desperate was the need for help. Whether they could actually help someone face-to-face or not, there was plenty they could do to make sure the commission and other such agencies had everything they needed. Mr. Hay helped me add a few things that they wanted to make sure people knew.

Then I said a few words just to my fellow Californians, reminding them of things Mr. King and I had said, and encouraging them to continue giving aid however they could. A sickening feeling of guilt crept in when I thought of the money Cal stole. But it just made me all the more determined to make up for it now!

As I put the paper down, I smiled to myself. All I could think was what it was going to be like around the house when Pa and Almeda and the others opened the paper and saw *me* there.

The very thought made me cry. When I sat down at my writing table again fifteen minutes later, it was not to write anything for the papers, but to begin a long overdue letter home.

A Tiring Agenda
CHAPTER THIRTY-THREE

*B*efore I knew it I was writing more articles and traveling around with Mr. Vargo to fund-raising events on behalf of the Sanitary Commission, and with Mrs. Harding to help her get people to become part of the volunteer "army of helpers," as she called it.

When I was introduced to Mr. Vargo, he shook my hand with a momentary puzzled look on his face.

"This isn't *the* Corrie Belle Hollister?" he said, glancing toward Mr. Hay.

"I'm not sure what you mean," replied Mr. Hay. "She *is* Corrie Hollister, of that much I am certain."

"But are you the Corrie Belle Hollister who writes . . . are you the author?" he said, to me this time.

"She writes for the *Alta* . . . in San Francisco," said Mr. Hay.

"But the book—are you the young lady who wrote the book about the little town in California . . . about the gold rush and your coming across the desert and the cave falling in on the young boy?"

I nodded sheepishly.

Mr. Hay looked puzzled. He hadn't known anything about my journals.

"My wife read your book, Miss Hollister," Mr. Vargo went on. "It is such a pleasure to meet you! She told me all about it! She has a friend in Chicago who sent it to her. She will be very excited when I tell her you are here in Washington and are going to be working with me."

Mr. Hay asked a few more questions, and Mr. Vargo told him what he had heard about me from his wife. I must say it was dreadfully awkward and embarrassing to hear the two men talking to each other . . . about *me!*

My days were taken up with so many activities that I scarcely had time to sit down and do much more writing. I did, however, manage to keep a regular series of articles appearing and being sent back to California. By then it was clear to me that I might be in the East for quite some time. I began writing letters home, too, so they would know more about what I was doing than they would find out from reading the stories in the paper.

I had to laugh when Mr. Hay brought me a copy of the *Alta* with that first story in it about Gettysburg. Mr. Kemble had changed the byline. Above it, and with every article that appeared later, were the words *By the* Alta's *own Corrie Belle Hollister, on special assignment in Washington to cover the war effort.* It was obvious he wanted everyone to think *he'd* sent me himself!

There wasn't any more fighting anywhere close by all the rest of that summer. The battles of Vicksburg and Gettysburg had exhausted both armies, and they spent the following months recuperating. Word did begin to come to us, however, about movements in and around Tennessee, the last great Confederate stronghold now that the North and West were securely in Union hands.

President Lincoln continued to be frustrated by General Meade's allowing Lee to escape so easily after Gettysburg. As Lee retreated southward, Meade followed but made no attempt to inflict any further damage. When Lee came to the Potomac River, he found it swollen from heavy rains and he was unable to cross. Meade caught up and found the Confederate army trapped. Once again he could have overcome Lee and possibly ended the war for good. But he did nothing. The water level fell, and Lee got his army across to safety.

Mr. Lincoln was furious. It almost seemed as though his own general had been trying to *help* Lee survive so that he could regain his strength and try still another invasion of the North! Later in August, General Meade came to the Capital for a meeting with Lincoln. I happened to be in Philadelphia at the time with Mrs. Harding and Mr. Vargo and several young nurses of the Sanitary Commission. But Mr. Hay told me about their meeting later.

Mr. Lincoln had said to the general who'd won the battle of Gettysburg, "Do you know, General, what your attitude toward Lee for a week after the battle reminded me of?" Meade said he didn't. "I'll be hanged," the President told him, "if I could think of anything other than an old woman trying to shoo her geese across a creek!"

I made enough friends that I had people to talk to and to keep from being too lonely. I even began to feel at home in Washington. The landlady at the boardinghouse, Annabelle Richards, really did make me feel as if I were coming home every time I returned after I'd been away for a few days. After a while I didn't think of myself as being a "boarder" but rather that her house was where I lived. I did go back to visit Mrs. Surratt from time to time, though she continued to try my resolve.

There just didn't seem to be any way to get "inside" her and establish any kind of a friendship. I continued to pray for her.

I wrote to the convent and was so happy to get word back that Sister Janette was recovering nicely and was nearly returned to full strength. They invited me to come back soon, and all the sisters signed the letter and added personal words of their own. Every letter from California made me cry, and so did the one from the convent. I did think often about the time I'd spent there. I still couldn't help but wonder if God might someday want me to follow that same life myself. Part of me hoped so.

In the meantime, I knew such a life wasn't for me *yet*. Right now I had enough to occupy my time just keeping pace with the tiring agenda that had been set before me. I did take a week off from the Commission work in early September to go back north to visit the Convent of John Seventeen and the Sisters of Unity. They treated me like one of them, making me even more homesick for the sense of belonging I had known when I was with them.

But I returned to Washington, and then visited the headquarters of the Sanitary Commission in Boston later in September. I traveled there by train with Mrs. Harding and Eliza Ireland, a nurse who supervised much of the training of the volunteers and who had become quite a good friend.

In Boston, I first saw Dorothea Dix. I'd heard plenty about her and was frightened at the prospect of her seeing me and maybe even telling Mrs. Harding to get rid of me. She had volunteered her services to the Union just five days after Fort Sumter fell and was put in charge of all female nurses used by the Union. She was tireless but autocratic and unbending—so much so that eventually she began to be called "Dragon Dix."

She was especially hard on young women wanting to help the war effort because it seemed like a romantic, adventurous thing to do—which was the mentality of many of the young men who joined up, too. I don't suppose that was so much of a problem after the war had been going awhile, but from everything I'd heard of her, she even turned down nuns some-times. "No woman under thirty years need apply to serve in government hospitals," she had always maintained. "They are required to be very plain-looking women. Their dresses must be brown or black, with no bows, no curls, no jewelry, and no hoop skirts."

She didn't actually work for the Sanitary Commission but for the army itself. She was in Boston for the same plan-ning and training sessions as I was attending. So even if she'd wanted to, I don't suppose she could have had me thrown out. After we were introduced, she looked me over from head to foot without a smile, without so much as a word. When Mrs. Harding mentioned that I was a writer who'd written a book and several articles on behalf of the war effort, the dragon lady's only remark was a noncommittal "Hmmph." It wasn't hard to tell that she thought I was too young to be doing what I was doing and if she had her way I wouldn't do it anymore.

Far more pleasant was my meeting with Mary Ann Bickerdyke, a Quaker widow who *was* a Sanitary Commission agent. She had traveled with the Union army for over three years, through sixteen battles. After Gettysburg, she said, she wanted to take some time in the North to round up more support, to encourage the volunteers, and to assist Mr. Vargo in raising desperately needed funds. As soon as she was able, she said she intended to be back with the soldiers on the front lines where she could do the most good. She had visited with

President Lincoln, too, and laughed when telling me that he'd heard of her nickname and had called her "Mother Bicker-dyke," just like the boys in the hospitals all did.

The most widely circulated story about Mrs. Bickerdyke related her response when a surgeon she was helping asked her on whose authority she was acting. She answered, "On the authority of the Lord God Almighty. Have you anything that outranks that?" She was the only woman General Sher-man allowed in his camps. When he was asked why he al-lowed *her*, he replied, "I make the exception in her case for one simple reason: She outranks me."

The trip to Boston was the only time I ever saw Doro-thea Dix. Our paths never crossed again, much to my relief. But I did see a great deal more of Mother Bickerdyke. Several times we spoke in Washington together on behalf of the Com-mission. And because we both were working for the Sanitary Commission, we remained in loose touch with each other through Mrs. Harding and Mr. Vargo, even after she returned to the front lines.

We spent two weeks in Boston before returning to Wash-ington via New York, Philadelphia, and Baltimore, where we held meetings featuring Mrs. Bickerdyke. While in Boston I wrote Almeda a long letter that took me several nights by candlelight after the others had gone to sleep. Being in her home city of Boston had turned my thoughts toward her in a deeper way than ever before. My heart filled with such vol-umes of love for all she had been in my life, and I had to try to tell her.

I realized too that it was time I tried to say to her, as one adult woman to another, how deeply appreciative I was of everything she had built into me spiritually—with her patience and her love and her understanding and the many long talks we had had together. She had been a mother to me after Ma's death. Much of my own relationship with God I owed to her loving nurturing of me as I grew from girlhood into adulthood. Not until you're older do you realize how deeply people have affected you as you've grown. I needed to tell her again, even though I had told her some of my feelings before. I wanted to tell her, too, how much it had meant to me that she'd shared so openly about her past and about Mr. Parrish and how she'd come to know about God's love for her. Being in Boston reminded me of that all over again and carved out new depths in my love for her.

When I was in Boston I also wrote to Mr. King to tell him what I was doing. I sent the letter to Governor Stanford's office in Sacramento. Mr. King had been involved in many activities in and around Boston before he had come to California, and I thought he'd like to know that his work with me in 1860 had led me back to his old home.

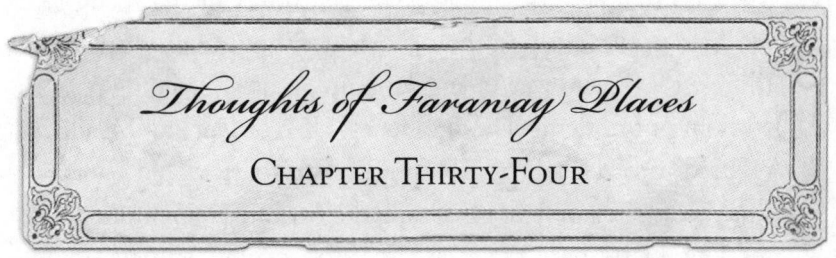

Thoughts of Faraway Places

CHAPTER THIRTY-FOUR

*T*he temperature began to cool steadily, and it became obvious that fall was approaching.

Still I was busily involved, meeting more and more people, traveling to new places, seeing cities I'd never dreamed of being able to visit. And somehow the time continued to pass. I wasn't consciously thinking of staying on the East Coast, but the days slipped by, then weeks . . . then months. Whenever anyone would ask me where I was from, I'd immediately answer, "California." I never stopped to think about actually *living* somewhere else. And yet I was growing older, and my writing *was* paying enough that I could support myself and wouldn't *have* to go back to California if I didn't want to.

It always took me off guard, but more and more I would encounter people who recognized my name. "Oh, I read your article about such-and-such," they might say. Some knew me from political articles, others from gold rush stories. I even met one lady who remembered my story about Katie coming from Virginia and the little apple seedling. And the book was making its way to the East Coast from Chicago, too, and the few people who knew about it and had read it were always so nice about what they said.

We usually don't see big bends and forks in the road of our lives until we're past them. No matter how much we plan, things still have a way of sneaking up on us and sliding past without our noticing. I doubt General Lee or General Meade realized how decisive the battle of Gettysburg would be on June 29 as they were approaching the town from opposite directions. Gettysburg itself wasn't part of anyone's strategy—it just happened to be there in the way, and then people looked back later, as they were doing this fall, and said that stopping Lee had been a major turning point.

Well, now it *was* fall, and it had been over four months since I had said goodbye to my family in Miracle Springs. And when in every one of their letters they'd ask me when I was coming back, I'd read the words lightly, not thinking about them too much. Without knowing it, I suppose I was gradually working my way around one of those bends in the road that I didn't even know was there. If very much more time went by, I'd have to start realizing that I was *living* and *working* in the East, not just "visiting" for a short time. Because I felt a great purpose in what I was doing, I knew it was important. And to be truthful, I *wasn't* thinking of returning just yet. There was still so much more to be done, and I felt I needed to be part of it.

This was especially true once reports began to come to us that General Lee's army was, as Mr. Lincoln had feared, rebuilding itself to full strength. And once the fighting flared up seriously again, it would cause terrible casualties and increase the need for medical care.

All the while, I was writing and was being paid for my stories. Several years earlier, Mr. Kemble had been sending my stories about California and the gold rush and West Coast politics to the East so folks here would know more about the West. Now I was writing about the East and about the civil war, and the articles were being sent back to California so folks *there* would know what was happening through the eyes of one of their own—me!

Then came a day, in early October, when suddenly all this dawned on me in a flash.

"What am I doing here?" I thought to myself. "How long am I going to stay . . . how long will the war last . . . what will I do when it's over . . . where *is* my home now?"

As significant as the questions were with regard to my future, even more significant was the fact that I knew I didn't have the answers. I didn't know.

Would I return to the convent? If I did, would it be the same, or had the experience struck so deeply in me simply because of how and when it had come? If I did go back to Miracle Springs, what then? What would I do—live forever with Pa and Almeda, writing and working at the Mine and Freight?

Or did my future hold something I still couldn't see, around bends in the road of my life that I hadn't even come to yet?

Then I realized that writing was something you could do anywhere. It paid enough for me to rent a room and pay for board anywhere, and the government was taking care of my expenses now, so I could save my article money. For all these reasons, it suddenly dawned on me that if I wanted to, I could go *anywhere* to live and keep writing.

Just think . . . anywhere! Now that there were telegraph lines all across the country, and now that Mr. Stanford and his men were working so hard to get a railroad line built all the way from the Pacific to the Atlantic, I could stay in touch with my family and Mr. Kemble and even President Lincoln from just about anywhere on the whole continent.

The thought was staggering!

Women didn't usually have the opportunity to mark their own path any way they chose. But it seemed that I *could!* How could I be so fortunate? Why had God so blessed me as to give me a freedom that so few people knew? Ma certainly had never known anything like it. She had had to work hard just to keep us five kids alive! And now here I was, her eldest, experiencing a freedom she could not even have imagined.

It all made me feel humble and thankful, adventurous and bold and daring—all at once!

I could go to Alaska or Colorado and write stories about the new gold rushes there, or to Canada or Oregon . . . maybe I could even travel to Europe someday!

But the very next afternoon my thoughts took an altogether different and equally unexpected turn.

The moment my eyes fell on the envelope that Mrs. Richards handed me, I recognized my sister Emily's handwriting.

I had heard from every one of my other brothers and sisters, but not Emily. The only news of her I'd received had come from Almeda, and that wasn't much.

It was not a long letter, but pleasant and newsy, and it was so good to hear that she and Mike were doing well, that she was happy, and that she saw the rest of the family once a month or so.

But the most important reason she'd written, she said, didn't come till the last of the three pages of her letter.

You'll never believe it, Corrie, but guess what—I'm going to have a baby. I just found out from the doctor two weeks ago—sometime in the spring, he says. Oh, Mike and I are so happy, and I wanted to tell you first of all. I haven't even told Becky or Almeda or Katie yet. Nobody else except Mike, that is. Of course he knows!

You've always been the best sister a girl could have. You took care of us, you were always so patient with us, and though we didn't know it at the time, you were practically both Ma and Pa to all four of us there for a while.

I don't suppose I ever said it enough to you, and I'm sorry
I waited so long. But knowing there's new life inside me
has awakened me to lots of things I never realized before.

So I wanted you, my older sister, to know before anyone. You are so special to me, and I'm so proud of you!
Every time I see something of yours in the newspaper, my
heart just gets big inside and I can't help but smile on account of my famous sister, the friend of the President!

Oh, Corrie, I love you so much, and I hope and pray
you'll someday know the joy I feel right now of being able
to bring a new life into the world.

> God bless you, my dear sister,
> EMILY

I was sobbing long before I was through reading.

I laid the letter down on the bed and went outside. I had
to have some fresh air, and walk.

Why had her words of happiness stung me so deeply?
Why couldn't I rejoice and laugh with her?

I knew why. And it made the tears streaming down my
cheeks all the more difficult to ignore, because Emily's letter had come immediately after my enthusiasm about going
wherever I wanted to.

Perhaps I *could* go to faraway places. Perhaps I *had* shaken
President Lincoln's hand and written newspaper articles, and
perhaps even a few people recognized my name when they
heard it.

But what did all that matter? What difference would that
make if my life wasn't complete?

That was the hardest question of all to face—one that
I now wondered if I'd always been afraid to look at. *Could*

a woman's life be complete without being married? Ma had always tried to prepare me to not be married, but I could tell from her tone that it was a sorry pass for a young woman to come to, and somehow we ought to be making plans to make the best of it. I had always just accepted it as my fate that I wouldn't be married, and I even began to like the idea.

But maybe my experience with Cal had wounded me more deeply than I wanted to admit. The way I'd gotten my hopes up about him showed me that down deep I *wanted* to be married just like everyone else.

During my time with Sister Janette at the convent, I thought I had put the question to rest once and for all. I felt as if I truly understood for the first time that the *deepest* meaning a woman's life could have, and the most eternally significant, was to be devoted to Jesus in as complete a way as if married to him. I had been excited about that prospect, eager to give myself and all the rest of my life to him with that abandoned totality.

Why, then, did Emily's words bring tears of anguish and loss to my eyes? *I hope you'll someday know the joy I feel. . . .*

But I never would know it! And why should it make me cry? Why should I feel saddened by it? Sister Janette wouldn't. She had chosen to live a life that would never bring the things Emily was speaking of. I thought I had wanted to make that choice, too. And yet . . . Emily's words rubbed something raw within me.

I *did* want to know the joy she spoke of! I couldn't deny it! I wanted to know what it felt like to have a man's arms wrapped around me, to hear the words spoken in my ear, "Corrie . . . I love you!"

Oh, God, I'm sorry, I thought. *I want to love you and serve you and be content that YOU love me, I'm so sorry . . . but I do wish that someday I might know the love of a man, too.*

But I would never know it. I was too old already, and I didn't know any young men, and I wasn't pretty . . . worst of all, I wasn't the marrying kind—just like Ma had said. I wasn't fun and lively. I was a reading, thinking kind of person, not the kind of girl any young man would ever look twice at. And I wasn't interested in doing nothing but making a home for a man and having ten children. What man would want to marry a woman who was always doing man-things, like writing and making speeches? None of any of that mattered anyway. I was twenty-six, and that was too old. Ma'd said I wasn't the marrying sort clear back when I was ten or twelve, and I guess she was as right about that as she was about most things.

I wiped my sleeve across my eyes as I walked, but I couldn't stop the tears from coming.

I hope you'll know the joy I feel right now of being able to bring a new life into the world. . . .

No, Emily, I thought to myself, *I'm afraid I never will know what it's like to love a man, to be loved in return, or to have a baby and to be a mother.*

How much did being a woman depend on such things? Would I be complete without them? *Could* a woman be complete and yet remain alone?

I don't know if it was wrong to think it, but I couldn't help wondering right then what it was like to be intimate with a man. What did it *feel* like in your heart to be that deeply bonded with another human being? What was it like to love someone that much?

I began to think of Emily and what it would be like for her. What was childbirth like? Was it as painful and yet as joyous as women said? How could it be both excruciating and exhilarating at the same time? What was it like to hold in your arms a newborn son or daughter, the child of your own womb?

I couldn't imagine how wondrous a thing it must be! And I couldn't keep my tears from starting up all over again.

What was it like to be a parent, to watch that son or daughter grow and learn to walk and talk and begin becoming a person with individuality and character all its own? What were the emotions that a mother's heart would feel?

I had been so close to Ma, and now felt so close to Almeda. And yet for the first time I realized what a huge gulf there had always been between us . . . and always would be. Emily had bridged that gap already in many ways, and in another six months or so she would share womanhood with Ma and Almeda in a complete way—a completeness I would never be able to enter into.

The realization was too painful for me to think of further. I turned and walked briskly back to Mrs. Richards' boardinghouse, still crying but determined not to sink any further into the despondency that was threatening to overwhelm me altogether.

Forgetfulness and Remembrance
Chapter Thirty-Six

I didn't do very well at keeping the tears and self-pity away. Both remained with me the rest of the day.

I *couldn't* go down to dinner looking the way I did. As soon as the other guests were served, Mrs. Richards came to my room and knocked on the door to see if I was coming.

"No, I don't think I'll be down tonight," I said through the door. I'd never missed supper the whole time I'd been there.

"Corrie . . . are you all right?" she said.

"Yes . . . I'm fine," I answered, knowing I wasn't being truthful. "I'm just not feeling too well."

"What can I do for you, child?"

"I'll—please, I'll . . . I'll be fine in the morning. It's just a headache, and . . . I'm not hungry."

"You'll tell me if there's something I can do?"

"Yes . . . yes, I will. Thank you, Mrs. Richards."

She went downstairs to the dining room, and I lay back on the bed and started crying all over again. Oh, I would have given anything to have Almeda at my side right then! I was miserable!

But I just couldn't stand to be such a victim of my moods. One minute I was happy and excited about life, and everything looked so bright. Then the next I would find myself knocked off my feet and knee-deep in a slough of despair and hopeless-ness. Pa had said to me more than once, "All that thinking's bound to tie your brain in knots now and then, Corrie. Just take life as it comes, and don't cogitate so much on it."

But I couldn't help thinking about everything. Besides, I didn't *want* to just take life as it came. I wanted to have a hand in the process. I figured I knew better than anyone else—anyone except the Lord, that is—what I did and didn't want to be doing.

But if thinking was part of looking your life in the face and getting on with it, and if up-and-down feelings went along with thinking about things, then I suppose I was stuck with it.

Uncle Nick always said, "Aw, that's just the way women are. Men are the *doers,* but women are always gettin' all emo-tional about everything. If there weren't no men, why you women'd make one fine pickle of it, and you'd never get nothin' done!"

Even while Alkali Jones' cackle was sounding through the room, I could see Aunt Katie biting her lip to keep quiet!

Almeda had a different explanation, and she and I had talked about it plenty of times. "Yes, Corrie, we women do have a more sensitive emotional nature. And we're prone to violent fits of unpredictability now and then—usually about once a month!"

We both laughed.

"Men think they're so smart, but they don't know any-thing about how a woman's body and mind and emotions all work in a delicate balance. And neither do they know how much a mess of things *they'd* make if we weren't quietly hold-ing everything in *their* lives together. Though don't ever ex-pect a man to realize that . . . or to say it, if he did!"

I smiled through my tears as I recalled the conversation. Yet I wasn't willing to accept that answer for my moods either, that I was just a victim of how women happened to be made and I couldn't help it.

I *wanted* to help it! Whatever explanation there might be to account for it, I didn't like it. I wanted to be more consistent and steady, and yet here I was again, suffering through a terrible case of the doldrums!

The following morning an open-air meeting had been scheduled on the lawn surrounding the Washington Monument. I was going to talk for about five minutes on the importance of people volunteering to help with the recent fighting down in Tennessee, even if they knew absolutely nothing about doctoring or nursing, telling how I was able to be of some use to the sisters at Gettysburg, although I'd had not a minute of preparation ahead of time.

I awoke early and decided to go out before breakfast to try to clear my brain of yesterday's cobwebs and depression. Maybe I wouldn't ever marry or know real intimacy or experience childbirth or know what motherhood was like, but now was not the time to worry about it. I had responsibilities, and I couldn't neglect them by wallowing around in the hole I'd dug for myself as a result of Emily's letter.

The air was crisp and chilly. Fall was definitely in the wind. There would probably be rain by evening.

I walked and walked, trying to be stoic and strong and brave and not give in to those womanly "emotions" that had knocked me to the ground yesterday. I would fight them, whatever their source. If it was my destiny, my fate, my lot in life to remain single and alone, then I would be brave about it. I would endure it like . . . well, not exactly "like a man," but like a strong woman, anyway! Nobody ever promised that life would be everything we might want. People faced lots of hardships many times worse than I ever had. Hundreds of thousands of boys were dying in this terrible war. And hadn't I just realized two days ago how blessed I was? What business did I have thinking otherwise?

I was walking along, breathing in deeply, keeping a stiff upper lip about all my troubles of the day before, and I never thought of God once. I didn't pray, I didn't talk to him about any of it, I didn't ask him what I ought to do or think. Worst of all, I didn't even realize it. I hadn't thought of him once since reading Emily's letter! I was just determining within *myself*, with no help from him, to be strong. I never realized that when you're trying to summon up strength *only* from within yourself, there's no strength there. There is no weaker position for a man or a woman—for anybody—than standing alone. Yet that's what I was trying to do, deceiving myself that I was being strong.

All of a sudden I remembered God. I remembered that he was there, that Jesus was walking right beside me, that he had never left me. I remembered that he had been there all through yesterday, too, that he was beside me in the room as I'd read Emily's letter, and had been with me all night as I slept, and even through the hour I'd been walking this morning, even though I hadn't been aware of his presence for so much as a second.

A new wave of heartbreak swept over me. This time it was not the despair of self-pity but rather the mortification of what I'd done, that I had forgotten him so completely.

All the strength I'd been trying to summon up only a moment before evaporated in less than a second. I felt so small, so weak, as if I'd betrayed him, even though he had been good to me and had never left me.

Tears filled my eyes—tears not of self-motivated sadness but of remorse and grief.

"Oh, Lord . . . I am so sorry!" I whispered.

There was nothing else to pray, no more to say. I felt so low. How could I have doubted that he would take care of me, that he knew what was best, and that he would do the very best for me in every way? How *could* I forget? Yet I had.

My heart heaved with wave upon wave of unspoken and faulted attempts to convey my sorrow over forgetting to trust him and doubting that my life was utterly in his hands. But no words escaped my lips.

Then, just as suddenly as I had remembered the Lord's presence with me, I remembered something else—my own words, words I had prayed while at the convent:

. . . Whatever future you have for me, whether married or not, I will be happy just to know I am with you. Let me just know that I am only yours. I want to be your bride. . . . Oh, God, use me and fill me with yourself. I want to be yours completely.

How could I have forgotten so quickly?

I had given myself in marriage to Jesus. I had given him my heart and my future. I had meant every word of those earlier prayers . . . and I knew that I still did.

"I *do* want to be yours, Lord," I said softly through my tears. "I am sorry I am so weak. Help me . . . help me to be strong—strong as you would make me strong, not trying to be strong by myself without you. Please, Lord, help me! I don't have that kind of strength alone."

Asking for his help calmed me some, and gradually I was able to breathe in deeply and stop crying.

By now I was walking back toward Mrs. Richards'. I felt
drained, both emotionally and physically. I was aware of the
Lord's presence with me, but was too spent to be able to ar-
ticulate the prayers my heart was feeling. Then a new realization came upon me. And I know he put it into my mind in
answer to the pain and questions that had engulfed me from
Emily's words.

*Corrie, I will make of you a complete woman. You need have
no fear of anything missing from your life from being married or
being a mother or not. Complete womanhood comes from joining yourself to me, and in no other way. There are many wives
and mothers who are incomplete, broken, lonely women. They will
never know the completeness of their womanhood until they join
their hearts to mine and allow me to make them complete. I alone
can raise up my daughters into the fullness of their being, their per-
sonhood, their womanhood. None but my daughters will become
true women, and they must become my daughters before all else.*

"But why, Lord," I found myself saying, "why can't I remember? Why is this so hard for me when my heart truly does
yearn to be only yours?"

*I have allowed you to suffer these things, Corrie, I felt I heard
him saying, so that you will know the cost, and know the worth
of womanhood as my daughter—full womanhood as you yourself
long for—so that you will be able to speak of these truths to others
of my daughters.*

My thoughts were silent. My heart was still at last, and
at peace.

*L*ate in October, one evening when I arrived back at the boardinghouse—which by now I had begun calling "home"— there was an envelope awaiting me. It had no stamp, however. It had been hand delivered, Mrs. Richards said, by John Hay himself. It bore the insignia of the presidential seal.

I opened it hurriedly.

Dear Miss Hollister,

President Lincoln would like to see you again. Please come by the White House tomorrow. Ask for me, and we will set up a time as soon as possible. Thank you.

> I remain,
> Sincerely yours,
> JOHN HAY,
> Secretary to the President

I went the next morning, and Mr. Hay asked me to come back that afternoon at 1:45. Shortly before two, I was shown into the presence of Mr. Lincoln.

He was just as kind as the first time, and I think I was no less awestruck.

"Miss Hollister . . . Corrie," he said, shaking my hand warmly. "Thank you for coming to see me again."

"Of course, sir," I answered.

"Mr. Hay has kept me apprised of your work here in Washington, and I have read some of your articles. Again, as I attempted to express before, I am most appreciative."

"Thank you."

"I have another request to make of you," he went on, "although this one is in a slightly different vein."

"Anything," I said.

"I am planning a visit to Gettysburg in about three weeks, to dedicate a new Union cemetery there. I am hoping to be able to talk you into accompanying me, along with the rest of the ever-present presidential retinue."

He *hoped* to "talk me into it"! As if I were so busy I'd have to think twice and consult my schedule to see if I had room to squeeze Abraham Lincoln in! I was speechless!

Somehow I heard the words coming out of my mouth, "I'd be honored, Mr. President."

"Good, I am delighted to hear it. We will travel by train, of course. Mr. Hay will fill you in on the details. The day's schedule is not finalized yet, as I understand it, but I hope there will be an opportunity for you to say a few words. I trust you would have no objection?"

"Not if that is what you would like, sir," I said.

"I knew I could count on you."

The President looked tired and dejected. At my last interview with him in July, despite his irritation over how things had gone at Gettysburg, he had been full of life, and his eyes had glowed, even with anger at times, as he'd spoken of the possibility of ending the war.

Indeed, a quick end to the war now seemed as remote as ever. Robert E. Lee was rebuilding his strength, and Mr. Lincoln continued to have trouble with his generals being timid about dealing the death-blow to the Confederate army. It seemed the North had the more courageous president, while the South had the shrewdest general. Lee's hands were tied by an ineffectual President Jefferson Davis, while Lincoln's decisive military strength was blunted by hesitant generals who did not share the scope of his vision. The two greatest military minds in the country—Lincoln and Lee—were fighting on opposite sides of the conflict, and their mutual skill and determination only extended the killing in a prolonged stalemate. Time, of course, favored Mr. Lincoln because of sheer numbers of men and quantities of supplies. But in the meantime, the South fought bravely and determinedly on, with the result of a *huge* loss of lives.

The hoped-for end of the war following Gettysburg and Vicksburg faded through that fall of 1863. The Confederacy was not dead yet! In September they routed Union forces in the small Georgia town of Chickamauga in one of the bloodiest battles of the war. Lincoln was not only frustrated with his commanders, but sorrowful personally as well. His wife's brother-in-law, Confederate Brigadier General Ben Hardin Helm, was killed in the battle. Mrs. Lincoln wept but was overheard to say to a friend that she wished *all* her Confederate relatives would be killed. "Any one of them would kill my husband in an instant if given half the chance," she said, "and completely destroy our government."

I'm sure the war was on his mind a great deal when I saw him in October. Oppression seemed to hang about his countenance. I also learned that just a few days earlier he had taken the bold step of naming General Grant commander of all Union forces between the Appalachians and the Mississippi.

Here was a general who would follow his President's orders, who was brave and a shrewd tactician of nearly Robert E. Lee's caliber, and who could hopefully unite the Federal effort.

And I was a little more than fond of him for the simple reason that he had once been to Miracle Springs! That was a long time ago, of course, and how could he possibly remember? Yet in my secret heart I hoped that *someday* maybe I'd have a chance to meet him again.

I was glad when I heard the President and Mrs. Lincoln had gone to the theater a week before we were scheduled to go to Gettysburg. I hoped it might be a sign he was feeling better and that the stress I'd seen on his face was perhaps lessening. He had gone to see a play called *The Marble Heart.*

"It's got to be young Booth playing in it," remarked Mrs. Richards.

"I don't know anything about it," I replied. "And who's Booth?"

"Oh, a young actor, John Booth. Not as good as his father, Junius Brutus Booth, or even his brother Edwin for that matter. But he's young and ambitious and on the rise. Who knows, the world may hear of young John Wilkes yet."

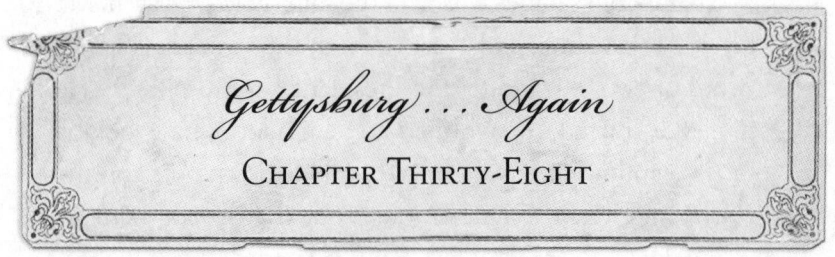

Gettysburg . . . Again

CHAPTER THIRTY-EIGHT

$\mathcal{T}$he train ride to Gettysburg was certainly nothing like coming across the country alone. There were newspaper people and reporters and politicians and military men. Gettysburg was a town of only about two thousand people, but they expected a crowd of some six thousand. And a lot of them were on the train with us!

I sat next to a man who was a correspondent for the London *Times*, living in the United States to cover the war. We had a lively talk, although I'm not sure what he thought of a young woman calling herself a reporter as if I were on *his* level. Neither did he seem to think very highly of Mr. Lincoln, which annoyed me. I told him I happened to think Abraham Lincoln the greatest man on the continent and that I was going to Gettysburg to speak along with him, at the President's *personal* invitation. I don't suppose it was altogether humble of me, but I just couldn't tolerate people criticizing the President after all he'd stood for, and being the great man he was. I suppose he wasn't impressed with the backward colonies that still had slavery, after it had been banned in the British Empire for over twenty years. I don't think the fellow believed a word I'd said about being invited there to speak.

Mr. Lincoln sat in the back of the same coach I was in. Mr. Hay was beside him, and every so often they would exchange a word or two, but mostly the President kept to himself. He seemed distracted, thoughtful. He spent a lot of time looking out the window, after which he'd scribble down notes on the back of an envelope. Later I found out that he was actually writing down his speech as we bounced and clattered along!

His mind was probably on General Grant, too. However much the purpose of our trip was to commemorate a battle whose echoes had long since died away, the fact of the matter was that even then, at that very moment, huge troop movements were amassing tens of thousands of soldiers in Tennessee in what would prove to be Ulysses Grant's first test of generalship since his promotion a month earlier.

The date was November 19, 1863. It is a day I shall never forget, and I doubt the citizens of Gettysburg will forget it, either.

The huge mass of people assembled in town, then walked and rode in a great procession to the new cemetery. Mr. Lincoln and other dignitaries rode horses, some rode in carriages, most walked. I was pleased to see some of my friends from St. Xavier's, and I rode with Father McFey, along with Jennie Wade's mother and sister, in a large black-draped carriage.

Everyone was dressed in black—the men in suits and tall black top hats, the women either in black dresses or draped with black shawls. Even though the mood was solemn, on the outskirts of town local entrepreneurs, some of them only ten or twelve years old, had set up tables and were selling drinks and cookies and battlefield relics they'd collected—even dried wildflowers, which had grown up since July.

Most everyone stood. Some of the women and families from town had brought blankets to spread out and sit on. A wooden stand had been built for the speakers so they could be seen. Several dozen chairs stood just below the speaker's stand, where I sat next to Mr. Hay. I was the only woman among those seated in front, and I felt more than a little conspicuous!

The main speaker of the day was Edward Everett, a noted pastor, diplomat, and politician, who had served as governor of Massachusetts. He was now seventy years old and mostly traveled about the Union giving stirring, patriotic orations.

He was introduced, stood up, and began the longest speech I have ever heard in my life—before or since! It's a good thing it wasn't as hot as it had been during the actual battle, or the death toll might have mounted still further among those in attendance. As it was, they didn't drop from the heat but gradually sank to the ground from sheer boredom! After an hour, most of the listeners who had begun on their feet were seated on the ground. And he was only half through!

Finally Mr. Hay leaned over to me.

"Corrie," he whispered into my ear, "I'm afraid we are going to have to eliminate your remarks from the agenda. If Everett doesn't sit down pretty soon, everyone will be asleep and even the President won't be able to speak!"

I smiled and nodded. Actually, it was a great relief.

Occasionally during Mr. Everett's speech, the President had continued to write on the envelope he had been scribbling on during the train ride.

At long last, Mr. Everett began winding down his passionate oratory, and then finally stopped—just a minute or two short of two hours since he'd begun—and took his seat next to President Lincoln. There was scattered applause—mostly because the speech was finally over, not because of anything Mr. Everett had said.

Then President Lincoln stood up. A great silence descended upon the crowd. The words that came from his mouth
were so brief, and yet so powerfully forceful—especially to my
ears, because I had actually *seen* this battle—that I could not
keep tears from coming to my eyes. Every face from these terrible days came back to me—Jennie Wade's, Alan Smith's,
Isaac Tomlinson's, as well as faces of the dead whose names I
had never known and whose voices I had never heard. I cry
every time I remember Mr. Lincoln's words, some of the most
magnificent words ever spoken:

Fourscore and seven years ago our fathers brought
forth on this continent a new nation, conceived in liberty, and dedicated to the proposition that all men are
created equal.

Now we are engaged in a great civil war, testing
whether that nation, or any nation so conceived and so
dedicated, can long endure. We are met on a great battlefield of that war. We have come to dedicate a portion of
that field as a final resting place of those who here gave
their lives that that nation might live. It is altogether fitting and proper that we should do this.

But in a larger sense we cannot dedicate—we cannot
consecrate—we cannot hallow—this ground. The brave
men, living and dead, who struggled here, have conse-
crated it, far above our poor power to add or detract.
The world will little note, nor long remember what we
say here, but it can never forget what they did here. It is
for us, the living, rather, to be dedicated here to the unfinished work which they who fought here have thus far
so nobly advanced. It is rather for us to be here dedicated

to the great task remaining before us—that from these honored dead we take increased devotion to that cause for which they gave the last full measure of devotion— that we highly resolve that these dead shall not have died in vain—that this nation, under God, shall have a new birth of freedom—and that government of the people, by the people, and for the people, shall not perish from the earth.

He turned and went back to his seat. People were still shifting around trying to get comfortable, and his short address was finished.

Not much more happened. Afterward Mr. Lincoln was introduced to Jennie Wade's family, to whom he gave his regards. He'd heard about Jennie before, as the only citizen of the town to be killed as a result of the fighting.

On the train ride back to Washington I saw the *Times* man again.

"I had a feeling you were trying to pull my English leg, telling me you were going to take to the podium with your President," he said.

"I told you the truth," I insisted. "But after Mr. Everett had gone on for an hour, they decided they should shorten the program, and mine was the one they eliminated."

He shrugged as though he halfway believed me but still wasn't sure. "Whatever you say. Might have made it a more memorable day though."

"How do you mean?" I asked.

"Not hardly worth our coming all this way for, wouldn't you agree?"

"I wouldn't have missed it!"

"I could have found ten more useful ways to spend the day. Your President was an abject failure. It's a wonder to me you Americans have managed to keep your country from blowing apart all this time, considering the mediocre men you thrust up into leadership from the most unqualified of backgrounds."

I couldn't believe what I was hearing. The gall of him to say such things about Mr. Lincoln!

"It was the most wonderful speech I've ever listened to!" I said.

"Ha! It will be forgotten by next week!"

The article he sent back to be printed in his own London *Times* was circulated through the papers of Washington and New York, too. About Gettysburg he wrote: "The ceremony was rendered ludicrous by the sallies of that poor President Lincoln, whose ridiculously brief remarks were hardly fitting for so momentous an occasion. Anyone more dull and commonplace it would not be easy to produce."

I was furious when I read them.

I hoped Mr. Lincoln never saw the disparaging words. There was at last some good news for him from the South. His appointment of General Grant had paid off! Just six days after his speech at Gettysburg, the two-day battle of Chattanooga began. When it was over, Ulysses Grant had scored another brilliant Union victory.

Three great turning points of the war had come during 1863—Gettysburg, which beat back Lee's invasion of the North. Vicksburg, which gave the Union control of the Mississippi. And now Chattanooga, which solidified General Grant's leadership and gave the entire Tennessee line into the control of the Federal army.

As the fateful year ended, it seemed impossible that the South could hope to win the war militarily. All the advantages were with the Union.

Yet still the stubborn Confederacy refused to yield. And as a result, thousands more would have to die. . . .

A Night to Remember

CHAPTER THIRTY-NINE

*C*hristmas of that year was one of the loneliest times I had ever known. Christmas was always such a special day in our family, and I was so far away! All I could think of was what they were doing, and I couldn't help feeling sorry for myself. But even if I did want to go back, once winter set in, travel across the country was no longer possible. I would be in the East at least until the spring—maybe longer. As long as the war lasted, nothing was certain.

But I didn't have to spend the day alone. I enjoyed a nice morning with Mrs. Richards and some of her family. The afternoon I spent with Mrs. Harding and some of the other Commission people. We had planned several Christmas events at both Harewood Army Hospital and the Armory Square Hospital. We'd arranged for decorations and what extra food the citizens of Washington could donate. We had a small band to play Christmas carols and a choir of nursing volunteers to sing to the men.

By evening I was too tired to remember that I was lonely. None of the wounded men or the soldiers in the field could be with their families for Christmas, either. It was a time of sacrifice for everyone, and mine was hardly to be compared with all the suffering and misery I'd seen.

A little over two months later, in the first week of March, 1864, President Lincoln announced that he had promoted General Grant again, above brigadier general, placing him at the head of *all* Union armies. Grant would be coming to Washington to personally receive from the President the specially created rank of lieutenant general. No one since George Washington had held such a high military rank.

I was thrilled to receive an invitation to attend a reception at the White House on the evening of March 8, at which General Grant would be honored!

I immediately made plans to take some of my article money out of the bank, and asked Mrs. Richards if she would help me select a new dress for the occasion.

When the day came I was so excited I could hardly wait till evening. What a birthday present this was—even if it was two weeks early—to be invited to a fancy reception at the Executive Mansion *and* to see General Grant!

He was just as I remembered him—older, of course, and now with some gray in his hair and beard, but short, strong-looking, stocky, with piercing eyes.

After Grant left California, he had resigned from the army altogether. He'd done lots of things since, but had failed at all of them—farming, selling property, peddling firewood on the streets, bill collecting. Finally he went to work as a clerk in the family leather store, working for his brother in Galena, Illinois. That's where he was when the war broke out.

He reentered the army, was put in charge of a small band of volunteers, and gradually began to be noticed by Union leaders when he started winning battles while most of the Northern generals were suffering humiliating defeats. Within two years he was in command of the whole Mississippi theater of the war.

The instant he walked into the room, all the guests began applauding. The President immediately approached him, took his hand, and vigorously pumped it up and down. "Why, here is General Grant!" he exclaimed. "This is a great pleasure, having you here, General, I assure you."

Everyone was pressing around to see him and greet him, but he could hardly *be* seen because of his height. There was Mr. Lincoln, easy enough to see above most of the heads. But Mr. Grant was eight inches shorter than the President. Most of the women were taller than he was!

All at once, from near the back where I was standing, I suddenly saw the general's head appear—taller even than the President's. He had stepped up onto a crimson-covered sofa where he could be seen. And there he stood for over an hour, shaking hands with everyone in the room.

What a sight it was! For once the President of the United States was *not* the central figure, but stood back while all the attention was directed toward this apprehensive man who disliked crowds, disliked Washington, D.C., and who even then, he confessed later, was eager to get out of all the hubbub and back to battle. But then he stood on a sofa while the most important people in the national capital treated him like a hero.

And, in a way, I suppose he was. He was the first general, at least, that President Lincoln was entirely pleased with. And to have the confidence of a man like Abraham Lincoln was no small accomplishment for *any* man.

I waited patiently in the stream of people moving steadily toward the crimson sofa.

When at last the moment came, and I found my hand in his and his piercing eyes looking down into mine, it was all I could do to find my voice.

"I'm happy to see you again, General," I said. "I saw you out in California in 1853."

"Where was that?" he asked.

"North of Sacramento. You stopped by in our little town to see your friend Simon Rafferty."

His eyes brightened. "Yes . . . yes, of course. I do recall the day."

"You were on your way up to Eureka."

"Ah, yes . . . Fort Humboldt—a dreadful place. Drove me to the bottle and straight out of the army!" He laughed.

"I'm glad to see you didn't stay out," I said.

"Under the circumstances, so am I, young lady, although if I do ever catch up with Robert E. Lee, I may live to regret my decision." He paused, then bent down a little and added softly, "But don't tell the President what I just said!"

"No, sir, not a word."

I moved on, but he stopped me. "Wait, young lady," he said, "you forgot to tell me your name."

I turned back toward him. "Corrie Hollister," I said, "Corrie Belle Hollister."

"I'll try to remember it," he said. "I hope our paths may cross another day, Miss Hollister."

"Thank you, Mr. Grant," I said. An instant later I was past him, and he was busy greeting someone else.

Ulysses Grant had not only come to Washington to receive his new rank from the President, he had come quite literally to take charge of the Union army of the North—which had until then been led by General Meade—and to do what no other Northern general had been able to do—advance upon the Confederate capital of Richmond. Five different generals had attempted it. All had been repelled by Robert E.

Lee, who was already being called the greatest general of the war—on either side.

But now it was time for the greatest Union general to take on Lee's army face-to-face. It seemed almost inevitable that one day the two men would square off and do battle against each other. It was fitting, I suppose, that the war would culminate in such a way. The Union controlled every other major front—the seas, the Mississippi, Tennessee, and Georgia. The only area the Union could not gain control of was northern Virginia and the Rebel capital of Richmond.

Only Robert E. Lee stood between the Confederacy and utter defeat.

And at last the moment had arrived for Ulysses S. Grant to take firm command of the armies that had been placed under him, and march south to meet Lee.

In April General Grant reviewed his new troops, then retired to confer with General Meade and discuss strategy for the planned campaign. As they met, members of his staff told of his great exploits and triumphs in the West and at Vicksburg. The veteran soldiers of the Army of the Potomac were not impressed.

"Everything you say may be true," one man said. "But you never met Bobbie Lee and his boys. Grant'll have his match in him, and that's the truth."

Following Grant into the Wilderness
CHAPTER FORTY

For months I had been talking and writing about helping the war's wounded and donating money and supplies to the Sanitary Fund. I had helped Mrs. Harding recruit and train people, and worked at the organizational duties of the Commission. Then one day it dawned on me that I hadn't really *done* any of the work I was telling other people *they* ought to do. What had happened at Gettysburg had come upon me almost by chance. I just suddenly found myself in the midst of it. I began to wonder what business I had saying what I said to others when I had done only two days of it myself.

The very next day I went to see Mr. Hay, then I talked to Mr. Vargo, and finally I discussed my plan with Mrs. Harding. I told them all the same thing—that I thought it was time I joined the Commission volunteers myself, and put the nursing and medical training I'd been giving into practice on the actual battlefield again. I told them that I was going to go south with the Commission brigade that was getting ready right then to follow General Grant's movements as he marched toward Richmond. I would continue to help them in any way possible, I said. I would continue to write articles and send them back to Mr. Hay. But in the meantime, I felt I needed to be near to offer any *real* help that I might be able to give.

They all said they would be sorry to see me go, and that they would miss me, but they understood.

I wrote to Pa and Almeda about my plans, too, although I didn't tell them how close to the actual fighting the Commission tents sometimes were. I figured they would probably worry enough without my adding to their troubles by talking about the potential danger.

General Grant launched his move into the wilderness of northern Virginia during the first week of May. He hoped to force Lee into a showdown that would end the war quickly. The Confederate capital was only seventy-five miles away, but General Grant could not take Richmond. Supreme general faced supreme general. Neither would give up, neither would retreat, both continued to wage skillful and canny warfare—Grant offensively, Lee defensively. Neither could defeat the other.

It was the military chess game of all time. There had never, in all the years of the war before this, been such a period of sustained, day-after-day, unrelenting savage fighting. Over 90,000 men were killed in the first month alone. All Americans, all young . . . all dead. And still the war was no closer to being over.

The Confederacy could not possibly achieve a victory now. The numbers against them were too strong. Yet Lee fought on, determined, it seemed, not to lay down arms as long as a single boy wearing gray was left alive. In truth, the South's greatest general also cost the South countless lives and great destruction of property. How many Rebel boys could have gone on living had Robert Lee not been so stubborn to continue after defeat was inevitable?

Lee's strategy was not to defeat Grant. He knew he could never do that. To make up for Grant's superior numbers, his strategy was to fight a skillful defensive game, making Grant attack him at the worst possible positions, and make the cost of Union losses so high that eventually the Northern public would turn against the war effort and sue for peace. If he could just stall Grant's march until November, until the presidential election, thought Lee, and if he could inflict enough damage on Grant's army, Lincoln's prestige would be hurt and he would be defeated in the election. With Lincoln gone, Lee was sure the North would eventually tire of the war and decide to let the South go her own way.

But if that was Lee's hope, Grant's determination to win a decisive victory for his President was just as strong. Some called him ruthless, others called him brutal. But Lincoln had made him the President's supreme commander because of the general's willingness to fight. And fight he did!

Through the summer, into the fall, and toward the end of the year, the great and terrible bloody standoff between Lee and Grant continued. Richmond still remained in Confederate hands, with Jefferson Davis still President of a rebel nation.

The same week when Grant had plunged into the wilderness after Lee, General Sherman in the South left Chattanooga for Atlanta. This was the second objective in the North's final two-pronged offensive to end the war. Once Atlanta and Richmond were in Union hands, the end of the war would not be long behind.

But neither was easy to gain. The fighting on both fronts lasted all summer.

When I left Washington with the Commission brigade, I envisioned being gone for months and perhaps traveling hundreds of miles. But the battle was so tightly confined that

we were able to transport many of the wounded back to the
Washington hospitals, and to travel back regularly ourselves
for needed supplies. We never went more than a hundred and
fifty miles from the Capital.

Nevertheless, the wounded came faster than we could
nurse them—two thousand a day for a month! The atrocities
of war are too horrible to describe. I will spend the rest of my
days on earth praying to God to erase those images from my
memory.

I saw huge mass graves filled with bodies. I had to walk
across battlefield trenches strewn with so many corpses that
I could scarcely make my way without stepping on them. I
literally stumbled over the bones of the unburied dead from
a year earlier while trying to make my way through the dense
woods of the wilderness. I witnessed amputations, saw crates
piled high with hands and feet and whole legs, waiting to be
carted outside the camp and piled atop the mound from the
previous day.

I held men in my arms the moment they died. I prayed
for the mercy of death to overtake some who couldn't die. I
listened to the screams for death while holding down panicked
and demented men with all my strength, in the fiercest heat of
battle. And I even had to take the knife in my own hand to cut
away tissue down to the bone, making it ready for the surgeon.

More than once I remember thinking it was the lucky
ones who lay there dead. Ordeals more horrible and appalling awaited the wounded in the hospitals and our makeshift
wards than they had encountered in the thick of enemy fire.

Sometimes there was more peace among the dying than
among the living. When the cannon fire and shelling would
stop for a while, the doctors and surgeons and medics, if they

could be spared, would go out onto the field of recent battle to see what could be done for the freshly wounded. Accompanying them was never pleasant, for despite all I had seen, I feared some new horror that was more awful yet.

Following the doctors a few paces behind, we came upon the poor men the moment after the doctor had seen there was no hope and had moved on. Usually by this time the pain was past and life was quickly ebbing away. Sometimes fear filled their eyes, and they looked to us beseechingly, imploring us to do what the surgeon could not. Most seemed to show no fear. All had forced themselves to accept the inevitability of death, and to accept that it could come to them any day. Those who could do so usually mouthed only two words, "How long?"

It was no good lying to them. Everyone knew what was coming.

"Twenty minutes," a doctor might say. "Soon . . . not long, son, be brave . . . only another fifteen minutes. . . ."

And then to those of us who followed came the task of looking into those same eyes and communicating in those final moments something that said to them that life had been good. Mine was often the last human face a young man would ever see, mine the last eyes he would gaze into, mine the last voice his ears would hear.

Not mother, not sister, not wife, not father . . . but *me* . . . me—a girl he didn't know, had never seen before. And yet here I was, kneeling at his side, having to be the wife and mother and sister that he would never see again.

In those few brief, awful seconds, with but a look into the eyes, how can you speak of love, of hope, of *life?* How can you tell a boy whose life is draining out of him and soaking into the dirt beneath him about a Father in heaven who loves him?

Never was my faith so tested as in that furnace of terrible affliction when I followed the army of General Ulysses S. Grant into the wilderness of Virginia. I knew it had to be done. The war had to be won. But I hated it. I hated the death, even as I tried to give life in the midst of it.

Usually there were no words—only a look from my eyes into theirs. After a while the tears even quit coming, and for that I was sad. My heart wept, but for a time after that awful summer of 1864 my eyes were dry.

And then I would move on . . . to the next boy who perhaps could be saved and about whom the doctor was already giving me instructions . . . or on to the next pair of waiting eyes, and lips murmuring, "How long . . . ?"

We "fixed" the corpses by pinning the toes of their stockings together after their boots were taken off. That way, when they hardened from the rigor mortis, their legs were straight and more bodies could be laid out and more easily carried off to burial.

One boy the doctor had just passed looked up into my eyes as I knelt for a moment beside him. There was no fear in his face. Just a pale, white calm, the peace of knowing that it was nearly over.

"Fix me," he said softly to me.

My heart tried to rise up into my mouth, and I stifled a great cry of anguish.

Then he crossed his arms over his chest as he knew we did with corpses, and with the last strength of his legs managed to pull his feet together and touch his toes. I pulled off his boots, laid them beside him, then pinned his stockings together. He smiled thinly, then closed his eyes, looking so pleasantly at rest I thought him asleep.

I leaned over and gently kissed his forehead.

Not a muscle twitched as my lips met the grime-encrusted skin of his boyish forehead. He was so young!

I stood up, looking down again at his face. I knew he was dead.

*I*n the wilderness of Virginia, behind the trenches and for-
tifications and siege works of Grant's army, in our mobile field
hospitals where we moved about doing what we could to al-
leviate the massive suffering, I met Clara Barton.

I had heard of her, of course. Everyone involved in the
medical and nursing aspect of the war knew of the bravery
she had already demonstrated. When I suddenly found myself
working beside her one day in a hastily erected tent, my first
thought was not that I was meeting someone well known but
that here was the first person I'd ever met who was like me!
When we had the chance later, we talked about what had
brought us here, and discovered so many similarities that we
became fast friends at once.

She was in her early forties and, unmarried like me, had
gone through almost all the same quandaries and doubts and
frustrations over that very thing—being unmarried and working and living alone, when everyone except nuns seemed to
think it a completely unnatural thing. We had a good laugh
and several long talks about that.

She kept a journal, too, and that was as nice as finding
out that she wasn't married. My only regret was our meeting
like this, in the midst of battle, where it was impossible to find

enough time to talk. She was so sweet and pleasant, always with a kind word to the men, always smiling, it was no wonder she had come to be known as the angel of the battlefield.

"How did you get started in all this?" I asked her one day when our hands were sharing a pot of warm water, scrubbing at the clothes that had been taken from the dead to use for bandages and slings.

"I was a clerk in the Patent Office in Washington when the war began, Corrie. Actually, I am from Massachusetts. My first exposure to the troops came when I met some boys who were down from my home state. I'd visit them and talk to them and try to help ease their homesickness."

"I'm sure they were glad to see such a pretty, smiling face," I said.

"Pretty? Corrie . . . come now. If you and I are going to be friends, we mustn't lie to each other!"

I laughed. It was easy to see from the twinkle in her eye that she was teasing me.

"Well, you're as pretty as I am, anyway," I said.

"Then I'll take your words as a compliment!"

"Now who is stretching the truth?" I said back.

It was time for both of us to laugh. It felt good to joke and laugh for a change in the midst of all the blood and death. These days there weren't too many opportunities to see the bright side of anything.

We were both silent a minute. Then a very thoughtful look came over Clara's face.

"Corrie," she said seriously, "I don't know what it's like in California, if it's anything like Massachusetts or Washington, but—"

She paused, trying to find the right words.

"Do you ever feel *odd*," she went on, "strange, out of step with the rest of the world, because, you know—because you're not married? Especially, do you think people look at you and think you a bit peculiar because you *want* to do other things in your life besides just marrying and having a family?"

I nodded, relieved to find someone at last who understood my predicament.

"You asked how I got started," she said. "As soon as I began meeting those poor, homesick men, I *wanted* to do something for them. How do you explain that kind of thing to someone whose only thought is to have a little place to call home, where they can stay for their whole life, always cooking over the same stove, always going to sleep in the same bed at night? There's nothing wrong with any of that, but I wanted to *do* something more than just go back to my boardinghouse every evening after my work at the Patent Office. . . . Corrie, I don't even know *where* I would call home now . . . do you understand me?"

How well I understood! After this last year, living in boardinghouses and traveling all around the North and visiting new cities and staying with people I'd never met before, and now here, following the fighting and sleeping outside under the stars or wherever there was room in one of the tents . . . I didn't know where to call home, either.

"So I started collecting things to take to the men—nothing much . . . soap and candies, tobacco and brandy when I could get it, lemons, supplies for sewing, homemade jellies. Oh, but you should have seen their faces! They were so appreciative.

"And then came Bull Run, and the wounded poured into the Washington hospitals. Before I knew it I was doing more than just helping with homesickness with little treats. That's when I began trying to help with nursing and assisting with the wounded in the hospitals, although at first I knew nothing whatever about it or what to do."

I thought of my own experience at Gettysburg. "When the blood is pouring out before your very eyes, I don't suppose it takes long to learn where to put the bandage," I said.

"I remained in Washington for a time," Clara went on. "I wanted to do more. I so hungered to help save lives, whether I knew anything about nursing or not. But I was afraid to follow the troops. I didn't want to be seen as a camp follower. I'm sure you understand, Corrie. I knew what they'd all think—the surgeons and officers and commanders, and even the regular army nurses like old Dotty Dix—they'd all think I was after nothing more than a husband."

I smiled. "I have a very dear uncle who thinks like that, too," I said.

"I don't want a husband, Corrie. There's too much to be done, and a lot of it takes a woman to do it, not a man. Nobody questions Mary Ann Bickerdyke—have you met her?"

I told her I had.

"A dear, isn't she?"

"Yes."

"But she's older and a widow," Clara went on, "so nobody thinks it strange of her to be involved. And Dotty Dix—how about that woman?—have you met her?"

"Yes, but I don't think she thought too much of me."

"She doesn't want women like us around," laughed Clara. "That's exactly what I mean—even she, one of our own kind, thinks all we have on our mind before we're fifty years old is marriage, and it's just not right."

"You don't call her Dragon Dix?" I asked.

"Not that I haven't wanted to a few times," replied Clara. "I've been around her enough to know why she earned the title. And frankly, it's not that far wrong! But I owe her the courtesy of treating her more nicely than she treated me."

Neither of us said anything for a while. It was time to rinse out the trousers and shirts and change the water. Fortunately this was one occasion when we *had* fresh water to begin a new batch with. In another ten minutes we were back scrubbing in the pot again, with white, wrinkled fingers and palms.

"Have you ever thought about becoming a nun?" I asked her.

"I'm not Catholic."

"Neither am I, but I still find myself thinking about it." I told her briefly about my time at the Convent of John Seventeen.

Clara was quiet a long time. Finally she spoke. "You know, it's funny you should ask that," she said. "I'd nearly forgotten about it, but now that you remind me it comes back to my mind that I *did* think about it for a time back when I was nineteen or twenty and didn't know what a young, unmarried girl ought to do with herself. But then I went to Washington and later got involved in the war and found nursing more to my liking than praying and Bible reading."

"I don't know if I could make a lifetime of being around blood," I said.

"You seem to be doing fine here."

"It's what's needed, and there aren't enough hands. But I don't think I could ever get used to it. My stomach is always in knots. Are *you* used to the blood, the death, the screams, the pain?"

"Used to it—no," replied Clara. "I hope I never become *used* to it. It's unnatural, wrong. War is an evil thing. But the blood doesn't bother me any more than lots of things. When there's fighting, young men are wounded and need tending to. I suppose it's something I feel called to do, why God put me on the earth. It's when I feel most . . . I don't know what to say exactly, most—*myself* . . . most at peace with who I am supposed to be . . . and least concerned with what anyone else—Dotty Dix or the generals who don't think women ought to be near the fighting, or anyone else who thinks someone like me should be finding a husband and living a quiet life as somebody's wife—might think. My place, Corrie, is anywhere between the bullet and the battlefield. I'm happy here. It's what I want to do. It's what I know I was meant to do."

She stopped, and her hands stilled for a moment. She looked across at me, then asked, "When are you most yourself, Corrie? When are you most at peace with what you want to be doing?"

It was a hard question to answer. I had been trying to figure it out ever since meeting Sister Janette.

"I suppose when I'm writing," I said at length. "I love to think about ideas and try to put them on paper."

"What kind of ideas?"

"Anything . . . all kinds. Things about God, mostly—how the truths in the Bible give meaning to life, how God speaks and moves and is involved in what we do. But I like to write about anything— describing how something looks, or telling about people I've met. When I get the time, I'm writing right now about what it's like trying to help the wounded. I may even write something about you!"

Clara laughed. "And then what will you do with what you have written?"

"Give it to the newspapers, send it to my editor back in San Francisco to be printed there. To me it's important that people are told how things are, what it's like. And when I'm doing that—whether I'm telling about the war or describing something I've seen or even telling what I'm thinking and feeling inside—I suppose *that's* when I feel, as you called it, most *myself.*"

"I write in my journal whenever I have the chance, but I've never thought of writing for a newspaper. Women aren't supposed to *do* that."

"Neither are they supposed to be on the battlefield during a war!" I said.

"You're right," laughed Clara. "And I suppose as long as women like you and I have it in our heads to be doing things that women don't do, and have it in our hearts that we want to spend our lives doing them because we feel it's right that we do, I don't suppose we can ever get away from folks thinking of us as just a bit peculiar!"

I joined in her laughter. It was nice to have a companion who shared some of the same feelings and could understand. For once, even if briefly, I didn't mind being different than other young women my age.

Lincoln vs. McClellan
CHAPTER FORTY-TWO

George McClellan was one of the Union generals with whom President Lincoln had grown extremely frustrated early in the war, long before the star of Ulysses Grant began to rise so brilliantly onto the horizon. He had been the President's top general early in the war, and had led the first Union assault on Richmond back in 1862. Had Grant been in charge then instead, the war might have ended quickly. But McClellan was cautious, fearful, and indecisive. Rather than an all-out attack, he waited and probed timidly, sending message after message back to Washington for more troops, more supplies, more guns, more horses.

His hesitation gave Lee the time he needed: time to defeat McClellan and prolong the war for several more years. President Lincoln had put up with his failure to lead a decisive way long enough. Finally, in October of 1862, in frustration and anger, he relieved McClellan of his command for good.

The general was embittered, always felt he had been judged harshly and unjustly, and never forgave his Commander-in-Chief. When 1864 arrived, he ran for president, won the Democratic nomination, and thus was pitted head to head against his old rival, whom he still hated—Republican President Abraham Lincoln.

It was an ugly, bitter campaign throughout the late summer and fall months. Republicans accused the Democrats of treason because many of them were calling for peace even above the preservation of the Union. Even McClellan did not go quite that far, although he did agree with the stinging democratic editorialists who charged that the true objective of the "Negro-loving, Negro-hugging worshipers of old Abe" was miscegenation, a new word coined for the mixing and blending of white and black. Whatever the North as a whole may have thought about slavery itself, and however willing its people were to fight the South to outlaw slavery, it was clear that prejudice against the Negro race was as deeply ingrained in the cities of the Union as in those of the Confederacy. The election of 1864 proved it.

The South was elated at McClellan's nomination. Confederate Vice President Alexander Stephens called it "the first real ray of light since the war began." If McClellan could defeat Lincoln, they were confident, the war could be brought to a swift end, and terms of peace could be arrived at which would ensure the continuation of the Confederacy as a separate nation. The people of the North were ready for the war to end. Only Abraham Lincoln stubbornly insisted on prolonging it, the Southerners thought. If Lincoln could be defeated, slavery and the Confederacy could both be preserved.

Such was Robert E. Lee's hope. Such was the hope of all loyal Southerners, every one of whom hated Abraham Lincoln passionately. Every white man and woman, that is. To the slaves, he was the liberator.

At its core, the election was a struggle not between ideologies but between two men—one a President, the other a scorned general, still resentful over his dismissal from command. McClellan publicly called Lincoln "the original gorilla."

It did not look good for Mr. Lincoln. There had never before been an election for a nation in the midst of a civil war. No President since Andrew Jackson had served a second term, and the public mood in the North did not bode well for reversing the trend.

In August, President Lincoln said, "I am going to be *beaten*." Then he added, "And unless some great change takes place, *badly* beaten."

His only hopes seemed to lie with his two generals, Grant and Sherman, now engaged in the final fight to bring the Confederacy to its knees, hopefully before November.

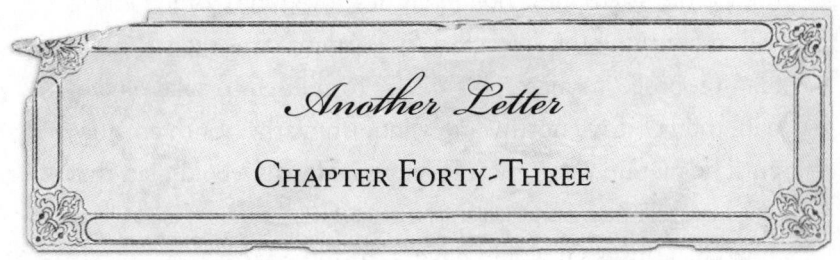

*W*hile Lee and Grant slugged it out in Virginia, without noticeable success for either side, General Sherman was making more progress in the South. He and his 100,000 men made it to the vicinity of Atlanta in early August.

The siege lasted a month. But finally he hurled everything he had at the starving, beleaguered city, forcing the Confederate army out once and for all.

Sherman moved in to occupy it for the Union, then sent telegrams north to both his President and his friend and commander, Ulysses Grant: *Atlanta is ours and fairly won.*

But Atlanta was only half of Grant's final objective. The fall of the great "Gate City of the South" and second most important manufacturing center of the Confederacy could not alone seal the victory for the Union. There was still Richmond to be won. Sherman's victory, however, did boost morale in the Northern states, so that President Lincoln's election prospects began to brighten.

And Lincoln, Grant, and Sherman had all learned the lesson of Gettysburg—that the enemy army must be destroyed so that it could not rise to fight again. Meade and McClellan were not commanding this time, but rather two determined fighters—Grant and Sherman. And they would ensure that the victory at Atlanta completely destroyed the Confederacy's will to continue the struggle. Once Atlanta was secure, Sherman proposed to march his troops to the sea to take Savannah, then to drive northward, vanquishing the South entirely, until he met up with Grant in Virginia. It was a bold plan that would surely bring an end to the war. The South *refused* to lay down its arms, so it would have to be forced to do so.

In the meantime, a break came from the field hospital where I had been working, and I suddenly found myself traveling back to the Capital.

The message that had come to me was as unexpected as was the stir it caused in our camp. Only, moments after the courier had arrived with newspapers and letters and a few supplies, Mother Bickerdyke came hurrying toward me.

"Corrie . . . Corrie," she said, "here's something for you— it looks important!"

As I took the small envelope from her hand, I couldn't imagine who could be writing to me here—or what could be so important. I was hardly aware of the other nurses and assistants following right behind her with looks of wonder and anticipation on their faces. It didn't dawn on me that they were all following her on account of *me*, and to see what the letter could possibly contain.

"The courier said there were two important messages from the President," Mrs. Bickerdyke went on as I took the envelope from her. "'One of 'em's in here,' he said as he threw down the hospital pouch onto the ground. 'The other's marked *Urgent*, and it's for General Grant!' Then he galloped off on his horse toward the front lines."

"Hurry, Corrie," said one of the nurses. "Open it. We're dying to see!"

I fumbled with the edges of it and finally succeeded in pulling out the paper inside. I couldn't help glancing immediately to the familiar signature at the bottom, and it took me two or three readings to absorb the words that preceded it.

MISS HOLLISTER,

The reports reaching us here tell me you and Mrs. Bickerdyke and Miss Barton and all the other faithful servants of the Union are doing a brave and courageous job of healing in the midst of terrible suffering and anguish. I commend you, and all your colleagues of the Sanitary Commission and other agencies involved in the relief and medical efforts, and would ask you to personally convey my appreciation to all those with you there on the battlefields of Virginia. I only hope the brave soldiers under General Grant can sustain their valor under the terrible conditions of this mighty battle for freedom.

As I read the words aloud, I paused and glanced around. A few shouts and cheers and whoops and clapping broke out at the President's words, which they all knew had been addressed to them as well as me. How could we not be encouraged and uplifted to know that Mr. Lincoln had heard of and appreciated our efforts!

Sadly, I too am facing a mighty battle—this one political in nature. It appears more than likely that I will be defeated for reelection in November, and I fear such a result bodes extremely ill for the future of the nation, and could mean defeat for everything we have been fighting for.

Loathe as I am to remove you from such important work as you are doing, there are many capable hands who can carry it on. There is, however, only yourself who has the experience, both in politics and in reporting, to assist my campaign in the unique manner of which you are capable. You have campaigned on my behalf before, with good result, and I would like to call upon your assistance once again. Your experience on the battlefield will only add to the estimation in which you are already held by the growing readership in this nation, which recognizes your name as one they can trust.

I look forward to a speedy reply from you, and trust it will be an affirmative one. Please make an appointment to see me immediately upon your return to the Capital, and we will discuss our mutual ideas to ensure a victory in November.

As always, I am indebted to you for your help, Miss Hollister.

> I remain,
> Sincerely yours,
> A. LINCOLN

All the friends who were gathered around listening as I read began talking and congratulating me the moment I was through. So many things were flitting through my mind. Then I heard Clara's voice beside me.

"It would seem your writing *is* what you are to be doing," she said, "just as you told me. President Lincoln seems to think it is even more important for you to do than helping here with the wounded. It looks as if you're going to have the chance again to do what you *like* to do as well as helping the country."

"Just like you," I said, looking at her with a smile.

"I'll help with bandages, you with words from your pen."

Back in Washington

CHAPTER FORTY-FOUR

I left the rear line of the camp the next day for Washington. General Grant's army had been stuck for more than two months outside Petersburg, south of Richmond, and it did not appear likely the Confederate capital was about to fail anytime soon. I went north, but the siege for the two vital cities went on.

After the front lines of fighting and the terrible condition of our camp hospitals, even the drab room at Marge Surratt's place would have seemed spacious and clean. But when I walked into my former room at Mrs. Richards' and set down my bag and looked around, I truly thought myself in a palace! Everything looked the same, and yet it seemed almost tinged with a heavenly cleanliness and purity.

Clean sheets! I can hardly describe what it felt like that first night to slide down between them and pull the quilt up and snuggle it in between my shoulders and neck, stretching my legs back and forth and knowing everything was *clean!*

And the quiet during the night! No moaning, no distant cannon fire, no sudden screams from a waking amputee who was feeling about for his hand or foot or leg in the night and suddenly realizing it wasn't there. No foul smells of smoke or gunpowder or wet hay, no smell of men coming in after months without a bath. No mud . . . no rain . . . no dirt and blood . . . no death.

Even with the quietness, I slept fitfully my first few nights back in the city. I could not rest comfortably and peacefully. Part of me somehow felt that I still ought to be back there in the hospital tents with the others whom I now considered my friends, helping with the work that was always more than we could possibly do. And in truth, part of me still *was* there with them, even if only in my heart and my prayers. I would never forget . . . *could* never forget the experience. I felt that I would never be completely whole, completely at rest or at peace again after the things I had seen and heard and been part of.

But there was work for me to do here, too—important work, after talking with the President.

His campaign was in trouble, he said. Sherman's victory in Atlanta had helped, but McClellan was still traveling about the North claiming to be the only man who could succeed in putting the war-ravaged country back together. He wanted me to write—to write as fast as I could and as much as I could—to tell where I'd been and what I'd seen, and to write as openly as I cared to, expressing my support for the President and my conviction that his reelection was vital to the country.

"You mustn't underestimate the mighty power of your pen, Corrie," he said. "Women can't vote for me, but they are the morale booster throughout the whole country. Without their hands we would have no stockings, no shirts, no trousers, no uniforms for our soldiers. You know as well as I do that without the women of the Union, there would be no Sanitary Commission, fewer nurses, fewer hospitals, fewer lives saved. Your words have a wide audience among women *and* men, and I'm counting on you to speak—with your pen and your mouth—to help those others who are engaged in like effort to rally the spirits of our people to persevere in this fight to the end, which is nearly at hand. McClellan must not be elected. It would mean doom to the Union, and, I fear, permanency to the Confederacy."

"Will the papers publish my articles if they're obviously and blatantly political?" I asked.

"We'll make sure they do!" interjected Mr. Hay.

"We have a very shrewd man on our staff who manages affairs with the press," added Mr. Lincoln. "You write what you can, Corrie. The Democratic papers, of course, won't touch it. But there are enough who are on our side that your words will be read in all the major cities."

"And California?" I asked.

"Yes, there, too, and Oregon as well. Your own paper— what's your editor's name?"

"Mr. Kemble," I said.

"Yes, Kemble—well *they'll* print your articles, surely, and I'll make a note to him personally, asking him to circulate them around the state."

"To the competition?" I asked.

"I'll make a personal request. And . . . well, if he's not in agreement, you can tell him we'll file your articles with *another* of the major California papers."

"I'm sure he'll be happy to do as you ask," I said, smiling.

"What do you say, Corrie? Are you with me in this? Will you write . . . for the Union cause . . . and for *me*—to help us with this reelection?"

"Of course, Mr. President."

"Do I still detect some hesitancy?"

"Oh no, not about you, or my belief in the country or your presidency. It's only that I don't suppose I'm as confident as you seem to be that anything I say or do will make that much difference."

"You leave that to us," said Mr. Hay. "We have many skillful people hard at work on the election. We have enlisted the support of a number of other known reporters—men, of course. There will be many people speaking on behalf of the President. And all of it together, including what you will be able to do, *will* carry the day. You mustn't worry about results. Do what *you* do best, and we will do what *we* do best."

I began immediately to do what Mr. Lincoln and Mr. Hay had asked. I didn't know what result it might have, but I could and would write about what I'd seen, about what I thought, and about the importance to the country of Mr. Lincoln getting reelected.

Everything now was so different than the two previous times I had been involved in campaigns—for Mr. Fremont in 1856 and for Mr. Lincoln in 1860. I'd never really stopped to think about whether I ought to be a Republican or a Democrat. But I had supported the Republican candidate for three elections in a row because of the men themselves and because of the slavery question.

That very afternoon I sat down to try to begin a new article about the war and the election and Mr. Lincoln.

In 1860 I supported a man I'd never met for President of this great country we call the United States of America. I didn't know Abraham Lincoln, but I believed slavery to be wrong, and I felt strongly that we needed a President who would seek to rid our nation of it and would stand up for the truth that our country was founded on—freedom.

So when they asked me to help, to speak out on behalf of his election, I agreed, even though I was young and timid. Mr. Lincoln was elected. My home state of California voted for Mr. Lincoln, as did most of the rest of the states of the Union.

Now, four years later, a lot has changed for all of us. We've been fighting a terrible civil war almost since the last election. Hundreds of thousands of our sons and friends and brothers have been killed. Mr. Lincoln has freed the slaves and declared slavery illegal.

But the most important thing that has changed is that we are now *two* countries instead of one. As important as the question of slavery is, we are fighting now to preserve the United States of America as *one* nation. And after all this fighting and all this killing, we are still a country at war, and the South is still unwilling to come back and be part of the Union it should never have left.

If we quit now, these last four years will have been for nothing. At Gettysburg ten months ago, Mr. Lincoln delivered a dedication speech for the young men who had died there. He said that we had to resolve that they did not die in vain. He said that we had to dedicate ourselves to the great task before us of *finishing* the work that they began.

That work is the preservation of freedom. That is what they fought for, and died for. And for us to give up now will mean that all who have given their lives these last four years will have given them for no result. For nothing will have been gained.

If we give up now, the things we have been fighting for will not come to pass. We will remain *two* nations—the Union and the Confederacy. Slavery will remain in the South, and the dream of freedom for all men and women will vanish.

Four years ago I supported a man I did not know because I believed in what he believed in. Today I support a man whom I *do* know because he is the only man who can lead this nation forward—this *entire* nation—into the full measure of the freedom we are fighting for, and into the full stature of nationhood that is the destiny of this land. To turn our back now on Mr. Lincoln and all he has stood for on our behalf will be to invalidate the lives of all those who have sacrificed for the cause of freedom and unity.

I urge you all, men who can vote and even women who cannot, to continue supporting our President, Mr. Abraham Lincoln, until this battle, now drawing to an end, is fully won and freedom is restored throughout our *whole* land.

"That's it exactly!" exclaimed Mr. Hay when he had read the two sheets I'd handed him. "Yes, Miss Hollister . . . yes, this is wonderful—the President will be most pleased!"

I couldn't help being a little embarrassed. He continued to look over what I'd written with an expression of surprise, but also with a smile.

"The President might want to use some of your phrases himself—*the full stature of nationhood . . . the destiny . . .* you've really touched upon some remarkable concepts, Miss Hollister—*invalidate the lives of those who have sacrificed . . .* yes, I'm certain some of this will find its way into the President's own remarks. Very well done!"

"I'm happy you like it," I said.

"It is perfect—just what we were after. Within a week we will have this running in as many of the papers sympathetic to our cause as we can."

"And the *Alta?*" I reminded him.

"Of course. I'll arrange to have it wired to San Francisco, too. Now, Miss Hollister, do you have other ideas for more such pieces?"

"I . . . I suppose—that is, yes, I always have ideas, but I never know exactly what's going to come out until I sit down and start writing."

"Well, however you do it, you get to work on some more of it! If *this* is what comes out when you put your hand to the paper, I would like to see, perhaps, a new article once a week—or even more often, if possible. With Sherman's victory and your articles and the President's campaigning, I think we may turn this election around yet. If only Grant can keep Lee from running him out of Virginia. A Lee victory now would be a devastating blow to our whole effort."

He rose and led me to the door.

"So, Miss Hollister," he said, "continue just as you have been doing. Bring me whatever you come up with. And in the meantime, I'll also be contacting you about making some campaign appearances."

"You mean . . . speaking?" I said.

"Somewhat, perhaps. But don't be anxious. I've heard that you are a fine speaker."

"I do better with my pen."

"Well, we'll see. But just be ready—I may want to call on you to accompany either the President or one of our Republican senators on a campaign swing or two—Ohio, New York, Pennsylvania, New Jersey . . . these are states we must not let McClellan win."

"I'm sure nobody would pay much attention to—"

"Come, come, Miss Hollister. I know better than that, even if you do not. There have been reports, even from as far away as California, about some of the appearances you made on the President's behalf four years ago. I happen to know that you are very effective on the stump as well as at a desk."

I could feel my face turn red. How could I convince him that I really disliked standing up in front of a crowd of people?

"Besides," he went on, "you won't always have to *say* anything at all. Your mere presence says something, too—a woman sharing the platform with the politicians, a woman whose name people recognize, a woman who has been on the front lines where the fighting is, and now who is writing and appearing on behalf of the President—not to mention that your book about California when you were younger is beginning to circulate a bit. It all speaks very well for the President."

"I'll do whatever you would like me to," I said finally.

"Then you keep writing articles and editorials for President Lincoln, and I will be in contact with you."

He shook my hand and I left.

I did as Mr. Hay wanted, and kept writing. Ideas kept coming to me, and I wrote them down. Sometimes they turned out to be an article that was printed, sometimes not, but I sat down at my writing desk every day to see what I might be able to say. I wrote about Mr. Lincoln, about how I saw the country, about some of my personal experiences both at Gettysburg and recently in Virginia, and even now and then about something relating to California, because there were voters back on the West Coast too, and they had to vote for Mr. Lincoln as well as those closer by.

A week and a half after my return to Washington, Mr. Hay asked me to accompany several congressmen and their wives, two senators, and the vice presidential candidate, Mr. Johnson, on a train trip to campaign in Pennsylvania and Ohio, then back through Buffalo, New York, and south to Philadelphia before returning to Washington.

"There will be other women along," he said. "All arrangements for lodging and the like will be taken care of. You'll have a wonderful time, and we hope it will be a very effective opportunity to sway the vote in these crucial states."

"Do you want me to stop writing articles?" I asked.

"Oh no. You should still have time to continue that work as well. You will not have to speak more than a few times. We simply want to be able to introduce you and let people see your face. But we want fresh new articles to continue to appear as well. The President himself will be joining the party in Philadelphia for two major campaign addresses."

I agreed, and told Mrs. Richards of my plans. Since we'd be gone three or four weeks, I told her I'd move my things to one side of the wardrobe and the bottom drawers of the dresser so that she would be able to rent out the room to other travelers or visitors to the city in my absence.

The very morning we left, a letter arrived from Clara Barton. I waited until we were on the train north to Baltimore and then Harrisburg before reading it.

> Everyone here sends you greetings. We all miss you, though we are glad you do not have to see the suffering for a while, and we know the work you are doing for the President may help the war end sooner.
>
> But oh, Corrie, the suffering is so dreadful. With every new attempt at Petersburg, more men are killed and wounded. Where will it all end? The battle is a tactical one, with standoff after standoff. There have even been reports of spies in our midst, even plots against Generals Grant and Meade. Yet our work in the hospitals goes on much as it was when you were with us. We have had to continue to move with the army, making use of homes and buildings in the surrounding towns whenever we can. Yet the means we have of helping is woefully inadequate!
>
> I saw, crowded into one old sunken hotel, lying upon its bare, wet, bloody floors, five hundred fainting men

holding up their cold, weak, dingy hands as I passed, and beg in heaven's name for a cracker to keep them from starving (and I had none); or to give them a cup that they might have something to drink water from, if they could get it (and I had no cup and could get none). As much as comes to us daily from the faithful women of the Northern states who labor making bandages and supplies, we have so much less than is needed.

I saw two hundred six-mule army wagons in a line, stretching down the street to headquarters, and reaching so far out on the Wilderness Road that I never found the end of it; every wagon crowded with wounded men, stopped, standing in the rain and mud, wrenched back and forth by the restless, hungry animals all night. Dark spots in the mud under many a wagon told all too plainly where some poor fellow's life had dripped out in those dreadful hours.

A man came through the camp just last night, following the battle with his wagon, an itinerant embalmer. Oh, just to read the words of his dreadful flyer made my flesh crawl: "Persons at a distance, desiring to have the bodies of their deceased friends disinterred, embalmed, disinfected, or prepared and sent home, and have it promptly attended to, apply to the office of Simon Garland, 35 South 13th Street, Philadelphia. No zinc, arsenic, or alcohol is used. Perfect satisfaction guaranteed."

To think of human death being reduced to such a grisly business! He was prowling about the hospital looking for the bodies of those he had been hired to fix. It was all too terrible to think about!

Do whatever you can, dear Corrie. Tell our President, tell the people of the country, how awful it truly is. This cannot go on . . . it *must* end! The killing and destruction must be put to a stop. Tell them, Corrie—from all of us!

I was wiping away tears even before finishing her words. I determined then and there to somehow find a way to include some of what Clara had said in my very next article. In fact, within ten minutes I had pulled out my pen and paper and began right there on the train, as best I could without spilling the ink.

The trip was long and tiring, yet exhilarating too. I met many new people and saw places I'd never seen before. Our first major stop was in Pittsburgh, then on to Columbus, then north to Akron, Cleveland, Erie, Buffalo, and Rochester before heading south. When I stood up to speak for the first time, I tried to remember what I'd said the first time I was on the platform in Sacramento four years earlier. Afterward, people came up to talk to me, especially women, and a lot of them had read either my book or some of the articles, and they were all so nice and kind with their words. After that it began to get easier, just as it had when I'd traveled with Mr. King, although I still preferred when the congressmen and Mr. Johnson did the speechmaking and only introduced me or said something about my articles.

I did manage to find time to keep writing, although it wasn't quite as easy as if I'd been back at Mrs. Richards'. During the campaign trip, I sent four articles back to Mr. Hay. One of them appeared in the Buffalo paper the day we arrived. One of the senator's wives came excitedly into my room of the hotel where we were staying, carrying it in her hand.

"Corrie, look," she said, "here's the article you sent back to John Hay when we were in Pittsburgh. I've brought you a copy of the paper."

"Thank you," I replied.

I glanced at it, but was embarrassed to read any of it just then.

Later that night, after I was alone and ready for bed, I opened the paper up to the second page and read what I'd written on the train as we'd traveled across Pennsylvania. As we'd gone through Harrisburg and Gettysburg, so many things were in my mind. I thought a great deal about Sister Janette and all she'd told me about Pennsylvania and William Penn and others of the early leaders of the country. Then I began thinking of the founding of our nation as a whole and of the men who had written the Constitution and organized our government. And I thought about slavery and what part it had played in our country right from the beginning.

When the fathers of our country wrote the Declaration of Independence, they said, "We hold these truths to be self-evident—that all men are created equal; that they are endowed by their Creator with certain inalienable rights; that among these are life, liberty, and the pursuit of happiness." When they later wrote the Constitution, by which we've been governed ever since, they again spoke of "the blessings of liberty" as the reason why the Constitution had to be written.

These documents have been the very foundations of this nation ever since. Yet what was the *liberty* they spoke of? What did they mean when they wrote *all men are created equal*? Who were the *all men* they spoke of?

Many of the very men themselves who signed the Declaration of Independence and the Constitution owned slaves. Five of the original thirteen states were from what is today the Confederacy. Four of our first five presidents were from Virginia, what we call today a "slave state."

These men, our very founding fathers whom we revere, obviously didn't think there was anything wrong with slavery. So what are we to make of their words *liberty* for *all men* and *created equal?*

As I read, I could not help but be reminded of Miss Stansberry, now Mrs. Rutledge, and how she had drilled us from our history books, making us memorize the first part of the Declaration of Independence and the Preamble to the Constitution, as well as the names of all the Presidents. Zack had hated it, but I was glad now for all the hard study she'd made us do.

If our nation truly was founded on "liberty" and "equality" for "all men," why are we now engaged in this terrible war?

Perhaps something was wrong from the very beginning, something that the founding fathers didn't know was wrong, but something that was eventually going to have to be fixed. Perhaps Abraham Lincoln is the man who has taken upon himself the task of completing what the founding fathers only began.

This great nation was founded and built upon principles known to few other nations on earth—principles of liberty and freedom and justice. And yet perhaps there has been a crack in that foundation, a crack barely visible, and indeed *invisible* to many, a crack which has from the very beginning of our nationhood weakened the structure of the nation we have been trying to build. That crack is the existence of slavery.

Why has there been a crack? Why has the foundation been weak?

Because something was established as a truth in the foundation of the country which *wasn't* a truth in the way things actually were. The Constitution and Declaration of Independence spoke of equality and liberty, and yet the laws of the land permitted slavery and inequality. Two opposite and contradictory things have been allowed to exist in this country all this time. Yet we still talk about this nation as the land of the free. But it has never been truly and completely a land of freedom.

Four years ago, our brave President said, "It is time to fix this crack of inconsistency . . . it is time that we at last make what have been truths in principle truths in fact . . . it is time we make *all* people in this land we call a land of freedom—it is time we make *all* people free at last."

Now we are fighting a dreadful and awful war over whether this crack is worth fixing. We must find out what kind of a nation we really are, and what kind of a people we really are. Do freedom, and justice, and equality really matter, or will this nation be satisfied to say that our government is founded upon such principles but in fact deny those very rights to a large number of people because of the color of their skin? Do we *really* believe that "all men are created equal"?

I think we *do* believe that. I know I do, and I think most Northerners, and probably a lot of Southerners do, too. Therefore, we must continue to support President

Lincoln. The crack is nearly healed. If we do not return him to the presidency now, it will be to give up when we are so close to making our land truly a land of freedom to all, when we have paid such a great price and fought such a great battle to do so.

We must now complete building what the founding fathers only began. And to ensure that the foundation is strongly built and that its cracks are completely healed, we *must* reelect President Lincoln to another term of office.

A Fateful Night

CHAPTER FORTY-SEVEN

For the rest of the campaign trip, everyone seemed to treat me just a little differently. Something about the article made them look at me almost with a look of astonishment. The women complimented me on what I'd written and said they'd never read anything like that before from me. They asked how I knew all those things to say and how I'd thought of it and how I knew so much history. But the men seemed to wonder to themselves if I was really the person writing those articles. In person I probably seemed shy and didn't say too much. And then when they read what I'd written, it didn't sound at all like the same person.

I suppose I had changed some. Being around Washington and important people, and listening and talking to them, I suppose I didn't sound quite so much like a little girl from the backwoods, as I once had. My writing was getting a little better, too, at least people told me so. I wondered sometimes what Mr. Kemble and Mr. MacPherson—who always said he liked my "homespun" style!—thought of it now. Maybe they didn't like it as much as before!

Afterward it seemed that this article, more than any other, was one people remembered reading. In Philadelphia, they introduced me as the young woman who wrote "so eloquently about the crack in our nation's foundation." Everyone had been nice until then. But after Buffalo, people treated me with greater courtesy and respect. Maybe for the first time some of them realized what Mr. Hay had been saying to me all along, that the written word was just as able to influence people as speechmaking.

Our itinerary had been somewhat uncertain. President Lincoln joined us in Philadelphia for two speeches; then he and Mr. Johnson and two of the senators went on to New York, while the rest of us returned to Washington. I hadn't been able to let Mrs. Richards know when I would be return-ing, and as a result, my room was occupied on the evening when I arrived back in the Capital. She offered to find me a place for the night in her own part of the house, but after thinking about it briefly, I realized that this might be an oppor-tunity sent by the Lord for some purpose. So I told her not to worry about me and that I'd see her the following afternoon.

Thus I found myself again knocking on the door of Marge Surratt's boardinghouse.

After everything I'd been through down in Virginia, and now after three weeks on trains and at meetings and in hotels, I was almost eager to see her. Hers wasn't exactly a friendly face, but there is something unique and special about laying eyes on someone you've been praying for. The moment I saw her, the most remarkable little stab of genuine feeling for the lady sprang up within my heart. I suppose praying for *her* had worked changes within *me*. But I thought I saw the beginnings of a smile as she saw me standing there in front of her.

"Hello, Mrs. Surratt," I said. "I need a room for tonight. Do you have anything available?"

"Turned you out, did they?"

"No, I just got back earlier than I anticipated."

"Well, you might as well come in, now that you're here. You can go to the same room as before. Supper's still at six."

"I remember," I replied with a smile. "Six sharp."

She almost smiled. I took my bag and went up to the room. Even its drab colors and ugly curtains didn't look half so bad this time.

Supper was uneventful. The men around the table were all faces I'd never seen before, and no more talkative than the others had been earlier. I helped her clean up afterward and tried to talk. But it wasn't much use. She seemed distracted and fidgety, looking toward the door and out the window as if she were expecting someone. Eventually I excused myself and went back to my room. If I was going to get anywhere with her, it would have to wait still longer.

I was tired and went to bed immediately. It was probably no later than eight o'clock when I lay down, and I think I was asleep within five minutes.

Dreams intruded into my consciousness. There were faces I didn't recognize, although they were familiar and I knew I should know them. A feeling of oppression came over me, but the dreams were fuzzy and undefined. There was more feeling to them than sights and activity—feelings of dread, of danger, and around and behind it a feeling of hurt and pain. I wanted to cry, but no tears would come. I had been hurt. I could feel it, but I didn't know why. And with it came the feeling that more hurt was coming, that danger was somewhere close at hand.

But where? I couldn't see it, couldn't find it. Danger to whom? I wasn't the one who was in danger. It was someone else . . . someone important. Who could it be? I had to warn them . . . then came again the hurt, the stab of pain in my own heart.

Visions of the battlefield began to distort everything . . . blood and screams . . . broken bodies lying everywhere, explosions of gunfire . . . mangled limbs and hands and feet . . . red bandages and blood dripping from them. Then came nurses all dressed in white. There was Clara and Mrs. Bickerdyke. They were talking in hushed tones. . . . Then again came the pain—were they talking about me? Had I done something they disapproved of? Why were they talking . . . ? I couldn't quite hear them, couldn't make out their voice . . . if I could just listen more intently. . . .

The white figures disappeared, and there were two men, leaders, commanding men, standing in front of thousands, trying to speak, but no words would come from their lips. I thought I recognized the two men, but why could they not speak? Why were such looks of sadness and pain upon their faces?

Then I did hear voices again . . . softly this time. Still the two bearded leaders moved their lips, but I knew the voices were not theirs. There were other voices, speaking in hushed tones . . . not wanting to be heard . . . speaking evil things. They were talking *about* the men in beards, whispering so as not to be heard.

And still over it all was such a feeling of dread . . . of pain . . . of suffering to come. But I couldn't hear them . . . I couldn't make out the words . . . if only I could. . . .

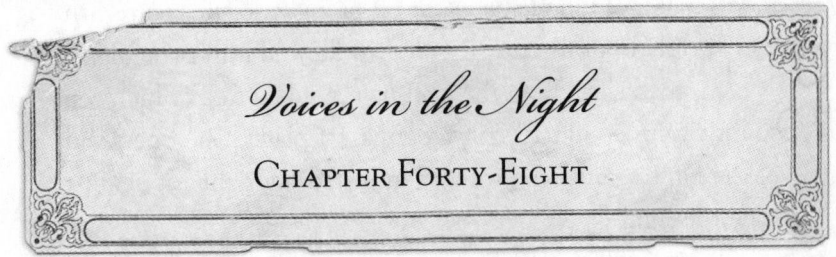

*S*uddenly I was awake!

The room was dark. It was the middle of the night. I couldn't even guess the time.

And there *were* voices!

Not voices from a dream, but *real* voices—speaking in subdued and hushed tones, yet above a whisper. Through the thin walls I could hear them plainly, although I could not make out the thread of the conversation. The discussion was fervent, but not exactly an argument.

I listened for several seconds in the blackness. Then all the feelings of oppression and dread and fear and hurt from out of my dream blanketed me all over again. But this time it was real! Now I knew why my dreaming consciousness had felt such pain at the sound of the voice that had intruded through the walls and into my sleeping brain.

My heart pounded, and my whole body broke into an instant sweat. Along with the pain, a new emotion rose up within me—anger! I was filled with such a tumult of feelings that I almost began to wonder if I really *was* awake!

I threw back the covers and sprang to my feet. In the darkness I sought a drinking glass that I'd set on the nightstand.

It was still half full of the water I'd brought to the room with me. Hastily I put it to my lips and swallowed it in two gulps.

I tiptoed silently to the wall near my bed from which the sounds were coming. With great care I placed the open end of the glass against the wall, then rested my right ear against the other end.

Again I strained to listen, and I could hear the voices in the next room clearly.

There was no mistaking it. I *did* know the voice. It was Cal Burton!

I couldn't believe my ears! How could it be? Yet I *knew* it was him!

". . . That may be, Surratt," he was saying, "but I don't think even your contacts could get you in that close."

"There are times when the protection breaks down. It only takes a second and the deed is done." The speaker must have been Mrs. Surratt's son.

Cal laughed. "And one more second for you to be killed too," he said.

"Kidnapping is the best plan," interjected another voice. "Then we could exchange him for every Confederate prisoner they're holding."

"That's still the wrong target, Booth," said Cal. "You're all a bunch of crazy malcontents—"

He was interrupted by a German voice I could barely make out. "Watch what you be saying, Burton, you swine, or I kill *you* first."

"Atzerodt's right, Cal," chuckled the fellow he had called Booth. "We outnumber you three to one."

"In everything but brains," rejoined Cal. "Look at the practicalities of this, Booth. When you aim too high and miss,

you've wasted your chance and you won't get it back. The kidnapping scheme's foolhardy. It would never work, and would
only rally people around him all the more. I know you think
you've been cowardly all this time for not joining up, and I
know you dream of being a spy like our friend Surratt here—"

"Be careful of the insults, Burton, or I'll give my German
friend leave to wring your neck."

"Are you going to deny what I've said?"

Booth was silent.

"Then like I said, look at the practicalities. No foolhardy
deed of heroic daring is going to do the Confederacy any good.
If we want to turn the tide of the war, we can't make a martyr
of the old gorilla. It's Grant we've got to concentrate on, I tell
you. If he's not stopped, he'll eventually push Lee back and
overrun Richmond and all will be lost."

"And what do you propose?" asked the man called Surratt.

"That we focus our efforts there, on Grant. If we can eliminate him, the will of his army will collapse."

"And are *you* going to infiltrate his camp?" asked a skeptical Booth.

"Of course not. I'm no assassin."

"Who then?"

"I have someone high up in his command whom I am
confident can be persuaded to see that there's an accident."

"You can get closer than you think I could?" said Surratt.

"Not me personally. One of Grant's officers. If you can
lay your hands on the sum of money you spoke of, and one of
the two of you, either you or Booth, can get it to me in Richmond, I have ways of contacting my friend, the lieutenant.
He will do it for us, I'm certain. Then none of you will face
the gallows."

"Or you," added the German voice.

"I have no intention of getting so close myself that my hands get blood on them."

"I don't know whether I trust you or not, Burton," said Booth, "but your scheme has a ring of sense to it. But believe me, if it fails, we will have to look to stronger measures."

"Have it your way, Booth," laughed Cal. "You and your demons of greatness! You would make the world your stage if only given half the chance. I, on the other hand, only believe in taking what opportunities are presented. Pragmatism, Booth. It's probably not a word you are familiar with. But I tell you, Grant is the target that *is* within our reach, and which will serve the Confederacy just as well."

"We will go along with you . . . for now."

"Good. Then meet me in Richmond. Will four days be enough, Surratt?"

The other mumbled something, but I could not make it out.

"We'll make it five then. You be in Richmond on Wednesday next. At noon, say. I'll meet you at Winder Supply. I'm on good terms with the owner. He'll have a room we can use."

"I don't know the place."

"Down the hill from the State House, on the river, about a hundred yards along the waterfront."

"I'll find it."

"Wednesday," repeated Cal. Then I heard him rise and leave the house.

Midnight Flight

CHAPTER FORTY-NINE

What could it be but a plot to kill General Grant?

My mind was racing a thousand directions at once. Even all the old anger and pain over what had happened with Cal disappeared. I temporarily forgot about the money he'd stolen. He had obviously gotten mixed up with some evil-sounding men and was still willing to do just about anything for the sake of his own personal gain. And it sounded, too, as if his allegiance to the Confederacy had grown considerably. Maybe he had become one of the South's important men, just as he'd wanted.

But killing? I could hardly believe that . . . even from Cal! Yet I'd heard what I'd heard, and by now I was wide awake— so wide awake I was shivering both from the cold and from the fearful things I had overheard. I was remembering, too, things Mr. Hay had said about the Surratts. I felt very alone and exposed and isolated.

And suddenly I felt very unsafe in this house!

I had to get away and somehow get word to General Grant of the danger. Should I notify the President? No, he was still in Philadelphia. Mr. Hay was there with him.

Whom could I tell? Who would *believe* me? If I went to the police or the army headquarters, I would sound like some crazy lunatic. They wouldn't know me, wouldn't know my connections with the President. And what difference did those connections make, anyway? Who would believe such an insane story?

As my mind raced over it all, my hands fumbled about in the darkness for my clothes. In a few minutes I was dressed.

Should I leave immediately? What if they heard me?

I hadn't heard the front door open or close. What if they were all staying here tonight? What if Cal himself were in the next room? If they heard so much as a peep out of me, they'd pounce on me in a second.

But how could I wait till morning?

There wasn't a moment to lose. One way or another, I wasn't going to wait for them to find me, and then do whatever awful things they might do to me!

I had already been stuffing my things into my leather bag, and now squeezed it shut and cinched up the leather straps. It was still dark, but I dared not light a candle. I was confident I could make it down the stairs in the dark and to the safety of the street outside.

I picked up my bag and tiptoed softly to the door. I didn't care how threadbare it might be, I was happy enough for the old rug on the floor to keep my feet silent.

Slowly I grasped the latch. With hardly a squeak it turned. I pulled the door open. It gave no sound and I breathed a silent sigh of relief. I stepped out onto the bare wood floor. Neither the landing nor the stairs were carpeted.

I swung the door closed behind me, then took two or three small steps across the landing, feeling about with my foot for the edge of the first step.

I found it, paused, then gingerly began making my way down the narrow flight. My heart was pounding so rapidly I thought it would wake the entire house!

Slowly, one step at a time, feeling my way with cautious steps, I inched down the stairs . . . one step . . . two . . . three. If only I could remember how many there were! Six . . . seven.

It seemed there were twelve or thirteen, maybe sixteen in all! . . . Nine . . . ten . . . I had to be over halfway. Any moment my foot would find the bottom landing and the outside door.

. . . Thirteen . . . fourteen . . .

Suddenly what sounded like an ear-splitting *creak* gave way under my foot. I'd forgotten how terribly the bottom three stairs squeaked! I remembered noticing it almost every time I climbed them!

I froze in sheer panic. The only sound in the blackened hallway was the beating in my chest! Maybe no one had heard it. I would wait, then would stretch my leg all the way to the bottom and avoid the first two offending slabs of loosened wood.

I remained stock-still.

"Who's there?" suddenly came from somewhere upstairs behind me.

My heart jumped into my throat!

"Who's there, I say?" It was Mrs. Surratt's voice. I heard the sound of her footsteps trudging across the floor of her room. "John, is that you? George? Who's there?"

For another moment I was paralyzed. Then I heard her hand on the latch. It was all I needed to jolt my legs into activity once more. Even as the light from her candle entered the hallway above and sent its inquiring rays down the stairs, I flew down the remaining steps, heedless now of either the squeaks of the wood or the echo of my footfall, and raced across the entryway to the door. My free hand found the latch and turned it hard. It was locked.

Behind me I now heard Mrs. Surratt's hastening feet and angry voice. "John," she cried to her son, "John . . . get out here now, I tell you!"

I had dropped my bag and was now fumbling with the bolt and latch of the door with frantic and sweating fingers, paying no more attention to the noise I was making. The metallic sounds echoed badly in the still night!

The door swung open! I grabbed up my bag again and the next instant was through and onto the porch. The cold night air slapped me in the face, but I was hardly aware of it. Behind me Mrs. Surratt's muffled feet were followed by the thick clomping of boots down the stairs.

"After her, John!" cried Mrs. Surratt.

I was running now, clumsily carrying my bag. The night was black. How thankful I was there was no moon!

I crossed the street in seconds, then ran to the left, staying on the dirt of the street rather than pounding loudly along the wooden walk. I sprinted as fast as my legs would carry me. It seemed like an eternity, but must have been only two or three seconds.

I heard the bolt and latch open behind me from where I had just come. That same instant I threw myself into an alley that appeared on my right, stopped, and leaned against the side wall of a feed store, out of sight of the boardinghouse.

I heard John Surratt take several steps across the porch and onto the street.

"Hey . . . what do you think you're doing?" I heard him call out into the night. "Come back here . . . come back, or I'll have to hurt you . . . you hear me?"

My lungs heaved up and down. My mouth was wide open, trying to gulp down the air as silently as I could. My chest burned with pain. I stood absolutely still, not moving a muscle.

I could hear Surratt's boots walking slowly across the street. Then the sound ceased.

In terror I listened for the next sound. I knew he was looking up and down, trying to figure out which way I had gone. At any moment he could appear at the entrance of the alleyway beside me. Then his hands would grab me and close around my neck!

"Come back, and I won't hurt you," he called out again.

The sound was still some distance away. Then he began slowly running again along the street. His footsteps receded. He was going the other direction!

I let out a long breath. When he was about a block away, I slowly stuck my head out from behind the edge of the wall. The door to Mrs. Surratt's was closed. At least she had not followed him outside. I craned my neck out a bit more to see if I could see her son in the distance.

It was too dark to see him, but I could still hear his booted feet. They were even farther away than before.

I crept out of the alley and back into the street. If I couldn't see him, neither could he see me from the same distance!

As rapidly as I was able without breaking into a noisy run, I began walking along the street in the opposite direction. I walked the rest of the way to the next street, took it to the right, and, now that I was well away from the boardinghouse, eased again into a gentle run.

I went on for two or three more blocks, turning several times.

All at once I realized I had arrived at the railroad yard.

I was still too close to the boardinghouse! Where could I hide?

I glanced around. Everything was still and quiet and mysterious. The vague shadows and outlines of the silent trains and buildings gave a spooky and frightening look to the night.

I listened behind me, sure that at any moment I would hear John Surratt's heavy feet chasing after me!

I had to get out of sight, out of the open. I had to conceal myself somehow!

I kept moving slowly, without direction or a plan, across the yards, stumbling across the huge iron tracks.

Suddenly looming before me were the huge boxcars of an immobile freight train. I squinted into the darkness. One of the cars appeared empty, its great sliding door standing open.

I approached slowly, trying to quiet my feet on the rocky surface below.

"Is . . . is anybody in there?" I whispered up into the car as loudly as I dared.

No sound came back through the night.

"Hello . . . anybody?" I repeated.

Still there was no answer.

I hoisted my bag up onto the floor of the car, then felt about for an abrupt edge or a hook or anything to get my hands on. In another few seconds I was scrambling up into the freight car. In another second or two, I had my bag beside me and was safely hidden away in the blackness inside.

John Surratt would never find me now!

I leaned back against the wall of the car, finally aware of my exhaustion, breathed deeply, and closed my eyes.

Uncertain Thoughts

CHAPTER FIFTY

When I next came to myself, the gray of dawn had spread over the city of Washington.

How long I had been there I could hardly guess. I stretched the kinks out of my muscles and tried to rearrange myself, then glanced about. The car was empty.

I stood up and poked my head out.

The freight yard was still silent, and the city still slept. But I could hear a few voices and clanking sounds in the distance. Morning was approaching, and I knew there would be a great deal of activity around here within an hour as the trains were readied for their various destinations.

I sat back down inside. I had to think.

Cal had said five days. Now there were only four. Yesterday was—what was it? We'd arrived back in the Capital on Thursday afternoon . . . that made today Saturday . . . no, that was only yesterday. Today was Friday!

There were *still* five days!

Five days to get word to General Grant!

There must be someone else I should tell! I couldn't go chasing off as I'd done two or three times in the past. I was older now, not so impulsive and foolhardy, as Pa had called me then. I'd been lucky that everything had turned out so well when I'd ridden off to Sonora after Derrick Gregory. But now there was danger to more people than just me. I had to settle down and think through what would be the wisest thing to do!

I could go to Mrs. Richards' house as soon as the sun was up. I could talk to her about—

No, I thought to myself. By now they would know it was me who had left in the night. Mrs. Surratt had probably rummaged through my room within minutes of my flight. They would suspect I had overheard, with my room right next to the parlor. I had mentioned to her earlier where I was staying.

No, her son—or even Cal or that mean-sounding German fellow!—was probably hiding somewhere nearby, watching for my return, waiting to nab me!

And if they did know it was me, and suspected what I was planning to do, might they accelerate the timetable? Maybe they wouldn't wait the five days after all! That is, if Cal was still there . . . or if they could get word to him.

There could be no delay! The danger to Mr. Grant might now be ever closer than next Wednesday.

Should I telegraph him?

They would be sure to think it a hoax! He would never remember my name. I could send it anonymously! No . . . that would be even worse. They would think it a Confederate plot to distract him and cause him to change his plans.

Worse still, any message I tried to get to him, by telegraph or through somebody else, could easily be intercepted before it got to the general, either by the lieutenant spy Cal was talking about, or by somebody else who didn't think the message valid enough to bother the general about.

No . . . somehow I had to see General Grant myself. . . . I had to tell him face-to-face. Otherwise he wouldn't know how serious it was if I didn't tell him what I knew of Cal and how high up his Confederate connections were. It was the only way. . . . I had to get back to Petersburg and the front lines!

But how?

I'd have to go by horse. But first I had to get out of the city. The train would be the safest and quickest. The lines behind General Grant's army were safely in Union hands. I could take the train as far as Culpeper, then rent or buy a horse there and ride behind the lines the rest of the way south to Petersburg.

I sat down on my case. I couldn't do anything for several hours, until the station opened. I was certain a train would be heading south out of Washington before noon.

As my thoughts cleared, my body began to remind me that it had been a long night. I needed to find either an outhouse or a clump of trees before the sun came up and too many people were about! If only there was someplace I could wash my face and comb my hair. The hunger pangs in my stomach didn't bother me. Food I could do without for a while, if I had to.

Again I peered out of the car. The yard nearby was still completely deserted. It was probably not later than five-thirty or six. Leaving my bag where it was, I carefully jumped down.

Boxcar Accommodations

CHAPTER FIFTY-ONE

*W*hen I got back and had once again climbed aboard the car where I had spent the night, I sat down to wait as patiently as my stirred-up mind would let me for morning to come.

It wasn't long before another thought struck me. If they knew who I was—which they did—and they suspected I'd overheard their plot—which I was sure they did—and if they were looking for me at Mrs. Richards' . . . then they were just as likely to look for me at the train station too!

Even if Cal had left the house before I had, there would still be two of them, and they would be sure to be searching for me wherever they thought likely. And where more likely than the train station?

No, I couldn't just walk in and ask the attendant for a ticket. One of them was sure to be hanging about the place—maybe even Mrs. Surratt herself, if she was in on it too.

If I was going to take the train, I would have to find some other way to do it. I'd have to find an open boxcar like this one going south, at least until I was out of the city.

I got up and went to the door again. This time when I climbed down I took my bag with me. The car was on a side track and was clearly going nowhere anytime soon. I began walking toward the back of the station, keeping behind other cars and buildings so as to stay out of sight as best I could.

I thought I knew which tracks were northbound and which southbound. In the central part of the yard, I saw men loading several cars about two-thirds of the way back in a long line of cars. The engine at the front I was positive was pointing south. *Of course,* I thought. The southbound train would be taking provisions to General Grant's army. It would have come in mostly empty or else bearing wounded to Washington's hospitals, and it would return with supplies. There would likely not be many passengers traveling *toward* the fighting.

I inched my way closer, keeping out of sight.

Before long I began to hear the voices more plainly. I got as close as I dared, then stopped to wait.

"This one be full," a man called out two cars down from where I was standing on the back side of the train opposite from where the doors opened toward the loading yard.

I bent down and looked underneath through the wheels. I saw a man's feet walking away from me. Then he stopped at the next car and joined another man there. I walked slowly down until I was at the back of the car he'd just finished loading, then stood directly behind one of the huge iron wheels so they wouldn't be able to see my legs even if they should look under the train.

In another fifteen or twenty minutes I heard them move on down the line to the next car. I stooped down and glanced underneath again. They were walking back to the building where the supplies had been brought, while a third man jumped up on the board of the wagon from which they'd been unloading, and from the sound of it yelled a command to a horse to head back to the supply building for another wagonload.

Now was my chance! They all were sure to be looking the other way. I crouched down, got on my hands and knees, and, dragging my case along behind me, crawled under the car and peered out the other side. The two men were just entering the building about thirty yards away. I looked the other way, squinting into the sun, which was just coming up in the east. That way was also clear.

I crawled out from under the train, stood up, threw my bag up into the open door of the boxcar, scrambled up behind it as fast as I could, and in another few seconds was safely inside and crouched behind sacks of flour, a bunch of wooden barrels, and crates marked "Explosives." There could be no doubt left that this train was heading south toward the war!

I got as far toward the back and out of sight as I could manage, then hid down as low as I could, trying to find a way to make myself halfway comfortable.

Two hours later, from the sounds of the voices outside I gathered that all the cars were loaded. I heard footsteps approaching, then saw the shadow of a figure beside the door of the car I was in. I held my breath. The next instant a loud clanging crash echoed through my ears from the heavy wood door being pulled shut on its clamp with a slam.

Suddenly I was left in the darkness. The only light came through in tiny gleaming shafts through the board and the edge of the door. For a moment a new fear surged through me. What if I was locked in and *couldn't* get out! As long as the train was going in the right direction, I suppose it wouldn't matter. We were sure to get someplace before I starved to death.

I continued to wait. About an hour later I heard the sounds of the engine starting up. By this time many voices filled the yard outside. Another thirty minutes went by. Then the unmistakable jerking motions and clanking and creaking all indicated that the train was getting under way. Gradually it picked up speed.

After some ten or fifteen minutes, once we were safely out of the station and I thought probably out of the city as well, I got to my feet and worked my way over the sacks of flour to the door. In the dim light I located a lever that looked as if it would unhook the latch from the inside. I put both my hands against the end of it and shoved upward with all my might. It didn't budge. I tried again, harder this time. I felt it give slightly. Encouraged I gave it one more huge effort.

All at once the lever flew upward, the latch unhooked, and the sliding door sprang back and opened two or three inches.

Now I could shove the door open on its bottom rail at will. I did so, opening it to a space of six to nine inches. We were still not up to full speed, but had left the city. The rising sun of the morning was looking straight in the opening at me as we moved to the right. We were heading south!

Relieved, I took a seat closer to the opening and sat down on one of the canvas sacks. I had a long ride ahead of me and I might as well make myself comfortable. It was too dreary and spooky in the darkness, however, so I left the door open as it was.

I didn't know when or where the train would stop, but Culpeper was, I thought, some sixty miles away. We were sure to be there sometime that afternoon.

Culpeper . . . and South

CHAPTER FIFTY-TWO

*T*he train rumbled on slowly for several hours without a stop. I didn't exactly know the route or where we were bound, but as long as it continued south, I was moving in the direction I needed to go. There was no direct rail link yet between Washington and Richmond. Now that the Army of the Potomac under Grant had been dug in for so long in a wide swath arching down from Spotsylvania and Fredericksburg down through Cold Harbor and to Petersburg, most of the supplies were sent to them by ship down through the Chesapeake Bay and up the mouths of the Rappahannock, the York, or the James. Where this trainload of supplies was headed I wasn't sure, but it couldn't go much past Culpeper without getting dangerously close to being exposed to the rear lines of the Confederate troops and General Lee's position. I assumed it was bound for the northernmost of the Union troops flanked out between Culpeper and Fredericksburg. If I could get a horse there and ride around behind the lines, it would still be another hundred and fifty miles, through rough terrain, to the siege position of the army outside Petersburg.

At the first town where I felt the train starting to slow, I managed to close the door and latch it again so as not to be seen. We stopped briefly twice. I listened, but was unable to hear anything that indicated where we were. But the third stop, which must have been somewhere around two or three in the afternoon, had to be Culpeper. Moments after we'd pulled in, the engine let out a huge and final-sounding burst of steam, and I knew we'd arrived at our destination. Down the line I heard the boxcar doors being opened.

There wasn't anything they could do to me for stowing a ride now, so I decided to just jump down and be off. If someone tried to question me, I'd make a run for it.

In fact, why should I wait until they opened the door at all? After all, they might take *me* for a Confederate spy!

I got my bag right beside me—wishing by now I'd left it and whatever it had in it to the dubious care of Marge Surratt and her cohorts!—then gave the door lever a mighty shove. It gave way. I pushed against the door with my shoulder, got it open about two feet, grabbed my bag, and jumped down.

"Hey . . . what the—" exclaimed a voice only about five feet away.

Out of the corner of my eye I saw a large Negro man with a crate hoisted over his shoulder. He couldn't have chased me even if he'd wanted to, with that heavy load. But I didn't wait to answer his unfinished question. My feet hit the ground running and I bolted straight away from the train.

Nobody else seemed close by, although I heard a couple more cries that sounded as if they were meant for me. But I didn't look back, and I heard no footsteps giving chase. In less than a minute I was out of sight of the station. I slowed to a walk and tried to take stock of my surroundings.

The poor little town looked as if it had been ravaged by the war and had come nowhere near recovering. The only men were recent arrivals and wore the dark blue of the Union. The only natives of the place that were left were women, children, and the elderly. No one smiled.

There were two hotels in town. One looked pretty badly shot apart and was boarded up. The other was still open, though who traveled this way now in the vacuum created by the armies I didn't know. I went inside, found a table, sat down, and enjoyed three cups of water before ordering an early supper that, judging from the woman's expression, was far too much food for a young lady of my size to be eating. She said nothing, however, beyond many curious looks and glances, and I offered few words in return.

When I was through I asked her if there was a livery stable nearby. She directed me up the street, the curiosity on her face turning to outright suspicion. I determined that I had better make haste away from this place!

It was a good thing I had some money with me when I'd made my escape out of Washington. The old man at the stable was only too glad to part with one of his horses for hard Yankee cash, and threw in a sorry old saddle for five more dollars. The horse looked as tired as the town, but once I got him used to my voice and to the idea of carrying me on his back, he did just fine. I missed Raspberry more than ever, but this sturdy fellow ought to get me there in one piece.

I asked the man for a couple of long straps of leather, tied my clumsy bag onto the back of my saddle where it would rest on the horse's rump, bought a canteen and a bag of feed, and after about forty minutes of transacting business and making all the impromptu preparations I could think of, I thanked him and sped down the street on my way.

I glanced back and saw him wiping his forehead with his sleeve, holding his crumpled, dirty hat in one hand, with an expression of bewilderment on his face.

I figured I had a good three hours of daylight left, maybe four.

I took the road due south out of town. Having no idea how close I was to the very spot where fierce fighting had taken place back in May, and how close I was, in fact, to where I had earlier been when helping behind the lines, within an hour I was crossing the Rapidan River.

Fredericksburg and the safety of the Union position lay southeast of Culpeper. But somehow I missed the Fredericksburg road and continued south.

Danger was closer than I knew.

*M*y first inkling of my predicament came too late for me to avoid it. Suddenly I found myself riding straight into a Confederate camp!

My first reaction was fright. If I'd had time, I would have wheeled the horse around and galloped back the way I'd come. But I was past the sentry before I knew it, and it was suddenly too late. My heart leaped up into my mouth.

"Well, hey there, little lady," drawled the lookout, standing up from his post. Within a second or two I was surrounded by six or eight others.

"Where y'all bound?"

"Uh . . . south," I said.

"No need to be afraid, we ain't aimin' to hurt you none," said one.

"If you be headin' south, ma'am, then you're among friends now. Get off your horse and stop a spell. Y'all both look like you could use it."

The others all laughed good-naturedly. By now the group had grown to ten or twelve, and I realized I was right in the middle of a whole unit, not just a handful of men.

My first reaction was: *This is the enemy!* I'd been involved with the North and the election and Mr. Lincoln and the whole point of view that we were "at war" with the Confederacy for so long that I forgot that these men clustering about me were Americans just like me. There was no difference between us. I had come only a few miles into Virginia. This was George Washington's home state! And yet I was looking at them as if they were from some foreign country! When I later realized all this, I hated all the more what this awful war did to us. The unity that was the whole purpose of the Convent of John Seventeen was being trampled to death every day on the battlefields of this war—and I had succumbed to it, too!

I sat there on my horse too terrified to move, or even to speak, but trying desperately not to show it. If they found out what I was doing, what awful things might they do to me? I was, after all, a spy—trying to outspy Cal and Surratt and the others with their scheme!

I had heard they shot spies on sight, or hanged them, without even a trial!

And I knew they must be able to read all over my face every single thing I was thinking!

"It's nigh on to nightfall, ma'am. You'd best get down and join us. We got us some beans an' biscuits you'd be welcome to."

"Join us for the night!" shouted out somebody from the back, and the comments from a few of his companions were too awful to think about. I had to get out of here before they took me prisoner!

"I . . . I, uh—I have to keep going," I said lamely.

"Ain't no place to go, ma'am," said one of the gray-clad men who was being nice and courteous. "We're the rearguard unit, and if you was to keep on this way, you're gonna get yourself all tangled up in the rest of our army. There's some nasty fighting going on down that way. You tryin' to get to Richmond?"

"Uh . . . yeah," I nodded.

"It ain't safe down there, ma'am."

"I . . . I reckon I took a wrong road back a ways," I said, trying to put on a Southern accent. It sounded ridiculous in my own ears, but none of the men seemed to notice.

"Spend the night here, little lady," called out the man who had said it before. "*We'll* help ya find your way, all right!"

"I . . . I have to go back," I said. "I've got to get to Fredericksburg."

"Fredericksburg! Why, ma'am, the blame Yankees has got Fredericksburg! Ain't you heard? We got a war on—and you're right in the middle of it!"

One of the men, who looked a little older and might have been an officer, now walked around, eyed my big brown leather case strapped behind me, patted it once with his hand, then asked, "Where you come from anyway, Miss?"

"Uh . . . Culpeper."

"You don't sound very convinced."

"I came from Culpeper all right," I repeated.

"Well, the corporal here's right. It *is* nearly nightfall, and we *do* have food left, and you'd be welcome and safe here. I can promise you that none of these louts will bother you in the least . . . and neither will the Yanks. You'll be as safe here as anywhere for miles."

There was a slight pause. I didn't know *what* to do! If I did stay, I'd never be able to sneak out of *here* in the middle of the night! They kept sentries posted all the time, and if they saw me trying to make a run for it, then I would *really* be in for it!

Meanwhile, the man's hand was still resting on my bag. "What you got in here anyway?" he asked.

"My clothes," I answered, feeling myself starting to sweat. What if they opened it? My letters from Mr. Lincoln were in there, copies of several articles I'd written in *Northern* newspapers, and notes for new articles . . . not to mention my journal. They would hang me for sure if they found all that!

"Mighty big bag for coming down just from Culpeper," he said. I didn't at all like the suspicious sound in his voice.

Just then, from farther into the camp, a man approached who looked even more important yet. Some of the men fell away to make room for him, and he came straight on toward me.

"What's going on here, Lieutenant?" he said to the man who had been talking to me. Then he glanced up at me where I still sat on the horse, tipped his head slightly, and added, "Ma'am." Then he looked back to the lieutenant.

"This young lady just came riding in here like she was in a pretty big hurry," the lieutenant said to him. "She says she's from Culpeper, Major, and bound for Richmond. But she's not altogether making sense. Then she said she's got to get to Fredericksburg, which the Yankees got now. I don't know, sir, she just seems a mite confused. And then there's this bag of hers," he said, patting it a couple more times.

The major glanced up at me.

"You confused, young lady?" he said. "Or maybe just frightened?"

I nodded, and whatever else may have been said, he knew I was telling the truth about that!

"Well, I'll tell you one thing, these men of mine may be a hard-fighting and a rough-tongued bunch. But if there's one thing we Southerners know, it's how to treat a lady. I promise you, you have nothing to be afraid of."

He paused, then added in a more serious tone, "But these are dangerous times, ma'am. I'm sure you're aware of that. There's Yankees and spies and patrols and marauders prowling around through these woods for miles in every direction. So you see, we've got to be mighty careful, and we've got to know where you're going and where you come from, and what your business is. We're under orders from General Lee himself to let no one past us on this road here. No one. So you see why my men are asking you all these questions. We got our orders, ma'am. And besides, we can't just let a young woman like you be riding out loose any old place you want. Why, you might run into a patrol of Yankees and get yourself killed! They're a ruthless lot, and we'd never forgive ourselves if we let something happen to you."

"Let us open up her bag, Major," called out the man whose sound I didn't like. "It's been a long time since we seen any *women's* duds! We'll find out what she's up to all right!" He gave a terrible and suggestive laugh.

Suddenly I found my voice, though I was shocked to hear what came out of my mouth.

"I was just trying to get some warm things down to my husband before winter!" I cried. "I haven't seen him in four months, and I was desperate to get word to him that we was going to have a baby!"

I burst out crying, yanked back on the reins, spun the horse quickly around, and without waiting for another word from any of them, kicked at the horse and galloped off as fast as I could northward along the road I'd come in on.

The last thing I saw out of the corner of my eyes was the group of gray-clad Rebel soldiers standing where I left them.

I heard a few comments and some laughter. But just as I rounded a turn and was nearly out of earshot, I thought I heard the major say, "Well, Lieutenant, you'd better go after her. Make sure she gets headed back to Culpeper all right."

Retracing My Steps
CHAPTER FIFTY-FOUR

I rode the poor tired horse as fast as he would go, but it wasn't near as fast as I wanted him to go! Oh, for Raspberry right then!

It was five or ten minutes before I heard hoofbeats behind me. My mount had slowed noticeably. The moment I heard him I knew it was no use. I reined in and let the rider behind me catch up. He galloped up alongside, then eased to a gentle canter beside me. I glanced over to see the Southern lieutenant.

"Whoa . . . whoa there!" he said, as much to me as to my horse. We both slowed to a stop.

"You really didn't have to chase outta there like that," he said. "None of us meant you any harm."

"I know," I said. "I was just nervous and scared."

"Well, now that we all understand, the major wanted me to ride along with you awhile, just to make sure you was going to be all right."

"I can find my way," I said.

"And I'll just make sure of it." He eased his horse forward. Mine followed.

"Are . . . are you going to ride with me all the way . . . to Culpeper?" I asked.

The lieutenant laughed.

"No, missy," he said. "Culpeper may be in Virginia, but that's Yankee territory now. No, I'll get back to my unit before this night's well settled in, as long as I know you're safely on your way. The clouds have lifted and the moon should be out. I think you'll make it before it's been dark more than an hour or two."

"It's very kind of you to be so concerned about me," I said.

"Like the major said, we Southerners know how to treat a lady. Being a Virginian yourself, ma'am, I wouldn't think you'd be surprised."

I said nothing. What he'd said reminded me of Katie and Edie. I wondered where Edie was right now, and if she was safe.

"And I still can't rightly see why you was so jittery back there," he went on. "Us Southerners gotta stick together, not be afraid of each other."

Still I didn't reply. I was getting all the more uncomfortable having him think things about me that weren't true!

He rode along with me for about another thirty minutes. We talked some, but I felt so awkward that I don't suppose I exactly encouraged a lively conversation. Finally he turned his horse around.

"You just keep straight on this road, ma'am," he said. "It'll take you straight into Culpeper. If you meet any Yanks, don't tell 'em nothin' about your husband or you'll never know what they might do to you. Just tell 'em you lost your way, or tell them anything. And if they do try to start bothering you, like Yanks'll sometimes do to women, well, you just tell 'em, you know, ma'am . . . tell 'em as how you're in a family way. Even them brutal Yanks won't bother a woman that's carrying a child."

I thanked him again for his concern, and told him to thank his major for me, too. Then the minute he was out of sight, I dug my heels into the horse's sides again. He'd had far too long a rest. And I had urgent business I had to get back to!

I had no intention of riding all the way back to Culpeper. The thought of a night in that hotel with that suspicious lady wondering about me was not one I relished.

Within another thirty minutes I came to a crossroad. It didn't look like much, but it was running east and west. It was nearly dark by now, but I saw a small hand-painted wooden sign a little off the road. I moved up beside it, leaned forward in the saddle and squinted. I could just barely make out the words *Locust Grove* and beneath it *Fredericksburg.*

That was all I needed to see. I wheeled my tired but trustworthy steed to the right and off through the wooded thicket along what wasn't much more than a wide path. I'd ride as long as I could be certain of my way, then find some place to hide out of sight and sleep until dawn. It didn't cross my mind until later that I was in the very vicinity of the battle back in December of 1862, which Cal had received the telegram about when I was following him in Sacramento. It had been the Confederate victory at Fredericksburg that had convinced him to defect to the South's cause. Now here the two armies were again, nearly in the same place, with the outcome of the entire war hanging in the balance.

I made it the rest of the way without incident.

After I'd settled onto the softest grass I could find for the night, using some of my clothes as bedding and blankets as best I could, I found myself reflecting on the events of the day.

Suddenly it occurred to me what I'd done an hour and a half earlier. I'd *lied* to get away from the Confederate soldiers! Not only had I lied, I'd done it naturally, without even thinking about it.

A part of me tried to justify it, but without much success.

Whatever the result, even though I had gotten safely away, I *had* done wrong. If I hadn't told the lie, perhaps God would have found some other way to get me out of there. Or maybe he *did* have some other way in mind, just waiting to perform, and then I snatched it out of his hands. Perhaps I had *prevented* him from helping me by helping myself instead!

By the time I finally fell asleep, I was feeling bad for not trusting him enough to know that he would have protected me. But I was too tired to be miserable about it. And I did trust him enough to know that he would forgive me and would keep taking care of me from now on, if I would let him.

"I'm sorry, Lord," I said finally. "I got so caught up in what was happening that I didn't think to pray and ask for your

help. Forgive me for lying. Help me to remember your presence. Wherever my steps go from here in this thing, please
guide me and keep me exactly where you want me to be."

The night passed tolerably. By early afternoon the next day
I was in Fredericksburg, where I got food, water, and a new supply of feed for the horse. A few suspicious looks came my way,
but I paid no attention, took care of my business, and headed
south, confident now that I was well behind the stretched out
line of *Union* troops. By taking my way southward in an arc behind them, I would eventually arrive at the Southern position
outside Petersburg, where the intense fighting was still going
on. That's where I was certain I'd find General Grant.

It took me a day and a half more to reach the front
lines. It was evening when I rode into the hospital camp. I
was amazed to find it virtually unmoved from where it had
been when I'd left well over a month before. The siege of
Petersburg and Richmond hadn't had much result. Most of
my friends from the Commission were still there, although the
fighting had abated considerably and many of the wounded
had been transferred to hospitals in the North, so it wasn't
nearly so horrid as before. I was surprised to find Clara Barton
still there. Even before I left, she had been talking of going
down to Atlanta, where there had also been a great amount
of bloodshed.

I went immediately to the army doctor who was in charge
of the hospital and medical units.

"How far are we from the field headquarters?" I asked.

"You mean General Grant's quarters?"

"Yes. I have to see him."

The captain could not help laughing. "*You* want to do
what?" he asked.

"I've got to see him," I repeated. "It's extremely urgent. How far away is it . . . could I get there tonight?"

"I don't know, Miss Hollister," he said, still chuckling. "I'd say it's three or four miles. But at night, with all those trenches, unless you had an escort, it could be a mite risky."

"Could you take me?" I said.

"Me?"

"Yes. I need to get there, I tell you."

"I suppose I could," he answered slowly. "But not tonight. I wouldn't go out there toward the front in the dark. They're liable to take you for a Reb patrol and shoot you dead before you had the chance to say a word."

I thought to myself a few seconds. This was only Sunday night. There was still plenty of time.

"How about at dawn, then?" I said after a pause. "Will you take me there first thing in the morning?"

"Maybe I could. Say, what's this about, anyway?"

"I can't say. I've just got to see the general, that's all."

"He'll throw you out. You're never going to get close to him . . . at *any* time of the day."

"Will you take me?"

"All right, all right! You've patched up enough wounded around here, I guess you're entitled. But I tell you, you're not about to get inside General Grant's tent."

"Let me worry about that," I said. "I'll be here at sunup."

I turned and left his tent and returned to the nurses' quarters, where I spent the night.

The next morning I was saddled and ready to go just as the sun's first rays were coming over the ridge in the east.

True to his word, the captain was also ready. We set off westward toward the front lines, passing through the regiments and units of thousands of Union soldiers. General Grant's army had been encamped here so long that everything had a look of permanency. Along with hundreds of tents and camp-fires, there were even a few small buildings that had been con-structed, stables for the animals, blacksmith shops. In places it resembled a real town—except that there were no women or children, and everyone wore blue and carried guns. In a way it *was* a city—a mobile city of eighty or ninety thousand men . . . a city whose only purpose was to wage war on the Confederate capital.

There had been no fighting the day before, and none was expected today. Guards and cooks were about, of course, but many of the men still slept or else were just rousing them-selves. Everywhere the white smoke of campfires lazily filtered upward into the still frosty morning air, but it was a far calmer scene than I might have expected when riding through the middle of the Army of the Potomac.

Occasional stares followed us as we passed, now and then a salute to the captain. But these men had seen more already than a lifetime would allow them to forget, and the sight of a woman riding through camp, even when they were just get-ting dressed for the day, was hardly enough to surprise them. Most hardly seemed to notice me at all.

At length we came to a collection of larger tents, two or three buildings, and a farmhouse that had been comman-deered, and I knew we had arrived at our destination. In the distance I could see the edges of the maze of trenches that had been dug around Petersburg where the men in the front stayed.

We rode up to the house. "We're, here to see General Grant, Sergeant," the captain said.

"I don't know if the general is up yet, Captain."

"Then find out, Sergeant. We'll wait."

The sergeant disappeared inside, then returned about a minute later. He was followed by a major.

"What's this all about, Captain?"

"Only that we have to see the general."

"The general is barely out of bed," replied the major, "and is not seeing anyone all morning."

The captain glanced over at me—apologetically, yet with an I-told-you-so look.

"I'm afraid you're stuck, Miss Hollister," he said. "I brought you here, but like I said, they don't let just anyone into the general's headquarters."

"Especially not before 7:00 a.m.," added the major curtly. "Good-day, Captain." He turned and began walking back toward the house.

I was off my horse and after him in an instant.

"Wait . . . wait, please, Major!" I called, running after him and grabbing his arm. "I've *got* to see General Grant! It can't wait . . . it's *very* important!"

He stopped and spun around, pulling his arm away from my grasp and casting down a look of extreme annoyance at me. He bored into me with his eyes for several seconds. Then, apparently not thinking I deserved so much as a word in reply, he turned again and with deliberate step began walking again to the house.

Once more I hurried after him, grabbed his arm and held on tightly.

"I've *got* to see him!" I repeated.

The major spun around and glared at the captain still sitting on his horse watching the scene. "If this is your idea of a prank, Captain," he spat, "it has gone far enough! You get her out of here or I'll have you court-martialed. The affections of this schoolgirl for the general hardly befit your commission, Sergeant!"

But I was not about to be hauled away by the major and the guard. And by now I was more than a little upset myself! *Schoolgirl affections!* I was trying to save the general's life!

I let go my hold on the major's arm and dashed for the door. I was onto the porch before he realized it, and now he sprang after me. But by the time he had a chance to grab me, I threw open the door and bolted inside.

"I must see General Grant!" I cried. "Won't anybody listen to me? The general is in danger!"

There were two or three other men inside what looked to be a parlor or sitting room just inside. They glanced up, but before anyone could say a word, the major burst through the door after me and had hold of me in a vise-grip within seconds. I tried to scream out again, but felt his large hand clamp tightly over my mouth. Then he dragged me toward the door.

This was awful! I was going to be sent off, probably to a stockade. If I didn't do something drastic—and soon—the general would never hear of the plot against him.

The major's strong right hand was over my mouth, and his left clutched me around my midsection. But one of my arms was halfway loose. With a great heaving effort I lifted my right arm and slammed my elbow into the major's stomach. I don't suppose it hurt him much, but the jolt of it took him by surprise and he lost his breath momentarily.

It was all I needed! I kicked at his legs, struggled free, and again bolted away, this time for a closed door on the opposite side of the room. I heard shouts and curses behind me, as well as the major's running feet.

Just as I reached it, the door opened, and I suddenly found myself running straight into a man's chest, and then toppling to the floor at his feet.

The steps of the major behind me stopped instantly, and the shouting ceased.

"I apologize for this most bothersome intrusion, General," the major said. "I assure you, this tramp and the man who brought her here will be punished severely."

I looked up from the floor. There, towering above me, his fingers still fiddling with the suspenders over his long underwear, stood General Ulysses Grant himself!

An Early Morning Fracas
CHAPTER FIFTY-SIX

Again I felt the major's hands grab me. He yanked me to my feet and away from the general.

"General . . . General, please!" I cried in desperation, "I *must* talk to you . . . it's extremely urgent! I came all the way—"

"Shut up, little girl!" cried the major, and once more his huge paw closed down over my mouth. I struggled to try to bite it, but he pressed down all the tighter.

"Major!" commanded General Grant, and it was the first time he had spoken. "That is hardly the way to treat a young lady."

"She has disregarded my every command, General. There's only one thing no-goods like this understand!"

I was furious, and was struggling and twisting fiercely to get free. "Hey, one of you men—Sergeant—" the major was saying, "help me with this contemptuous little vixen. She's as feisty and strong—"

"Major," came the general's voice again. "Major . . . let her go."

I stopped struggling. The major stopped dragging me across the floor, but did not loosen his hold over my mouth.

"I said let her go," the general repeated.

"But, sir, she has—"

"Major."

"Yes, sir," said the major. His grip loosened. The instant I was free I sprang from him and ran across the room, nearly crashing into the general again. Now that I was standing instead of looking at him from on the floor, I was almost shocked to find that I was as tall as he was.

"General Grant, please," I implored him, "please listen to me before you have them throw me out!"

He eyed me intently, looking over my face.

"I'm sorry," I went on. "I know I had no right to storm in here like this, but I didn't know how else to see you! It is extremely important, General!"

Still he was looking me over, unconcerned about being only half-dressed, and not nearly so worried about the early hour or the incongruity of the situation as the men of his staff.

"Don't I know you, young lady?" he asked after another moment's pause.

"Corrie . . . Corrie Hollister," I said, trying to make myself as calm and presentable as I could. "We spoke a little at the White House earlier this year." I took a breath and made the attempt to look mature.

Suddenly his face broke out in recognition. "Of course . . . yes, I do remember you, Miss Hollister."

At almost the same instant, he looked past me to the major and his face turned stern.

"Don't you know who this is, you fool?" he barked.

"She never identified herself, sir."

"Did you give her half a chance, Major?" rejoined the general. The major stood silently.

"I just happen to have spoken to her at the White House," the general went on. "This young lady happens to be a well-known writer for the Union cause, and is working personally for the President on his reelection campaign. Now, do I hear any more words about no-good tramps?"

His booming voice filled the room. When the echo died down, only the silence of the morning was left.

"Now . . . what's this all about, Miss Hollister?"

"A matter of great urgency, General Grant," I answered. "I've come all the way from Washington."

"Did the President send you?"

"No, sir. I'm afraid he knows nothing about it. He was out of town when I heard, and I didn't know what else to do but come straight to you."

"Heard what?"

"That's what I must talk to you about."

"Go on."

"Not here, please, sir," I said. "I think we ought to talk in private."

General Grant's face indicated that he was ruminating on it for a moment; then he nodded slightly.

"Fair enough," he said. "You don't mind if I finish dressing first?"

"No, sir," I said, smiling.

"Good!" he laughed. "I'm happy to hear it isn't *that* urgent."

He turned to the other men in the room. "Is the coffee on yet?"

"Yes, sir," barked out one of the sergeants who had been silently observing the drama.

"Good . . . good! Get me a good strong cup ready, and see if Miss Hollister here wants anything. She is my guest, and I want no more of what went on earlier, is that clear?"

Without another word, General Grant turned and disappeared again into the room from which he had come. When the door had closed behind him, the sergeant left for the kitchen.

A Frightening Plan

CHAPTER FIFTY-SEVEN

ifteen minutes later I was seated in General Grant's office in another room of the farmhouse. The door was closed. We were alone.

He was completely attired in his dark blue uniform and boots, although not wearing his hat. He took a long swallow of his coffee, then turned his eyes upon me.

"All right, Miss Hollister," he said. "You've got your private hearing. Tell me what was so urgent you had to bring it to me direct from Washington personally?"

I recounted the events of three nights earlier, repeating everything I had heard.

"And you say you know this fellow Burton?"

"Yes, sir. We worked together closely back in California before the war broke out and in the first months of it."

"And you say he defected to the South?"

I told him as much of the story as I felt I needed to. He listened to the whole thing very patiently. If he looked worried about his life, he didn't show a trace of it, though his expression was certainly serious.

"And the other fellow's name again?"

"Surratt," I replied. "I think it's *John* Surratt."

"Hmm . . . Surratt," mused the general. "It has a vague ring of familiarity to it. I seem to recall the name in connection with an intelligence report about Southern spies our people had identified."

"They said they would meet on Wednesday, General. It's Monday now—you've got to *do* something, sir! They're going to try to kill you. They said one of your own lieutenants—"

"Right . . . yes, I heard everything you said, Miss Hollister," said the general. "And I see why you insisted on seeing me alone. Hmm . . . ," he muttered again, obviously thinking very hard, "it could be any of a hundred men . . . there's no way to find out the identity without—"

He stopped abruptly. His eyes were wide open and his face animated. Even behind the beard, I could tell he was hatching some plan to undermine the plot against him.

"Hmm . . . yep, there's no other alternative . . . what we're going to have to do is nab your friend and bring him back here. If I've got a Reb in the ranks of my command, I've got to find out who it is!"

Before I could reply, he was on his feet. He strode quickly to the door and opened it.

"Sergeant!" he called.

A moment later one of the men I'd seen in the house before appeared at the door.

"Get me Captain Dyles."

The sergeant disappeared as quickly as he had come and again I was alone with the general.

"We have a man on the staff who's been infiltrating the Confederate ranks the whole time. He's been with me since Fort Henry. I'd trust him with my very life—which, I suppose, is what I'm doing now! He's from Alabama, talks with as thick a Southern drawl as you please, but loyal to the Union as I am. I've sent him behind enemy lines a dozen times. He's never failed me yet. And a scrappy fighter when push comes to shove. You won't be safer with anyone."

I didn't know what he meant, but he kept talking, and before I had the chance to ask, a knock on the door came, and a moment later he was introducing me to Captain Geoffrey Dyles, who was dressed in plain clothes instead of a uniform.

"Geoff, we've got to get into Richmond," General Grant said. "Gotta get in and back out again safely . . . and soon. Before Wednesday. Can you do it?"

"I reckon so, General," replied Dyles. It was indeed one of the strongest Southern accents I'd ever heard—perfect for a Union spy.

"You'd have forty-eight hours."

"I can manage it."

"You got another man or two you can trust?"

"The more men the more danger, General. You think I gotta have more men?"

"You're going to have to grab a high-placed Rebel agent— nephew of their vice president, no less—and bring him back here. I doubt he'll take too much a shine to the notion, so I figured it might take more than one of you."

"I'll take Crabtree."

"The Negro?"

"Plays as good a compliant slave as there is. I've used him before."

"Big man, isn't he?"

"Huge, General," laughed Dyles. "Three hundred pounds, if he ain't eaten for a week. More if he has! A better man in a pinch I couldn't have. Saved my life half a dozen times."

"Doesn't he call too much attention to himself?"

"As long as I treat him like a slave, and he keeps his head lowered, all we get is comments about his size. That way, nobody pays me the least attention. Best cover I could have."

"Can you smuggle in a gun?"

"Crabtree's so big, General, I've smuggled whole cannons stuffed inside his clothes past the stupid Confederate sentries!"

"Good. You might need a cannon to kidnap this fellow. It'll be broad daylight—what time did you say the meeting was, Miss Hollister?" said the general, turning to me.

"Noon," I answered.

"Hmm . . . yep—broad daylight. And you say in a scrap, Crabtree's a good man?"

"As good as four others!"

"Good. I want to make sure nothing happens to this lady. I may owe her my life."

Both Captain Dyles and I looked up at General Grant with looks of amazement. The captain's was one of question, but mine was one of fear!

"You want her going into Richmond with us?" he asked.

"Of course."

"But it's behind enemy lines."

"That's why I want to make sure she's safe."

"She'll slow us down and add to the danger, General."

In reply, General Grant just smiled. "Don't bet your horse on it, Geoff," he said with a knowing grin. "This lady's been through some scrapes of her own. From what I hear, she can take care of herself."

All this time I was listening to their exchange with mingled astonishment and terror. Me . . . go *with* Dyles and Crabtree . . . into the middle of the Confederate capital?

"But why, Sam?" asked Captain Dyles. I'd never heard anyone use the general's nickname before, but I noticed that there were no other officers around.

"How else you gonna know the man?"

Dyles shrugged. "I figured I'd have some description."

"It's too risky. Time's short, and we have to be sure. Miss Hollister here's the only one who knows this Burton on sight. There's no other way to do it but to have her there to put you onto the right fellow. Then you bring him back to me, and we'll make sure he gives us the name of the spy who's infiltrated my command."

Two mornings later, at dawn on Wednesday, I sat on the board of a rickety old wagon, dressed in rags intended to make me look more Southern than I had before. Beside me sat a plain-dressed Geoffrey Dyles. The wagon, pulled along by a tired old workhorse, entered the outskirts of Richmond, Virginia, along the road from Lynchburg and the west. Jacob Crabtree sat behind us on a load of hay, ropes tied around his feet. There were also several large wooden barrels in the back, and another horse clomped along behind us, tied to the back of the wagon.

Captain Dyles had spent all Monday morning devising his plan and getting together everything necessary—the horses, the wagon, our clothes, and the barrels. After lunch, the three of us had left the Union camp on a course due south, which would take us below Petersburg, away from the positions of both armies. It took us the rest of the day to work our way down to Stony Creek, where we made camp. Tuesday morning we headed westward to McKenney.

Only a few people gave so much as a second look at us, and anyone we did chance to meet, Captain Dyles talked to like a friendly Southerner trying to get his wife and slave away from the fighting, all the while cursing the Yankees who were trying to take all his land. No one thought a thing about it. Neither Jacob nor I said a word, and we just kept on moving.

By Tuesday evening we had come up on the rear of the Confederate lines holding the perimeter around Petersburg and Richmond. This was the touchier part of Dyles' plan. Most of the southern flank, however, was concentrated between Richmond and Petersburg, so he hoped by getting far enough to the west we would be able to move into the city without opposition.

We were nearly to the city before anyone said more than a few words to us. But as we drew to within sight of Richmond, we approached a unit of Confederate soldiers guarding the main road. They were stopping everyone.

We inched our way forward.

"What's your business in Richmond?" the soldier asked Captain Dyles when our turn came.

"Can't y'all see?" drawled Captain Dyles lazily. "We got us a horse to deliver."

"I see the horse all right," rejoined the soldier. "Looks like a nag to me."

"You mightn't oughtta let th' genrul hear you say that, son," drawled Dyles.

"What general?"

"*The* genrul. How many genruls we got us left? Genrul Lee, of course."

"What's he got to do with you?"

"That's what I been trying to tell you, son. This here's his horse."

"General Lee's! I don't believe you. It's just an old nag!"

Dyles started laughing, slowly and calmly at first, then gradually rising for effect. Finally he seemed to be struggling to stop and get control of himself.

"What's your name, son?" he asked, still laughing.

For the first time the soldier looked a little uneasy.

"Uh, Gibb . . . Lieutenant Jacobson Gibb."

"Well, Lieutenant Gibb, nag or no nag, Bob Lee bought this horse offen me last week, down t' my farm where I raise nags like this. Why, he's been getting horses from me for years. Afore the war I took 'em all the way up to him at his place at Arlington. You have heard of Genrul Lee's fondness for horseflesh now, ain't you, Gibb?"

"Yes, sir . . . yes, I have."

"And you want me to tell Bobbie Lee that it was one Lieutenant Jacobson Gibb who held me up when I was trying to deliver his latest purchase?" Captain Dyles wasn't laughing now, but eyed him sternly.

"No . . . no, sir."

"You want me to convey to th' genrul what you think of his nag?" Dyles asked.

"No, sir. I'm sorry, sir. You're free to move through."

I breathed a sigh of relief, and was surprised when the captain kept sitting there and made no move to go on.

"Ain't you gonna ask me about the hay and the barrels?" he said.

By now Lieutenant Gibb was so flustered he didn't know what to do! I don't know if it was hearing General Lee spoken of with such familiarity or the captain's commanding tone that was more upsetting for him.

"I, uh . . ."

"You want me to tell the genrul you let us through without a proper search? That's as bad as calling his horse a nag. For all you know I'm a no-good Yankee lying to you. Why, Gibb, I might have me a spy in them barrels back thayere."

"Yes, sir. Tell me, sir, what's the hay for? And what's in the barrels?"

"I thought you said you knew horses, Gibb! You ain't as bright as you look, son! The hay and feed in the barrels is for the horse, what else you thank they'd be for? Bob Lee always orders a wagon of hay and two barrels of my special mixed feed so the horse feels at home in his new surroundings. That make sense to that feeble brain of yours, Gibb?"

"Yes, sir."

"Hey, you ornery galoot," Dyles shouted, turning around to Jacob in the back of the wagon, "open up one of them barrels and show the lieutenant here th' special mix of grain."

"Yes, massah," replied the big black man in his laziest and most compliant tone. He took the lid off the barrel he'd been sitting on, plunged his thick hand inside, and lifted it high, with the grain pouring through his fingers.

Jacob sat back down on the barrel.

Once again Lieutenant Gibb motioned for us to pass.

"Ain't you gonna ask to see the bill of sale for that nag, Gibb?" drawled Dyles. "You wasn't planning to let us through without proof, was you?"

"No, sir."

"Well, here 'tis." Dyles pulled a sheet of rumpled paper from his coat and shoved it toward the lieutenant. He eyed it briefly, then nodded.

"What about her?" he said, nodding his head toward me.

"What about her?" said Dyles.

"Why's she along?"

"Why, Gibb, she's more important than the horse! What do you thank she's got under that towel there. More feed for the horses? My wife *always* bakes the genrul a fresh huckleberry pie to go along with the horses he buys! And she insists on delivering it personal, war or no war!"

Suddenly Captain Dyles clicked his tongue and flicked the rein and we jerked into motion, leaving a bewildered and relieved Lieutenant Jacobson Gibb standing alongside the road watching us go.

Slowly we continued along until we were out of sight. Then from behind me I heard a gradual rumble of low laughter coming from Jacob, which grew and grew until he could no longer contain it. I glanced over at the captain. His eyes were sparkling and he could hardly contain himself either. I had been terrified every second, but it was obvious both of them enjoyed this!

Captain Dyles glanced back at his large black friend, then started laughing himself.

"That poor lame-brained Rebel kid! Why, he was about to let us go without even having to use the bill of sale!"

"Why didn't you just go?" I asked. "What difference did it make, after all that?"

"Why, Miss Hollister," Captain Dyles replied. "I *had* to show him the paper! General Grant's orders."

"General Grant? Why . . . I don't understand."

"General Grant's been practicing ol' Bob Lee's signature for two years waiting for a chance to try it out. He told me just before we left to make sure I had a chance to show this to somebody. If we got captured and they hanged us, then he said he'd know he had to practice a little harder!"

Jacob roared with laughter.

I didn't think it was so funny. At the word *hanged,* a shiver of dread shot through me.

"Hey, quiet back there," Dyles said back to Jacob. "We're coming into the city. These folks around here don't much like their colored folk looking like they's having fun."

"Yes, massah . . . anything you say, massah."

A faint chuckle followed his words.

Winder Supply

CHAPTER FIFTY-NINE

$\mathcal{B}$y the time we reached the middle of Richmond it was about nine in the morning.

Captain Dyles drove the wagon to the street along the waterfront, and after about a mile I saw ahead of us a building with the words "Winder Supply" painted on it. He seemed to know Richmond pretty well. I wondered if he had been here before.

We went slowly past the building, the captain eyeing it carefully, then around the corner onto the adjacent street.

"You say they said there was a *room* here they were going to use?" he said to me. "But nothing about where it was?"

"No, all I heard was 'he's got a room we can use,'" I replied.

"Probably in back somewhere. There's bound to be another door back here we can get in."

He took the wagon along the side street, glancing about, looking over the side and rear of Winder Supply, which stood on the corner and then extended down the adjacent street as well.

We went past the end of the building, down to the next street, then turned and headed back toward the river. He reined the horse in at the back of the supply building, glancing around. Several men were carrying bags in and out of a small warehouse, and two others were loading up a wagon.

"Probably in the main building someplace," Captain Dyles mumbled to himself. "But we can't stay here too long or we'll attract their notice."

He flipped the reins and we began moving again.

"Where you figure to ditch the hay and feed and the nag, Geoff?" asked Jacob behind me.

"Don't know. We gotta keep it long enough so we're not just driving around in an empty wagon and attracting notice."

"Gotta be rid of it before that fool Gibb sees us again," added Jacob.

"We'll ditch the stuff. Hate to cut the horse loose, though—nag or no nag," said Dyles.

"I reckon the general figured one horse was a small price to roust out a traitor."

"Reckon he's right at that."

We were still riding along slowly as they talked, and I could tell the captain was thinking at the same time.

After two or three minutes, a look of resolve came over his face. "I've got it!" he said, and immediately pulled at the reins and began leading the horse back around yet again. This time when we approached the rear of the Supply Company building, he pulled the wagon to the side of the street, then stopped, in full view of the men and workers who were about. We sat there and waited.

A few minutes later a man came sauntering our way.

"Anything I can do for you?" he asked.

"We's just waitin' on master Jim," answered Captain Dyles, this time with the sound of an ignorant field hand.

"Jim who?" asked the man.

"Master James T. Bow*reee*guard," said Captain Dyles, stretching the name out slowly. "Master Jim, he done tell me to hitch up the horses an' take the darkie an' meet me at Winder Supply an' he'd be there directly, maybe sometime 'bout noon."

"It's three hours till noon."

"He done tol' me t' wait for him no matter how long he was. He said we had a heap o' stuff t' get."

"What about the woman?"

"She's powerful strong for her size," said Dyles. "We kinda short o' darkies now, what with all of 'em leavin' t' fight or go North. Master Jim, he tol' me t' bring her along t' help with the loadin'."

Apparently satisfied, the man turned and began walking back to the supply building. "Just keep this area clear," he said. "We've got a lot of loading that'll be going on this morning."

"Yes, suh," replied Dyles, following his retreating figure with eyes that were shrewdly taking in everything about the place in spite of his backward-sounding tongue. It was becoming more and more obvious to me all the time why General Grant had sent him on this mission. He was adept at playing just about any role.

As the thought of his acting came into my mind, so did the name *Booth.* Suddenly I made the connection between the actor Mrs. Richards had told me about and the name I'd heard in conversation with Cal. Was it the same man? I wondered what a well-known actor was doing mixed up with Cal and John Surratt.

My thoughts were interrupted by the voice of Captain Dyles beside me. "Time's come, Miss Hollister," he said. "You up to your part in this little charade we're playing?"

"I'll try, Captain," I said.

"Then here's what I want you to do. We'll stay here, but we can't see the front door of the place from here. I want you to walk up the street, and cross over there by the river. Find yourself someplace to sit down where you can see the front door and me at the same time. Then you sit there and look bored and tired, and if anybody comes around you put on as thick a drawl as you can. You keep your eyes peeled for your friend. I reckon he'll use the front, but there's no telling. But keep your head down underneath that bonnet so he can't see your face."

"He'll never expect to see me here," I said.

"Keep the brim of that bonnet over your eyes regardless. When you see him, you take off the bonnet and give me a little wave—that is, *after* he's gone inside. Then you get back here to me."

"What will we do then?"

"I don't know. Reckon we'll have to go inside, find 'em, and then do a little improvising."

I got down, but then Captain Dyles spoke up again.

"One more thing, Miss Hollister," he said thoughtfully, still running options through his mind. "Tell me about your friend."

"He's not my friend," I said.

"No matter. I want to know . . . is he likely to fight? Is he a hero or a coward? With a gun in his gut, is he bound to do what we say or risk his life for his cause?"

It didn't take much reflection for me to answer.

"Unless he's changed, Captain," I said, "under those conditions, I'd say he'd do whatever you tell him. Cal Burton's only cause is himself. I can't see him risking his life for anybody."

*L*ate in the year as it was, after more than two hours sitting in the sun, I was hot, tired, and sweating.

But when I first saw Cal striding up the street, suddenly all my senses jerked to attention. My heart started pounding and I could feel my whole body tense up. I hadn't actually laid eyes on him since the end of 1862. All the same emotions I'd felt five nights earlier were suddenly back—but this time even stronger! I was angry, afraid, and hurt. But I managed to keep it all inside instead of jumping up and running over and yelling all the things I was thinking. I kept my head down, and watched as he approached and then went inside the front door of Winder Supply.

The next instant I took off my bonnet, gave it a little wave in the direction of the wagon, then stood and walked hurriedly back in that direction myself.

By the time I got there, Captain Dyles and Jacob were out of the wagon and moving toward the back door of the place. I joined them, and we walked inside. None of the other people around paid us much heed, and I didn't see the fellow who had questioned us before.

We walked in. It was dark and smelled of grain and hay and boxes and wood and leather. Gradually my eyes became accustomed to the dim light. There were people around. Some of them glanced at us, but no one said anything.

I was afraid, but both Captain Dyles and Jacob acted as if they belonged there, and we didn't seem to attract any notice.

Suddenly I spotted Cal at the other end of the large room. He was coming straight toward us.

"That's him!" I whispered to the captain, then turned sideways and bent down my face to the floor. I was so glad it was dark!

We kept shuffling along. Cal was talking to another man and brushed right beside me. I could have grabbed at his arm, he was so close. As he went by, the captain followed him out of the corner of his eye. Cal and the other man entered what looked like a storage room off the large one we were in. The door closed behind them.

"You recognize the other one?" the captain whispered down to me.

"Surratt?" I replied. "I only heard him, but never saw his face."

"We'll have to get a listen, then."

Dyles turned and began sauntering aimlessly in the direction Cal had gone. I stuck as close to him as I could. We edged toward the closed door. He motioned to me to get up next to it and listen.

"Is it him?" he whispered.

"I can't tell . . . I think so."

Dyles thought a moment. "Doesn't matter if it's him, anyway. All we need is your Burton fellow. You ready, Jacob?"

The big Negro nodded.

"We gotta get the both of 'em before they can yell out, so we gotta be quick."

Jacob nodded again.

"Then let's go. Hollister," he said to me, "you follow us in and get the door shut pronto so nobody hears nothing."

Even as the words were coming from his mouth, he opened the door and he and Jacob burst through. I was right behind them.

Cal Burton glanced up, and his eyes fell straight on me. A shocked look filled his eyes and a pallor spread over his face. It was almost worth everything I'd been through to finally see the tables turned on him.

"Corrie—" he breathed. But it was the last word he spoke. Jacob's huge hand clamped down across his mouth. Cal's struggle was momentary. One look told him he was no match for Jacob. At the same time, Captain Dyles had overpowered the man I took for John Surratt.

"That him, Hollister?" said the captain, nodding his head toward Jacob's prey.

I nodded, feeling suddenly sick to my stomach. Despite what Cal had done to me, I felt all at once like Judas!

"Then get that rag outta my pocket," he said.

I found the pocket of his coat and pulled out a length of rag.

"Stuff it in this swine's mouth," he said.

I moved toward them. The captain slowly moved his hand aside. But before I could get the rag in, Surratt started to cry out. A slap across the side of his head from the captain silenced him again.

"You try that again and I won't be so gentle! Now, Hollister, get it in there!"

"I'll get you for this, little lady," growled Surratt through clenched teeth. "You may have gotten away that night in the street, but I'll—"

I jammed the rag in between his teeth and lips. He tried to spit it out, but I shoved it in tighter. Suddenly he chomped down on rag and fingers together and bit me hard.

"Ouch!" I cried, jumping back.

The next instant Surratt lay on the floor unconscious from another blow from Captain Dyles' fist.

"I warned the varmint," he muttered. He stooped down, took another length of rag from his coat, and tied it so tightly around Surratt's mouth I thought his lips were going to bleed. Then hastily he pulled out some rope and quickly bound Surratt's hands and feet, leaving him lying in a heap on the wood floor. Then he got up and turned his attention to Cal.

"Now, Burton," he said, "you can make this hard on yourself or you can make it easy. You've seen what I can do when I'm crossed. But Jacob here ain't half so nice a feller as me. Besides, Jacob's got a gun in your ribs too—Jacob, be so good as to show Mr. Burton what you got aimed at his heart."

Jacob brought around his left hand, which cradled a small revolver, in front of Cal's face.

"Now then, Jacob's gonna let you go. You make so much as a peep, and you'll feel his hand again. You make any ruckus when we're outside, and you'll feel the bullet from his gun, and it'll be the last thing you ever feel. Now move!"

Jacob removed his hand from Cal's mouth, then grabbed him by the arm and pulled him toward the door.

"We're going for a little walk, Burton. And like I said, if you know what's good for you, keep quiet."

Cal threw me a look of mingled fear and disbelief at my betrayal of him. All I could think of was what I'd felt in Sacramento to discover him gone—but it didn't help me feel any better.

Dyles opened the door, and with Cal between the two of them, he and Jacob made their way out into the large warehouse and immediately began walking toward the doorway through which we had come. Jacob stuck so close to him that the gun was invisible, but every once in a while I saw him jab Cal in the ribs as a reminder. I followed behind them.

The moment we were outside and in the sunlight, Captain Dyles ran nearly headlong into the Supply Company man who had questioned him before.

"We found Master Jim," the captain said, slackening his pace but continuing on.

"Everything in order, Beauregard?" he asked, looking straight at Cal.

I saw him wincing as the steel pressed against the back of his rib cage.

Cal nodded and, encouraged by Jacob's bulk next to him, continued moving.

The man eyed our small entourage with a question in his eyes. Yet what could be wrong in a well-dressed Southern gentleman accompanied by two poor white field hands and his Negro slave? We kept walking. I went past him, and we all moved straight to where the wagon was still sitting. The man continued to watch us.

"Tell us to load in some bags of oat feed," whispered Dyles to Cal.

Cal was silent.

"You heard the man," growled Jacob, again reminding Cal of the gun.

"You . . . you men get some oats in there," Cal said half-heartedly.

"Louder, Cal," I said. "I think he wants the man to hear you."

"You heard me," he said, louder this time. "Get those oats loaded."

Dyles and Jacob stood shuffling around the wagon another moment or two. I glanced back at the man who'd been watching us. Finally he turned and headed back toward the building.

"He's gone!" I whispered.

"Into the back, Burton!" said Jacob, practically throwing Cal up and onto the hay as he spoke. The next instant he was beside him.

Captain Dyles sprang up on the board, and I scrambled up to the seat next to him. He flicked the reins, and we bounded into motion.

I glanced back. Cal lay on his back on the floor of the wagon, hay strewn all around him, with Jacob's boot against his chest, and the gun in his hand pointed toward his head.

Captain Dyles urged the horse as fast as he dared, first up the street to the riverfront, then left, and then along the same route we had followed into the city a few hours earlier.

*N*ow that we had actually kidnapped Cal and were making our escape through the Confederate capital, I was assaulted by many thoughts and feelings.

Mainly, I was just plain scared! What if Cal shouted out? What if someone thought we looked suspicious—which it seemed to me we did—and stopped us? What if we ran into a unit of Rebel soldiers? They were all around Richmond in the outlying districts! What if someone from Winder Supply followed us? What if Surratt got loose and suddenly all of Richmond was on the lookout for us!?

But mostly I felt an awful feeling in the pit of my stomach about what I'd done. Somehow it didn't matter that they were trying to kill General Grant, or even that Cal had stolen the money in California and had done what he'd done to me. None of that mattered right then. All I could think of was that I had betrayed another human being, someone I had once cared about! I had *betrayed* him!

It was no lingering and misplaced loyalty to Cal I was feeling. He was a rat in my eyes. Even worse—he was a spy and a criminal against the Union and a participant in a murder plot. I had no feelings left other than anger for what kind of man he'd allowed himself to become.

Yet what was even more despicable than a spy and mur-
derer? The stool pigeon, the traitor . . . the Judas! How could
I have stooped so low! *Was* this justified to save a man's life?
Was it forgivable to betray a traitor?

And then, right in the middle of my thoughts, I heard
Cal's voice.

"Corrie," he said behind me, "I'm surprised at you. All
that religious talk . . . I thought you were different."

His words stung me. But any tears I had left for Cal Burton had been wept and were dried up long ago. And the
patronizing, disdainful tone of his voice snapped me out of
my self-recriminations. Cal had, indeed, changed! His voice
was cold—hard, callous, and biting. If I'd thought he might
have repented of what he'd done, I could not have been more
wrong! The sound of his voice told me that he had continued
his downward slide, and that perhaps he had become a man
even capable of murder if it suited his selfish purposes.

I turned around and looked down at him where he lay.
Seeing him so vulnerable and helpless filled me with a sudden
sense of pity. All the pain from the past was gone.

"I'm sorry, Cal," I said sincerely. "I haven't changed . . .
it's *you* who has changed. And whatever you may think of
me, I couldn't let you kill General Grant. The future of this
country is too important to me."

"Bah, Corrie, who are you trying to kid?" he spat back.
"There are no noble causes. It's every man for himself in this
world!"

"I don't happen to agree, Cal. I think the future of this
country *is* a noble cause, and I intend to keep fighting for it,
whatever you may think."

"You always were a starry-eyed idealist."

"I'll still take my ideals over your principles, Cal."

"Do *your* principles include betraying a friend?"

"A *friend*, Cal? After what you did to me, after what you have tried to do to the Union? Whose friend are you, Cal—anyone's but your own?"

"You're a fool, Corrie, if you think—"

But Jacob had had enough of his derision, and the rude coarseness of his tone toward me.

"Shut up, you!" he snarled, jabbing Cal with his boot.

"You big ox," Cal snapped back. "You're not going to shoot me in the middle of town. A shot would bring soldiers down on you like a swarm!"

"You'd be just as dead though, wouldn't you, *Massah Cal?* But before it comes to that, I'll stuff your mouth full of hay and tie it shut like your slimy friend back there. So shut your mouth, or I'll get down there and start feeding you like I do my hogs back home!"

Apparently Cal believed the threat and said no more.

We went on a while longer in silence. Beside me I could see Captain Dyles glancing furtively about, his eyes scanning the streets and buildings, looking for any signs of threat or trouble. At the same time, I knew him well enough by now to know he was thinking about how we were going to get out of town, through the sentries watching the roads, and safely back to the Union encampment on the other side of Petersburg with our kidnapped quarry. Even though we had Cal, the hardest part of the whole plan might still be ahead of us!

"We gotta get rid of this stuff back here before long, Geoff," said Jacob at length, as if reading both my mind and that of the captain at the same time.

Dyles nodded. "Yeah . . . I'm thinking. We still got about a mile to go."

The houses and buildings of Richmond were thinning and we were reaching the outskirts of the city.

"You'll never get away with it," said Cal. "They search every wagon in and out of the city!" His voice was cocky; I wondered if *anything* would ever humble him!

"I told you to shut up," said Jacob, grabbing a handful of hay and throwing it in Cal's face. "One more word, and I'll make it so that mouth of yours can't utter a peep!"

We bumped along another few minutes, then the captain noticed a barn off to the right side of the road that looked unused. At least there was nobody anywhere nearby, and the fields next to it were vacant of cows or horses. Immediately he pulled at the reins and steered our wagon toward it. He drove around to the back side, stopped, handed me the reins, then jumped to the ground.

The great door had no lock. He swung it open and nodded to me; I flicked the reins and the horse pulled us inside. The moment the trailing horse was through, Captain Dyles closed the door behind us, then jumped back up onto the wagon.

"Miss Corrie," said Jacob, handing me the gun. "If he makes a move, shoot him."

I knew my eyes widened and my heart started beating hard. I was glad for the darkness of the barn. I didn't want Cal to know I was afraid.

"Nobody'll hear it now, Burton," he added to Cal.

"She'd never have the guts!" shouted Cal, given new boldness by seeing the gun in my hand.

"You don't have to kill him, Miss Corrie," said Jacob. "Just a bullet in his leg someplace'll be fine."

Already the captain and Jacob were struggling with the barrels. Jacob popped the lid off the first. The next moment I heard the *swish* of the grain falling onto the floor. Then they did the same with the second, and within two minutes we were ready to leave the barn and be back on our way.

Again I was at the reins and Captain Dyles began to open the large rear door of the barn.

Suddenly he stopped.

"Hold on, Miss Hollister," he said.

I pulled back and stopped the wagon.

"I just don't like the idea of leaving a good animal for the Rebs," he said, looking back into the barn at the horse he had untied from the back of the wagon. "Not to mention your safety being a mite worrisome to me . . ."

He thought a few seconds more.

"There just might be a way . . ." he mumbled to himself. "Yep . . . it might work." Then he glanced up at me. "I haven't been too comfortable with your part in this, Hollister. If anything was to happen to you . . . well, there's got to be some way to ensure that if anything goes wrong, you can get safely away. Yep, it just might work. . . ."

Even as he was talking to me I could tell he was still thinking about what we might do.

"That's what we'll do," he said finally, with a sound of resolve, closing the door again. "Get down from there, Miss Hollister and unhitch that mare. We're going to swap her for Lee's nag."

Having no idea what he meant to do, I obeyed. Jacob remained where he was, watching over his charge in the back of the wagon.

Five minutes later we were set to go again. This time, however, I wasn't sitting next to Captain Dyles on the board of the wagon, but was on the bare back of the mare that had pulled us faithfully all the way from Petersburg.

"Okay, let's be off," said the captain, flipping the reins and leading the wagon through the open door of the barn. I followed on the mare.

"I hate to leave behind the pie the sergeant made us," Jacob said, laughing.

"It'll make some Reb farmer happy when he finds it," said Dyles. "And we don't need it now. It won't do us no good, but the horse still might."

A few minutes later we were back on the road. Half a mile farther on, the soldiers from the guard unit appeared up ahead of us. I inched the mare up alongside the wagon.

"You stick close, Miss Hollister," said Captain Dyles, "but keep to that side of me so the Reb don't get too good a look. We can't have him recognize that white star on the mare's forehead."

"I'll try to keep her nose turned away from him," I said.

"If anything goes wrong, you save your own neck."

"Nothing will go wrong," I replied, wishing I felt as confident as my words.

"You hear me, Miss Hollister—you don't worry about us if anything happens. You get that mare back to General Grant in one piece, and yourself along with her. That's an order. That's why I put you on her . . . just in case."

"Yes, sir," I said.

Five minutes later we approached the gray-clad Confederate guard.

"Howdy thayere, Lieutenant Gibb," drawled Dyles in such a heavy accent that I almost had to laugh. "We're on our way back to th' farm."

"General Lee like his new horse?" said the friendly sentry with a smile.

"Shore did. *He* didn't think it was no nag, neither."

Just then I heard a faint groan and a kicking sound from the back of the wagon. I glanced over and saw Jacob kicking against an empty barrel lying on its side—rolling it back and forth to drown out the sound of Cal kicking against the inside of the other.

Poor Cal! Jacob had finally stuffed his mouth full of hay, tied a rag around it, put him inside the empty grain barrel, replaced the lid, and sat down on top of it himself. No one would be able to budge it with Jacob's weight holding it down.

Both Dyles and the guard glanced over at the sound. The captain barked out angrily at his black friend.

"If you can't keep that empty barrel from rollin' round back thayere while I'm talkin' to the lieutenant, I'll whip your hide when we get home, boy!"

"Yessuh, massah," mumbled Jacob, casting his eyes down, but managing to keep making enough noise to cover Cal's.

"What's she doing?" asked the guard, glancing over at me.

"My wife?"

"Where'd that horse come from?" he asked, eyeing my mount carefully, then looking at the one hitched to the reins the captain held in his hand. He seemed to be turning over something in his mind, but it hadn't quite occurred to him that we'd just switched the two.

"Why, that there's the genrul's old horse. We was tradin' the two of 'em."

"Why's she riding it?" he asked, now beginning to look back and forth between the two horses.

"Genrul Lee wanted it that way."

I didn't like the suspicious look in Lieutenant Gibb's eye. But before I had a chance to worry about it further, Captain Dyles spoke again, to me this time.

"You might as well get goin', dear," he said. "We'll catch up with you in a minute or two." With his eyes he motioned me to go. I saw that he was worried.

Out of the corner of my eye, I could see the guard starting to object. I think it might have suddenly dawned on him that we still had the same two horses as we'd gone into the city with that morning. But I wasn't about to look at him. Instead, I urged my horse on and moved gently forward in front of the wagon and along the road leading out of town.

Then suddenly everything started to happen fast.

I heard Lieutenant Gibb's voice yelling at me to stop. And I heard more ruckus than ever coming from the back of the wagon. I knew Cal was kicking at the barrel where he was crumpled up underneath Jacob's weight, and I knew Jacob was kicking and rolling the empty barrel about to keep Cal from being heard.

But a third sound seemed to mingle with the sound of my horse's hooves on the dirt road, Cal's kicking and the barrel rumbling about, and the sentry's shouts.

Unconsciously I began to quicken my pace.

The noise increased . . . there was more shouting . . . the sound of galloping hooves!

I glanced back.

A rider was approaching from the city, galloping hard, shouting, calling out to the guard.

The sound of his voice sent a chill of fear up my spine. Still turned, I squinted to see if I could make out the figure atop the fast-approaching horse.

It was John Surratt!

In panic I hesitated, then stopped. *What should I do?*

My question was answered the next second. Seeing my uncertainty and that I had stopped, Captain Dyles shouted above the din.

"Go, Hollister . . . I gave you an order . . . now ride!"

Already I could see that Lieutenant Gibb had his rifle aimed at the captain and Jacob, and that one of his men was helping Cal out of his temporary imprisonment.

A cloud of dust from Surratt's approaching horse swept over the scene as he reined in to a frantic stop amid more shouts.

Everything was a confusion. *"Union spies!"* Someone shouted, *"After her! Don't let her get away!"* But my mind and arms and legs all seemed paralyzed, and images of jail cells and gallows flitted through my imagination like a dreadful nightmare come to life.

Then the sound of Jacob's enormous booming voice raised louder than all the rest echoed thunderously through the air.

"Get out of here, Miss Corrie!" he cried, and I don't think ever a voice sounded so commanding or penetrated so deep into my bones. "Ride like the wind, and don't—"

His voice was cut short. The butt of Surratt's rifle clubbed him alongside the head, and he slumped to the ground unconscious.

It was all I needed. Suddenly I was awake again!

I spun around on the mare's back, dug my heels into her sides, and galloped away, my eyes filling with tears for Jacob and the captain.

Behind me I heard more voices and shouts. Then came a shot from Surratt's rifle!

Still riding, I glanced back. He was mounting his horse to follow me. I heard Cal's voice calling after him. "Let her go . . . she's of no more use to us."

"I've got a score to settle with the lady, Burton!"

I was well down the road now, probably two hundred yards away and riding with a desperation I'd never known.

Another shot came! Though I heard nothing, somehow I knew the bullet had whizzed by me not more than inches away.

"Stop, Surratt!" I heard Cal's voice faintly in the distance.

There was no answer, only the sound of Surratt's horse, now galloping after me. I knew he was making up the distance rapidly.

Another shot . . . closer yet!

This poor mare was no match for whatever Surratt had under him! I could feel his approach with terror.

Suddenly I felt a slamming sensation in my back. My right arm went limp and dropped to my side. The pain was different than anything I'd ever felt before.

The explosion of sound which followed the bullet seemed hazy and slow and dreamlike, as though it were coming ten minutes after the impact. My fading consciousness somehow was still alert enough to realize that the sound and the bullet had left Surratt's rifle at the same time, and my confused mind tried to make sense of the contradiction . . . but couldn't.

The pain lasted but a moment. Then followed only numbness.

All sounds began to fade.

I heard several more shots, then I heard nothing more of Surratt's hoofbeats. I could not even hear my own horse . . . all was quiet and still.

Still I rode, though I hardly knew it. Vaguely I was aware of my hair flying out behind me.

I was slumped over the mare's neck, struggling to maintain my grasp of her mane, trying to stay on her back.

I only knew there was danger behind me. I had to get away . . . had to keep riding. Why was it so quiet? Was I asleep? And if so, why did this dream seem so real?

Let me sleep a few minutes more, Almeda . . . be up soon . . . had the strangest dream . . . about a war . . . men dressed in black . . . they both have beards . . . they are in danger. . . .

I'll be awake soon . . . Ma . . . what are you making for breakfast . . . strange dream, Ma . . . I thought I saw Pa . . . he was somewhere far away . . . we were all with him, Ma . . . all except you . . . I didn't see you there, Ma. . . .

The quiet of the dream grew quieter . . . all was still . . . nothing but silence . . . peace . . . no pain . . . everything was white . . . bright. . . .

Then even the silence faded into nothingness.

Slowly the brilliant whiteness turned pale, then ashen . . . then gray . . . and finally gave way to blackness.

Epilogue

*W*hen I next woke up, I found myself staring into a face I had never seen before.

How much time had passed, I didn't know. The room was clean and white, and I was lying in bed. The first sensation I felt was a slight pain in the back of my shoulder. It didn't occur to me immediately that it was from the wound where I'd been shot.

This, however, was not the biggest surprise of all. That was the simple fact that when I woke up and looked around, I couldn't remember who I was!

But that is another whole story, and I'll have to tell you about it later!

About the Author

MICHAEL PHILLIPS is perhaps best known for reawakening interest in the writings of George MacDonald. In the 1980s Phillips embarked on a campaign to reacquaint the reading public with the works of the forgotten Victorian novelist and Scotsman. Phillips edited and published more than fifty of MacDonald's works in twenty years, including his own acclaimed biography of the man. Combined sales total two million copies, inaugurating a renaissance of interest in MacDonald's work. Phillips also began writing fiction of his own, and now it is as a novelist he is primarily known. He has authored and coauthored (with Judith Pella) more than seventy titles in addition to his volumes of MacDonald. His best-known novels include those of the Phillips-Pella writing team, THE STONEWYCKE SERIES, THE JOURNALS OF CORRIE BELLE HOLLISTER, and THE RUSSIANS, as well as his solo THE SECRET OF THE ROSE, AMERICAN DREAMS, and SHENANDOAH SISTERS. Michael Phillips and his wife, Judy, alternate their time between the U.S. and Scotland, where they are attempting to increase awareness of George MacDonald and his work.